THE ROAD TO
LAGOA SANTA

PARACATU

CATALÃO

SÃO FRANCISCO

RIO DAS VELHAS

CURVELO

LAGOA SANTA

SABARÁ

OURO PRETO

JEQUITINHONHA

VILLA FRANCA

SÃO CARLOS DE CAMPINAS

SÃO PAULO

RIO DE JANEIRO

SANTOS

100 KM

THE ROAD TO LAGOA SANTA

a novel by
Henrik Stangerup

Translated from the Danish
by Barbara Bluestone

Marion Boyars
New York · London

Published in Great Britain and the United States in 1984 by
MARION BOYARS PUBLISHERS
457 Broome Street, New York N.Y. 10013.
and 18 Brewer Street, London W1R 4AS.

Distributed in the United States by
The Scribners Book Companies Inc.

Distributed in Canada by
John Wiley & Sons Canada Ltd.

Distributed in Australia and New Zealand by
Thomas C. Lothian Pty.

Originally published in Denmark under the title
Vejen til Lagoa Santa by Gyldendal, 1981

British Library Cataloguing in Publication Data
Stangerup, Henrik
The road to Lagoa Santa.
I. Title   II. Vejen til Lagoa Santa. *English*
839.8'1374[F]   PT8176.29.T3
ISBN 0-7145-2797-1 cloth

Library of Congress Cataloging in Publication Data
Stangerup, Henrik
The road to Lagoa Santa
Translation of: Vejen til Lagoa Santa.
I. Title.
PT8176.29.T3V3613 1983   839.8'1374   83-6025

Typeset in 11 point Baskerville by Essex Photo Set, Rayleigh, Essex.

To Jacob; to my mother; and to my friends Erik Bøtt zavw and Per Johns who encouraged me all the way through. And to Gitte.

(Fazenda Lagoa/Marienborg – April 1980–April 1981)

Publication of this book has been supported by the Danish
Government Committee for Cultural Exchange.

Also by Henrik Stangerup

The Man Who Wanted To Be Guilty (a novel)

The poems on pages 20, 59, 117, 253 and 267 were
translated by John Muckle.

I

It all merged into one. Uncle Wilhelm told sailors' yarns about his voyages to and from Brazil. He had encountered many Indians over there. He himself was the main character around whom everything revolved . . . I too was there when the expedition in the virgin forest threaded its way forward, guided by a Negro armed with a knife to hew a path. I admired the mysterious magnificence of the stalactite cave illuminated by the light of the torches. And in the rainy season I sat quietly with Uncle Wilhelm in the lonely room with the sloth in the corner while by turns the lightning flashed or the rain beat down incessantly . . .

Little by little, as the years went by, the tone in the conversations about Uncle Wilhelm began to change. As ever, there were love and admiration, but the once so golden aura was now more and more infused with sadness and concern . . .

Something was wrong; something which he glimpsed over there but did not mention in his letters, a misfortune threatening him which Father and Mother discussed but would not speak freely about to me.

Troels-Lund, *A Memoir, 1906.*

1

The time of the cave expeditions is nearly at an end. The modest little house in Lagoa Santa is cluttered with bones on the floors, on the tables, in the outbuilding. Some of the bones are packed in newspapers and others in boxes, but many are still lying about with labels attached. One heap lies in a corner of the garden and has not yet been catalogued. There are bones which Dr. Lund cannot fit together and which, he suspects, are from historical time. Dr. Lund is tired but pleased. In almost ten years he alone, with the help of some slipshod negro assistants and Brandt, when he was not busy with his painting, has accomplished the work of ten diligent scientists. He has journeyed thousands of miles on horseback or by mule, spent nights on small ledges deep in caves with an oxhide beneath him and a ragged blanket over him, with torches and tallow candles placed to show him the way outside, into the fresh air, if in the middle of the night his chest pains should suddenly trouble him.

He has denied himself every sort of comfort. Months could go by without his tasting a decent meal, and only under waterfalls or at home in Lagoa Santa could he wash off the dust of months of travel. He has had attacks of fever, thirst has caulked his throat when he was lost on the *campos cerrados*, and at times the sun has burned so fiercely that blisters have formed on his forehead. He has been scratched by plants, bitten by insects and attacked by fearsome stomach pains which have confined him to his bed for weeks. Yes, Dr. Lund is proud that he has persevered for those ten years. He is looking forward to returning to Europe soon, to cultivated society, to paved streets, sidewalks, restaurants, libraries, cheerful smiles, alert eyes, serious newspapers, bright schoolchildren, tradesmen. To Copenhagen, where he can be together with H.C. Oersted and Schouw and Forchhammer and Reinhardt and spend evenings with his family; to Paris, where he can meet French colleagues and assist in evaluating the scientific testament left

13

by Cuvier. But his heart lies in the south of France. Provence. There he will live most of the year, in a fragrance of lavender and thyme, with occasional excursions to Rome, Paris, and Vienna. Six months from now Dr. Lund will once more be the European he feels himself truly to be.

But first all the bones must be packed. It will take months. And he must sell the house and speak with Brandt about his future plans. This will take more than just a week or two. Honest, nervous Brandt. Why is he so busy predicting that Europe, from the North Cape to Sicily, will soon be consumed by the flames of revolution, and that only in Lagoa Santa will eternal peace reign, while the cities of South America are also drawn into the madness because Man, broken paving stone in hand, dares defy the natural order? Dr. Lund feels responsible for Brandt, deeply responsible. He does not like the word 'guilty'. What should he do? Should he insist that Brandt return to Norway, the country from which he had fled over ten years ago, a Norway veiled in mists from the unhappiness of his innermost self? Will Wilhelmine take him back after so many years? Will she understand him? Understand what had driven him to Brazil, far from the condemning eyes? What is the alternative to Wilhelmine? To advise Brandt to remain alone in Lagoa Santa? To move to Rio and try his fortune as a portrait painter at the risk of never being accepted by the proper circles and of dying of all sorts of ills, forgotten among the blacks? Dr. Lund himself would never dream of settling in Rio. On his way back to Europe he will visit the imperial city for a couple of weeks at the most, after having first obtained information regarding the health conditions prevailing in the city. He will visit his old travelling companion Riedel, now director of the Emperor's parks. The Emperor, a mere boy, will receive him in audience, and he will enjoy the first taste of how civilized people behave. If only yellow fever does not break out in Rio, as it has so often before. If so, he will have to put off his journey for yet another year.

It is a long time before the rainy season begins, time enough to pack everything and have the boxes sent off with the *tropa* - the mule train - to Rio. From there they can be shipped to Denmark when the corvette Galathea in due course reaches Brazil. However, once he is caught by the rain, nothing can be done for another four months. The muddy red earth will flow down through Lagoa Santa, the garden will be transformed into a waterfall, and, if worse comes to worst, the water will tear out the flowers and the sweet potatoes and hollow out the ground beneath the coffee bushes, making them topple at the merest touch. Suddenly Dr. Lund feels that there is nothing worse than the tropical rain. That merciless rain which submerges his caves, gouges deep holes in the path down to the lake, and causes the lake to overflow its shores. Unceasingly, week after week, it drums upon his roof as he lies there gazing up at the tiled ceiling swarming with geckos while in the next room Brandt potters about with his easel, grunting to himself. As he lies there, Dr. Lund dreams about the rain falling at home in Denmark, the rain of his childhood and youth, over Lake Peblinge and Lake Furesø, the rain which comes like a blessing after brief cooling gusts of wind, with a scent unimaginable here in Minas, and with a play of color from the palest green to golden and dark brown.

No, Dr. Lund does not wish to live through another rainy season in a godforsaken little town inhabited by dull provincials. The locals repel him: the blustering fazenda owners whose heads are filled only with cattle prices, the unshaven priest who never opens his mouth, and those others, the children of Nature, the slaves with their missing teeth, their primitive minds and their superstitions. They are all beings of another world, incapable of enlarging their horizons; creatures who spend their lives doing absolutely nothing, passively letting the rain trickle into their palm huts and their children roll in the mud with the black pigs. Were they to be given an education it would hardly help. They would never attempt to read a decent book or engage themselves in serious matters. The Englishmen who manage the gold mines are the only ones whom Dr. Lund actually likes. Even if the sky were ripped apart by a hundred thunderbolts and the earth to crack open into a flaming abyss, an Englishman will always be an Englishman. Dr. Lund approves of that. They refuse to swallow any of Brazil's random stew of a culture, and their mines, created under inhuman conditions and at the cost of innumerable lives, are miracles of the art of engineering. So are their railways. Perhaps in a hundred years, the *godems*, as the

15

Brazilians refer to the English in their vain attempt to pronounce 'Goddamn it', can manage to civilize Brazil. If only they can take charge of things, crush the corruption, and truly open the country from Pernambuco to Rio Grande do Sul.

2

Dr. Lund thinks about all this as he rides his mule over the open campo. Perspiration drips onto his spectacles, and his collar cuts into his neck, causing a slight pain. His straw hat with the wide curved brim is fitted firmly onto his head. The leather bag over his shoulder contains his indispensible hard-boiled eggs, bread, chunks of unpalatable Brazilian cheese, some dried meat, a bottle of boiled water, and a bag of candles. He has no need of large torches, for the scientific work is finished. And he continues musing, 'Thought is one thing, another thing is . . .' That other thing is Nature. Nature everywhere. Dr. Lund can see nearly one hundred eighty degrees around him. He perceives the slightest movement, a frog stirring behind a leaf, a bird on the distant horizon plummeting down after its prey. At the same time he can see the endless carpet of bluish green grasses underlying the campo vegetation, a carpet abundantly scattered with plants and small shrubs ornamented with bright flowers. Larger bushes jut up here and there above the shrubs, but to Dr. Lund the strangest of all are the dwarf-like trees with their low twisted trunks. Their branches contort into curves which merge to form a top wider than it is tall. The bark is like thick wrinkled cork.

Dr. Lund has often blackened his fingers by touching these trunks. Not a day has gone by without huge fires, and they have been raging for centuries. At first he thought that the fires were lit by Brazilian farmers, but he had to reject this explanation after careful study. He has examined the documents of the campo estates dating back to the first settlers in this region, and seen that the proportion of open campo to forest was exactly the same then as it is today. The vast campos de Araraquara, which no white man had ever visited before he and Riedel, had first been wrested from the Indians during the last fifteen years, and the first Brazilian settlers had assured him many times that the region looked then exactly as it does now. But not until he studied the trees was Dr. Lund convinced that the burning had gone on long before the first scattered traces of civilization. He had found gigantic trees with crippled, twisted branches – the same sort of trees which in the virgin forest, the *calanduva*, soar straight and tall. Yes, for centuries, perhaps millennia, ever since the time of prehistoric man, Brazil has been burning. Then as now, about one hundred miles away, and over there also, only twenty miles away, huge clouds of smoke suddenly billow up to the sky, dying down, rising again, for days, for weeks. Over there it is Cain upon whose fire God casts his mantle of wind. Over there is Abel to whom God grants joy.

And still Nature returns, after the burning, year after year. Plants, bushes and shrubs shoot up through the carpet of grass. An excursion through these sea-blue regions would reward any botanist with a bounty of marvelous flowers. Once again Dr. Lund feels privileged. Once again he knows that he did right in returning to Brazil's nature and that Providence was with him then just as it clearly beckons him back to Europe now. The memory of the rich treasures which he has gathered in these regions enchants him more than the memory of the meadows at home in Denmark. He may miss Denmark during the rainy season, but in Europe he will always yearn for the blue-green carpet of grass of the campos. Soon, towards the end of the dry season, the campos will take on a new garb, the grass will turn to straw, the flowers will wither, and Dr. Lund will imagine himself in a field of oats. And then it will burn everywhere, not a single campo will be spared, but after just a few weeks the earth will again be covered by a sparse carpet of the freshest green, and Dr. Lund will delight in seeing how one side of the red clay path he is now riding will be barren wintry soil, white as ashes, while on the other side the landscape will unfold in all the magnificence of germinating spring. And then, as now, there will be no plant, bush, or shrub which he does not recognize. Not one of them is an annual. The same condition which prevents the formation of annual plants, namely the hardness of the earth's crust, protects the roots of the perennial plants from damage by fire. And yet! Dr. Lund has also discovered this: that the essential means of protection lie in the very substance of the roots themselves. With few exceptions the roots of these perennial plants develop into a bulb, often mealy as touchwood, but juicy. Into this refuge, sheltered from destruction by drought and fire, the life process withdraws and from this succulent vessel shoots will be sent forth with renewed vigor, enticed by the night dew or the rain which always follows the fire.

It is growing late. Dr. Lund estimates that the temperature has dropped to between eighteen and twenty degrees. There have been only two days of rain in the last month and the ruby sky is nearly cloudless. Dr. Lund's route runs southward, through an ever denser campo forest, down toward a marshy plain bordered to the north and west by the ascending highland, and to the south by the last branch of the mountain ridge Serra do Espinhaço. There lies one of the caves he loves most, Lapa da Cerca Grande. Only the chattering of the parrots, the lamenting of the anús, and the hoarse cry of the caracará break the silence as he rides down toward the meadow where the Indian crag Mocambo rises like the huge gothic castle of a robber baron amidst the greenery, the entrance to the cave well-concealed to the northeast. Dr. Lund's rump is sore after the day-long ride. He opens the leather bag, takes a sip of water, and taps two eggs together. He is looking forward to spending the night in the little shelter he has had built against the rock. As darkness falls, the meadow now spreads before him, and he can still picture all the trees and bushes of the campo, as in his mind the dry, sometimes leathery, sometimes brittle, consistency of their dull dingy green links up with their names: *Murcia, Eugenia, Psidium, Cassia, Mimosa, Acacia, Byrsonima, Kielmeyra, Davilla, Bombax, Anacardium, Zeyheria montana.*

The place in his brain where all these names are preserved is his succulent vessel, the spring from which new vigor issues

18

forth every day. He may drop from fatigue or lie ill for days, but the strength within him always wells up again, to fill him with curiosity and the certainty that God is guiding his steps. All has been created, all is controlled by Divine Will. To call anything in God's plan supernatural or contrary to reason is to isolate it from God, who is at one with the Order of Reason. Superstition, to which the Brazilians abandon themselves, is a mere lack of faith. 'A faith must be capable of being articulated,' Oersted would say. *Murcia, Eugenia, Psidium* . . . that is to articulate the faith. *Cassia, Mimosia, Acacia* . . . from a modest corner, to the best of one's ability, humbly, to describe the Creator's Plan, of which he, Dr. Lund, is also a part. From these campo bushes to the bones from the caves now awaiting shipment to Denmark. From the gravel pits by Jagtvejen and Vibens Hus where he played as a boy to the day when he walked out along Vesterbro and saw the Word of God in the sky in glowing letters and knelt down, trembling with awe but also fearing that someone may have seen him and thought him mad. From all the lectures he has followed to his own doctoral thesis, from the walking tours on Sicily together with Schouw to that day in Paris when he met Alexander von Humboldt. From his first visit to Brazil to now, nearly twenty years later, as he rides out over the meadow while the sun sends its last flames over the horizon directly over yet another smoldering campo. In all these events, there has been a profound truth, a coherence woven of the finest threads.

Brandt, thinks Dr. Lund. There must be a solution to the problem of Brandt! Europe, thinks Dr. Lund, and for once he does not long for paving stones. He dismounts the mule, hitching it to the post of the shelter. What is wrong? A faint shudder passes through him. Presently it becomes a pain spreading from the nape of his neck down into the small of his back. But it is not a physical pain originating anywhere in particular. There is nothing wrong with him, and yet there is something wrong - somewhere. His nerves are quivering. There is a chilly wind. Dr. Lund feels faint, but not, as so often before, with delight. He is faint because he suddenly feels empty. There is nothing within him, nothing around him. Will God unexpectedly punish him because he has just presumed himself to be an inextricable piece in His Plan of Creation? Everything is dark. An anú cries a few yards from him. It ought to be sleeping now!

It is Wilhelm who is suddenly aching in him. Wilhelm inside the Doctor of Philosophy, Peter Wilhelm Lund. He thinks of his mother and of that day in Palermo when he received the package of letters describing her illness and death. He thinks about all those in the family who died young.

Dead, they are all dead.

He thinks about . . . no. He draws the blanket around his shoulders and enters the hut and prepares for the night. No longer does he shiver. The wind is still blowing, but not coldly. The restlessness has gone just as quickly as it came. Dr. Lund notes with satisfaction that the anú is now sleeping as it ought to do. He spreads out the oxhide and lies down warily after having stamped about noisily several times to frighten off snakes. Through the chinks in the roof of palm leaves he will soon see the southern firmament. One of the countless verses which he knows by heart occurs to him, to help him fall asleep. In this poem Goethe, despite all his rhetoric, expresses the true love in an understanding of Nature:

> *So you dabble in Botany, in Optics? What a farce!*
> *Poets should stick to touching tender hearts.*
> *Such hearts! A charlatan can make them flutter.*
> *No, let my joy be this, to touch you, Nature.*

3

'Troglodyte! Troglodyte!'

Even when Dr. Lund thinks himself alone, news of his whereabouts always spreads far and wide. He did not see a single person from yesterday noon until he reached the Indian cliff. Can trees tell tales? Can flowers point the way? Dr. Lund has descended deep into the cave, down to where the stalagmite crust abruptly dips like a frozen waterfall, after he went through the part of the cave where the stalagmite formations created enormous snowy mounds covered with a crystalline crust of brilliant white. He has hardly put down the candles and noted that there is no part which he does not know like the back of his hand before he hears, reverberating from all passages and chambers, one echo catching another and magnifying it in an ever more overwhelming wave of sound, a chorus of *'Troglodyte! Troglodyte!'*

Presently he sees the light of torches, and then three grinning toothless negro boys between the ages of ten and fifteen come into view, disturbing him just as he is about to seat himself upon the stalagmite crust to bid a silent farewell to Lapa da Cerca Grande. This is by no means the most beautiful cave or even the one which has yielded the richest fund of scientific information, but it is the one which most strongly imparts to him the feeling of primeval times, by the primitive paintings outside on the cliff and by the knowledge that wandering Indians still spend nights here on hunting expeditions over the meadowland. Dr. Lund wishes to sit here alone for hours, deep in reflection, filled with gratitude. But now these boys are here, standing in front of him and hitching up the poor spotted rags they use for trousers, even though they can very well see that there are no more bones they can help him dig out of the saltpeter layer, for a few coins apiece.

'Troglodyte!' they repeat, still smiling. Can the wind gossip? Can it whisper from fazenda to fazenda, from senzala to senzala, and all the way out to the tiniest, most isolated caboclo huts? Hardly a year has passed since the first time when, home in Lagoa Santa, Dr. Lund was called "Troglodyte" by a flock of boys. This word for cave man, overheard in conversation with Brandt and childishly mimicked, has become his nickname and has spread from village to village, perhaps over most of Minas province. He smiles. First the *godems* and now Troglodyte. Will they never learn!

Dr. Lund informs the boys that he does not need them, but they are unperturbed. All three sit down on the stalagmite crust, waiting. What are they thinking? The youngest one scratches himself between his wide-spread abscessed toes, painstakingly, his tongue outstretched, as if this were the very meaning of his life. What are they hearing? There is nothing to hear except their own breathing. What are they seeing? Now and then they look up to the ceiling where the bats are hanging in clusters, then gaze at him with no change of expression. The biggest boy has a long red running gash across his forehead. He probably never washes it, and he scratches it with his unclipped amber-yellow nails with their coal black crescents. They will sit like this for hours if Dr. Lund does not chase them out with shouts and gestures. Once in a while they grin at him, immediately afterwards erasing any expression from their faces. They have no food, not even a piece of bread, or any water. They can wait till evening, till the next morning if necessary. If they are sleepy they will roll onto their backs and doze for a few hours, then awake again and, without blinking, sit up and gaze at him as before.

It amuses Dr. Lund to ignore them. The candles shed their soft wavering light onto the ceiling, as if an angel were standing there fluttering long veils of luminous tullé. He recalls all the days and nights he has spent here in the cave digging out the bones of the prehistoric dog, a beast of prey whom no animal approached unpunished, always stalking the paca, its favorite victim. This cave was its impregnable dwelling, in which it concealed its bones, many of which through the millenia lost their organic substance and were transformed into calcite, so that when dropped, they produce the same ringing sound as hollow stalagtites. How can the primeval past be explained to these three boys? How can proper education be introduced to this country in order to furnish it with just a fraction of the knowledge he possesses?

Suddenly the bats flock in panic towards the exit. A rumbling is heard somewhere in the Indian cliff, like the beating of enormous Stone Age drums or hollow tree trunks. The three Negro boys glance at each other, then the eldest motions them off with his torch, and in no time they have disappeared up toward the entrance. One of them drops his torch, which rolls down over the frozen waterfall of the stalagmite crust, down into the depths where it is extinguished with a hiss in the water accumulated from the rainy season. Dr. Lund is not afraid. He convinces himself that it is a violent unseasonable thunderstorm. But when the sounds continue, while the candles begin to flicker, although there is no hint of wind, he thinks of an earthquake and rises. He can barely rise, and when erect at last, his body is so stiff that even the slightest movement is painful. He looks about fearfully and sees that there are no falling stones and that the stalagtites show no sign of loosening. The cave is completely calm, not the least movement is transmitted from the stalagmite crust up through the soles of his boots. But the bats are gone, each and every one. And the candles are still flickering. Dr. Lund looks straight into his own vaporous breath and on the wall his monstrous shadow stands immobile, as if it would do everything in its power to prevent him from taking the slightest step. The rumbling continues. Is the passage about to collapse. *Has* it collapsed already? Will he never get out?

He feels the chilly draught from the passage on the back of his neck, just where it aches most. He must escape as quickly as possible before the earthquake reaches the cave. But then, suddenly the rumbling ceases. Soon the battalion of bats returns. Each bat knows its own flitting erratic path and the spot on the ceiling to which it will cling. The candles do not flicker anymore. Everything is as it was an hour ago, except for the ache in his body, from the back of his neck to the tips of his toes. His insides have tightened into knots and only by summoning up all his energy does he manage to place one foot in front of the other and wrest himself from the hypnotic power of the shadow. He arrives at the passage leading upwards to the outside. He howls in pain and his howl echoes everywhere. It takes him over four hours to move up the passage. The moment he steps outside and sees the meadow steeped in the afternoon sun, the pain abates and he can crawl down the cliff and hobble the short distance to the shelter. A flock of golden-winged parrots flies up towards the peak of the cliff, overgrown by jungle. His attention is drawn to a little *Cassia*. Beside it grows the light rosy *Melochia*. He is breathing freely again, and yet it feels as though everything in him has slackened, as if his body is disintegrating within. Earlier, he had had difficulty making the least movement because of the excruciating stiffness. Now he is exhausted by simply trying to straighten his weak back. His shins and arms feel as though they would snap like brittle twigs, and when he pokes at his gums, they bleed.

When he arrives at the shelter, the mule is lying rigid on its side, congealed foam seeping from its nostrils. It has been bitten to death by a snake.

4

Dr. Lund drags himself along through the campo bushes. He has drunk the last of the water and long since eaten the eggs, cheese, and dried meat. He does not know what to do now that night is approaching. Yet he continues along the path as his glance glides from bush to bush. The track narrows, broadens again, and forks into three small paths, each running in a different direction. There, where the northerly path winds out among some rocks, the three boys are standing. They will carefully show him the way, and having found a stick to lean upon, he follows them, still feeling as if he is disintegrating inside. Long after nightfall they reach a little hut where an old caboclo with snowy white stubble and a ragged straw hat seemingly glued to his scalp receives them in the glare of a torch.

5

Dr. Lund is sleeping in a corner. No one speaks to him, neither the old man nor his pregnant wife nor the three boys. There are no beds or furniture in the hut, only the bare red earth, some pots and heaps of rags piled up along the clay walls. But the old man had solicitously swept together some palm leaves as a bed where Dr. Lund now lies. Dr. Lund grips his jaw and mouth as a little black pig snuffles at his feet. Sleep comes to him and bears him away to the gravel pit of childhood, but he is not searching for swallows' nests, nor is he studying the dance of the mosquitoes on the little lake. He is seeking something, he does not know what, and if he crouches by the lake he sees strange nameless larvae struggling not to be sucked down into the black depths. Nothing is revealed. Everything is chance and darkness is the master of the universe. The next morning Dr. Lund is served water and a bit of bread. The boys help him out onto an oxcart.

'Lagoa Santa', he whispers, and the old caboclo prods the oxen with a pointed bamboo stick, setting the cart slowly, creakingly, into motion.

6

Brandt is there to meet him when the cart pulls up in front of his house. They do not know what to say to one another. Brandt, dressed in his smock and spattered with paint to his wrists, regards Dr. Lund aghast, offers him an arm, helps him down from the cart, and leads him into the house, past the piles of bones not yet catalogued and packed. In the stained old mirror by the door Dr. Lund catches sight of a face with hollow cheeks, porous, slack skin like parchment, and vacant red-rimmed eyes, rheumy with age.

7

Wilhelm is forty-four years old.

II

You know how keen was my interest when I heard you speak at that time, how enthusiastic I was about the description of your stay in Brazil, and in that regard not so much with respect to the mass of individual observations with which you enriched yourself and your science, as with respect to the impression which your first foray into that wondrous Nature made upon you; your paradisical happiness and delight. Such things will always have a sympathetic influence upon every person who has any feeling and warmth, even though he believes that his satisfaction, his occupation, is to be found in quite another sphere, but especially upon a younger man, who as yet only dreams about his destiny. Our first youth is like a flower in the morning dawn with a lovely dewdrop in its cup in which all the surroundings are reflected in a harmonious and melancholy way. But soon the sun rises on the horizon, and the dewdrop dries up; with it disappear the reveries about life. Now the important question is whether the person is able once more, to borrow an image from the flowers, to develop – through his own strength, like an oleander – a drop which can form the fruit of his life. Above all it is necessary to find the soil in which one truly belongs; but this is not always easy.

Søren Kierkegaard, *Letter to the naturalist P.W. Lund, Copenhagen, 1st June 1835 (never sent).*

1

Brazil, Java, Spitzbergen, the North Pole. Where does the Earth begin? Wilhelm makes the globe spin round and round. Suddenly he stops it with his finger. The Earth begins there! And the Earth turns round the Sun and the Moon turns round the Earth. And both the Earth and the Moon turn on themselves. But right now the Earth is standing still because he has stopped it just where Europe merges into Asia. What if he had been born there? Would he have had slanting eyes and high cheekbones? Would he still have been named Wilhelm – just in a different way? He once lived out on a star, said his father after he had climbed the stairs from the draper's shop, changed to his slippers in the corridor, and come all the way through the apartment into the room where Wilhelm has been lying in bed for almost ten days. Now he is feeling a little better. The worst fever attacks are over. His father's globe has been placed on a small low table by the head of his bed so that he can learn all about the countries of the world. It is brown where there are mountains and has yellow markings where there are steppes and white ones indicating desert and stripes and dots across the oceans where Columbus and Vasco da Gama sailed with their men.

His father has seated himself on the edge of the bed. In one hand he holds a bag full of striped candy from the confectioners over on Nytorv, in the other a book with engravings of all sorts of flowers described by Linnaeus in *Flora Suecia*. And his father tells him more about the time when all people lived on the stars just as all those not yet born are living out there right now. Out there had lived the *idea* of Wilhelm, and the *idea* of Troels Frederik and of Christian and of Carl and of Henrik Ferdinand and of his father and his mother. When Wilhelm asks what an idea is, his father answers that it is almost the same as the soul. An idea is simply *something more*, something which is very difficult to describe in a few words. One day God had sent the idea of Wilhelm down to Earth where early in the summer of 1801 it landed on Nygade and became that same Wilhelm with arms and legs, a head and a body who is now lying and listening to his father's story as he spins the globe thinking over the questions which his father answers so well.

But sometimes his father becomes angry or looks as if he is. This is when Wilhelm asks about things he cannot answer. Questions whirl about in Wilhelm's brain. One leads to another, and the more he asks, the more all things around him become alive, especially when he has a fever and does not know when he is awake and when he is asleep and if it is really true that Nelson intends to catch him and put him in the hold of his ship to sit chained to a barrel of gunpowder till he grows old with a tangled gray beard, wild white hair, and nails like long rotten stalks. Why does he dream such things if they are not true? Why are there dreams inside his head? Why are they not *outside*? His father can answer none of these. He grumbles crossly. He scratches his thigh. He wrinkles his forehead and looks out of the window, at the snow falling in large bluish-white clumps melting against the windowpane and turning into drops chasing each other in zig-zags. The wind howls in the chimney and loosens a tile on the roof opposite, causing it to slide down over the gutter and fall onto the street and shatter into pieces with a crash. This calms Wilhelm because for a moment he pictured the tile hitting the head of a passerby so hard that he himself felt a stab of pain. But the tile hit no one and Nelson is not thinking of capturing him and perhaps his father is not as angry as he looks when once more Wilhelm asks why dreams are inside our heads and not outside and presently asks,

'Why do we *ask*?'

His father stands up. Yes, he is angry after all. He strikes Wilhelm's quilt and snatches the bag with the striped sweets out of his hand and puts it under the globe.

'There aren't answers for *everything*!' says his father and goes out, mumbling, 'Why do we dream inside our heads and not *outside*! Why do we ask! Who invented the question mark! That boy can ask about more than . . . It will help matters when he goes to school!'

The doctor has paid a visit. He has given Wilhelm medicine and peered deep into his throat. The coating on his tongue is gone.

'Those eyes! Those eyes! He'll be a professor someday!'

Wilhelm hears these words all too clearly and suddenly he is afraid again, even more than before. He is afraid that the doctor is speaking loudly just to make him think that there is nothing wrong with him. The doctor, his back turned, in his heavy overcoat with small sparkling raindrops on the fur collar, speaks to his father with one hand on his father's shoulder, and Wilhelm feels that it is now only a matter of days. Or perhaps it will happen tonight or early tomorrow, and the doctor knows it, and his father knows it. It means nothing that the fever has dropped and his tongue is no longer coated – he knows, he knows that he is going to die just like his oldest brother Troels Frederik will die and just like . . . just like the two sons his father had with the woman he was married to before and just like . . . And as the doctor packs his things and snaps his bag shut, everything begins to swim before Wilhelm's eyes. Fatigue overcomes him, and he slowly forgets that he may die tonight because now his mother is bending over him in a fragrance of vanilla, kissing his cheek and his mouth. There is nothing better in the world. He looks directly into his mother's eyes and asks her why people always look into each other's eyes when they talk together. She answers that it is because the eyes are the mirror of the soul. She becomes the name he loves most because it sounds like a golden flower out in the fields near Rosenlund. Sara Lisa. His father had once told him about Linnaeus who knew all about the flowers and married Sara Lisa. While his mother smooths his pillow, strokes his hair and says that he should sleep, just sleep, he sees Sara Lisa in Sweden with a basketful of flowers, the most beautiful flowers which Linnaeus has found and with which he speaks when he wishes because he knows that flowers also have souls.

Sara Lisa. Linnaeus.

Linnaeus and Sara Lisa.

Wilhelm is sleeping.

At Borgerdydens School in Klareboderne there is no time for

asking questions. Lessons must be learned by heart and headmaster Nielsen gives floggings for poor marks and detention for the least offence. In wintertime the classrooms are so icy for the first two hours that some of the teachers shiver in their coats while the pupils sit with their teeth chattering and blue cheeks, waiting for the stove to heat up. Greek. Latin. Mathematics. Dates. German. Verses. Recitation, recitation, and more recitation. Borgerdydens is the only school in Copenhagen which also teaches natural history. Wilhelm (or Peter*wil*helm, as the other boys call him, as one word like a rifle shot whose sound he likes because it signifies respect) is clever in all subjects, and in the course of a few years he has the highest marks in the school. Nobody can surpass him, not even the older boys. Headmaster Nielsen always pats him on the back when they meet in the halls or on the stairways, and Peter*wil*helm can even make the grimmest teachers smile just by looking at them with his bright blue eyes. His natural history teacher has become his good friend, and sometimes accompanies him the last part of the way to school because Wilhelm not only learns his lessons better than the others but also knows about all kinds of things in Nature which do not even have to be learned. 'Confound that Peter*wil*helm!' says the natural history teacher in admiration to the rest of the class when Wilhelm has told them all about the difference between staminate and pistillate flowers, about the five parts constituting each flower, or about the time the Botanical Gardens were moved from Amalienborg Castle to Charlottenborg. Wilhelm has already compiled his first herbarium in which everything is arranged according to Linnaeus's method, and he has memorized over forty Latin names. Peter*wil*helm never gets caned.

Carl is in the class above him. Carl is Wilhelm's favorite brother. He does not get on nearly so well with Christian, Henrik Ferdinand, or Troels Frederik. Christian never says anything, Henrik Ferdinand relaxes and brightens up only when the talk turns to new ships for the fleet or counting money, and Troels Ferdinand is always ill. But Carl is curious about everything, and he is also better than all of them at gymnastics and sports. He can run away from the big boys on Nygade, he can beat up all the boys his own age, and he can do twice as many push-ups as Wilhelm, and twice as quickly. In the summer when the whole family moves out to Rosenlund near Vibens Hus, Wilhelm has lots of time on the way to and from Borgerdydens to tell Carl what he knows, not only about Linnaeus, but also about the great Danish naturalists: Henrik Harpestreng, who discovered medicinal plants to cure the most dangerous diseases; Niels Steensen, who was the first (in the whole world!) to describe the fossilized plants and animals which lived thousands of years ago; Martin Vahl who was so much cleverer than his rivals that they were angry and refused to give him a key to the greenhouse in the Botanical Gardens; and Fabricius, who in a number of large books (which his father has promised him as a Confirmation gift) has written everything about how the Earth was created. Wilhelm likes Niels Steensen best, even more than he likes Vahl, because he became a saint who helped the poor and refused to wear fine clothes. But Fabricius' natural history, parts of which his father has read aloud, makes Wilhelm's imagination run wild, and he dreams of the day when he will be old enough to travel to Kiel and see his famous insect collection.

Wilhelm simply cannot stop when telling Carl about everything Fabricius discovered by studying night after night. He points to each tree, catches sight of every roadside flower and sees every cloud in the sky, as his school bag bounces on his back and his polished ankle boots kick up the fine dust on the way to Klareboderne. Sometimes he is forced to stop and hold tight to Carl's elbow to catch his breath; his skin prickles with excitement and his words stumble in his mouth because he can picture it all. First there were the very *simplest* substances of which many *minerals* were formed and then the *terra firma*. Covering the Earth there was *water* as far as the eye could see, waves as high as the Round Tower, even higher, which dashed against one another with a deafening crash and sprayed up to the clouds. There was *no life*, not even a little fish. There was nothing. But then the first *mountain peaks* appeared, and on the first mountain peaks the first *plants* came into view, formed by the minerals and the air. The *animals* were slowly formed by the plants, first some strange *insects* with long horrid antennae, then the *amphibians*, and

. . . the *racoons*. When not only the mountain peaks but also the *plains* and the *valleys* and the *fields* had appeared, then God created *Man*. But not the Negro. Fabricius knows all about this too: that the Negro is a hybrid of the ape and Man. And the two brothers grin, especially Carl, who still recalls the day he saw a negro from St. Thomas with two foreheads exhibited in a cage on a pushcart on Gammel Torv.

While Wilhelm tells Carl all about the Earth and the animals and the flowers, Carl protects Wilhelm on the way to school. Their mother would never allow Wilhelm to make the long walk past the Common by himself, nor would he dare to do it. Among the trees there exists a world utterly different from the one which he describes to Carl. A world of sinister ambushes and sudden hoarse grunts from brawling roughs with pock-marked faces, filthy knees, and ragged pants. There is a band of gypsies encamped around illegal fires, roasting flayed hares and handling the silverware they have pinched and packed into old sacks full of holes. They smell, these gypsies . . . And they lie. And they prophesy death and misfortune, so Wilhelm turns pale with fear when one of them, usually the oldest and ugliest of the women, comes swaying toward him, arms outstretched and a single tooth in her head and tries to catch hold of his left hand, the heart hand, to stare into it and smile evily after she has seen when he is to die. But each time Carl is brave enough to frighten off the roughs or shield Wilhelm behind his broad back when the gypsy woman approaches him. Meanwhile shouts and yells are heard from the Common where the recruits are drilling. Fortunately they are not as loud as before because one summer day his mother, not being able to abide the racket, had taken Wilhelm by the hand and driven directly to Princess Caroline. Immediately granted an audience, she had described the sufferings of the poor soldiers in such a way that the princess had clasped her hands in consternation and had spoken to her father, the King. The canes were then forbidden and now officers appear regularly to make certain that everything goes properly.

Yes, with his mother who always gets things done and Carl by his side, Wilhelm has nothing to fear. He loves to write their names on a slip of paper which he folds into a little lucky ship as he bends over his lessons thinking of the fleet which the English defeated, of the time Copenhagen was bombarded, and of last year when there was a national financial crisis which forced many families from their homes – some even put a bullet into their forehead before dawn. When Carl is sitting over at his table nibbling on his pen, Christian and Henrik Ferdinand are in the next room working out their calculations, Troels Frederik is lying in bed, and his mother is pottering about in the kitchen, sprinkling water on the clothes to be ironed or singing a song in German, then Wilhelm knows that Denmark will regain strength and prosperity when Carl grows up and that Holstein, his mother's homeland, will always be there to protect the country.

To Wilhelm, Holstein means endless fields of wheat, farms twice as large as those of Zealand, thatched roofs reaching down to the ground, lakes which take days to sail across and millions of dragonflies among the rushes, wide roads with wagons drawn by four-in-hands at a full gallop in the turnings, and more birds than one could count in ten lifetimes. His mother's maiden name is Lohbeck. It evokes sunshine from morning till evening, and a large bowl of stewed strawberries and thick cream. Marina. It is like her hand on the nape of his neck and a dish of honey cakes sprinkled with chopped almonds to gladden him and his brothers. Magdalena. It is the Bible and she who consoled Jesus. But also she who can cheer everyone in the family no matter what happens, and no matter how many bombs the English aim at Copenhagen. It is she who gathers the family round the long dining table in Rosenlund and lights the candles in the candelabras and acts as if the crash did not exist. Thanks to her, Uncle Jens can bear to be forced to sell his refinery on Norgesgade. Uncle Ole forgets his money worries and launches into stories about the poets he met at Rahbek's Bakkehus; and his father with pride once again tells about the bombardment in Copenhagen when a cannon ball fell right into his office in Nygade where he had stayed behind alone while the rest of the family fled to Rosenlund. 'A Lund is never afraid! *Never!*' growls his father with satisfaction and makes whistling sounds like a cannon ball speeding through the air before it lands with a BOOM.

Green Lund is Uncle Ole, Blue Lund is Uncle Jens, and Gray Lund is his father. Wilhelm is all ears when out walking with his mother, as she tells him all about his father's family, how they moved from Jutland and became prosperous in Copenhagen and that his father is the one who is most cautious with money as he still wears his modest gray clothes, while Uncle Ole insists upon apparel greener than the greenest beech forest, and Uncle Jens is not content with a costly royal blue coat, but must have an entire wardrobe of blue, from his socks to his singlet. But when his mother speaks about the family before they came to Copenhagen, a dark shadow seems to cross her face. Wilhelm knows that the family has frightful secrets, and he thinks that the reason why so many in the family die young is because the Bible says that the punishment for sinners is passed down for seven generations. Wilhelm suddenly sees black thunderclouds gathering over Jutland, skeletons dancing on the moor, a door creaking on the rusty hinge of a barn in which a man with a blue face dangles from a rope bound to the tie beam. Every ghost story Wilhelm knows passes through his mind when the shadow crosses his mother's face. It is the name Markvor Lund which terrifies Wilhelm. Markvor Lund who, many many years ago, murdered his wife with an axe, leaving blood stains on the floor that could never be washed away, and buried her in the scullery. Before Markvor Lund, the family had been a true noble family with a coat of arms displaying a spread eagle with a star for a head and a real knight's helmet above the escutcheon. But as punishment for his crime Markvor Lund was brought to Copenhagen and beheaded in the presence of the King. The family, deprived of its coat of arms, sank into the deepest poverty, and, as beggers, were forced to migrate from fertile Southern Jutland to Northern Jutland, there to begin again as common smallholders.

'Do we all have to die young because of Markvor?' asks Wilhelm, thinking of Troels Frederik, who is growing paler and paler.

'*Schluuder!*' His mother brushes the shadow from her face, and once more it is she who prevents evil in the world: 'We are not all going to die!' she says and tells him that God has declared that once the family learns obedience it will be elevated again. She smiles, and again Wilhelm thinks about Holstein. When they are walking along Jagtvejen and the sun is shining, she gives him an affectionate prod and he runs over the fields out to the gravel pits to catch butterflies with his new net.

Peter*wil*helm has earned his school-leaving certificate with distinction, and headmaster Nielsen has named him the finest student ever to attend Borgerdydens. There is no doubt: Peter*wil*helm will study medicine and surgery in preparation for a brilliant career as a doctor. Student Wilhelm plunges eagerly into his studies, and elegant, erect, and precise as he is, he rapidly becomes the admired focus of his fellow students and the volunteers at Frederik's Hospital. PW, they call him, a name Wilhelm likes even better than Peter*wil*helm because it signifies not only respect but also a strong-willed man who cuts through to the heart of the matter. PW says. PW suggests. PW thinks. Yes, Wilhelm is delighted to be done with Peter*wil*helm's long years of school and, as PW, to know that the future awaits him with an official residence, study trips abroad and his own textbooks on surgery in German and French translations. Wilhelm dissects crayfish, mice, and rats with a facility unmatched since Niels Steensen. In a year and a half he has done three years of his work. But once in a while he grows dizzy, particularly when he has worked from morning till evening at the hospital. Then he must be looked after by someone, not for very long, but long enough to arouse worry about his health. Nasty cases of disease among the patients make his stomach turn. One day when a patient was taken by a violent attack of cramps, he nearly fainted. The older doctors take council, as they wish to protect him from it happening again: a patient lying on the floor with eyes staring upward, frothing at the mouth, his limbs jerking wildly. They also warn him that he must take care that his childhood consumption does not develop dangerously and become the disease which, as expected, carried off his oldest brother Troels Frederik.

Professor Reinhardt most strongly urges him to abandon the study of medicine and instead devote himself to natural sciences. Reinhardt has been a friend of the family for many years and is Wilhelm's teacher in zoology. Wilhelm admires his lectures – studded as they are with knowledge and new observations – at the Royal Museum of Natural History in the new quarters on Stormgade where Reinhardt reigns supreme. There he personally sees to all the practical tasks of keeping the collections neat while carrying out his own scientific work in his official residence in the same building. This is where after lectures he gathers a circle of young men for whom he enthusiastically describes the day when all animals and all plants will be set into a gigantic system which will reveal to mankind God's Plan of Creation.

True understanding of this plan will create eternal peace on Earth because, where confusion once reigned, order will now be seen. If Man could learn from this order and realize that he is part of the whole, then a new era would dawn in which every nation and every religion would fit into its place in the universal organism and cosmic harmony. Disease would be eradicated. All the continents would become civilized. All men would be able to read and write and thus contribute to the world awakening to consciousness of itself. 'Nature is individualization and individualization leads to coherence and centrality!' Wilhelm takes these words to heart and often stays behind alone with Reinhardt in the museum, so that in peace and quiet, for hours at a time, they can talk as night comes on. Wilhelm can actually *hear* the falling of the dust, representing all that Man must combat because it is decay, oblivion, confusion. Finally Reinhardt convinces him that his future is that of the natural scientist. Wilhelm gives up the study of medicine and instead determines to submit papers to the two competitions held by the university, one of them on a medical topic, entitled *A Description of the Benefits Gained in Human Physiology by the Vivisections Made in the Past Ten Decades,* the other concerning natural science, entitled *An Investigation Carried Out by Knife and by Injection of Danish Decapod Crustaceans Intended to Answer Questions Regarding the Blood Circulation of these Animals.* On the same day, Wilhelm is awarded the prize for each paper. He is praised above all for the latter, in which he compares the so-called heart of the crayfish with the dorsal vessel of the insects and demonstrates

that the venous and arterial system of the gills conducts air.
   PW has become a scientist.

His father's death came as no surprise to the family. Henrik
Gray Lund had been ailing for a long time. Perhaps he could
have been granted five years more, but he died as he had
lived, gently and peacefully, without complaint, his family
gathered round his bed, confident that God would receive
him. Yet the size of the fortune which he left was a surprise,
and after the first period of mourning Wilhelm feels that
Providence is truly with him because now he can face the
future without worrying about money. His money is invested
in safe bonds, in houses in the city, and in business ventures
now flourishing again after the crash. Henrik Ferdinand, who
has been given a position as assistant in the National Bank
after having abandoned his dream of traveling to China for
the East India Company, is charged with administering the
estate and it could not be in better hands. Wilhelm knows
this: that if he does not show respect for the memory of his
father by becoming a scientist who will make the name Lund
famous far and wide, he would be a wretch. Both in Paris and
in Berlin they will one day know the worth of a Lund and
what it means to come from a family which after a terrible
curse worked its way up from generation to generation by
such simple occupations as selling wool and knitting
stockings. Wilhelm can visualize the spread eagle with a star
in place of the head. He will make himself worthy of the
family's old coat of arms. Soon, with Carl as his second in
command, he is busy gathering a group of students to make
excursions out to Frederiksdal whenever the weather permits.
   There, in the Gamekeeper's House by Lake Furesø, they
set up a small laboratory, where Wilhelm has planned
everything down to the last detail. Here, insects, butterflies,
and flowers are classified. Catkins, beechnuts, and acorns are
collected. Descriptions are made of the songs and nests of
birds, the behavior of earthworms, and the hiding-places of
hedgehogs. And together with Carl, Wilhelm attempts to
work out the numerical system according to which the cuckoo
calls. For nights they sit facing one another in the light of the
tallow dips, adding and subtracting - *nothing* in Nature is

accidental. One day, through methodical work, they will discover the secret of the cuckoo. Knowledge, knowledge, and more knowledge is their motto. *Alles lernen*, as Alexander von Humboldt says. From the particular to the general, from the unconscious to the conscious, the spirit which permeates the material, and the subject and the object which permeate one another. Wilhelm seeks to master the great organizing principle. He does not tolerate anyone in the group shirking or speaking about irrelevant matters.

The group includes one student to whom Wilhelm quickly takes a dislike: Beck. He jumbles up all his observations, speaks about ideas where there are no ideas, and does not see them where they really are, convinced all the while of his own superior perception. One day Wilhelm resolves to put him to the test. While Beck is down by the shore of the lake and the others are in the Gamekeeper's House, Wilhelm carefully peels the end off a greenish twig, to make it look like an insect, and places it casually on the counter among a handful of butterfly larvae and millipedes. When Beck returns, he is in an exalted mood. Nature is beating in his breast. He is at one with Nature. He points to the larvae and names them correctly. He pokes at the millipedes. Then his finger hesitates by the peeled twig and he puts on his spectacles. Catastrophe. Beck does not know his facts. Nature does not speak through him, and Wilhelm rejoices. The others in the group laugh mockingly and Beck cringes in fear.

'So, it seems that student Beck cannot *classify*!' says Wilhelm, making the others laugh even louder.

Student Beck grows pale. He is excluded from of the group. He removes his spectacles as the tears begin to roll down his cheeks. He puts on his coat, bows with exaggerated politeness and leaves the Gamekeeper's House, his head awkwardly erect. Wilhelm glances at the other students, feeling he has overplayed his role. He wants to run after Beck, who has now become a dot in the forest, but pride restrains him. What's done is done. The others look at him with even greater respect than before, but mingled now with fear – a fear which spreads to Wilhelm. It makes the hairs rise on the back of his neck; he has discovered a side of himself which he did not know before. He has felt the pleasure of being evil. He is seeing with

Markvor's eyes, hearing with Markvor's ears, feeling Markvor's blood freezing within him. He hastens to think about something else, and after dinner, together with Carl, he again begins to await the cry of the cuckoo. It is late in coming tonight. Then, suddenly, it is there, with one cry. One single cry. Afterwards it is silent for an hour, perhaps two, and Wilhelm and Carl only hear the sighing of the wind in the treetops as they regard each other fearfully.

'Superstition!' says Wilhelm and strikes the table, surprised at the vehemence of his voice, and just then the cuckoo calls once more, and then over and over. Both of them are relieved, and Wilhelm does not give a thought to the little episode till a month later when Carl returns, ill, from a walking tour in Sweden. A storm had taken him by surprise and he had sought refuge in an inn where all the beds were taken, forcing him to make do with a cart shed as shelter from the rain. Exhausted, he had fallen asleep on a wood pile and awakened from that sleep, never to regain his health. Less than a year later, at the age of twenty-five, he dies, smiling, brave, and cheerful to the end. Wilhelm feels that his own turn will come soon. There is no family coat of arms to win back. Markvor is eternally victorious, and Death has its own numerical system which no one can comprehend. Why *Carl*? Wilhelm is frantic with sorrow, as unable to console his mother as she is to console him. At Rosenlund or Nygade they converse in low voices, and their cheeks are pale. Henrik Ferdinand and Christian seem to bear the sorrow better and, together with Reinhardt and the family doctor, they urge Wilhelm to travel to a warm country and carry on his scientific work there. There is already word that a doctor in Milan will translate his prize essay on the significance of vivisection. His mother listens and nods. She knows that Wilhelm knows that her only thought is when will Death come for the third time, this time to snatch away her favorite son? Is. *Was*. Is. *Was*. Wilhelm begins to think of himself in the past tense. He sees the obituary in the newspaper, he hears the minister preaching over his coffin. PW was the most promising student of his generation. Would have gone far had God willed it. Is his future in warm countries? Will Italy keep Death from his door? Or France? Or the magical tropical South America of

Alexander von Humboldt and Auguste de Saint-Hilaire? How far away must he go so as not to go - away?

Wilhelm has no volition left. He loses interest in science and thinks that he ought to have been a poet. Then at least he could have left a volume of poetry. *Poems 1825!* He pays regular visits to Bakkehuset, where Rahbek had gathered his third circle of young poets. Wine, song, and passionate discussions. Slowly life awakens within him again, after weeks of wandering about the Common thinking of Carl and all the gypsy women from whom he had protected him. No one has read his heart hand yet. Late one afternoon as he walks along Vesterbro on his way to Bakkehuset, he sees the Word of God blazoned in the sky. He kneels down, trembling in gratitude. At once he leaps up again, hoping no one has seen him kneeling in the mud. God has shown him the way. He must go to Brazil, to the place he first saw on the globe when he was small and sickly and wondered where the Earth began.

Wilhelm no longer asks why one asks. It is answers he must find now.

Peter Wilhelm Lund does not want to die.

Senhor Lund, the Brazilians call him, and Wilhelm dreams of nothing but the day when he can put 'Doctor' in front of it. Here in Rio de Janeiro that is the grandest one can be, after count or baron, general or admiral. But will he ever achieve it? Every single day terror strikes him – the terror that he too may be afflicted by *the* disease. By comparison, yellow fever is a blessing because it brings instant death. Consumption is an honorable illness although it too ends in death. Leprosy is a misfortune, but a misfortune God has willed. All sorts of stomach infections, muscular atrophy, articular rheumatism, and gangrene are to be preferred because the Devil keeps a respectful distance. But *the* disease is his work, if anything is. It means eternal damnation and a madness that ends by twisting the convolutions of the brain the wrong way. It transforms the face of a man, the noblest of all forms, created in God's image, to a spongy, pustular mask of evil with wildly bristling hair and bleeding eyes bulging from their sockets. Some days Wilhelm hardly dares leave the house of the merchant to whom his letter of credit is addressed and with whom he is lodging. These are the days following the nights when, sweating all over, he has tossed about on the damp sheet, haunted by nightmares because suddenly he feels that no one in Rio de Janeiro can escape *the* disease.

They all have sores on their lips or at the base of their finger nails. Or rashes covering their faces and their arms and the backs of their hands. The rich, with straddled legs and golden slippers bobbing on their toes, have themselves carried about in sedan chairs by muscular negro slaves. With enormous diamond rings on all ten fat fingers, they sport the evil mask of old age, although they could be hardly a day over thirty. And even so they pretend that there is nothing wrong. They may even be proud of their sores and rashes and scratch themselves without restraint while they kiss and hug one another, lascivious like no other nation, without considering that they thus spread the infection. Children also have the disease, especially mulatto boys fourteen years old and more.

45

Grinning and screeching, they run about the dusty streets of Rio de Janeiro, in and out among the sedans and the handcarts loaded with coffee sacks, showing off their sores as if they were jewels – the mark that they have become men. The blackest of the negroes do not seem to have the disease, but Wilhelm knows that this is only because their skin better conceals sores and scars, and he knows that the disease comes from them above all. Had Brazil been colonized by the sanitary North Europeans, or even by the French, and not by these depraved and unwashed Portuguese, the disease would not be nearly so widespread. Nonetheless, Wilhelm is fond of the negroes, of their humor, their gaiety, their songs, their infinite patience. He cannot bear to see them whipped in public for the pleasure of some raging obese fazenda owner, or kicked like dogs by a hysterical female. They belong to a wild offshoot of humanity, ignorant of the Fall of Man, from a remote past which makes them resistant where the civilized European succumbs – the negroes are the unknowing bearers of disease.

Wilhelm keeps his distance from the negroes. Especially in the evening when, in the cool breeze from the South Atlantic, they crowd together in plazas and squares of Baroque churches where they move in a trance around lighted candles amidst bottles of sugar-cane liquor, birds' wings, beads, coffee beans, and small heaps of sugar; offerings to the gods from the Africa they can never forget, where, it is rumored, primeval monsters still survive in the last steaming fern forests. When the spirit roars out of the mouths of the blacks when they dance more and more wildly, the men with bare chests, the women in their white dresses with crocheted veils over their shoulders and waving glowing cigars in the air to invoke the good will of the powers, then Wilhelm is seized with wonder as, from a safe distance, his back pressed against a pink or pastel blue church wall, he wipes the perspiration from his palms or his neck with one of the perfume-sprinkled cloths he always carries. Nothing here is as it is in Europe. Nothing indicates that he exists in the present, on the threshold of an utterly new era in accordance with the Plan of the Creator. Up is down, the past is the present, and the present is a remote future.

46

Even the church seems strange to him, and not just because he is a Protestant. In the Mass things are jumbled together beyond recognition. People kneel incessantly for all sorts of queer saints and pray to guardian angels black as heathen statues, bearing golden crowns and swathed in azure shawls from top to toe. Everything must be kissed, everything must be sprinkled, be it a splinter of bone from a moldy glass-lidded shrine or a blood-stained handkerchief in a murky little niche. One procession succeeds the other, marching in and out of the churches and mingling with the throngs of negroes. Jesuit priests, with week-old stubble, and tiny little nuns unconcernedly pass the negroes' witch doctors and howling spirit mothers. Their cigar smoke to honor Africa's antediluvian gods merges with the Christian incense. Mists from the ancient past blend with the sweat of the brow from the Fall, while now and then the tropical rain washes the offerings of the negroes over to the snout of some black-spotted pig without the negroes noticing because they have long since been lost in a trance. Meanwhile, from the open church doors a European falsetto is heard chanting: *Gloria in excelsis Deo et in terra pax hominibus bonae voluntatis . . . laudamus te . . . benedicimus te . . . adoramus te . . .*

Although Wilhelm cannot but be fascinated by this religious bedlam, his days consist in all other respects of valiant attempts to avoid and evade everything. He never touches railings, he turns handles with his elbows, he never drinks water without first having it boiled, and he demands to examine his meat with a magnifying glass before it is cooked for him in an eating house. He sniffs eggs cautiously and throws them away at the merest odor or blood speck on the yolk. When not invited out to dine and spend the night at the home of members of the European colony, he returns to his room before the abrupt tropical night fall, when the streets and roads become dangerous for anyone who appears to have a bulging wallet or a gold watch in his vest pocket. If he must relieve himself, he has developed a special technique to avoid touching the seat. He places his hands wherever he can and thus supporting himself on extended arms he hangs directly over the soil tub and evacuates until he turns blue in the face with exertion. Thus the weeks pass for Wilhelm, fluctuating

47

between fear and wonder, without accomplishing anything of note.

At the end of September he had sailed directly from Copenhagen on board a ship which a wind from the southwest had forced to sail north of the Faroe Islands and which was delayed off Scotland for sixteen days due to headwinds and unexpected frost. Not until December did the ship reach Rio, which was illuminated in honor of the birth of the heir to the throne. Cannons boomed from a naval fleet gathered in the harbor to set sail for Montevideo to crush the rebellious Uruguayans. In this year of 1826 and, as the Carnival approaches, every day is a new celebration which provides Wilhelm with excuses for not collecting birds, fish, insects, flowers, and plants, and sending them together with detailed bulletins to Reinhardt. Behind Rio lies vast Brazil, this newborn empire which bears little more resemblance to a nation than do Antarctica or Siberia. A few coastal towns, some thousand plantations and fazendas, a population of a few million, most of them slaves, and a wild and undiscovered country patiently awaiting him, student Peter*wil*helm and prize-winner PW from the capital Copenhagen and now Senhor Lund, destined to become for the Portuguese part of South America what Alexander von Humboldt became for the Spanish.

Amazonas! Mato Grosso! At home in his room Wilhelm spends hours poring over the newest printed maps. He cannot comprehend how borders can be drawn between Brazil and its Spanish-speaking neighbors in regions where no white man has yet set foot, winding borders painstakingly drawn, round mountains, over lakes, along rivers, zig-zagging through impenetrable jungles. But he is not going to be a cartographer, he is going to be an explorer whose speciality is Nature, and therefore he will no longer waste time. He decides to experience the Carnival, which everyone speaks of as if it were the Eighth Wonder of the World, and then there must be an end to it. Henceforth he will depart from this filthy, noisy capital where no one keeps an appointment, where orchestras play with wretched delapidated instruments, where the Italian opera has no decent repertoire, and where no bookshop but the German one in Rua da Quitanda attempts to stay up to date with the latest scientific publications.

One thing consoles Wilhelm: that his chest seems healthy. He has not coughed a single day since arriving in Brazil. The tropical climate has done wonders in this regard, and he writes about it in great detail to his mother, who has now moved into a small apartment by the shore. If she is content, he is content. And he adds and subtracts so that the Brazil which she reads about is a country in which everyone is polite and drowses all day long in hammocks while being waited on by well-nourished slaves as the palms cast their cool shadows and all sorts of gaily colored birds offer delight to those who bother to open their eyes. Reinhardt on Stormgade must wait for his bulletins for another month or two.

The imperial and royal Austro-Hungarian Consul General has the honor of extending an invitation to a ball at his country home upon the occasion of the arrival in Rio of the Countess Viktoria Ritter Meduna von Riedburg und Langenstauffen-Pyllwitz and Count Ghyzy von Giecz, Assa und Ablanczkürth, on their journey home to Europe from Tierra del Fuego. Among the guests is Doktor Pedro Guilherme Lund. The invitation has gone via the Dutch vice consul Hindrich, a cultivated man and an ardent collector of insects who has become Wilhelm's good friend and who has helped him with advice and letters of introduction. Wilhelm is chagrined to see himself addressed by a title which he has not yet earned. He feels like a fraud and hopes that no rumor will reach home that he is going about here calling himself doctor and - why not? - professor. But otherwise he is looking forward to the party which, he has decided, will mark the end of his stay in Rio. Afterwards, again with the aid of Hindrich, he will take up residence in a secluded house half a league inland, at the foot of a mountain upon whose slope - he has been told - a plantation of coffee, oranges, plantains, and pineapples stretches until merging with the virgin forest. For the rest of the year Wilhelm will concentrate on his work, after the party at the home of the Imperial and Royal Consul General, where from the start everything proceeds in the most lavish style in the elegant suburb of Catete.

Immense fish of all colors are borne in on tortoise shells, carved into filets as thick as bricks, garnished with langoustes, lobsters, crabs, snails, and oysters. Suckling-pigs are rotating on spits, the desserts are coconut and chocolate delicacies from the great fazendas in Bahia, which have taken days to prepare. The beer has been brought in barrels from the German colony in Uruguay. The wine comes from Chile and France; choice bottles unsurpassed in Europe. Everything is served upon golden dishes and poured into silver goblets encrusted with aquamarines, tourmalines, and amazonites. As an extra refinement there is a marble table in a corner where those who wish can taste paper-thin slices of raw fish, carved by a Chinese chef. The women's gowns are of the costliest silk, their hair is set in the latest European fashion, their throats are encircled by clusters of rubies. At a mere snap of their fingers, a negro slave woman comes running with smelling salts or perfume. The men are dressed just as ornately. They too are perfumed and powdered, and they carry thin cigars in long ornamented ivory holders.

On a dais a chamber orchestra is playing Louis Spohr's *Quatuors brillants*, which in Wilhelm's opinion has moments which measure up to Clementi, his favorite composer – and which is played *nearly* in tune and almost as the music is written, offering a touch of Europe, a fragile hope that in this country too, civilization will one day gain a foothold. But it will take many years, he realizes gradually as the evening wears into night and manners become coarser, and the guests strain to keep up conversation in their poor English, French, and German. In one room the dance begins, out of step, and the women laugh too loudly, as if they wished to be heard on the other side of the Atlantic. Wilhelm sends a fond thought to his mother. She would be ashamed of her own sex if she were here. In another room they are playing games of cards and dice, pounding on the tables and spitting on the floors like in some rowdy sailors' pub. Belches fill the air, and now and then a guest calls for his slaves to carry him to the nearest balcony so he can vomit. There are innumerable *doctores* present who claim to know everything about philosophy and science, but when Wilhelm enters into conversation with them, proud to be able to speak the three major languages without mistake or accent, he discovers that they know less than pupils in the middle school in Borgerdydens. When they realize that they have revealed their ignorance by confusing Descartes with Linnaeus – oh, that Europe which everyone yearns for, dreams of, kneels to, is ready to sacrifice everything for, oh to be returned to its embrace! – then they avoid him as if he were armed with a poisoned rapier and stumble off to the tables, fanning themselves with embroidered handkerchiefs to overfill their cups with more wine. And now Wilhelm thinks of his father, old Gray Lund, who knew that woollen stockings and savings are better for mankind than all the diamonds in the world.

Then suddenly a young man is standing directly in front of him, first sideways, seemingly preoccupied and slightly weary, as if he wished to converse with all others but him, but presently turning and smiling as if they were old acquaintances. His thick black curly hair is littered with confetti, his silk shirt is unbuttoned far down his chest, on which drops of sweat catch the light from the multitude of candles in the crystal chandeliers. And on his little finger gleams the most glorious diamond of the night. His eyes are brownish black but soft and yielding. His lips are formed like two classic Cupid's bows, his complexion is pale, but not from illness. No doubt he is one of those who purposely keep in the shade to avoid the suspicion of having mulatto blood in their veins. He strives to emphasize the European in his appearance by his way of holding the goblet as if it were light as a feather, with the wine filled to just above half, as is proper, and by nonchalantly placing one foot in front of the other. The proud curve of his back, the half upturned shirt collar sliding under the hair at the nape of his neck – yes, here at last Wilhelm feels that he has met an equal, one of his own age, sensitive and perceptive.

Soon they have introduced themselves to one another, exchanged compliments and inquired with interest about each other's occupation. The young Brazilian comes from one of the wealthiest fazenda families in the hinterland. However, years of longing for culture and refinement drive him time after time to Rio de Janeiro where for weeks he strolls about the harbor, awaiting the day in the near future when he will sail to his motherland Portugal. From there he can set off by coach, on horseback, by foot, *n'importe comment*, on his grand tour to Francois-René Chateaubriand's lucid France and Johann Gottlieb Fichte's powerful and learned Germany. *Reden an die Deutsche .Nation!* Wilhelm is impressed by the young Brazilian's precise choice of quotations by Fichte – '*Aber wirke, als wenn kein Gott sei!*' – and his persuasive ability to describe, on the basis of his philosophy, the dawn of a new poetic and political day in which all men will be equal and the lion will slumber next to the lamb. Clementi? Of course! No composer can surpass him, not even Mozart – about this the two agree completely, whereas something within Wilhelm tightens into a black knot of fear when the talk turns to Fichte and the revolution which would set Man in God's place. Even though the Brazilian is not fanatic and describes Clementi as accompanying mankind's hope for equality and fraternity, as if a mere magical snap of the fingers could make the doors of Paradise on Earth swing open, still Wilhelm is relieved when their conversation turns to Nature and Cuvier, the master from the Collège de France whose *Tableau eléméntaire de l'histoire naturelle des animaux* Wilhelm knows by heart. They talk elatedly while the Brazilian takes him by the arm and carefully, continually excusing the vulgar behavior of his countrymen, gently leads him out onto a balcony from which they can see the slaves amusing themselves on the muddy roads leading to the illuminated palaces.

Confetti is showering down from the balconies, and buckets of water are being poured onto the dancing and singing negroes while they are throwing at one another balls of wax as large as breadfruits which explode with their contents of perfumed goat's milk. Others are flinging sand, flour, rice, egg shells, and rotten eggs. One group of slaves prance off, dressed like doddering Europeans with white-painted faces and yellow paper vampire teeth jutting from their mouths and exaggeratedly high-heeled Baroque shoes, waving to the left and right as if they were the lords of the world. The musicians are also dressed like Europeans, with moth-eaten wigs, and the main procession, the *entrudo*, carries at its head the giant doll of a white prince, half ghost, half fairy tale figure, with savagely staring conch eyes and arms flopping about its body. Mulatto girls are being chased among the trees, dogs are howling, cats are spitting from the treetops. The negro music grows louder, with its droning monotonous rhythm of guitars, dulcimers, and primitive violins not exactly pleasing to a trained ear, yet the atmosphere is filled with a sweetness, a fragrance of cinnamon and melted sugar which charms Wilhelm – or *Guilherme* as the Brazilian calls him – in a way that makes his name sound like a rhyme in an ode or an elegy. For the first time in Rio, Wilhelm feels at ease. It is like an exotic and arousing dream, and an unfamiliar tingle runs up his arm when his new acquaintance lightly places his hand upon it. While he drains his goblet, the slaves caper beneath them, and Wilhelm does not know where he is because he hears himself speaking on and on about Nature. But now it is not Nature as Cuvier describes it in his works but the Danish nature as he himself sees it and remembers it and which his friend does not tire of hearing about – the red-footed falcons and the marsh harriers and the blackberry butterflies, the beech forests, the meadows and the hundred small islands, the fogs, sunsets and the spring's romantic . . .

'*Dänemark!*'

Wilhelm comes to himself, startled to hear a deep rusty female voice. He turns his head. His friend is gone. Instead, the Countess Viktoria Ritter Meduna von Riedburg und Langenstauffen-Pyllwitz is standing beside him, asking about that country which was the only one in Europe to have the indescribable stupidity to side with Napoleon. Wilhelm is speechless. Before, Denmark was beautiful and now it is poor and oppressed. The Countess smiles ironically at him, her rouge smeared out over her lips and a tiara set with brilliants jammed askew onto the coiffure which must have taken three hairdressers nearly a day to set. Wilhelm thinks of Jutland in the dead of winter and of his family on its way northward, clutching beggar's staffs, as mounted soldiers from the south burn farms and pillage for food. The country is stripped first of its eastern part, then of Norway, and perhaps soon also of the rest, including Copenhagen to which the Countess mockingly refers as a little provincial North German town in comparison with the Vienna from which she comes, the

Vienna of the Congress, the true, elegant capital of Europe. And she laughs wickedly, obviously tipsy, while with two fingers moistened with spittle she twists a lock of Wilhelm's nape hair into a curl and the negroes in the plaza below send him big toothless grins from their white-painted faces.

Is Wilhelm also intoxicated? He has emptied three goblets, he who usually never drinks anything but tea, milk, and water, and a violent disgust rises in him at the foul breath of the Countess, her fingers at his neck, and her perfume mixed with the reek from her bare, hairy armpits.

But then all is transformed again when his friend returns and with a single glance causes the Countess to retreat in a huff. His friend is holding a bottle of wine and pours for both of them and says that after Wilhelm's description he has now placed *Dinamarca* as the first destination on his itinerary. He kisses him very lightly on the lips and Wilhelm feels as though they have been brushed by a butterfly. Then the horror comes over him, a horror which he has never known before. The ground beneath him gives way, and in a flash of fireworks he suddenly sees that his friend's face is not that of a friend. His eyes are not soft and brownish black but black as ebony, soulless, as if they would pierce him. The diamond on his little finger swells up like a shapeless living creature, and on his upper lip, slanting down towards the corner of his mouth, zinc ointment poorly conceals the rough scabby sore. Wilhelm bangs his goblet down onto the balustrade and flees through the salons and the halls, now filled with dancers. In the corner sofas, couples are lying entwined, the members of the chamber orchestra slouch drunkenly among their toppled instruments, and everywhere it seems as if the Countess Viktoria Ritter Meduna von Riedburg und Langenstauffen-Pyllwitz is grinning at him. Going down the stairway he stumbles several times over some of those who had introduced themselves as doctors and who now sprawl on the steps pawing at giggling negro slave girls. Footsteps sound behind him unceasingly. But he will not turn.

'*Guilherme! Guilherme!*' he hears. Lamenting, entreating.

Wilhelm rushes outside and the terror within him mounts. He runs after the frolicking blacks who are now setting their course toward the heart of the town. Soon he is struck in the back of his head by the first wax ball, then the second, then one hits his temple and the sticky stinking goat's milk drips down his cheek and underneath his shirt. Wilhelm must go home – 'home' to his spartan room at the house of the merchant, not far from the main street Rua Direita, but there is still far to go and he does not know the way. First the road runs abruptly into a wall. Then it leads him directly out toward the jungle. Then it is filled with holes deep enough to stand in, and sometimes it winds back towards Catete so that Wilhelm must start all over again. New processions appear, more wax balls are cast at him. He trips over beggars while mulatto girls leap out of the darkness and clutch his shirt and spit angrily when he desperately pulls himself free. Spluttering fireworks land in front of his muddy running feet while everything in his brain turns into Fichte – that Fichte who says that the self creates the non-self, who says that everything which exists is the result of the productive imagination. Everything is invented. Everything is self-activity. He is like the spider in its web, racing frantically up and down the threads he has spun from his own self, past houses imagined by himself which collapse onto plazas which he himself has fantasized and in which everyone is chasing him. The names he says aloud so as not to lose his mind as his heart hammers in his throat from exhaustion are only names, invented in another age, in a happier dream – Vibens Hus, Nygade, the Common, Rosenlund, Klareboderne, Lohbeck. There is no Holstein to protect him, only the rocking and pitching, stinking and riotous tropical capital, a notion from the depths of his darkest self in which everyone, and now he as well, has *the* disease.

Then at last Wilhelm reaches the home of the merchant. He fumbles with his keys and tears at the door handles on the way to his room, where he falls over all the costly measuring instruments given him by the Royal Danish Academy of Sciences and Letters before he flings himself onto his bed. And vomits.

It was a bagatelle. Wilhelm knows it. Never again will he touch a drop of alcohol. Never again will he discuss philosophy based solely upon speculation. Precision, observation, collection of data, classification – these are the important things. Away from the brain, out into Nature. Wilhelm sets to work with furious energy. He has moved out to the little country house and rises with the sun at five in the morning. He works in his room until six o'clock, drinks tea, then goes off on his excursions, armed with his double-barreled piston rifle as defense against human beings as well as beasts. He hacks his way forward step by step in the dense high and thorny brush covering the surface of the uncultivated earth. One excursion in particular into the wild dark virgin forest into which the rays of the sun never penetrate and where no man has ever set foot surpasses in ruggedness but also in beauty everything he has ever known. About dinnertime he returns home and studies his new finds. After dinner, prepared by the kindhearted old negro slave who is a permanent fixture in the house, he continues to work until it grows dark and then descends to the sea to bathe. He no longer even thinks of Rio. The city was a necessary evil to arrive at this place, the best he could wish for, with a view of the deep bay on which Rio lies.

Everything is within his reach, mountains, forest, rivers, and the sea, and finally he has sent the first detailed reports home to Reinhardt and packed plants and bird skeletons into specially built crates. He has also become interested in fish. He catches a great variety of them and pulls off their skin after having rubbed them with snuff and dried them in the sun. Moisture is his enemy – a few days later the heads and fins are covered with mold. He has better luck when he soaks them in alcohol, in 'Omega-sign'. Before immersing them, he notes their colors down to the most delicate nuances so that Reinhardt can compare the fresh fish with the dead, faded ones. A special delight for Wilhelm is the study of the lower marine animals. Among these he discovers a number of new ones, some of which cannot be classified under the known main genera. Among the asymmetrical specimens he is especially pleased to have discovered the living representative of the extinct genus *Favosites*. He observes physiological phenomena in this creature which are utterly incomprehensible to him. Among the articulate worms he finds a genus which forms a new group. Among the earthworms he distinguishes three species, one of which is between *Lumbricus* and *Thalassema*, and another of which is remarkable for its gigantic size as it measures twenty-four inches when immobile and thirty when it crawls.

The more Wilhelm observes the products of Nature and not of speculation, the dizzier he grows at the thought of how infinitely much more there is to investigate, and how little he knows as a botanist, an ornithologist, an entomologist, and an ichtyologist. Every stone he picks up at the beach, when the incoming tide permits a seaside excursion, is covered with a foam-like substance always differing in consistency, color, shape, and structure. His study of these colonies of small organisms is like an enchantment. He can hardly imagine a painting lovelier than these rocky basins whose crystal clear waters appear in the vertical searing sun more transparent than air itself. Their walls are carpeted several inches thick with small creatures of the purest hues from azure and scarlet to orange and vermilion, and whose floor is ornamented with thickets of algae and corals. Wilhelm describes all this for Reinhardt and even allows himself to get carried away with poetry, as when he receives a letter from Henrik-Ferdinand notifying him of the royal resolution according to which 'We have most graciously ordered that from the fund *ad usus publicos* the annual sum of 400 rigsdaler in silver coin be used for the collecting of zoological and other natural specimens in Brazil by *Candidatus philosophiae* Lund for the Museum of Natural History of this city.'

Peter Wilhelm Lund is far from being the only European scientist exploring Brazil in the footsteps of Sainte-Hilaire, Johann Baptiste Spix, and Karl Friedrich von Martius. By the mail which arrives every other week by donkey driver or from travelers passing through, he learns all about the European expeditions being organized in Rio to set off for all corners of Brazil, with costs borne by the Czar of Russia or by the European royal houses. In some cases colossal sums are at stake. A certain Langsdorff has two hundred thousand roubles at his disposal, a sum which sets Wilhelm dreaming. The urge to exchange scientific experiences wells up in him. There must be somebody who would understand the value of the considerable collection he has gradually accumulated and which awaits shipment to Copenhagen.

The desire to communicate makes Wilhelm restless, and there is nothing he would rather do than go along on one of the great expeditions, either with Netterer to Pará, or with Langsdorff to Mato Grosso. Or even with the world-famous African traveler William Burchell who is preparing a major journey via São Paulo and Rio Grande do Sul to Buenos Aires and thence diagonally up through Paraguay and western Brazil to Lima in Peru.

Wilhelm hastens to Rio, his experiences at the Carnival happily forgotten. But he is advised against joining Burchell who has no idea of how to manage finances. In just a few years Brazil has become the most important field of investigation for European science. Everything in Rio is touched by the spirit of discovery, and everyone who intends to map new areas is lured by gold mines or rivers full of diamonds. Wilhelm determines to make his own expedition with no thought of becoming rich. He has tired of his worms and the lower marine animals; he wants to go inland, and he decides that his first destination will be the Swiss colony Nova Friburgo. For four days he rides from morning till evening. At times he must ford rivers with water up to his waist. The strong currents and round smooth stones paving the riverbed make it nearly impossible to keep his horse and pack donkeys from slipping. At times they must struggle onward for miles through mire halfway up their legs. Some of the rivers he must cross have risen so high from the rain that he can cross them only by swimming or in a canoe lent to him by local negroes. To add to his difficulties, there are no inns. In the evening, when Wilhelm arrives, exhausted, at a venda more wretched than most wretched European hovels, there is nothing to eat but dried meat and black beans. There are no beds. Wet and dirty as he is, he must lie upon the floor, and only the toils of the day enable him to fall asleep quickly. On the last day, with a six-thousand-foot-high mountain chain to cross, the difficulties culminate. Here the road is mostly a dried-out riverbed paved with loose stones among which the horses and pack donkeys have to pick their way with the utmost effort. Where there is a dirt track that has become so mired from the constant rain that it costs him even more trouble. It rises steeply, it drops downward diagonally, it winds so close to the precipice that the horse and donkeys are forced to climb, jump, crawl, and even worse, to slide on their rumps. Wilhelm has no idea how at last they manage to get over, dripping with perspiration from physical effort and from fear.

His reward awaits him in Nova Friburgo near the rivers Rio das Bengalas and Rebeirão do Cônego in a wide wooded valley. Here Wilhelm meets people of far greater integrity than in Rio, responsible, clear-skinned, and busily occupied with cultivating maize, churning butter, making cheese, fabricating cuckoo clocks and meteorological instruments of a precision that has won them fame throughout most of South America. The houses are freshly painted and newly washed, and the inhabitants all wear the costumes of their native cantons.

Exhausted, Wilhelm is shown the way to the *Gasthof* of the colony, which has a quotation from Schiller in Gothic lettering above the entrance:

Everywhere the world is a perfection
Man's tormented soul can never reach.

Wilhelm spends several weeks in Nova Friburgo, frequently invited to gatherings where inspiring European conversation is given pride of place. Then he moves on, to Fazenda Rosário some miles away, where the guest house is placed at his disposal. Here he enjoys the most rewarding time yet. He obtains a live three-toed sloth, and he studies passionately the nature of the animal and writes its biography in extenso: the ideal of an unsuccessful physical and spiritual organization whose sluggishness and stupidity are scarcely to be credited. He dissects the black urubú, the turkey vulture. Beneath its skin, on the forewall of the craw, he finds an opening large enough to poke a quill through, and he is convinced that it is not a pathological malformation. He describes the roadside plants and weeds and records the life of the Brazilian carpenter ant, as well as the remarkable deviation from the normal structure of the alimentary canal which he finds in specimens of the family *Euphones*: these birds quite simply lack the gizzard or craw.

For a year and a quarter Wilhelm remains in Fazenda Rosário, with only one long journey, to São Salvador dos Campos and São Fidélis by the Paraíba River inhabited by the half-civilized Indians of the Coroado and Coropó tribes. Every day is a gift, no matter where he wanders with his rifle, his vasculum, and his insect clips. He hunts everything, even the tapir which often does not drop before being shot many times and chopped vigorously with a machete, leaving Wilhelm streaked with blood. At home in the guest house he spends his time recording what he has shot and observed, anatomizing, skinning, skeletonizing, drying, arranging, and packing while the negro slaves flock in curiosity to his windows.

At first the negroes clearly thought him mad and could not comprehend what he was doing. But gradually they have gained respect for him, especially after the day when the surgeon from the nearby town with whom he has had some 'scientific' conversations admitted that the 'damned Englishman' knew more than he himself, while the schoolmaster confessed the same regarding Latin. This respect verged upon awe when the negroes saw that his piston rifle could spit fire without stones. Often Wilhelm has a whole troop at his heels when he is out shooting, and he takes great trouble to maintain his esteem, so that it is rumored that the 'Englishman' never misses a shot. His diet is simple, consisting mostly of eggs, meal, and fish from the streams on the fazenda lands – but even with his modest food he is on public display, as if his meals were imperial feasts. The slaves besiege his windows, exclaiming in wonder about his manner of eating with a knife and a fork, and with a napkin spread on his lap. If, the following day, he goes by a field of sugar-cane in which negroes are laboring, he can hear that the most important local news is how much the *godem* has eaten in the past week and which kinds of fish.

But Wilhelm misses his family. How does his mother look after all these years? How does her voice sound? And how are Henrik Ferdinand and Christian as married men, the husbands of Petrea and Nicoline Kierkegaard from Nytorv? Wilhelm receives many letters from home, and sometimes he breaks down in tears, overpowered by yearning. He ought to return home soon. But just as he has decided to write enquiring about ship's passage, he is afflicted with a violent skin disease. He is covered by a rash and then struck by other ills. He has stabbing stomach pains, dropsy in his knees, aching feet when he stands up, dizziness for the slightest reason. He is in a constant sweat, even at night when it is cool. Wilhelm dares not think it through to the end, even though he hears within him, unceasingly: sin, guilt, *punishment*, sin, guilt, *punishment*. For three weeks he does not step outside the guest house, and he eats nothing but bread. The sloth lies curled into a ball and the piston rifle stands by his headboard, loaded. He mobilizes all his courage to look Death in the eye.

Then, gradually, his ills disappear. Bony and pale, Wilhelm notes with relief that there is no trace of a sore on his lips or at the roots of his nails. Providence is with him once more, the blood again surges in his veins, and in the middle of January 1829 he departs by ship for Europe with his collection, drawings, and notebooks, and with tanned warm cheeks.

Senhor Lund is on his way to his doctorate.

3

P.W. Lund, D. Phil., soon realizes that with a Danish father and a Danish upbringing he is not highly regarded in Holstein. There is opposition to the government, and the students, who refuse to speak Danish, have written protests against being forced to study a language and a literature which, they feel, have little relevance. There are riots in the streets of Kiel and more than once rotten apples and brimming chamber pots have been thrown on the Danish professors at the university, behavior about which Christian Flor, Peter*wil*helm's old teacher at Borgerdydens School, complains most bitterly.

Professor Flor is a man whom Dr. Lund values highly. However, after Flor's participation in the conspiracy of 'The Dozen' who sided with Oehlenschläger in the war waged against Baggesen, whom Dr. Lund considers to be Denmark's most universal poet, Flor has a tendency to talk about the 'slumbering' Nordic spirit, about 'forebodings' and 'ardent strivings'. Such things are hardly to Dr. Lund's tastes, and particularly not now. For with the University of Kiel's acceptance of *De genere Euphones* as a pioneering doctoral thesis elucidating the unsurpassed fauna of Brazil, he is strengthened in his belief that precision is the only means of progress and also helps to overcome those ridiculous misunderstandings between nations which inevitably lead to chaos and war. It hurts Dr. Lund to see how isolated Flor and the other professors are in their outpost. It hurts him even more to be advised against spending several weeks exploring his mother's native Holstein, the place of his boyhood dreams, because it is said that many inns refuse to accommodate Danes. There are even rumors that Danish envoys have been beaten bloody on deserted country roads and in Kiel harbor pubs. Dr. Lund therefore decides to depart at once for Berlin and Vienna on his first grand tour of Europe.

He cherishes the recollection of the reunion with his family in Copenhagen. His mother is doing well, far better than he had dared to hope, in her new apartment by the Canal.

Gentle and unchanging in her starched gown, she keeps alive her memories of his father. Christian lives with Nicoline on Nygade and carries on the draper's business, whereas Henrik Ferdinand, having married Petrea and advanced steadily in the National Bank, has purchased a house in Nørrebro, outside the city rampart, with a lovely garden running down to the shore of Peblinge Lake. Here Wilhelm spent most of the summer. Evening after evening, he recounted stories of Brazil while gazing out at the noiseless dance of the mosquitoes beneath the treetops and the flight of the ducks across the sky. Now and then a pair of swans with their young come all the way to the garden table to be fed on biscuits, while a litter of German boxer puppies romps amidst the roses and the honeysuckle arbor with no fear of snakes or poisonous spiders. Not much has changed in placid Copenhagen. The summer was unusually long and warm, but when the church bells pealed at sunset, the cigars and candles were lit, and the West Indian rum toddies appeared on the table, a pang would at times pass through Wilhelm because, in the midst of the family circle, he would feel that it might never befall him to settle down as a husband and father, surrounded by children of all ages, to wake each morning, in times of joy and sorrow, to see the cheek of a faithful woman upon the pillow. 'Uncle Wilhelm,' Henrik Ferdinand's newborn daughter Henriette will soon be saying in a clear childish voice or in letters, 'Uncle Wilhelm, tell me about everything that has happened to you alone out in the world.' But his mother is content and that is most important of all. She asks of him only that, at the age of twenty-eight, he live up to his growing reputation. And that he take care of his chest.

During his short stay in Kiel, Dr. Lund no longer dwells on his fate as a bachelor. He thinks above all of Europe, of the energetic, progressive Europe of science, museums, academies, colleges, journals, libraries, and dissertations. In Berlin there is a ringing frost, and Dr. Lund dresses warmly. He is impressed by the seriousness which reigns in all government branches, and he even admits the justness of the notorious military system because every subject, regardless of rank or position, is also a soldier. What Berlin has done for art and science ought to serve as a model for Copenhagen. There is something inexplicable about the way culture can blossom here. It is a potato land, poor in resources, ravaged by wars, and forced by its geographical position to maintain a disproportionately large army, yet it generously supports the arts and sciences. Officials receive the wages of princes, parks are trimmed and lush, and monumental public buildings are erected, all because effective government can work miracles. To be sure, the castle cannot measure up to Christiansborg, but Dr. Lund is struck dumb when he enters the Armory, which offers a display of weapons unequaled by anything he has ever seen. The most scrupulous order prevails, and visiting schoolchildren, caps in hand, whisper in awe. Every cannon barrel is polished, every rifle butt shined, every uniform spotless and brushed free of the least speck of dust. Dr. Lund finds the atmosphere in Berlin more courteous than hospitable – except when he pays a visit to the Zoological Museum, converses with its director, the indefatigable, systematic, ambitious collector Rudolphi, presents him with a copy of *De genere Euphones* and persuades him to open the sealed jar containing the viscera of the black urubú. It is a great moment for Dr. Lund when he fishes out the craw with tweezers and finds its structure to be identical to his Brazilian specimens, with a hole large enough to contain a quill. Rudolphi growls like a bear and claps his hands, looking like he could hop with excitement in his lambskin-lined bison boots. The next day he sends a messenger to Dr. Lund's hotel with a set of keys and a letter stating that the museum is at his disposal and that he may open any sealed jar he might wish.

In just a few days, Dr. Lund's reputation has spread throughout the cultivated circles of Berlin. He is greeted on the street and invited to tea-rooms and to chamber-music concerts. He finds that his reputation has preceded him as he journeys down through Europe, via Dresden and Prague to Vienna, where from the very start he must strive diligently not to be drawn into an all-consuming whirl of social distractions. He is dragged from dinners to suppers, from suppers to the theater, from operas to operettas. The city reminds him a good deal of Copenhagen. Like the citizens of Copenhagen, the Viennese are fond of a certain degree of soft comfort, and they too possess an appealing modesty, quite unlike the vulgar behavior of the Countess Viktoria Ritter Meduna von Riedburg und Langenstauffen-Pyllwitz in Rio de Janeiro. Is she not a native of Vienna? Perhaps she is not listed in the authorized peerage? Dr. Lund has no wish to enquire. She was an evil character in an evil dream. For when he recalls Brazil, it is the nature of the country which he remembers – and can still smell, still sense in his body like a hint of fever, still feel tingling in his fingertips as the sensation of the skin being pulled off an animal and the welter of intestines, of the dusty fur of the sloth, of the algae and corals, and of the slime on the scales of a fish and the chill of a snake's skin. Can the highly praised nature of Italy measure up to that of Brazil? He doubts it – but ever curious, he intends to travel to Sicily, and so, earlier than intended, and not without thought of avoiding the countess, he sets off from Vienna.

It is the harshest winter in the memory of man. Dr. Lund grows anxious and wraps his muffler high up to cover his nose and mouth. To be sure, he has brought good winter clothing, but five days and five nights of relentless, arduous traveling by stage coach to Venice is almost more than he can bear. The snow falls in whirling flakes, smothering the fields and farms of Italy. After the dusty streets of Vienna, lacking sidewalks and so crowded with carriages that he could not take two steps without risk of being run over, Venice is like a town of some submerged Atlantis, with its narrow shale-paved streets where horses and carriages are so rare a sight that the inhabitants have only heard tell of them. In disappointment he writes his mother about the frozen canals, the hoary gondolas, the Palace of the Doge, its facade hung with icicles, and the Piazza de San Marco, as fine for skating as Peblinge Lake. The doors and windows of his hotel room shut so poorly that there is a constant draught, the floor tiles have all cracked from the cold, and downstairs in his landlord's kitchen, the olive oil has frozen on the shelf.

Dr. Lund is concerned that he has alarmed his mother by giving her the impression that he had mistakenly arrived at the North Pole. So in his first letter from Rome he sets her worries at rest and makes much of having successfully come through the various stages of his journey before the Eternal City and the springtime welcomed him in good health. He proudly writes – and at last the sun is shining on his face – about the day the papal diligence had to travel the most dangerous route in all Italy. The road twisted through the Apennines on the brink of terrifying precipices. He and the other passengers, ten men in all, had to trudge in front and shovel the snow until they nearly dropped from exhaustion, while ten of the strongest men from a nearby village walked behind, holding the coach securely by a rope to keep it from sliding sideways. Two dragoons of the regiment which always accompanies the coach in the papal states rode to and fro, fearsome in appearance and ready to repel the attack of the highway robbers at whom Dr. Lund hints in the last lines of his letter. But his love of truth keeps the scoundrels at a proper distance, and Signore Dottore P.W. Lund, Café Greco, Via Condotti, Roma, closes his letter by assuring his mother of his deepest affection as the local church bells chime, marking time in the Italian way, from Ave Maria thirty minutes after sunset to the Ave Maria of the following day.

A heretical vermin from a country whose art is a sickly hothouse plant – this is how Dr. Lund describes himself in Rome, a city permeated by art. He manages to meet Thorvaldsen just before the great sculptor is to leave for Munich, but otherwise he keeps his distance from the Scandinavian clique so as to devote himself to the delight of the virtuoso Romans with their incomparable ear for music. He practises playing the piano diligently, and in an amazingly short time has taught himself to read and write Italian by studying Ugo Foscolo's novel *Le ultime lettere di Jacopo Ortis*, a passionate love story about a young Venetian nationalist and a protest against the mutiny in Campo Formio. In cultivated Roman society, nearly all of the acquaintances he makes belong to the *Il Risorgimento* movement advocating a united Italy independent of France and Austria. This is the heart of Europe. Pathos and clarity. This is the fusion of life and culture, of Christianity and the ancient world, of spirituality and sensuality, of song, lightness, and hospitality.

Once more Dr. Lund is drawn into a whirl of distractions, and when the Carnival begins he cannot help but compare it to the Brazilian one. Here in Italy it is like the innocence of a civilized person, displaying restraint in the midst of gaiety and a natural beauty and grace – exactly as described by Goethe. And one evening, at a masked ball given by the Duchess of Torlonia, the inevitable occurs: Dr. Lund falls in love. Ever since he was a little boy, girls have always seemed to be creatures from another universe – a universe with its own peculiar laws by which trivial matters become important and where what is important is lost in ceaseless bustle and chatter. But here in Rome the girls are somehow different, although he cannot say exactly why or how. Has Foscolo gotten under his skin? Has he himself become a character in a romantic novel in which every line is a taut fiber of emotion? Which chapter has Foscolo written for him? *This* one?

He arrives at the ball, with a half-open shirt, thin trousers and a half-mask dangling from his index finger. He feels feverish. He wants to hurry home to take his medicine and go to bed. But suddenly she takes him by the hand, and for the rest of the night Wilhelm forgets everything, his doctoral thesis, the viscera of the urubú, Vienna, the snow of northern Italy, and not least of all his chest and his mother's plea to watch out for himself. He would follow this girl to the end of the earth. Her name is Sarah. She comes up to his shoulder, and her long black curly hair is artfully drawn over her forehead. Her Egyptian eyes behind the mask and her round rosy cheeks delight him – and her laughter, which is slightly throaty but possesses a fullness, utterly enchants him. It hints at wisdom and playfulness and a sorrow which strikes him with longing even while they are holding one another by the hand as if they had always known each other.

She is only twenty years old. While dancing (Wilhelm forgetting to put on his mask) and later seated upon a sofa with refreshments served by two Nubian servants, she tells him how handsome she thinks he is, with his clear blue eyes which observe everything without wanting to possess it all, his erect posture, and his fine fingers. Wilhelm blushes. He has been brought up to believe that the man is to praise the woman, but he is at a loss for words even though he feels that Foscolo is doing what he can to prompt him. For this is the scene in which the wealthy merchant's daughter, as delightful as a fairy-tale princess, wishes to transform the shy bespectacled Danish scientist from a heretical vermin, a hothouse plant, into a natural outgrowth of the beauty all around them: a beauty which, however, can also bear witness to the suffering and persecution which the girl's family has known for centuries, in Spain and in the ghetto in Koblenz. When the girl relates all this, Wilhelm is overcome by contempt for human stupidity and brutality, the siblings of superstition, but when she tells about the warmth of her family circle, he thinks of Rosenlund and his own childhood and there is light everywhere. Sarah. Sara Lisa.

When the girl blows softly on his neck or, with two fingers, gently removes a hair from the leg of his trousers, or presses her glowing forehead onto his chest, the innermost strings of his heart are touched, especially when she tells him what *Schekhina* means, repeating it slowly, in a whisper: '*Schekhina . . .*'.

In her religion it stands for everything a child knows but forgets when he grows up. It means everything a person must strive a lifetime to remember. *Schekhina*, the first stars which God lit, the first heaven, the first sun, and the first springtime. The girl seems able to read his childhood in his face, can recall with him the time his father told him about the idea which exists for every human being and which no one must forget. No one. And Wilhelm kisses her forehead and savors the sweetness of perspiration and perfume on his tongue. Everyone is smiling at them as though they were the chosen couple of the evening. Only here in this capital of art can an intricately patterned carpet be woven of one thread going back to Nygade with the first snow of the year melting against the panes and another thread leading back to the ghetto in Koblenz and thence back to the Holy Land.

But where is this novel headed? What do the following chapters relate? Do the closing lines describe him settling in Italy with this girl Sarah and, quite contrary to expectation, siring children, many children, who will grow up in a world where the union of science and art leads to comprehension of the Creator's Plan and eternal peace among men? Or will it instead end with . . . the very opposite? Will he never see her again? Will he think of her to the end of his days as an enchanting face, a glance, a memory shrouded in melancholy? Or will arson, war, and revolution erupt, and will they perish together somewhere, fleeing over the Apennines, snowed in? The novel opens like a fan for Wilhelm, and as he kisses the girl's hand and caresses her fingers his fever mounts. In the costly Venetian mirrors he sees the guests dancing and dancing. Some come, some go. Some are still wearing their masks, others have removed them laughingly. Everyone is beautiful, everything is imbued with a spirit, and at last he offers to accompany the girl home. She grants him permission, and they rise and dance the last dance together. An unfamiliar joy sings in Wilhelm as they walk through the streets of Rome. The girl still refuses to remove her half-mask, and shakes her head and laughs to the stars when he asks why. They come to a modest little house with a rickety wooden stairway up to the first floor where she lives with her father and an aunt. He asks to see her the next day. She says she will come to his lodgings.

That night Wilhelm cannot sleep. His cheeks are burning and he is bathed in a cold sweat. He does not know whether it has all been a dream. Watching the stars fade and the sun rising and hearing the city awakening with a sudden deafening noise which reminds him of Rio de Janeiro, he tries one last time to sleep. Then he gets up instead, unmindful of his chest, unheeding the wrinkled clothing which he had forgotten to take off. He walks through Rome as if in a trance, but each time he thinks he has found the house with the rickety stairway, it changes before his very eyes in the harsh sun. When he makes enquiries, no one appears to know a Jewish girl named Sarah. He hurries home when it is time for her to come to him. But the hours pass, and thirty minutes after sunset, when the bells throughout Rome strike Ave Maria, she still has not come.

Wilhelm nibbles at a little sausage and bread in his room. On his night table lie his notes, his Italian grammar, his dictionary, his travel journal, the mask, and Foscolo's novel opened at the penultimate chapter. He is empty inside. The next day his fever disappears and, neatly dressed, he strolls up and down Via Condotti. He chats with the tradesmen, plays with the children, and tries to forget the restless dreams of the night. In one dream he was lost on the Commons, crying out for Carl, who had been kidnapped by the gypsies. In another dream he struggled, up to his arms in blood, to skin an immense fish which kept slipping away from him into a cluster of dead thorn bushes where it flailed its tail wildly, sending up a cloud of dust onto his spectacles. In yet another dream, he is walking across a deserted steppe, bare-chested, too weak to button his shirt and draw the flapping bison fur tightly about himself, when a violent snowstorm appears on the horizon and sending the first foreboding icy gusts toward him as somewhere in the distance his mother pleads with him to take care, 'Guilherme . . . Guilherme . . .'

Late in the afternoon Wilhelm makes his decision. He returns to the Café Greco with determined steps. He packs his valises and resolves to depart early the next morning for Sicily to join Professor Schouw, who has been sent out by the Danish government and is awaiting him in Messina.

Dr. Lund does not wish to be a character in a novel.

If only the amiable Schouw would keep to his botany and not talk politics all day long. If only he would not complain so much about the hardships. Both of these habits irritate his young colleague. Whenever Schouw, who is a highly competent botanist, finds a plant, presses it, and makes notes about soil conditions, he interrupts himself to discuss a new constitution being written by a group of leading professors in Copenhagen, including himself, aimed at introducing democracy in Denmark. In Dr. Lund's opinion a scientist ought not involve himself in matters outside his field and, accustomed as he is to rigors far worse than their day-long walks from Catania via Syracuse to Girgenti, he displays his disapproval by marching an extra five or ten miles each day so that Schow is forced to grit his teeth, cease his complaining, and faithfully plod after him without the merest mention of constitutional change. In all other respects the excursion is successful. In Messina they hire a mule driver and two mules to carry their baggage. In Girgenti they hire yet another mule to bear their multitude of plant specimens. Dr. Lund notes that, as he had expected, the flora of Sicily cannot measure up to that of Brazil. Compared with that of the tropics, the vegetation here is poor and the landscape is dry and bare. Yet the contours of the mountains and the sky appeal to him, and the climate is superb, just between the humid heat of Brazil and the chilliness of Northern Europe. In fact the most healthful climate for his chest.

In Palermo he parts company with Schouw, who will continue on to Naples and thence by ship to Copenhagen, and he wishes him godspeed on his journey and urges him to work for the establishment of a society for natural history instead of becoming embroiled in politics. Dr. Lund himself remains on Sicily for some time and sets out to study its fauna so zealously that in no time at all he has collected about one-hundred-and-fifty species of fish, all of which he sends home to Reinhardt. In Palermo he is invited by the Duke of Serradifalco to meetings of the local scientific society, but frequently he slips away, overwhelmed by the ignorance of the members. At one very comical meeting, an abbot, the oldest, plumpest and most highly-respected of the lot, went on for hours about some recently discovered stone layers of fossilized mammal bones and attempted to prove, with long quotations from Pliny, that these bones were not, as claimed by another wildly fanciful member of the society, the remains of Hannibal's elephants. Instead the abbot insisted that the *monstra* had been introduced much later by . . . the Saracens! And meanwhile the Viceroy of Sicily was present, listening politely!

But in the midst of his eager activity, Dr. Lund is once more struck by the feeling that he is part of a plot over which he has no control. He has more or less gotten over his unfortunate infatuation, and if he thinks about Rome it is, in spite of everything, with pleasure. Once more he is himself, working with great discipline towards his goals. But every once in a while, when bending down to pick a flower, he feels that 'he bent down to pick a flower', and sometimes, while standing delightedly in the sea with his trousers rolled up, 'he is delighted over the Mediterranean' to such a degree that a shudder goes over him and he must shake his head to convince himself that he is what he is. And after a message arrives from Rome that an unusually large packet of letters has arrived for him and he asks that they be forwarded to Palermo, his

initiative and energy disappear for days. He fears the worst –
fears the sorrowful chapter which he has never dared to think
about. The packet arrives, and in the first letters from his
mother, all of which arrived at the Café Greco shortly after his
departure for Sicily, he reads how happy she is for him about
his journey: about the triumph in Kiel, 'her' Kiel; about the
confirmation of his discovery in Berlin; and about the social
life of Vienna. In Venice she freezes to ice together with him,
in the Apennines she struggles alongside him through the
snow, but after his first days in Rome she ceases to write.
Instead he reads Henrik Ferdinand's and Christian's accounts
of her illness, up to the letter which he dares not read. The
bulkiness of the packet was due to the rapid succession of his
brothers' letters, and his eyes can no more than glance at the
opening lines of the last letter from Henrik Ferdinand about
'a sad message' before he lies down on his bed. He sees
everything through a veil of sorrow, but even then it is as if ' he
sees everything through a veil of sorrow'.

The next morning he musters his courage and reads the
letter. To prove that it is only a nightmare, he rubs his fist
despairingly against the walls, over a hole in the plaster
through which the bricks are visible. But the blood trickles
out over his knuckles. And now no quotation marks can help
him.

About a month after the July revolution, Dr. Lund arrives in
Paris on his way home. There are still riots in the streets, but
at first he barely notices them. He takes lodgings at a hotel on
Rue Corneille, with a view of the Théatre Royal de l'Odéon,
intending only to work. Most of the day he sits in his attic
room with his feet in a basin of water to alleviate the baking
heat, while working on an important treatise for *Annales des
Sciences Naturelles* on the life and organizational form of the
Brazilian giant ants. What Rome is for art, Paris is for science.
Here he has everything he needs, the best libraries, the best
reference books, the best museums. There are also detailed
journals offering up-to-date material and bitter controversies
sparing only the chosen few whose claims are supported by
irrefutable proof. In the beginning Dr. Lund likes the caustic
atmosphere of the city, the rapid pace, and the absence of any

sort of sentimentality. He takes pleasure in the drizzly rain and the falling autumn leaves and not least of all in the restaurants where he can sit in a corner collating his notes from Brazil with his steadily growing manuscript.

In Paris he finally reconciles himself to the death of his mother. Once more there is a firmness within him, a gathering of strength for new leaps forward, now that his painful journey via Milan to Paris, during which tears constantly flowed down his cheeks, is over. Brazil is in his thoughts daily, for now he has no one to think of except Henrik Ferdinand and Christian, and he is free to settle there again – and for as long as he wishes. If, to be sure, Providence leads him there! No longer does Dr. Lund feel like a character in a novel and no more does the mask of art keep him from looking reality squarely in the eye. Meanwhile, his faith in Providence has grown. It would never occur to him to defy God for taking his mother, and to *His* glory and as *she* would have wished it. With scrupulous order in his notes, a full bottle of ink, and pens in readiness to the right of his stack of fragrant, fine French paper, he describes the bloody wars which the Brazilian giant ants launch at the slightest provocation against their enemies, the termites, and against one another.

Dr. Lund recalls everything about them from the first time he saw an enormous anthill outside Rio de Janeiro, which ants of the species *Myrmica paleata* had captured from a division of termites. Out of this, at a nudge with the toe of his boot, enraged ants swarmed and attacked the termite larvae. They stung the termites who still remained and left them to the mercy of a battalion of the species *Myrmica eythorothorax* which presently came into view, marching in a long straight column. They took hold of the dead larvae and termites and dragged them down into holes in the ruined anthill. Throughout Brazil the ants are working, grouped into millions upon millions of republics, divided into commando divisions, soldier brigades, auxiliary troops, scouts, farmers, hunters, supply slaves, and engineer troops capable of repairing anything. Throughout the Empire they march forth, loaded with tooth-edged bits of fresh leaves, chunks of worms, small spiders, termite larvae, and the heads and severed bodies of enemy ants. In the aftermath of a horrible battle they might be missing a leg or two, but they never give up. When they resolve to undermine a house in Rio no one can stop them, and only the termites surpass them in swift destruction. When they attack a tree it is stripped bare in hours – the leaves fall, relentlessly, unnaturally, like green snow, with a muffled sound which mystified him the first time he heard it when taking a walk outside Rio, sounding as it did as if thousands of bits of wrapping paper were floating down from a nearby cluster of trees. The work of the ants. Or, for example, when he had shot a bird. It fell to earth no more than fifty yards from him. But before he could get there to skeletonize it, its feathers were already in wild commotion. The work of the ants. Nothing in Brazil can withstand them. The fences around the cemeteries, the railings of the sumptuous palaces in Rio, the sugar canes, the fazenda verandas, the coffee bushes, wherever the ants march and set to work, everything is destroyed. Chairs and tables crumble into moist sawdust. Statues of saints topple over. Bridges collapse.

Yes, Dr. Lund is engrossed in his work and hears only the scratching of the pen on paper. And quite soon his treatise is finished, and he is proud of it because everything is included; the red soil of Brazil, the primeval forest and the campo; the shapes of the anthills and their locations; the noises, trees, and bushes; the empire of the ants; the planet of the ants upon which lives Man, that gigantic mammal doomed to failure in his heroic struggle to prevent his dwellings from disintegrating and his fields from being consumed before the harvest. As the finishing touch he dedicates his treatise to Monsieur V. Audoin, a natural historian whose cool encouraging courtesy he respects. *Lettres sur les habitudes de quelques fourmis du Brésil* opens the doors of all the most exalted scientific circles in Paris to Dr. Lund, and he has soon received invitations to the celebrated soirées of the Baron Georges Léopold Crétien Frédéric Dagobert Cuvier.

At the home of Cuvier, everything is discussed in a relaxed atmosphere, and guests from all over the world bring him stuffed animals, fish, snakes in jars, and rare insects in lacquered boxes as tokens of their respect. The stairway up to his apartment, which is not far from the Collège de France, is lined with jars containing snakes from Africa and fish from the Ganges, with stuffed hyenas and lamas, with a cross between a zebra and a horse, with eagles from Peru and Ecuador, falcons from Iceland, and, on a little ledge, a multitude of shells decoratively arranged in front of a primitive painting of the Amazon. Dr. Lund is quite embarrrassed not to have brought a gift, not even a box with a regiment of *Myrmica paleata*, but at his first meeting with the master he promises to persuade Reinhardt to send him some extra specimens of the numerous Greenland fish at the Museum of Natural History in Copenhagen.

Cuvier is visibly pleased and forgivingly puts his arm round Dr. Lund's shoulders as he guides him about the apartment, showing him books, zoological illustrations, fossilized fish from before the Deluge, hardened lava from La Soufrière and rocks from the Aleutian Islands, a jumble of near-artistic fortuitousness. In Cuvier's home Dr. Lund meets with French notables from all branches of the natural sciences, most eminent among them Biot, Ampère, Milne-Edwards, and Thénard. The sun around which revolve the planets of comparative anatomy, zoology, and paleontology is here. In this serene crowded apartment with its dark creaking parquet flooring and – at the onset of winter – its frosted windows, the history of the Earth has been thought out and verified by a brilliant and generous mind. As yet no one has been able to sow the least seed of doubt about Cuvier's great Catastrophe Theory, as set forth in *Le Règne animal distribué d'après son organisation*: the theory that the Earth has been subjected several times to upheavals which annihilated all life – and that each time it was subsequently re-created exactly as before, though with certain omissions. Thus certain species had disappeared from one Creation to the next: had, in a manner of speaking, been *forgotten* in the great cosmic reckoning. In this way Cuvier is able to explain the many finds, such as the recent ones from the Paris Basin, of bones of previously unknown prehistoric animals.

To be sure, Dr. Lund is impressed by Baron Cuvier and delighted to be introduced to his circle. But he realizes that Paris is also the home of speculations which wander off into absolute nothingness; a school of thought led by the zoologist Geoffroy who, having returned from the Nile loaded with crocodile skins, has set out to prove an entirely different chain of events in the biography of the crocodile than the one endorsed by Cuvier. Dr. Lund attends Geoffroy's lectures and is deeply shocked by his constant criticism of Cuvier, from long tirades to small gibes, snide remarks, winks, and furrows of mock resignation in his brow. But fortunately most of the members of the audience side with Cuvier. At one point, when Geoffroy has entangled himself in a web of nonsense, strangled by his own philosophical threads, the audience begins to jeer at him, frightening him so badly that he crawls beneath the lectern. No student in a Copenhagen auditorium would ever dare to let such taunts pass his lips. As Geoffroy, from his hiding place, pleads for quiet, Dr. Lund feels himself getting carried away by the angry atmosphere, and he suddenly hears himself shouting in chorus with the others:

'Vive Cuvier! Mort à Geoffroy!'

He is immediately overcome by shame. To wish the death of a scientist, even one who persists in confused and false conclusions, even one who is in every way a charlatan, is no way to refute him. It is nothing but mob rule, the expression of a mentality of unforgivable violence, spawned by the mood which is increasingly taking possession of Paris, where hardly an hour passes without students thronging through the streets cursing their opponents with death and eternal punishment. Dr. Lund often takes refuge in one of Paris' twenty-four theaters when such violence erupts. He is amused by the vaudevilles, but the tragedies in which Napoleon is portrayed as The Dethroned World Spirit bore him. What sort of foreign bodies are swimming about in the blood of the Parisians? Why all the screaming and shouting after every performance, a hubbub which grows even louder when he emerges onto the street, buzzing with rumors of war? The Citizen King and the moderates are seeking to prevent the outbreak of war, whereas soldiers of the old guard tremble with eagerness to take revenge upon the English and they even roll out the cannons from Austerlitz in the Rue Corneille district. War or revolution, it is impossible for Dr. Lund to figure out what is actually happening. The entire French nation seems to be up in arms. Shops shut down, foreign trade ceases, and the public credit plummets. The Danish legation walls itself in and stops the delivery of letters and packages to Danes in the city. Dr. Lund is lucky enough to receive a letter from Henrik Ferdinand, informing him that he has become an uncle for the second time, just before the tumult approaches a climax.

'Aux barricades! Aux barricades!' is the cry he can hear outside his windows, as if his hotel were the target of them all, of the students, the republicans, and the Bonapartists, the Carlists, and the national guard. Whenever he takes a walk he is inevitably drawn into the center of events and forced to give his opinion. Being from Denmark and a natural scientist is no excuse. Nature too, in all its manifestations, plays a role in the great revolutionary drama, as a young anarchistic zoologist strongly impresses upon him at a chance encounter in a restaurant on Rue Racine where he usually orders fish soup. This zoologist suddenly lays hold of him, and no retreat to his coat and out onto the street is possible. At first Dr. Lund finds him congenial. He is knowledgeable and he is obviously cut out for a career at a museum. But then an imp takes hold of him. He criticizes Linnaeus for being a depraved monarchistic systematician, obsessed by the specific sexuality of plants. From now on, botany and zoology must be written afresh. No more shall the lion be called the *king* of the animals. The ant is every bit as significant as the mammal, the elephant is no finer than the rat. Why should some animals be called inferior? What a reactionary way of looking at things! All animals and all plants are equal, and the past was also revolutionary, a global bloodbath through the millenia to reach the definitive egalitarian classification which will soon see the light of day, written by a group of scientists inspired by Charles Fourier.

Dr. Lund politely enquires as to who this Fourier might be. Is he a zoologist? An ichyologist? And now he is no longer being instructed. Now he becomes the object of the deepest contempt. The eyes of the young Frenchman flame as he tells about FOURIER, Charles, the founder of *la science humaine*, who in his visionary writings describes the future universal society as a pyramid of cooperative communities, each unit consisting of about two thousand members. From the family level to all of mankind: in *le phalanstère*, the community, absolute equality will reign. No person will be private. Everyone will belong to the community. Everything – even the sex life of the individual – will belong to the community. There will be no professors or doctors separate from the whole. Artists and scientists, so individualistic in the past, will be apportioned the role of – *travailleurs de la pensée* . . .

A worker of thought! A worker of the mind! Dr. Lund protests indignantly and wrests himself free. He is going to return to the hotel. When he reaches the door the young Frenchman shouts after him,

'*Monsieur le Danois! Vous êtes de DROITE!*'

His comrades in the restaurant break into a roar of mocking laughter.

'*Et vous!?*' snarls Dr. Lund, dizzy with these words, this madness, this dreadful vision of the future. '*Vous . . . vous êtes une fourmi!* You are an ant!'

Right! Left! Right! Left! An icy wind blows as Dr. Lund makes his way along Rue Corneille. Where is Nature? Is everything in this city made of bricks, barricades, and demonic rhetoric? Where are the sky, the flowers, the living creatures? Where is God? Dr. Lund longs to be far from Paris. Longs for the light Nordic nights.

And for the interior of Brazil.

4

Wilhelm stubbornly argues with Peter Christian Kierkegaard, holder of a Danish theological degree and a German doctorate, that the first article of faith is sufficient. Why split God into three parts and write shelves of books full of Christian dogmatics and ethics, suitable only for giving generation after generation of questing souls premature gray hairs, when in fact God exists in nature for anyone who wishes to find Him? In the dewdrops of the flowers on an early June morning in Frederiksdal, in the babbling of the brooks, in the flash of a trout's tail, the song of the birds, and the whisper of the rushes along Sortedam and Peblinge Lakes. Is it not a miracle that the sun rises every day? Are the shifting of the seasons, the dramatic diversity of the continents, the paths of the planets, and the infinity of space not worth a lifetime of deep dedicated study for him who wishes to praise God? And the lucid eyes of a child, its first hesitant sentences, the moment it stands erect and totters forward – are not these things the best possible proof that human beings were created in harmony with everything else? And *not* for suffering, as the minister preaches!

Nature is the sanctuary of sanctuaries, as Wilhelm will insist to his dying day, more majestic than a Gothic cathedral, more profound than the collected works of the scholastics, more moving than Beethoven's symphonies and Schiller's dramas. But Peter Christian, Wilhelm's old schoolmate, refuses to accept this. To him, Nature is everything – and *nothing*. Can one discuss hermeneutics with a brook? Can one find consolation in the clouds when one implores infinity in agony? Can the rushes whisper about the absolution of sin, the resurrection of the flesh, and of life eternal? Inflamed by theological zeal, Peter Christian challenges the ever well-balanced and seeking Wilhelm during their walks from Blegdamsvejen where Henrik Ferdinand and Petrea, Peter Christian's youngest sister, have now moved into a mansion with innumerable windows, pillars, trees, and one of Copenhagen's loveliest drives – to Nytorv, the square in the heart of town where the Kierkegaards live. The two young doctors are seen together everywhere: in the Student Society, attending a crowded service at Trinitatis Church held by the royal confessor Jakob Peter Mynster, emerging from the Museum of Natural History, and sitting by the canal or at a café drinking a cup of cocoa with sweetened whipped cream.

Peter Christian Kierkegaard returned home from his grand tour of Europe about a year before Wilhelm returned from his. In Berlin Peter Christian had become acquainted with Schleiermacher and Herder. In Göttingen he had brilliantly defended his doctoral dissertation on *The Concept of Falsehood*, and was nicknamed *Der Disputierteufel aus dem Norden*. In Paris he was forced up onto the rebels' barricades and hastily departed from the city, little knowing that Wilhelm was on his way there. No European journal, no important philosophical or theological discussion has escaped the attention of Peter Christian, and no matter how hard Wilhelm tries to defend nature against theology, Oersted against Mynster, Peter Christian can always find a counter-argument. How can we understand a flower without language? What would heaven be if it were not p–e–r–c–e–i–v–e–d by man, *that is,* through thought, *that is,* as a philosophical concept? 'The spirit is ideality by which appearances are negated,' or 'The concept of the spirit can only be indicated as *in sich sein* and *bei sich sein.*' Peter Christian can go on like this for hours, and when Wilhelm occasionally catches a glimpse of similar opinions, he feels that they are both working towards the same spiritual goals, although along diametrically opposite paths.

But then once more the words stream forth from Peter Christian and float in the air together with the smoke from the cigar upon which he is continually puffing and from which he so often rips chunks with his front teeth while his cheeks redden, the veins of his temples swell, and the heavy-lidded close-set eyes in the square face stare out into the distance as if, at the far shore of a lake or the end of a street, there is a truth beyond all understanding, a secret door through which the soul can find a home and peace from all the consuming speculations of the world. Wilhelm actually feels sorry for Peter Christian when he throws his words about like a child hurls his building blocks, or constructs sentences like a ladder to heaven with missing rungs – then abruptly falls silent for long intervals during which everything seems to collapse within him, sucked down into the quicksand of gloom. At these moments, Wilhelm is grateful for the knowledge that nature is able to fill him with an inner serenity unknown to any disputant devil.

Yet, however much they may disagree in principle, they do agree that there must be an uncanny significance in the fact that their two families are now linked by marriage. They had played together as children, Wilhelm and Peter Christian and Nicoline and Petrea and Christian and Henrik Ferdinand and the now-dead siblings of both families and Niels Andreas Kierkegaard who had just left for New York to seek his fortune in commerce. Nygade and Nytorv. Nytorv and Nygade. The neighborhood of the stocking merchants, the wool hawkers of Jutland. The place where the Kierkegaard family from Sædding parish and the Lund family from Gjellerup parish rose to honor and power and survived the crash. At the same time, both families seem to lie under the same shadow, a thought which Wilhelm brushes away but which Peter Christian relishes discussing with self-tormenting persistence. This shadow rests most heavily upon the Kierkegaards, as Peter Christian insists. No ray of sunshine, no fresh breeze, is admitted to the room where old Kierkegaard, day in and day out, wrestles with fate, oppressed by the memory of that night on the Jutland moor when, as a boy, he had ascended an ancient burial mound and cursed the existence of God, his arms stretched up defiantly to the windy black sky. Is this not why God has taken his children, as filial sacrifices? First he took Søren Michael, after having afflicted him with a nerve disease. Then he took Maren Kristine, after having striken her with 'the cramp'.

From the street Wilhelm and Peter Christian can see the restless silhouette of old Kierkegaard pacing back and forth up in the apartment on Nytorv, just beside the Town Hall, and Wilhelm watches Peter Christian's eyes darkening. No womanly warmth can mollify his father, no lively aspect of street life can cheer him when he leaves the apartment to go to the Moravian Brethren Meeting House on Stormgade or to buy from farmers come to town with fresh poultry. When the two old schoolmates meet him in the street and Wilhelm tells him about Brazil, he listens politely, as if from a distance, all the while dangling a turkey from one hand. He is incapable of showing genuine interest. This is his square, his narrow world from which no imagination can help him escape, his prison which God has gilded, into the bargain, so as to persecute him all the more. Who will be *next*? says the fear in his eyes as he looks at Peter Christian in a way which makes chills run down Wilhelm's spine.

Sometimes they are joined by Peter Christian's little brother, Søren. Søren has just begun to study theology at the university, but he boasts that as a *quodlibetarius* he will study exactly what he pleases and attend only those lectures which will profit him the most. He is forever teasing his brother, and he can always find the weak points in his arguments, but when he has asked Wilhelm to describe the Brazilian wildlife, he listens raptly. Wilhelm feels that in Søren he has finally found a true listener. Without having to form opinions about the various categories of thought, Wilhelm freely and fully describes the entry into the harbor of Rio de Janeiro, the mountains, the Atlantic virgin forest, the Swiss colony, and the natural setting of the Fazenda Rosário, the heat, the diluvial rainstorms, and the fauna. Even Peter Christian is forced to pretend that he is listening when Wilhelm is questioned by Søren, who is all the while hopping in and out between the two doctors in his red-cabbage-colored coat with his thick hair, golden as wheat, brushed forward into an enormous tuft, one leg seemingly slightly shorter than the other, his hands in perpetual motion, as if they longed to touch everything he hears about. His eyes never gaze off into emptiness, and when Wilhelm tells about his pet sloth or the cobra which looks like it has two heads and of which even the Indians are terrified, Søren seems to see the creatures just a few yards in front of him.

Wilhelm likes this latecomer to the Kierkegaard family, whom he last saw as a boy, when the family would describe how every afternoon, before his lessons, he would go for a walk round the dining room table with his father, who forced him to imagine all the various landscapes and cities of the world and describe them in detail. But all the father's melancholy seems to bounce off this youngest Kierkegaard, thinks Wilhelm, and wonders how Søren could have inherited his singular appearance. It is as if he had wilfully gone generations back in time to find his true parents, this Søren with his snout-like protruding mouth, his receding chin, his enormous all-seeing eyes, and such abounding physical energy that he seems like a dancing doll from Nüremberg wound up to breaking point. Yet perhaps there is a touch of the shadow over him, as when, in straining to picture all that Wilhelm has described, he quite suddenly discovers, either because a fellow student has hailed him or because the wind has slammed a gate with a bang, that he is not in the midst of the wild silent landscape of Brazil but in Copenhagen, outside Henneberg's Hotel or on the way to Madame Børresen's restaurant on Vestergade.

'Oh! To live without Christ . . .' he might say, and Wilhelm hears the anguish in his voice.

But immediately afterwards he breaks out of it, as if refusing to be oppressed by melancholy, with one of the many barbed witticisms, feared by all the members of the family, who have given him the nickname 'Fork'.

'Yes, whereas natural history is the study of the evolution of all things, theology is the study of the involution of all things!'

And suddenly he is gone, dashing off to the university as Peter Christian gazes after him in bewilderment, looking as if he had unexpectedly been dealt Old Maid.

Wilhelm's discussions with his naturalist colleagues are far less lofty. Most of them still call him PW, and while he was in Paris they unanimously elected him a member of the Royal Academy of Science. Now they receive him with open arms, excited to hear the news from the capitals of Europe. Great things are expected of PW, and this at a time when Danish science is undergoing a renaissance. Reinhardt advises him to stick to zoology and follow in the footsteps of Cuvier. Forchammer would rather see him as a pioneer in geognosy. Schouw and Hornemann, director of the Botanical Gardens and publisher of *Flora Danica*, advise him to follow in the footsteps of Linnaeus and dedicate himself to the advancement of Danish botany after its period of stagnation due to – that Mynster! – the influence of bombastic German natural philosophy. In the naturalist circles of Copenhagen, Hans Christian Oersted is the uncrowned king in his attempts to unite Spirit and Nature. PW is one of his devoted admirers. Wherever he had gone in Europe, Wilhelm was asked about the author of *Ansicht der chemischen Naturgesetze*, the discoverer of electro-magnetism and of the element aluminum, and the founder of the Polytechnical College.

Wilhelm regularly attends Oersted's lectures and heartily applauds his repeated warnings against a natural philosophy which exclusively seeks nourishment from speculative thought. Only through a sincere (Oersted's favorite expression) cultivation of science, only by having philosophers learn mathematics and philology, can a true empirical natural philosophy arise. 'The efforts made by natural scientists within their own fields at the same time create empirical material for the use of philosophy.' These are words which Wilhelm can use. This is the way forward, here he feels himself to be on firm ground. 'Energy and reason, reason and energy exist in everything, and everything exists and will come into being through them.' It is like manna from heaven! 'Even the products of the mind of man are to be regarded as products of nature.' What heretical clear-sightedness, what a slap at Mynster! 'The fact that man's spiritual and physical development takes place in mutual harmony is a fact which those who deal with the spirit alone *would prefer to hide in a closet.*' (Laughter from the audience.) Yet another dig at Mynster and his brigade of brooding theologians! And always Oersted expresses himself with a natural delightful lack of aggressiveness, with warmth in his beautiful, somewhat melancholy eyes, with a round-cheeked humanity and a pragmatic insight which Wilhelm would like to describe as Socratic deism, rooted in the first article of faith. If only Peter Christian would *listen!*

Seated among the members of the audience at Oersted's lectures is the zoologist and poet Carsten Hauch. Wilhelm is at first rather uneasy about approaching him because in an article he had been compelled to criticize strongly some of

Hauch's thoughts on the order of development in the animal kingdom, as presented in a treatise called 'Miscellaneous from Sorø'. Hauch had first published an Italian version of this article in Naples, where the Church had banned it as heretical, and nothing would please Wilhelm more than to be able to comment ironically upon the judgement of the Church. But Hauch ascribes too great a significance to certain rudimentary organs. He argues for a zoological tripartite classification, namely reproduction, irritability and sensitivity, whereas Wilhelm supports Cuvier's four-part division, namely production, reproduction, instinct, and intelligence. In his response, formulated in the most polite terms and under the euphoric influence of an emetic which made all things appear bright and clear, Wilhelm had addressed himself for the first time to the problem of an overall order of development. PW to Hauch: 'It is most important to respect the main categories established by comparative anatomical zoology, whereafter one can venture out on speculative excursions.' Is Hauch the scientist getting carried away by Hauch the poet, since he insists upon opposing Cuvier? And what's more, he places the vile apes in the family of man!

However, Hauch appears not the least bit offended when, at the close of the lecture, he limps over to PW and courteously asks if they might not shake hands despite their differences of opinion. Wilhelm is greatly relieved. Ever since the episode with the student Beck in the Gamekeeper's House at Frederiksdal, he has had a deep-rooted fear of appearing haughty, and as Hauch is reluctant to abandon his tripartite classification, he smoothes things over and remarks that, in the end, only the Cosmos has the answer to the cosmic riddle, and that man can only hope to comprehend a millionth of the incomprehensible multiplicity of Nature. Wilhelm had once leafed through Hauch's verse drama 'The Power of the Imagination', which made no lasting impression upon him. He recalls Hauch's chivalrous Norwegian character from their student days, and he has often thought of him with sympathy after hearing the news of the tragedy which had struck Hauch. Half a year after Wilhelm had departed for Brazil, one of Hauch's legs had to be amputated in Naples in an indescribably painful operation following an infection with which he was afflicted while carrying out a scientific investigation of Mediterranean fauna outside Nice. With an extraordinary effort, Hauch had managed to regain his spirits after having been plunged so deeply into a state of hopelessnss that he had attempted to take his own life. Yes, Wilhelm would be an ingrate, a mask of ignorance, if he did not shake the outstretched hand of Carsten Hauch, and in the following weeks they come to take tremendous pleasure in each other's company, and particularly in spending many late nights at the Polytechnical College, amusing themselves with Oersted's instruments for forming sonorous figures.

On this point they do agree: that there is something deeply fascinating about forming a sonorous figure, the physicist's picture of the soul. Oersted has described how to make one: A plate of glass or metal is sprinkled with lycopodium, the plate is placed on symmetrically aligned metal strings, and a bow is drawn between the two strings. Then, as if by magic, as if in a fairy tale, a deep tone and and high tone are heard, and at the same time the lycopodium is seen to arrange itelf into a regular figure. The more symmetrical the supports, the richer the tone, and the more regular the figure! The two scientists note with satisfaction that a single arbitrary blow upon the plate produces only irregular lines in the lycopodium.

Hauch: 'Thus we see that every beautiful and euphonious tone is the result of an endless number of symmetrical vibrations, of . . . *a rich and well-ordered inner life!*'

PW, with a smile: 'Thus we can see that the pleasure which the tones convey to man is based upon a hidden wealth of manifestations of force . . . *arranged according to mathematical laws, those of Reason!*'

Both: 'This knowledge is hardly consciously comprehended by the soul, but it is charged with the feeling of a mysterious and wonderful magnificence, with the intimation of a deep accordance between the harmonious life and its own nature. Herein lies the power of the tones, their natural pact with the divine. Herein lies all Genius . . .'

However, the hours spent with Carsten Hauch, who bears his fate so heroically and who never allows a word of complaint to pass his lips, gradually bring Wilhelm into a state of yearning and melancholy. The deep yearning is for Brazil, the melancholy stems from the feeling of something holding him back, perplexing him, as if all his talents were starting to rust like fine weapons lying untouched. Now that summer is fading into autumn, Copenhagen is shutting itself up day by day, as if life were meaningless to its inhabitants. In their mutual relations there is a marked tendency towards the commonplace, a tendency of which Wilhelm does not approve – with the newspaper 'Kjøbenhavnsposten' striking the 'liberal' tone by completely eliminating titles and referring even to Oersted as 'Herr.' Herr here and Herr there. Soon everybody will be equally important, everything equally insignificant. Begone, begone! Remembered today, forgotten tomorrow, like the dead leaves of the trees whirling up in front of the horse-drawn carriages.

A feeling of the early onset of winter also brings out Wilhelm's fear of consumption. He had withstood the ice and snow of Italy, he had survived the chill of his Parisian hotel room – but can he last through yet another harsh European winter? Providence seems not to be illuminating his path as brightly as before, and he recalls, as if it were a century ago, his meeting in Paris with Alexander von Humboldt, a meeting arranged by Cuvier in the teachers' room of the imposing Collège de France. Von Humboldt, just returned from his great expedition through Russia, filled with impressions, bursting with the energy of a bull, a man for whom virtually no spot on Earth was unknown, a Prometheus whom nothing could stop, whom no melancholy could infect with doubt. There stood the giant, in an ankle-length wolfskin coat, snow melting on his shoulders, his back turned as he studied the wall map of Brazil, clearly out of sorts because his admirer had arrived late (for the first time in his life!) because of a stopped watch. Two minutes passed before he turned round, the longest two minutes in Wilhelm's life, but at last his good humor returned. He accepted the blushing apologies of his young colleague, and with a smack, placed his hand squarely on the map, on the province of Minas Gerais, and remarked that there, at that very spot, his instinct told him that a scientific talent as promising as Dr.

Lund's could accomplish his life's work.

Providence! Once again Providence, spoken through the mouth of von Humboldt! All the way up to Denmark, day by day, often on foot, via Frankfurt, Mainz, Cologne, Bonn, and Göttingen, Wilhelm felt himself prepared as never before for the great expedition to the interior of Brazil. But hardly had he arrived home than he heard the news that the country was in a state of revolution, the emperor had abdicated, and the federalist rebels were about to seize power from Saõ Paulo to Ouro Preto and Belem. Would it be a bloodbath? Would the harbors be closed down, as rumored? For some months, Wilhelm toyed with the thought of going instead to Jamaica, an island whose tropical flora and fauna had been strongly recommended to him in Rome by the zoologist Charles-Lucien Bonaparte. But then came the news that rebellion had erupted on Jamaica as well, a rebellion even fiercer than in Brazil. A veritable uprising of the blacks in which no white man was spared.

And the weeks go by. Wilhelm has the impression that the family is secretly plotting to make him stay in Copenhagen. Every day Petrea sets new knick-knacks in his spacious room at the top of the house on Blegdamsvej. His summer eiderdown has again been changed for the heavy winter ones, giving him the feeling of being packed in cotton wool from top to toe. A new stove has been installed, the houseboy Lars has already begun to build fires in it, and every so often Henrik Ferdinand mumbles that Wilhelm really ought to consider establishing a scientific career in Copenhagen. Only thirty-one years old, Wilhelm is starting to feel like an aging amiable uncle when, in the mornings, little babbling Henriette comes into his room, flings her doll at the foot of his bed, jumps up to him, and reaches out for his spectacles on the night table, commanding him to tell her about all the sloths he has seen. Petrea and Henrik Ferdinand have done everything possible to make him feel at home. Not a day goes by without one of his favorite dishes being served. The globe of his boyhood stands on a table in the corner of his room, surrounded by his notes and books. Within easy reach is *Reise in Brasilien* by Spix and Martius, the colossal three-volume work which he – having pored over it night after night – nearly knows by heart, from the grandiloquent dedication to the King of Bavaria, His Majesty Maximilian Joseph I, to the detailed maps. Spix and Martius traveled for three years, and each page is replete with descriptions: 'The traveler breathes more freely when he finds himself transported from the lowlands of the Amazon to the steep banks of the Rio Negro. Those clean sand banks...' Words!

Uncle Wilhelm! No, Wilhelm does not wish to be stranded here in Copenhagen, to live the rest of his life like an eccentric, with Spix and Martius as his bible. If he did, he would again and again make *their* journey, see the things with *their* eyes, live in the midst of family and friends incapable of understanding the lure of the tropics. Year in, year out, he would have to sit upstairs in the house on Blegdamsvejen, mollycoddled by the affectionate Petrea, his nose dripping, his ears assaulted by the everlasting din of the Copenhagen church bells, his head aching with Mynster's latest idea for hindering the progress of natural science, and his heart darkened by the shadow which lies over both families. He would again be discussed fearfully by all the family, now that Nicoline in Nygade had been taken seriously ill, and Christian had begun to grumble that old Kierkegaard, staff in hand, with tightly compressed lips and thunderous darkness in his eyes... *knows* it, *knows* it. And things do turn out just as the old man had feared. After the funeral no one can say a word. Peter Christian chews twice as many cigars as usual. Henrik Ferdinand demonstrably holds Petrea by the hand, and at the dinner table. To Wilhelm's irritation, he begins to hum an odd little tune, as if hoping to make everyone, especially Christian, forget their sorrow. Old Kierkegaard apparently refuses to die before his accounts books are perfectly balanced, before he and all his children and even his most distant kin have paid back what he has owed ever since that night out on the moor. Even Henriette has changed, she has lost the childish glow in her cheeks, and she whispers that death is like a ball, rolling slowly across the floor, touching everyone. Sometimes Wilhelm must excuse himself from the dinner table to wander for hours through the Copenhagen night.

What is it about this city? One day is it beautiful and everyone smiles; the next day it is like a scene from the underworld, with fog drifting through the streets and everyone scowling suspiciously. Even in scientific circles, discouragement is beginning to make itself felt in the wake of scientific disputes among the young scientists, disputes the like of which would have been unthinkable ten, in fact, even five years ago. *Who* is advancing? *Who* will be forgotton? Who is *right?* They all want to be right, as they sit behind their curtains accomplishing nothing, so unlike Oersted. Or is Wilhelm just looking at it all through a veil of sorrow, caused by the death of Nicoline? He even catches himself wishing that for just *one* night, *one* single barricade could be built here in the royal city of Copenhagen, just enough to jolt the citizens to their senses and make them drop their pettiness and their moping and make old Kierkegaard leap up from his bed and see the world with new eyes, forgiven. Wilhelm knows that he must depart. If he does not, he will start going in circles. And when reassuring news from Brazil arrives, he resolves to leave almost immediately, to embark from Hamburg. Henrik Ferdinand manages to conceal his disappointment and promises to take care of Wilhelm's securities and to once again arrange the forwarding of money to Rio de Janeiro. A tearful Petrea assures him that his room will be waiting for him with logs on the fire and well-aired eiderdowns and . . .

Oh when . . . when will he return?

. . . A month later? In Hamburg, as luck would have it, the ship which he had planned to take had sailed a week earlier than scheduled. His star is extinguished, and Wilhelm, downcast, takes a room at a modest hotel near the harbor. He is only able to eat one meal a day, and the rest of the time he wanders restlessly about the grimy crowded streets of the city. The Jews have set up their stalls everywhere, and he passes by four synagogues, and one late afternoon he sees a dark-haired girl being chased through the streets by two sailors. Just as she sees him and cries out to him for help she is caught and dragged away. Nobody pays any attention, not even her own people. For several days Wilhelm is haunted by the eyes of the girl, and when he sleeps she becomes a nightmare: barefoot and weeping, she stands behind a stall in a ragged cotton gown, flinging all her green and red peppers at him because he lost her early one morning in Rome. But when in anguish he tries to approach her with outstretched arms, he finds himself paralyzed, sinking into quicksand. And not far off, on a dusty street corner, old Kierkegaard stands shaking the Tables of the Law at him as if to say 'He shall not escape, not even he!'

Why did the ship sail from him, leaving him behind in this city? There are no museums, no decent institutions of learning. Klopstock died long ago, and everywhere here is misery and bartering. Here, so close to Holstein . . . ought he not visit it at last? But it is almost November. The birds have migrated southwards, there will be a morass of ploughed fields and muddy roads. Then suddenly he hears the news that the ship on which he was to have sailed sank in the Bay of Biscay and all men on board were drowned. No, Wilhelm will not use the word 'Providence' because God does not wish his good fortune to be founded on the death and misfortune of others. And yet he awakens to new life, he knows that the way is still being shown for him; he books a new passage and, on the 12th November 1832, sails out of Hamburg.

Now old Kierkegaard cannot reach him, and as the brig sets course for Brazil he must turn back to the Copenhagen which Wilhelm will not see for many years. But once more Denmark is bright in his heart, as the brig gradually approaches the Azores, as the sun takes possession of the sky and he can shed his heavy winter clothing. The crew of ten consists of Germans and Danes, and there is a pleasant atmosphere on board the brig, which is sailing out with a cargo of German white wine and will return home with cotton and coffee. Wilhelm walks the deck for several hours each day for the good of his constitution. To prevent seasickness he takes a dose of neroli oil sprinkled with rust from the anchor, an old skipper's mixture which he knows to work wonders. The brig sails at a speed of nine sea-miles per hour. The first flying fish leap above the waves. The ocean is indigo blue. Soon he will see the Southern Cross in the night sky.

When not out walking, Wilhelm spends his time studying the ocean. He observes how the surface temperature gradually increases in the Doldrums and sees for the first time what sailors call red fog: all white objects in the ship suddenly turn pink, a phenomenon which arises from the combination of fog and the east wind blowing directly from the deserts of Africa. He makes detailed observations of the light in the ocean. Many of its bright particles are caused by the weather, and they multiply when the air temperature is high and the sky overcast. In moonshine they disappear completely. But off the coast of Brazil he remembers that the gleaming particles increase, that they are somewhat different in character, and that nowhere else has he seen the ocean shine more brightly than by the bay of Rio de Janeiro. And late one night he knows that Brazil is near because the moonlight no longer quenches the brilliance. A thrill passes through him. He breathes deeply. The wake of the ship is now so luminous that by the clearing ports he can read a most delicate script. He realizes that it must be made by the tiny crustaceans. The next day the first pelicans fly over the foredeck. In the far distance a mountain chain comes into sight, and he stares at it for a long time until he can see that it is thick with trees. It is Cabo Frio, and the sailors cheer now that their voyage is safely over. The first colorful fishing boats appear. Soon afterwards a canoe, made of a hollow log, sails out to them, filled with black boys, shouting and singing. They have come to sell mangoes and watermelons. Some hours later, the brig sails by the Sugarloaf. There lies Rio de Janeiro, bathed in sunshine and a hazy pale-blue mist.

The sea is now dead calm. Dr. Lund unbuttons his shirt and wipes away the sweat running down his neck. In just a few days he will once more be in the virgin forest.

Never has Wilhelm felt such delight.

5

Columbus, Columbus! To think that so many centuries should pass before the vast American continents were discovered! When Dr. Lund thinks about it, Europe seems like a well-kept and handsomely furnished palace. France is the chattering parlor, Germany the dreaming bedroom, Russia the frigid cellar, Italy the veranda, and Denmark a sheltered little niche with a view out to the swan house of England in the garden pond. But Brazil! Unpopulated for thousands of years. Then a remote colony. Then all at once a Lusitanian kingdom during the Napoleonic wars. And now with a five-year-old emperor, Pedro of Alcântara, on the throne while a three-man civil council manages the practical affairs of the 'realm'.

Dr. Lund simply cannot take Brazil seriously as a culture of its own. No proud traditions, no history worth mentioning. No great poets, not a single composer or philosopher of any distinction. Even so, Dr. Lund is impressed by the energy expended by the white citizens of Rio de Janeiro upon transforming their city into a future world capital. In merely four years considerable progress has been made, despite the rebellion. Health conditions have improved. There are now sidewalks downtown. The harbor is growing. The national library in Ordem Terceira do Carmo's building has acquired a number of valuable new folios as well as a respectable collection of European, and particularly French, journals. The Italian opera performs more regularly, with a better orchestra and singers as good as middling singers in Europe. There is a shop on Rua Direita which specializes in sheet music and chamber music instruments. But at the same time the number of *doutores* has grown. Not infrequently Dr. Lund must discuss one thing or another with them, and it amuses him to test them to see if they are worthy of their degree, especially the ones who pass themselves off as botanists. The *Malvacea* family? A sigh. No answer. The *Compositae* order? A blush. And the *Euphorbiceae* family? Out with the smelling salts. No answer.

Dr. Lund landed some weeks before the Carnival, and to avoid being splashed with perfumed goat's milk and drowned in a flood of dancing blacks in a nauseating reek of sweat, head aching from their caterwauling, he rents a little house in the suburb Engenho Velho together with the German botanist Ludwig Riedel, a member of the ambitious Russian-supported expedition of van Langsdorff, bound for the Brazilian interior but curtailed due to illness. Riedel, whom Dr. Lund had met at a carnival gathering at the home of the consul-general, is a man of the finest European standards, capable in his field, curious and precise, with rather dreamy eyes, warm boyish cheeks, and a quotation from Goethe or Schiller ever ready on his lips. Whenever Riedel goes into Rio to supervise the packing and shipping of the most recently-collected material from Langsdorff's expedition, Dr. Lund eagerly studies the common wayside plants and weeds, the humblest subjects in the Brazilian plant kingdom. Whereas in Denmark the richest flora is nurtured by sunshine, here the sun burns away almost everything, leaving only a few miserable plants in the open areas. In vain does one seek a fresh sward, or flowers comparable to Danish poppies and cornflowers. To be sure, the verdant carpets on untrodden spots and around the houses are covered with grass, but it is neither the lively light-green turf which covers Danish fields in the spring nor the golden straw of the autumn. Instead it is strict and sombre in character like most of the plants in tropical Brazil, and the dark-green grass carpet forms a fitting front garden to the true capital of the plant kingdom: the virgin forests.

Footnotes? Trifles? That is what they say, those 'doctors' when every so often they take the trouble to drop by and find out what that Danish scientist knows so much more about than they. Why in the world does he bother kneeling there in the red soil with perspiration rolling down his face, making his spectacles continually slip down his nose? Why study so diligently and make notes on the difference between the light-violet heads of the genus *Eupatorineae* and the vine-like members of the genus *Vernonia* which grow among the hedges and sometimes completely cover them with a curtain of white fragrant flowers? What is so special about the *Tagetes minuta* species with elongated cylindrical flowers with tiny pale yellow ligulate flowers like vestments? What could possibly be interesting about the introduction of this insignificant flower? Along with *Leonorus tartaricus* it is without doubt the most common wayside plant, having arrived in Brazil as a pirate seed under the felt soles of the Chinese colonists. Can this be of interest to any serious rational being? What questions could those perfumed *doutores* Orlando Ribeiro Neto or Rubem de Albuquerque ask first, out of sheer good manners, maybe? '*Yes!* Yes, *precisely!*' Dr. Lund might growl, irritable in the humid heat, his nails caked with red soil, his spectacles spotted, and his trousers torn. But he must restrain himself from finishing his sentence, ' . . . if, to be sure, one *is* a rational being!' Instead he smiles politely and goes home with his vasculum full. A grain of sand is a stone *en miniature*; a stone, a tiny mountain. The detail leads to the whole and the whole leads to insight into the Creator's Plan.

Two, perhaps three volumes, of natural history, entitled *The Plan of the Creator,* this is what Dr. Lund hopes to present to the public in a few years, when he reaches the age of thirty-five, to replace the long outdated work of Fabricius. In his response to Hauch he had sketched his view of natural history, and for every passing day, even if he finds only some obscure wildflower which had previously escaped his attention – it strikes his eye when the sunlight glances off a little metallic stone – he becomes ever more sure of his idea: that everything in Nature moves toward individuality. First comes the crystal, which in a single happy moment was released from its obedience to the laws of gravity and, instead of striving toward the center of the Earth, adjusted itself to a new and upwards-seeking movement. Next comes the plant, the second step in the development, in which the life of the crystal is repeated in the *primary victorious struggle against the world.* Then comes the animal, which repeats the two lower steps – the life of the crystal and the life of the plant – and whose blood system resembles the roots and stem of the plant, but which, through feeling and will, liberates itself from the earth and thus reaches the highest form of individuality before the final step, in which the goal is attained in the realm of Freedom and Reason; the realm of Man.

Dr Lund is still proud of his definition of Man in his response to Hauch. Several lines, written early one morning in the house on Blegdamsvej while a symphony of birdsong and shouts of officers drilling soldiers on the Commons came in through the open window, often surface in his memory when he goes home to the little rented house in Engenho Velho. He passes negro women selling junket in cones of green leaves packed into square glass-paned boxes which they carry over their shoulders. Now and then twenty or thirty slave laborers overtake him at a trot, each bearing a sack of coffee on his head while their lead singer, marimba in hand, accompanies their lament. Dr. Lund conjures up again his views on Man: 'We have thus seen how step by step, Nature approaches its goal to release the individual from the earth. Man, the fruit of this final effort, is liberated. We step into the realm of freedom. For the first time on Earth the sound "I" is heard, and with this word the process of separation between the individual and the world is signed and sealed.'

I! The envious stones understand him. The trees nod to him in a melancholy way and longingly stretch out their branches to him. The flea-infested dogs loping about see him and sense dully where on the scale of creation they were stopped, and some of them begin to howl, tail between their legs. The clouds greet him as if he were their equal. The sun warms him with cameraderie while he wanders freely over the Earth. The humble wildflowers painfully comprehend that he has penetrated their innermost mystery as he carefully presses them into a herbarium and with his steel pen describes them in a detailed treatise to Schouw and Hornemann. They will applaud him in Copenhagen, little suspecting the extent of the work of which this is but the merest beginning.

I! No airy speculations, none of Peter Christian Kierkegaard's leaps in reasoning. Everything is related, logically. It is here in Brazil, on the expedition which he and Riedel are now planning, with all the newest maps spread out on tables and floors, that he, in unexplored regions, defying all dangers, undismayed by disease, poised as for a great tiger-like spring, will trace the chain of being all the way back to the first moment of Creation. Was it four thousand and four years before the birth of Christ, as the theologians have calculated?

Or was it perhaps six or eight thousand years before Christ? The search is on in heated competition with the other European scientists and explorers who are swarming to Brazil, including three Italian brothers whose ancestors allegedly date back to antiquity, a number of Prussians, still more Prussians, various Russians, and from England Charles Darwin, about whom there was so much talk in Rio de Janeiro, because the captain of 'H.M.S. Beagle' nurtured a very unreasonable aversion to Darwin's nose. Darwin has sailed further southward to Argentina and then down round Tierra del Fuego and up along the west coast of South America. This voyage provoked for a moment in Dr. Lund an unfamiliar pang of jealousy, which he however instantly transformed into fresh incentive. Is he not, here in Brazil, in the company of some of Europe's most eminent men and finest minds, a chosen among the chosen, a member of the vast new chivalry of the scientific age?

Dr. Lund is impatient to leave Rio now that his treatise has been completed and sent home, and because a certain memory of a certain countess sometimes returns to him with a sensation like the onset of nausea and an irritating flush behind his ears. Sometimes he trembles in anticipation as he and Riedel pack the precious measuring instruments, wrapped in several layers of velvet, into the boxes. Books, paper, gunpowder, shot, valises filled with traveling clothes, leather sacks with kitchen utensils and provisions, mainly rice, beans, dried meat, cheese, biscuits, coffee, sugar, and salt. Soon everything is in readiness. They hire four black laborers, one of whom had been on an expedition for the Prussian government, and they purchase a horse and seven mules. Six of the beasts are to carry the packs. The negroes place horse blankets over the boxes and valises. Each load is also furnished with an oxhide to protect it from the rain and for the members of the expedition to sleep upon at night.

The plan is to travel through the provinces of Rio de Janeiro and São Paulo, with a side trip down to Santos, where part of Riedel's equipment, which is of a quality far exceeding that of Dr. Lund's equipment, has already been shipped. There they will rest before continuing on through São Paulo and into the province of Goiás. From here they will again turn eastwards, cross the São Francisco River, and ride back to Rio through the gold districts of Minas Gerais. It is a journey of over five hundred Brazilian miles – *léguas* – or about three thousand kilometres. It will take them at least a year.

Does the rather pampered Riedel really understand what Dr. Lund is aiming for? He can hardly be said to possess much of an inspired vision. But he is accustomed to traveling. That is the important thing.

On the 12th October 1833 they depart from Rio, after several hectic morning hours of struggle to get the beasts to fall into line. First the horse galloped off by itself. Then a couple of mules kicked out their hind legs, throwing their loads off balance. But thanks to the negroes the horse was caught and the mules calmed. The month of October had been deliberately chosen because it is the end of the dry season, during which most of the vegetation has been burned off. The first signs of the rainy season will soon appear and bring nature to life. But the rain seems reluctant to come, and Dr. Lund and Riedel are forced to commence their journey under unfavorable conditions. Everywhere they go they are surrounded by burning forests, and the smoke, together with the dust of the road, constantly threatens to choke them. Not a blade of grass, not a drop of water in the brooks and rivers for the beasts. They are forced to feed the animals maize and to quench their thirst with sugar cane. But after a march of four days the situation begins to improve. They reach the first mountain range, and in its dark virgin forests there is both sufficient water and sparse food for the animals. Now, at last, the first rains fall, tropical, accompanied by overpowering thunderstorms. The lightning strikes around them, and Dr. Lund and Riedel must calm the terrified negroes, fleeing in all directions because they believe that every lightning bolt is tipped with a stone axe which could cleave then in a split second.

But otherwise the journey now goes at a regular pace. In the morning, at seven o'clock sharp, the beasts are saddled. A negro leads the way with Dr. Lund's piston rifle and his facão, a knife which can hack through the densest underbrush, to frighten off attackers. Next comes the horse, by itself, leading the mules, and therefore called *o capitão*. Then come the other beasts of burden, and after them come the last three negroes, one carrying Riedel's rifle, another his facão, and the third the travel barometer. The two naturalists, mounted on their mules, bring up the rear. Thus they proceed slowly. At noontime they make camp at a *rancho*, a roof of palm leaves on four posts, a structure found by most main roads in Brazil, beneath which the local landowners are obliged to set out a certain amount of maize for travelers. Usually there is a nearby *venda* selling sugarcane liquor, beans, dried meat and boiled eggs. As soon as they come to a shelter, the animals are unhitched to find their own food, after the boxes and valises have been placed beneath the roof. An oxhide serves as a table, chair, and bed all in one. Some of the negroes go off to gather wood in the nearest thicket, another is sent off for water. Then the fire is lit and the pot is hung over it with the daily dinner: black beans boiled with dried meat and a single piece of salted pork for taste.

This is the time when Dr. Lund and Riedel write in their journals or make notes on what they have collected and observed during the morning. After some hours, dinner is ready, and they eat reclining *à la romaine*. Afterwards, Dr. Lund shoulders his rifle and disappears into the forest, not to return with his bag till the early onset of dusk. The horse and mules are rounded up, foddered with maize, and then released for the night. By the firelight, the two naturalists relax after the exertion of the day and entertain one another with spirited conversation over a cup of black coffee and a cigar, until the chill night air makes them cover themselves with their blankets. Thus the curtain falls upon the day, and they sleep to the chorus of a thousand toads and tree frogs. Early the next morning, Dr. Lund is busy stuffing the birds shot the previous day. And at seven o'clock precisely, the beasts are once more saddled and ready.

During the first fortnight of their journey, the road went mostly through virgin forest of the sort familiar to Dr. Lund from his earlier stay in Brazil. But at the tiny village of Pindamonhangaba by the Paraíba River, he sees for the first time the Brazilian *campo*: the open plain, the savanna. These campos stand in sharp contrast to the virgin forest. After days

of murkiness, there is now light everywhere. Blue-green grass
and a multitude of flowers cover the plain as far as the eye can
see. It is enchanting. They cross the Paraíba River in canoes,
with the beasts swimming alongside, released from their
loads, which take almost a full day for the negroes to ship
across. Dr. Lund is continually making notes, shooting new
birds, studying them, and packing them into boxes. Then
their route goes up over a mountain range. There, two
thousand feet above sea level, lies the plateau, the *sertão*.
Never has Dr. Lund seen nature so varied as on this journey.
It is always astonishing, always miraculous, and sometimes he
feels as if he was witnessing the very moment when the Earth
first blinked its eyes, humming with inchoate life, the moment
just after Creation, when a delicate pearly net of dew was
gently spread out over the blue-green campo. The sun rises,
setting everything afire, and behind each stone a mystery is
concealed, each new flower smiles to greet him as it unfolds,
and each new species of bird respectfully submits to him a
specimen for study whenever he presses the rifle stock to his
cheek, often before his morning shave. He attempts to aim so
well that the bird will fall at once from the branch upon which
he spied it as he still lay, blanket drawn up to his chin,
awakening as one can awaken only in Brazil, not merely
rested but, morning after morning, reborn.

He has not yet winged a bird or – what would be worse –
been forced to follow for hours the blood-stained tracks of a
wounded animal into the virgin forest or out among the
bushes and thorny trees of the plateau. Precision and
perspicacity prevail on the trek from the towns of Bananal
and Taubaté and now to Santos, where he and Riedel ship
the first boxes, filled with stuffed birds and many herbariums,
back to Rio on a Norwegian vessel, the captain of which has
the deepest respect for natural science. From Santos they
travel to São Paulo, where they celebrate Christmas and the
New Year in an interminable pouring rain which confines
them to their modest quarters not far from the famous Jesuit
college, with no distractions other than their work and
playing cards. On New Year's Eve, the storm rages so
violently that the house is shaken to its foundations and the
pen splatters blots of ink onto the letter which Dr. Lund is

writing home to Henrik Ferdinand while he muses upon the fate which he happily avoided: of sitting for all eternity in a rocking chair, pampered by the affectionate Petrea, taken care of by his conscientious and increasingly paternal brother.

São Carlos de Campinas! How could Blegdamsvej ever compare to this? They reach the wild and noisy town, the gathering place of the greatest number of horses and mules in Brazil, at the beginning of the New Year. The dust drifts through the streets, red and shimmering in the sun, while in and out of the dense cluster of vendas tumble freed slaves, caboclos, and quarter-breed Indians, drunken, often brawling savagely, sometimes with knives, roaring out curses at one another as now and then a grimy Jesuit father attempts to separate them. Church bells peal unceasingly, probably because boys are amusing themselves by swinging on their ropes. Runaway horses frothing at the mouth gallop down the main street, over hens and chickens and snoring black pigs thickly encrusted with dried mud. A headless rooster jumps down from a chopping block and races about hysterically in a magic circle as blood spouts into the air from its carotid artery. Intermittent pistol shots are heard, first from one direction, then another.

The two naturalists ride with dignity into this swarm of beasts and natives. While Dr. Lund thinks how his family back home would fear for his life if they could see him now, he knows himself to be in every way under the protection of Providence, sitting straight and tall on his mule at the end of the procession, the sun reflecting on his spectacles, his hands placed firmly on his hips. The only annoyance so far is that Riedel, who apparently wishes to make the acquaintance of half the population since he insists upon swinging his straw hat in greeting to all sides, has the habit of grinding his teeth at night, producing a sound like a nail scraped against glass.

In São Carlos de Campinas they buy several more mules and more splint boxes for the herbariums and the stuffed birds. Mules are only half as expensive as in Rio de Janeiro, but the local economy is in a hopeless state. It is impossible to exchange bank notes of large denominations for gold and silver, which have completely dropped out of circulation, and

101

it is impossible to get hold of notes of smaller denominations. They are forced to use copper coins which, in addition to being of exceedingly little value, are so intermixed with false coins that on the average only one out of every five is genuine. And as on the remainder of their journey the natives will not be able to distinguish genuine coins from counterfeit ones and may therefore at will refuse to accept coins in payment, Dr. Lund and Riedel have to bring along four or five times as much money as intended, kept in large cloth bags fastened to their belts.

After a stay of several days, spent carefully planning the day marches of the coming weeks, they continue on the second half of their journey, curving northward in an immense semi-circle through the country.

Abruptly the landscape is different, merciless. Two days later they are deep into the highland desert, the true *sertão*. The undulating surface of the endless plain stretches far out to the horizon where a mirage of mountain ranges is formed. A poor sort of grass covers the plains. Riding over this interminable stretch, they see nothing but this grass, formed of two species, one resembling Danish oats just before harvest but providing no nourishment, and the other soaring from twelve to twenty feet in height. The air is filled with flying seeds, and Dr. Lund and Riedel protect their mucosa by covering their noses and mouths with scarves. The negroes do not seem to be bothered, for they are accustomed to this sort of terrain from Africa. They simply walk and walk in silence, scouting alertly for rattlesnakes and pumas, unsmiling, with none of their usual melancholy songs. Not a tree is in sight. The monotony is relieved only by isolated hills covered with stunted forests and depressions in the earth filled with swamps and underbrush. Day after day, week after week - the same. They find no shelter from the blazing sun, nothing of value for their collections. No sign of human activity, nothing which even resembles a human habitation. If by chance they meet some aged human creature, often no larger than a fourteen -year-old boy, toothless, with running sores below his nose and withered stubble, they at once take him into their service as a guide. At last they reach their destination, the hamlet of São

Bento d'Araraquara, where they are given a long shed in which to unpack their things and prepare for work.

Their first wish is for some decent food. But there is famine in the village, and not even the local plantations can provide them with anything to eat. The town is lifeless all day long. The children's bellies are swollen, the inhabitants gaze vacantly, and in the few vendas only bunches of sugar-cane can be bought, the bottles of liquor having long since been emptied. The guests sit on the clay floor, flies crawling over their faces, without looking up, some of them picking at their toes, others drawing lackadaisically in the dust with a rusty knife. The two naturalists are forced to live on their own emergency provisions. Several days later, perhaps because of the miserable water, perhaps from lack of nourishing, well-prepared food, Riedel collapses and lies trembling on his oxhide in their shed for nine days. His face grows paler and paler each day, he vomits and has diarrhoea, and Dr. Lund is kept busy scrubbing the oxhide, though little good it does. A stench of human decay fills the shed while Riedel unremittingly grinds his teeth and raves on about the work which he may now never write, his masterpiece, the book which would teach the Brazilians about planned rational agriculture, *Manual do Agricultor Brasileiro*. Dr. Lund is taken aback, for Riedel has never mentioned this work before.

Here then is Riedel's secret, *his* ambition.

Dr. Lund is relieved because he now knows that they are working in different directions and will never have to compete. They regard a plant with different eyes, they press it into a herbarium with different intentions. Dr. Lund senses that Riedel nurtures no idea of returning to Europe, for something about this land has marked and bound him. But is it only to lead him to an agonizing death in this godforsaken little village in whose crowded cemetery poor nailed wooden crosses jut up from the parched barren soil and holes have already been dug for the next dozen dead? Can this really be God's intention? Dr. Lund does everything in his power to nurse Riedel. He boils his water longer than necessary. He administers quinine in exact doses. He manages to obtain a single bottle of sugar-cane liquor with which to moisten his lips and, in the most unbearable heat, he fans him with damp garments. And a miracle occurs. Riedel is restored to health, virtually from one day to the next.

They continue on their way. Now they talk together without stopping, about the past and the future, about Denmark and Germany, Oersted and von Humboldt, about science and education. Yes, Riedel is possessed by the thought of bringing Brazil under cultivation, and with a glow in his now healthy eyes and a warmth in his boyish cheeks, he describes how some day ranch after ranch will flourish here, in the land which, just as before São Bento d'Araraquara, consists of dry grass all along the horizon. But after eight days of traveling, they suddenly come to a dense virgin forest covering the bank of the Rio Pardo. It takes them three days to traverse the forest belt along this river. At last they stand on the edge of the river. The sight is overwhelming, stirring, like an incomprehensible life-giving reward for the difficulties they have gone through. But now, with the onset of the dry season, the water in the river is diminishing and the shores, they have been warned, are notorious for the unhealthy climate which can cause virulent fevers. But neither Dr. Lund nor Riedel is discouraged, not even when they realize that they are nearly out of their fortifying provisions. Soon they will have no more coffee, sugar, liquor (for Riedel), strong tea (for Dr. Lund), or cigars left.

Undismayed, they pitch camp. Without warning a storm begins, a downpour which lasts most of the night. Their shelter is a roof of palm leaves borne by palm trunks, and the rain beats in from every side while they protect themselves as best they can by a large fire in the middle of the hut. The canoe paddlers who are to take them across the river the next morning have already been hired and at dusk their arrival is announced by a distant horn which, mingling with the echo of the forest and the silence around them, has a magical effect. Presently a flock of half-naked Indians and mulattos arrives. They are given leave to fill their empty bellies at the cooking pots of the two scientists and the negroes. Seated around the fire, they tell tales of all the dread monsters who live in the muddy waters of the river, including the gigantic fish with three snake heads, and sharks capable of illuminating the water from below like lightning, and the wandering beasts –

bichos – living at the bottom of the river, whose flailing reptile tails and tongues are so long and sharp that they can shoot up rapidly through the water and capsize or pierce any canoe.

For the first time, the two scientist's own negroes give their tongues free rein: they grin. They slap their bellies. They roll about on the ground with bulging eyes each time a new monster is described. And then suddenly hide their faces in their hands and send incomprehensible mumbled prayers to their gods. Together with the paddlers, they carve terrifying wooden heads to set in the prows of the canoes for protection on the crossing. Some of the heads have long vampire teeth, some have nostrils like those of Chinese dragons, and all of them stare straight ahead angrily with protruding pupils painted black in charred crushed wood mixed with water. The more heads the natives carve, the bolder they grow, and in the end they all break into song, waiting for sunrise, when the canoes can be loaded.

Lying close to the fire, Dr. Lund observes the natives in fascination, perhaps not unmixed with indulgence because of the power which superstition and mythical creatures exercise over them, yet also like a father might regard his children before a sound education has taught them to distinguish between what is important and what is not. They are, indeed, creatures of nature, checked at some point between animal and man, on a stage of their own which no one has yet described, a stage just before the word *we* becomes the word *I*. Tribal man, with a collective memory and identical reflexes. And yet a man. As he is wondering whether the secret is that they have a more viscous nerve fluid, one of the mulattos suddenly begins to shriek. Trembling from convulsive pains, saliva running down his chin, he grabs hold of one leg, just under the knee – where a bird spider the size of a fist has just bitten him. The spider scurries down his shin across his foot and rapidly vanishes out into the darkness. In the twinkling of an eye, another mulatto leaps toward the fire and snatches up a red-hot stick. Grasping the stick tightly with his greasy little leather hat, he presses it into the leg of the screaming mulatto, onto the spot where the spider had done its work. Three other blacks pin the wounded man to the ground. His screams resound far up the river. The first birds awaken. The sky grows lighter. An hour later, as the sun is rising, the mulatto has been cured and delightedly holds his *membrum virile* underneath the ragged loincloth. Smiling, he watches his helper place moist palm leaves on the burn and tie them firmly in place with small vines. Dr. Lund is filled with respect.

They reach Vila Franca, close to the border of the province of São Paulo, in the beginning of June, after a successful crossing and another eight-day trek. But hardly have they arrived in this hamlet, indistinguishable from São Bento in its deathly state of famine and hopelessness, its empty streets, and its deserted vendas, before Dr. Lund, in turn, becomes, ill. He is shaken by violent ague and it does not last a mere nine days. For over eight weeks his outer world consists only of the oxhide, which it is now Riedel's turn to scrub, a cracked clay floor upon which he gazes blankly in his vain attempt to lift himself onto his elbows, a ceiling through which a constant draught blows cascades of choking dust, and walls so full of chinks that in storms fragments of clay rain down upon him. Ants march to and fro across the floor with the half-eaten bodies of their enemies and jagged pieces of dead leaves. He concentrates on watching them to distract himself from the pains which seem to have emptied him of his very vitals.

He can take no food, only a little boiled water, and gradually he grows so thin that he would seemingly shatter into a thousand pieces if he could ever manage to stand up. Vila Franca. The name resounds in his head like small hard taps against a pane of glass which refuses to form sonorous figures. From outside the hut comes the sound of stones striking together in some game or other which the negroes play to pass the time, as every now and then they peer into the hut to ask when they will be moving on. Every day they enquire thus. And every day they quickly shut the three boards serving as a door when they see Dr. Lund's pitiful condition as he dreams wildly, in hours when the pains have slightly abated – dreams about everything which *he* will never be able to accomplish. Riedel, a shadow bent over his bed, a hand holding a moist garment, or a blurred coppery face floating high up under the leaky ceiling, thinks only of moving on.

106

He *feels*. In his lucid moments he knows that Riedel would never dream of deserting him, but then once more the nightmares come, and when they are blackest, old Kierkegaard appears, wandering after him over the plateau, unable to become ill. Unhurt by snake and spider bites, unmoved by storms, he catches lightning bolts and hurls them back in his tireless efforts to gather the family about him so that he can count them and cross them off with every death. And the wind blows even stronger. The winter storms are beginning, the highland will be blown to bits. The Earth itself will shake all life from its shoulders, and soon he will be flying through the black Cosmos. There is so much pain. There is no solution. There is no hope. And still he says to himself that it cannot be possible, not at his age, not just now as he as about to glimpse the coherence in the Plan of the Creator. 'I don't want to die' he says to himself. First he whispers, then he says it aloud. 'No, you're not going to die,' he hears, and it is not Riedel's voice but that of Providence. And as the storm mounts he feels that there is still life in his toes – he can move them – and in his legs and then in his thighs. He cautiously knocks his heels against the oxhide, eight weeks later. Nine weeks later he sees his hands close up for the first time, and there is life in them. Has the quinine, which he now takes in doses so powerful that a Danish doctor would throw up his hands in dismay, worked the miracle? Dr. Lund arises and repeats, 'I'm not going to die!' And now at last he can see Riedel's astonished face quite clearly. Presently a smiling negro with two yellow teeth in his upper jaw looks in and asks when they will be moving on.

Now that he has written letters home which the tropa will carry to São Paulo, from where they can be sent via Rio, Dr. Lund is able once more to mount his mule. Now he knows that there is nothing he cannot accomplish. He is new inside, the boiled water gurgles in his cured stomach. The dried meat tastes better than ever before, as tender as if it came from a freshly slaughtered cow. The oranges which they managed to buy in Vila Franca for an exorbitant price drip down his throat every third hour, when he presses them with his thin fingers, now becoming tanned and firmly fleshed about the knuckles.

Having lost nine days and nine weeks, the two naturalists resolve to alter their itinerary. Instead of penetrating Goiás, they decide to ride along the border of the province to the pioneer town of Catalão. From here they will take the shortest route to Paracatu, a few kilometres into Minas Gerais. Over one hundred leguas.

On the 17th September 1834, after two months of steady travel which yielded a rich harvest, the two naturalists left Paracatu in brilliant spring time weather, to enter the heart of Minas Gerais. As the stretch up to the São Francisco River is *terra ignota* and as it is vital for them to come out exactly at the site of a regular canoe crossing over the river, they hire a guide, a middle-aged sertanejo, a desert dweller who has made the journey before. Refusing to speak, he merely shakes his head when he has something to say, and as he leads the procession, with a rolling, swaying gait, he waves his hand in the air as if trying to catch mosquitoes. It is a strange landscape. Sandy steppes covered only by sparse tufts of grass, stretch in front of them like a becalmed sea. Nothing ruffles the horizontal surface, which is varied only by the many white conical termite nests and by the coppices growing at the swampy places on the plains.

Pools of water collect in even the very slightest depressions in the terrain, as if to preserve the perfect flatness of the surface. There is a multitude of lakes, large and small, all teeming with swamp and water birds. The choking heat given off by this sweltering desert, the stinking tepid swamp water which they must drink, the swarms of mosquitoes over the lakes by which they encamp, bring them into a constant but fortunately painless state of fever. They fear nothing now, and it charms them to hear – for now the sertanejo has finally opened his mouth – that the rivers and lakes in the midst of this unpopulated desert bear such pompous names as Córrego Rico, Rio da Prata, and Lagoa Dourada. And all the time they are guided by the unfailing instinct of the sertanejo with the rocking gait, who is silent once more.

They reach the tiny village of Arraial de Santa Anna five days later. Here their fever abates and they hope to rest from their hardships and find fresh food. But do peace and contentment exist only in the bosom of nature? Does hell break loose whenever many people are gathered? The day after their arrival, as Dr. Lund is sitting alone in his hut, busy writing in his journal, a mob of mulattos and negroes breaks in, armed to the teeth with ropes, daggers, maces, and homemade flint pistols. *'Death to the murderer! Blood! We will see blood! Revenge! Revenge!'* These are some of the mildest cries which bombard Dr. Lund's ears. Coolly he rises and enquires as to what their errand might be. But his question is drowned in the shout, *'Bring out the murderer!'* And they ransack the hut until, beneath Riedel's oxhide, they find the object of their rage, the quaking sertanejo who now, his legs dangling and his face already dripping with blood, is carried off amidst the most awesome threats.

Following them, Dr. Lund learns that on that very morning, the sertanejo had most brutally violated and murdered an old woman. Without interfering, well aware of the necessity of respecting the laws and customs of the land and of keeping a proper distance, he leaves the sertanejo, who is being dragged by the hair down the muddy main street, to his fate. Soon afterwards a howling wail of indescribable pain is heard, like that of a pig being slaughtered, accompanied by the victory fanfare of drums and trumpets. The next morning Riedel and Dr. Lund ride out of town, anxious about whether they will be able to find the right place on the shore of the São Francisco River with their unreliable map and with only a traveling compass. They see the sertanejo hanging from a tree just outside the smithy, his face blue-violet, his intestines spilling out, his eyes white and upturned. Shuddering, they once more commend their souls to the guiding hand of Providence.

The regions through which they now pass are among the most beautiful Dr. Lund has seen since the New Year. To be sure, the earth is again a tract of sand. But the hills are covered with sparse low woods whose trees flower with the most magnificent corollas imaginable. A number of the trees bear tasty succulent fruits. But most delightful of all are the valleys. Each is carpeted with fertile grass, and along the flowing brooks grow clusters of the charming fan palm called the buriti. They encamp each day on the slope of a buriti

109

valley. In the cool of the evening, after sundown, as the two scientists, having concluded their day's work, lie stretched out on their oxhides, the bright stars come out above them and the sky sprinkles its fresh dew. A ceaseless concert resounds from the surrounding valleys with mystical tones which touch them by turns with wonder, amusement, and terror. For hours they lie awake, listening, puffing on fresh cigars whose smoke rises like an omen of good fortune toward heaven, until the rustling leaves of the buriti palms lull them into a sleep so deep that they do not awaken until the songs of a thousand bird tongues are heard early the next morning.

But at times there are storms more violent than any they have ever experienced, storms which usually begin just when they have pitched camp. The weather may have been calm but the sky is choked with smoke and the heat is oppressive. Several hours after sundown, a little cloud appears on the horizon and mounts with incredible swiftness into the sky, while all around reigns a dead calm, a whispering that nothing will happen. Never having seen this phenomenon, Dr. Lund stands in mute awe till a bolt of lightning, accompanied by thunder, leaps from the cloud, now directly above his head. The negroes race to their posts, and in no time Dr. Lund has gathered all his boxes and covered them with the oxhide, which he folds lengthwise, lying down on its one half and covering himself with the other half. A few seconds later the storm begins. Riedel is unlucky. Not having managed to fold his oxhide, he desperately leaps onto his boxes and covers himself with the hide, which he attempts to grip with both hands. But lying thus he is at the mercy of the storm, which tears the hide out of his grip. From his hiding place, Dr. Lund watches it fly up into the air like a sheet of paper. Before Riedel can manage to catch his hide he is soaked to the skin by the cloudburst which immediately follows. Fortunately the storm lasts only an hour, but the beating of the pouring rain on Dr. Lund's oxhide, the roar of the storm, and the interminable thunder have nearly deafened him.

After a number of these abrupt assaults from a capricious heaven and, after spending two days crossing the São Francisco River which they do reach exactly at the landing

110

place of a number of large canoes whose prows are decorated with colorful monsters even more hair-raising than those carved by the negroes at Rio Pardo, they arrived on October 10th, following a storm which lasted nearly twenty-four hours, at the village of St. António de Curvelo. Times are hard in Minas Gerais. An *alequeire* of maize costing twelve *vinténs* in São Paulo costs eight *patacos* here, and a terrible fuss is made when they try to pay with their copper coins at the venda where they find a place to sleep, in a corner where they can spread out their oxhides for the night. Dr. Lund has already stretched out on his hide, for once wearier than Riedel, who is standing at the bar emptying his bags of copper coins, when a stranger enters with bold steps, his glossy leather boots reaching above his knees. The stranger towers at a height of more than six feet. His shoulders are like inverted shovel blades, and the ornamented rust-brown leather hat of the *vaqueiro*, the cattle driver, hangs at a dashing angle over one shoulder. The rain drips from his crimson cape, and one hand grasps a silver-handled riding whip. He is followed by two slaves of middling height who quietly seat themselves in a corner and begin to play a guessing game with pebbles and twigs concealed in their wrinkled fists. The stranger pounds the bar brutally, calling for his bottle of sugar-cane liquor. Without doubt he is one of the most powerful men of the region. Flinging out his arm to shake the rain from his cape, he offers – as a favor from one white man to another – to exchange all of Riedel's suspect copper coins for genuine gold.

He makes the freshly-minted gold coins dance in a row on the counter as he pours out a glass for himself and for Riedel, who has a hard time drinking the liquor brimming in the big glass which the stranger forces upon him. 'You speak with an accent!' says Riedel timidly to him. 'Are you German?' 'I'm Danish, but thank God no one here in this vale of tears understands *my* language!' responds the giant.

'Don't be so sure of that,' says a voice in Danish from the corner, where Dr. Lund was just about to fall asleep.

Ten days later, when they depart from Curvelo, Dr. Lund knows that he must return. He still faithfully investigates everything, shooting birds, stuffing them, mounting specimens, and making notes. But his thoughts revolve around the bones which the Dane had shown him in the saltpeter-rich soil deep within the caves in the low limestone mountains running through the region from the São Francisco River to the Rio das Velhas. There Curvelo lies with its exceptional abundance of caves in the very area in which the Dane's fazenda, the stock-farm Porteirinhas, is sited. Dr. Lund is convinced that nearly all the bones date from the geognostic period called the Diluvian. His head is in a whirl. Never before have remains from this period been found in any tropical land. These bones are like a gift from heaven to the man who can interpret their secret, and as they ride towards the village of Santa Luzia, through increasingly populated territory, on their way to the celebrated gold districts, Dr. Lund wrestles with the questions posed by the bones, provoking and goading. Can these remains of animal genera otherwise known only in the polar regions, be due to an abrupt drop in the temperature of the Earth? A contortion of the ecliptic? Could there have been some incredible migration of prehistoric animals down through North and Central America?

It was a wrench for Dr. Lund to obey his itinerary and leave Curvelo, even though from the very start he had nurtured an instinctive aversion to the Dane, Peter Claussen as he was called, despite Claussen's efforts to entertain them. Claussen always referred to himself in the third person, either as Pedro Claudio or Pedro Dinamarques. Pedro Dinamarques knows well enough how to deal with the natives. Pedro Dinamarques knows every mother's son in the hinterland, is on the best of terms with them, can make them hop, skip, and jump for him by merely snapping his fingers. Pedro Claudio, in short, gets what Pedro Claudio wants. And he boasts incorrigibly: that he had been a trusted officer in the Brazilian army; that he had been the true leader of the expedition of the Prussian Sellow; and to top it all, that he was a match for any scientist, being a corresponding honorary member of the Royal Belgian Scientific Society, a well-known archeological society in London, La Societé Cuvierienne in Paris, and La Societé d'Histoire Naturelle de Mayence – learned societies to which he frequently submitted treatises on geognosy (in which he claimed to be an expert), on zoology, botany, and prehistory.

But the strangest thing about him, and in Dr. Lund's opinion the most unpleasant, is his role as king in a colony of family members, all of whom at various times had followed him to Brazil, apparently having been enticed by his reports of having found the true El Dorado. Not only was there his wife, a timorous, stammering, wan, washed-out woman, there were also her two . . . what? sisters? cousins? and his own . . . what? brothers? cousins? who lived scattered about the farm, in dreary rooms, close by the negroes. Whenever one of them was alone with Dr. Lund, he or she would ask for Dr. Lund's help in returning to Denmark, especially the women, who actually begged him for assistance because time and time again they had to put up with Peter Claussen's pawing of the plump giggling mulatto girls with whom he surrounded himself. When he was not cracking his whip above the heads of the slaves and ordering his family about, as mulatto children with his own unmistakable curly blonde hair raced between his legs and pleaded for food, he would vie with Dr. Lund as to whose knowledge of the past was greatest. As his indispensable aid on their tours to the caves, he always carried beneath his arm a copy of Buckland's famous *Reliquiae Diluvianae*, underlined in red and green ink, with greasy dog-eared pages and black finger smudges. Who is this person? Dr. Lund tries to forget him. It is not the riddle of the Dane which he longs to decipher.

From the village of Lagoa Santa, a serene spot of red-tiled houses, and even one with real glass windows and a well-tended palm garden sloping down to a lake which reminds Dr. Lund of Lake Furesø, the two scientists continue on to Santa Luzia. There they send off their collections by tropa to Rio de Janeiro. Now they are in the heart of the gold district, and they progress rapidly towards Sabará and Caeté. The road leads once more through a narrow valley flanked by high mountain ridges, and the Ribeirão de Sabará which flows through this valley, resounds with the songs of freed slaves industriously panning for gold. The mountains amplify the clatter of the goldworks which by stages crushes the gold-rich stone and finally strains out the precious metal onto outstretched hides. In Caeté the two scientists decide to make

113

one last botanical expedition, to the mountain Serra da Piedade. The road climbs through a dark wood at the exit of which they are confronted by a steep cliff rising a thousand feet into the air. They pass the timber line. Low bushes, most of them in the blueberry family, grow in every depression where a bit of soil can collect, and from even the tiniest chinks in the bare rock, hosts of fragrant lilies bloom. They begin the arduous climb, encouraging one another with shouts of '*Keep going till you drop!*'

They must climb on foot, tugging the reluctant mules behind them. A piercing wind blows around the cliff and envelops them in a cold damp cloud which dimly arouses Dr. Lund's fear of consumption. After climbing for several hours, loaded with flowers, constantly struggling against the wind threatening to hurl them into the abyss, they finally reach the summit. There stands the little chapel for which the mountain of flowers is named, erected from the gifts of the pious in tribute to the faith which causes the loveliest lilies to grow out of even the most barren rock. And round the chapel, all round the summit, grows a profusion of flowers such as Riedel and Dr. Lund have never seen before. They carry bouquet after bouquet of specimens to the chapel, rapidly transforming it into a veritable flower market, and every so often they gaze out over the panorama of the gold district.

Some days later they visit the gold mine Gongo-Soco. This mine, the most renowned in the world, is run by an English company, and it comprises three sections, each forming a little town. The first section consists of the mines, with buildings, shafts, machinery, and flywheels three foot tall, all manufactured in Manchester and transported here first by ship and then on enormous mule carts, an accomplishment which Dr. Lund finds overwhelmingly impressive. In the second section live the slave laborers, in a squalor ascribable only to the blacks' inherent lack of order and cleanliness – even under English rule. Among the huts are swarms of wailing children with mud-stained mouths whose pregnant mothers slouch lethargically in the doorways, seemingly uncaring. Rats darting to and fro in the narrow alleys and an indescribable stench compel Dr. Lund and Riedel to withdraw with alacrity. They continue to the last section of the complex, the nearly perfect, prim, and thoroughly pleasant replica of a European village, where the English live. After a year of nothing but dreary, dirty, and depressing Brazilian towns, Dr. Lund is staggered to be surrounded by elegant English country homes. Two hundred Englishmen are employed by the company at the mine, and its yield is constantly increasing thanks to their efficiency, discipline, ingenuity, and unfailing spirit of enterprise. On the first day the two scientists visit the panning buildings, where they see nearly five pounds of gold in various troughs; millions of small grains and scales stamped out of the biotite schist – and it is still only morning. Before the sun sets, the yield will be three times as great. Recently, an Englishman, red-faced with pride, told him that the mines had produced one hundred and forty pounds in a single day, an event which was proclaimed in the world press.

At one end of the English village towers the palace, the residence of the governor. He is a colonel, in his mid-fifties, with small fat legs shaped like the handles of a soup bowl, bald as a billiard ball and clad always in the uniform he wore when he commanded India, gaining a reputation as one of Britain's harshest guardians. Without blinking an eye he will have a negro whipped, and with no further ado he will send Englishmen who refuse to submit to company regulations back to their motherland with no wages and, in the worst cases, with no money for traveling. Every day he posts handwritten dinner invitations to his most distinguished compatriots. Dr. Lund is flattered because on the day after their arrival he and Riedel are seated to his left and right, even though neither art, science, nor music interest the colonel in the least. But civilization also needs people of his sort, soldiers, and, thinks Dr. Lund, a gold mine like Gongo-Soco cannot be run by a child. The colonel offers them all manner of assistance. In the days which follow he has his private secretary guide them about, now and then making an appearance himself with a slave carrying three smoke-colored glasses and a bottle of the finest port wine, which they enjoy outdoors. Dr. Lund takes only a cautious sip or two.

However overwhelmed Dr. Lund may be at the accomplishments of a strong well-ordered culture in the heart of

Brazil, his thoughts still dwell upon the caves with the bones in the red-brown saltpetre-rich soil. One question leads to the next in an endless chain. Could there have been one catastrophe *at the same time everywhere on earth*? Not, as Cuvier believes, at different times on the different continents? But what could have caused it ? Do *you* have the courage to solve the riddle? he asks himself as he sits with his glass of port in one hand, the other clutching his sweaty handkerchief. Meanwhile a strangely silent Riedel drinks from his glass with an unnatural perspiration on his brow and a stiff smile on his pale lips whenever the English colonel relates another anecdote from his time in India.

Riedel is ill for the second time. And now it is he who is confined to his bed for weeks, in the guest house which the colonel has placed at their disposition. Dr. Lund spends his time nursing Riedel and writing a treatise on the campo vegetation which he intends to submit to the Royal Danish Academy of Science. When Riedel has recovered they depart immediately, after a cordial leavetaking from the English. At last, on November 23rd, they reach the capital of Minas Gerais, Cidade Imperial de Ouro Preto, The Imperial City of the Black Gold. Dr. Lund is still working on his treatise. Here Riedel suggests they part company, as he must return as quickly as possible to Rio de Janeiro so as to resume work on his *Manual*. Once again Dr. Lund is grateful to Providence because he feels healthier than ever. But on their last evening together a melancholy mood prevails. Riedel does not hide the fact that Dr. Lund has been the finest traveling companion he has ever had, and Dr. Lund returns the compliment with all his heart. They are sitting in a little restaurant on the plaza in the center of the sombre Baroque city, surrounded by impregnable mountains, with steep cobblestone streets lined with two-storey mansions embellished with delicate wrought-iron balconies. Priests and monks pass by in the pouring rain, a reminder that the Inquisition took place not so long ago. A solitary banjo player sitting in a gateway mirrors the melancholy atmosphere. Somewhere a child is crying. Suddenly all the church bells of the town begin to chime.

Riedel looks better; he is able to enjoy a cigar again. But the journey has drained him more than Dr. Lund had realized. His hands still tremble. Then, with a hint of a smile, he looks directly at Dr. Lund with his sensitive northern eyes:

To Man it is given
not to find haven;
legions of suffering
vanish, tumbling
from hour onto hour
like waters driven
from boulder to boulder,
to unknown destinations
on the darkening years . . .

. . . he quotes, almost inaudibly. This is not merely the respectful parting of two scientists. It is the way two friends bid one another farewell, with a verse from Hölderlin's *Hyperion*. Dr. Lund knows that from now on he will always miss the grinding of Ludwig Riedel's teeth in the silent and lonely tropical nights. But the call of the caves is growing stronger, luring him out to the edge of the desert, beyond the borders of civilization, to the realm of the loathsome Dane, Peter Claussen.

6

For the first time since that late afternoon ten years ago when
he had walked out along Vesterbro and seen God's word in
the sky above Bakkehuset, Dr. Lund kneels down and gives
thanks to God. His laborers, all mulattos in their prime whom
he has hired in Curvelo, are kneeling, repeatedly making the
sign of the cross with loud shouts: '*Milagre! Deus é grande!*' It is
their firm belief, which he is close to sharing, that this
subterranean temple can be nothing other than a dwelling for
the Lord, *o Nosso Senhor*. Never has Dr. Lund seen anything so
beautiful, so perfect, neither in the kingdom of nature nor
that of art. And he rises, brushes the dirt from his knees and
steps into the great chamber where all the magnificence of the
cave seems to fuse. He is followed by the Norwegian
vagabond and artist Peter Andreas Brandt, whom he had met
at Peter Claussen's unhappy court and with whom he had at
once allied himself.

Dr. Lund thinks of all the paths and detours which he had
to take, the works over which he had to pore late at night, the
plants he had to press and the birds he had to stuff, the
academies he had to visit and the mountains he had to climb,
the plains he had to traverse, and the diseases he had to suffer
in order finally, after ten years, to reach this enormous
unknown cave which reveals one surprise after the other in
hall after hall, passage after passage to arrive here at last in
the chamber in which the stalactite formations in the heavy
moist heat of the earth attain the sublime, and will soon
challenge all of Brandt's talent with brush and palette. They
light yet more torches and candles, causing thousands of bats
to awaken and flutter toward the exit. First they are
overwhelmed by an Indian temple, seemingly carved over the
centuries into the inner flank of the mountain by an army of
pariahs. Next they see Gothic altars like those of European
cathedrals. Then they see veils hanging from ceiling to floor,
concealing new sanctuaries or treasures from the bowels of the
Earth.

Soaring columns, as if designed and sculpted by Lorenzo Bernini, are embellished with mystical masks from the heart of Africa and ornaments from the Judeo-Mohammedan cultures. Everywhere there are borders, garlands, friezes, and crowns, all frosted with a thin, sparkling, sugary layer, infusing everything with the aspect of a fairy castle. Here and there other colors appear through the delicate covering of fissile calcareous crystals, hues of pale rose, of pastel green, but mainly of Chinese yellow to break the whiteness. The eye is constantly dazzled by the luminous reflection of the crystals and their infinite facets.

Dr. Lund knows that now and for a long time hence he will abandon botany and instead concentrate on the history of the Earth as it has suddenly revealed itself to him in what may be its most enchanting stage, here in the innermost rooms of Lapa Nova de Maquiné, which he and Brandt are the first humans ever to enter. His last treatise on the flora of Brazil, dealing with the campo vegetation, had been sent off by tropa to Copenhagen from the hamlet Cachoeira do Campo. One of the last trees which he had described in this treatise as yet another manifestation of the generosity of the almighty God was the garlic tree. Named for its pungent fragrance, this tree has a power of absorption exceeding any he has ever seen. Every morning, even long after sunrise, its top drips as copiously as a rain shower. And, contrary to all natural laws, the tree exerts a magnetic force powerful enough to make any compass within range quite delirious.

But not a thousand of these marvelous trees, no wondrously beautiful forest of carnivorous plants, no wandering trees without roots, no roses as large as pines, not even the most horrifying freaks or the most supernatural revelations in the floral kingdom can match this cathedral of geognosy, hidden under the southern slope of the mountain range Serra de Maquiné, not far from the Rio das Velhas where Córrego do Cuba separates itself and sinks into a basin-shaped depression. The entrance of the cave is three hundred feet above the brook, and only about one hundred feet from the verge of the mountain range. An enormous eriodendron with its crown of light-pink blossoms gives away the secret entrance. But, as if to bar admittance, there is a guardian at the gate, a forbidding trunk of the genus *Peroba*, struggling with the colorful flowering vines which have sided with the traitorous eriodendron.

Early one morning, while he and Brandt were roaming the lands of the Fazenda Maquiné, Dr. Lund had re-discovered the entrance of the cave. During the visit with Riedel, Peter Claussen had shown him only the first rooms. But on this second visit, the terrain kept playing tricks on him, and he had been searching for hours. Everywhere on the mountain-side bloomed the white flowers of the *Lippia*, celebrated for the delicious tea made from their dried petals – *chá de pedestre*. Just as he had dismounted his mule to pick a bag of these flowers, he had caught sight of a flock of birds, just fifty yards away, flying tirelessly in and out of the mountain.

Brandt pants heavily in the humid heat as he takes out his drawing pad and ensconces himself on a ledge. Again Dr. Lund thanks Providence that he met this unhappy, vulnerable, but thoroughly agreeable man at just the right moment of his life. On February 9th 1835, having paid off his negroes and sold his share of the mules, Dr. Lund traveled alone from Ouro Preto via Cachoeira back to Curvelo and spent over fourteen harrowing days at Peter Claussen's stock farm. Peter Claussen had been delighted at his return and showed him to the best guestroom, which he did everything he could to furnish as pleasantly as possible for his 'distinguished guest'. At first Dr. Lund believed, rather naively, that he could keep a proper distance from this monster and his family and take his meals alone on excurions to the caves. But Peter Claussen would always ride after him to see what he was up to, and Dr. Lund could never examine a bone in peace, what with Claussen's clamorous interference and wild flights of fancy. 'Wouldn't it be a good idea to join forces? We could publish a pioneering work on these relics of the past but also sell the whole lot to the great museums of Europe?'

Dr. Lund soon realized that innumerable valuable bones have already long since been scraped together pell-mell and sold by Claussen to the highest-bidding agent in Rio de Janeiro or even directly to Europe. And not only that. In some of the caves Claussen had scraped out all the soil to exploit its rich content of saltpeter. The damage was done. To make it worse, back on the farm, Claussen would interminably knock on his door and had once even kicked it in with a roar when Dr. Lund had politely asked to be left in peace. 'Pedro Claudio desires the company of Herr Doktor *now!*'

The negroes here worked harder than at any other fazenda Dr. Lund has ever visited. Peter Claussen was like a tornado, here, there, and everywhere, giving orders about everything under the sun, followed by his brothers (cousins?) who to the best of their ability sought to live up to the brutality of their absolute monarch. They had had no qualms about striking the negroes across the face, slapping them so roughly that even the Englishmen in Gongo-Soco would be shocked. And morning, noon and night, whenever Dr. Lund was not out in the caves, the wailing women would seek him out and beg for money so they could run away. In the end he gave these unfortunates enough money to make the trip to Rio de Janeiro whenever they wished and there, with the help of the consul-general, book passage on a ship to return to Denmark, their Paradise Lost. This feeling of being forced into the role of a good Samaritan made Dr. Lund feel that he was wasting precious time.

But in the midst of all this, Peter Andreas Brandt suddenly appeared with a bag full of sketches after a week-long excursion to the shores of Rio das Velhas. Hardly an hour had gone by before Dr. Lund had struck up a friendship with him. Dr. Lund then heard the sad story of *his* life, recounted in a stammering, guarded Norwegian, his large wondering but curiously lifeless eyes gazing out from a face clearly belonging to a man over forty, unshaven, with graying stubble and a patch of premature baldness on the back of his head, boiling red in the sun. Once Brandt had been a talented young man in Kristiania, full of good humor and ideas, a close friend of the leading poets and natural scientists of the Norway of his youth. Dreaming of becoming a journalist and an artist, he had founded a newspaper in Kristiania which was to publish weekly the freshest ideas from Europe.

But after just a few issues the newspaper went bankrupt. The promising young man had already married Wilhelmine and fathered three children who had to be fed, so he started a shop specializing in silks, cottons, and the finest tropical spices. But this shop too failed – and whatever else he touched. He was like Midas in reverse. In short, luck was not with him. His guilt at being a miserable father and provider festered within him like an abscess. People began to gossip about him, saying that he probably drank, that he dreamed strange dreams, that he had hopes of being a poet but had no talent for it, that he did not honor his wife properly, that he neglected his children, and that for days and weeks on end he would frequent the society of persons with whom one ought not be seen. Finally, when the promising young man was no longer young and not at all promising, he fled, in the hope of finding happiness elsewhere in the world. By some strange circuitous route he came to Chile, but after a time of some small success, things also fell to pieces for him there when the newspaper for which he did illustrations went bankrupt. He left Valparaiso and crossed the Andes on foot, taking with him only a rucksack and his last few coins, feeling it to be his death march, the march which leads everywhere and nowhere.

Driven by the energy of despair, he simply walked and walked, up over the mountains where the thinness of the air for a time halts the demons in their pursuit. Suddenly he was in Argentina. He worked his way further on to Paraguay, until one day it was no longer Spanish which the inhabitants spoke. Then he went along on an expedition returning from the southern Mato Grosso to Rio de Janeiro, but this too proved to be a disaster when the negroes mutinied and joined a *quilombo*, an illegal village for runaway slaves. And finally . . . finally he landed here, impoverished, famished, kept alive only by the little dry meat and beans which he could beg in churches and at fazendas, landed here, on Peter Claussen's stock farm as the 'supreme' and most cultivated slave, making drawings and land surveys for the Dane, an errand boy and entertainer all in one. He had no idea of *who* this giant, Claussen, really was, how he had come here, when, and not least of all, why. 'Swindle,' mumbled the brothers (cousins?) and then covered their mouths with their hands as if expecting a gruesome punishment for their indiscretion. 'Bigamy,' whispered one of the women late one afternoon, looking at him aghast as if Brandt had been the one to pronounce the shocking word.

Dr. Lund was moved by Brandt's story, recounted one peaceful morning at the farm while Claussen was in Curvelo on business. As he packed his first collection of bones into wooden boxes, Dr. Lund recalled Brandt's type from Bakkehuset and the Student Society in Copenhagen; the Bohemian, always attracted by the talk of poets and philosophers which, as he stands solitary with a glass of burgundy in his hand, he accepts all too readily, the day dreamer and the night bird: a difficult type if one permits him entry into the innermost mysteries, but also faithful and capable of conversing intelligently. He is precisely what Dr. Lund needs, considering the daily clashes with Peter Claussen.

Early one morning, as if they were naughty children, they stole out of their rooms while everyone else lay sleeping, and rode away silently from the Fazenda Porteirinhas, after Dr. Lund had guaranteed Brandt a regular monthly wage as his illustrator and scientific assistant. In Curvelo they made their base at yet another of the dreary rooming houses so familiar to Dr. Lund. From here they set out to visit the caves along the banks of the Rio das Velhas and thus arrived at the place where the white tea flowers bloom and the birds fly in and out of the mountainside.

The first large halls evoked in Dr. Lund a joyful rush of recognition. In the entrance, overgrown by cactus, a scrawny cow had pushed its way in to lick the saltpeter, a temptation to which other cows on the mountain slope had often yielded, as indicated by the many fresh cowpats scattered by the entrance and a little way into the cave. Later, people had followed their tracks and realized the value of the saltpeter. From a cartload of cave dirt, between sixty and seventy pounds of salt could be leached.

Inside the mouth of the cave, the first room, illuminated from the entrance and strewn with fresh cow dung some way in, expanded into an imposing hall which on his first visit Dr. Lund had measured to be eighty-eight feet in length, sixty-six feet in width, and an estimated twenty-six feet in height. Here the saltpeter-rich earth had been almost completely removed, and the calcareous crust protecting it had been broken up into a thousand pieces. On the floor lay enormous quartz boulders which had fallen from the ceiling, and at many places the stalagmites had merged with the stalactites. But long ago, when the red saltpeter-rich layer of earth had spread over the floor, the dripping water must have been like a flood, quite different from the motion which contents itself with one drip every half minute through the millenia. There had been no time for evaporation. This, Dr. Lund reasoned, was the cause of the thick, now broken, layer of lime on the ground.

From the first hall, a narrow opening lead deeper into a pitch-black cave in which their voices had resounded like a magical echo, especially Peter Claussen's triumphant roar. In the torchlight Dr. Lund had observed that this hall was even more spacious than the first one – he himself had cautiously paced to and fro, measuring one-hundred-and-twenty feet in length, seventy-four feet in width. In other respects, this room resembled the first one, and here too the calcareous crust had been broken through in the hunt for saltpeter. The hall was dewy with moisture and Dr. Lund and Peter Claussen kept on slipping, whereas Claussen's barefooted slaves could maneuvre far better. From a corner in this room, a long passage sloped down, lined with stalactite formations fashioned like regular lengths of drapery. This passage ended in a third hall, the most magnificent of them all, measuring two hundred feet long and one hundred and sixteen feet wide. Its ceiling was twice as high as the other caves, nearly fifty feet.

This hall was the most superbly furnished of the three. The left wall was almost bare, although by the entrance it was decorated with a drapery of chalk-white stalactites which reflected the torchlight like stardust. On the right wall there was a heavy bulging curtain which, like immense flames, shot up twenty feet into the hall itself. But most remarkable of all was the wall through which they had entered. Turning round, they saw that between two enormous pillars it formed a semi-circle with rows of round benches enclosing a base upon which towered a twenty-five-foot-tall bear. Despite the darkness, despite the bear which seemed to be awakening from its stony torpor when the torchlight shone in its eyes, here too traces of contemporary man could be seen. Scattered about lay the bones of bats and owls, but here and there they had been scraped aside, the calcareous crust broken through, and the red earth dug free. This was also the case in a fourth hall, a smaller one, a sort of side room completely littered with fallen limestone boulders.

Here every trace of human activity ceased, and here the cave appeared to end. But did it really? This question had troubled Dr. Lund ever since, and now that he had returned, no longer under the watchful eye of Peter Claussen, nothing could stop him. Brandt anxiously tried to dissuade him from entering a little opening which from the fourth wall led into the end wall of the fourth hall, an extremely narrow passage filled with water which indicated this to be a dead end. But 'Onward!' urged a voice in Dr. Lund, 'Onward!' And he rolled his trousers up to his calves, set his boots on a dry ledge and led the way into the water, which sent icy chills up his spine. He waded and waded. His torch raised high, yard by yard, thinking neither of consumption, water snakes, nor abrupt heart-stopping holes which would do away with him once and for all. As a vague stream coursing through his nerves generated a prickling sensation on his flesh, he knew that he was on the right track, that it was no dead end. And all at once, Providence fulfilled his burning desire: an utterly untouched room dating from just after the last global catastrophe. This was the deepest room in the entire cave, and from here, as he saw at once, new passages led up to new rooms. It was like a reward which he had hardly dared hope for. There were openings into yet other rows of rooms, chambers, and vast halls into which he climbed with the aid of the rickety rotting ladder which one of the mulattos brought him soon afterwards.

And all at once the torches were transformed, as if by a magic word, into a thousand candelabras shining from all directions. They illuminated the twinkling, sparkling, and dazzling calcite crystals of the fairy palace.

But the *bones* down in the red earth beneath the protective calcareous crust! What do they say? This is the question which gripped Dr. Lund as soon as he had thanked God and stood up, brushing his knees and smiling at doing so, for his trousers were already filthy. In the following days, he and Brandt and the laborers work in the cave, and only rarely do they make the trek outside to take a rest, to warm themselves in the sun, and to light the fire beneath their cooking pots. Often Dr. Lund insists upon doing the work by himself, leaving Brandt free to inspect the halls on his own and to sketch. The bones must be scrupulously investigated, *in situ*, as it is essential to note the position of every single bone and the position of the animal, possibly of the entire flock, at the moment of death caused by the all-annihilating earthquake which was followed by the floods. Floods which, as Dr. Lund is becoming more and more convinced, must have been worldwide, caused by melting polar ice-caps and shifts in the surface of the earth.

No, it is not enough just to fill sacks and boxes with these remains and ease them down the ladder and carry them back through the four halls and out into the daylight. They are not common soup bones or pieces in a meaningless puzzle. Each bone must be painstakingly dug out, often with a teaspoon and a sharp little knife, brushed free of dirt, tested, identified. Darkness falls outside the cave and Brandt's plaintive voice is heard, as if issuing from the very bowels of the Earth. Dr. Lund has remained in the secret cave room where no human being before him has ever set foot, perspiring and freezing at the same time, in a euphoric state of concentration which he has never before experienced. His clothes are wringing wet. His notebook separates like soured milk forcing him to stop making notes. His spectacles grow so steamy that in irritation he must lay them aside and instead peer like a hedgehog along the red earth where he has broken the calcareous crust. But his labors are rewarded. Out of all the bones, not a single one comes from any existing animal species! Most of the bones are from a species of ancient antelope, and the remainder are from the giant sloth.

As he digs, questions well up within him, one after another, enough, he feels, for a lifelong attempt at solving. How did these antelopes and these giant sloths penetrate so deep into the innermost heart of the cave? And not just *in* here, but *up* here? Surely the animals could not have come in by themselves, sick or old, to lie down and die a natural death. The bones all seem to come from healthy animals, although they are fractured here and there. Moreover, Dr. Lund knows that antelopes shun caves. Were they the prey of carnivores? But if so, where are the toothmarks of the beasts of prey? And why are entire antelope skeletons heaped together? The answer is the Flood and all the unsolved questions are swept before it.

And Dr. Lund sees it and knows that he is right. Long ago, a flood thousands of feet deep swallowed up the mountains like tiny rocks as it washed over the Earth, tore everything with it, bit out abysmal canyons, snapped the highland trees like dry twigs, ripped the primeval forests to pieces, dislodged the hills, and bore the animals at its head; a massive accumulation of carcasses which were washed deep into the caves, to be crushed against the cave walls. Then everything grew silent. The flood abated and the Earth breathed again. The water subsided to a slow drip in the caves, from stalactite to stalagmite. And God re-created all the animals and the flowers and the trees exactly as before, contemplating the day when He would create Man. But He also excluded various troublesome species which He felt to be unnecessary. Such as certain antelopes. Such as the giant sloth.

Or, had there been a *New Creation* after the catastrophe and the Flood? In Curvelo, as Dr. Lund works on his treatise on the Maquiné cave and the grimy urchins of the town peek timidly through the windows (now that people are talking about the strange thin man with the gold-rimmed spectacles who rides about on his mule collecting bones), this question, which is perhaps the most decisive of all, nearly takes his breath away. First it smoldered somewhere within his consciousness, then it sprang forth like lightning. It is this question which, if answered with a yes, would invalidate Cuvier's *Discours sur les révolutions de la surface du globe*. Furthermore, it would banish once and for all to the attic of superstition the theologians' belief in a Mosaic flood. Had God created an entirely different animal and plant life than that which exists today, then did He inundate the Earth because He realized that . . . *what*? That . . . that Man, his ultimate goal, would not have had a chance of survival among the prediluvian animals and the sinister fern forests? For God, everything is possible. Even the gigantic mistake which lasted perhaps a couple of thousand years and whose remains now rest in Dr. Lund's hands as he sits by the worm-eaten table in his lodging house, his brain still dazzled by the moment when the festive palace was illuminated – a mistake which God then erased by drowning it from pole to pole, from the Orient to the Occident, and thereupon, with the Sun and the clouds as His sole witnesses, caused an utterly new development to take shape, with man as the uppermost step, the liberated *I* in His image . . .

Is this the way it is? Is this the way it was? Can he prove it? Will Providence continue to guide his steps? At a stroke, Dr. Lund renounces all worries about his health – even though he knows that the Brazil which he intends to investigate is not that of its sun, but that of its dark dank interior. By every means in his power, on the path of duty, giving no thought to anything else, he will collect innumerable ancient bones. He will not be content with those he has found in Peter Claussen's caves and Lapa Nova de Manquiné. *And not a single cave must contain the bones of extant animals beneath the magic calcareous crust!* So far, the remains of the giant sloth are the jewel of his collection. He had found the skeleton of *Megatherium* in a little basin in the innermost floor of the fairy palace. Like many of the ancient antelope bones, it lay completely disintegrated in loose yellowish sand curiously different from the reddish earth. Only some toe joints, along with the teeth, were intact. The other bones had more or less crumbled to dust, and their moldered condition caused them to fall apart at the merest touch. But he did manage to take up various bone parts, not least of which were those which lay around the still visible excrement of the animal, which he would later describe in connection with a complete biography of the animal. The Deluge had astonished this animal to such a degree that its feces had virtually been sucked back into its intestines, out of pure fright – as Dr. Lund guesses. Many details will, for the moment, be hypothetical. The present task is to find a large enough quantity of bones from before the Flood so that he can answer the overriding question: did God create the world *as before*? Or did He create it *anew*?

Brandt is busy illustrating the Manquiné cave on the basis of his earlier sketches, and drawing the cranium of the ancient antelope and the bone fragments of the giant sloth which Dr. Lund has already described. He will send the drawings with the treatise to Copenhagen as the first instalment of what he hopes will be a long series which will constitute the foundation of his *Plan of the Creator*, a work which he now intends to divide into two sharply distinct sections, the prediluvian and the one in which man was created. An air of peace and quiet pervades Curvelo. Brandt has now seated himself outside in the sun and presently falls asleep. Dr. Lund lays the bones aside and sits down on the stone step of the rooming house to peel an orange. This town is somewhat more civilized than he is accustomed to, and a couple of the houses are painted, although in unattractive shades of green and red.

He has had some polite conversations with the priest. He and Brandt are greeted with respect at the venda, and when he strolls up and down the main street, everyone nods to him, apparently eager to ask what makes these bones so interesting. But he senses they lack the bright courage required to rebel against the dictates of Mother Church, which equates scientific questions with sin. Catholics are simply not born to be scientists. An ocean separates the Northerner from the Southerner, thinks Dr. Lund with no little complacency as he stands up to calculate the exact path of the sun. Then all at once the serenity is shattered by a sound in the distance, coming from beyond the town, from where the wind whirls the red loose dust up in disquieting spirals: 'Pedro Dinamarques!' 'Pedro Dinamarques!' The name is passed from mouth to mouth, most vociferously by a gang of black boys doing backward somersaults out of pure excitement. Presently Peter Claussen comes galloping up to the front of Dr. Lund's and Brandt's rooming house, followed by his two brothers (or cousins) and two slaves, also on horseback.

'So *there* you are!' roars Peter Claussen, leaping from his horse and pointing at Brandt, who jumps up from his chair. Dr. Lund puts on his spectacles, rises, and enquires what in the world Claussen thinks he is doing, intruding in such a fashion. Claussen scowls curiously into Dr. Lund's room, filled as it is with bones, all the while showering abuse upon Brandt, who quakingly steps back toward the entrance of the house. For a moment Dr. Lund is somewhat confused, somewhat frightened, as if there is something which he does not know about Brandt, something he has been hiding from him. Then it suddenly dawns on him that Claussen simply wants to retain Brandt as his slave. 'He's *mine*! Don't *touch* him!' bellows the giant, striking Brandt's shoulder repeatedly with the silver-mounted handle of his whip and shouting about all the money he has spent on him, all the feasts he has served to put some flesh on the bones of that skeleton of a Norwegian who had come crawling into Porteirinhas one day. Brandt still owes him innumerable drawings and a detailed map of his lands. Dr. Lund had better understand all this and act accordingly.

Soon everyone in town has flocked about them. But nobody understands a word of the hawking, coughing and gargling Danish spewing from Claussen's mouth as his beady eyes glare out from that chopping block of a head. It strikes Dr. Lund that *this* is how he must have ordered everyone about, intoxicated by his own power, that bull-necked nobleman Markvor Lund whose infamous deed brought a curse down upon the heads of his descendants for centuries. And suddenly, enraged as never before, enraged by his own rage, his blood boiling in his veins and the sun drilling into his forehead like an awl, as dogs howl, rats appear in the doorways, and cobras hiss in the dust, he slaps Peter Claussen on the cheek with his sweat-soaked handkerchief so that the ogre's eyes seem about to roll out of his head and fury makes his cheeks glow red. No one makes a sound. Only the wind can be heard. Even the dogs stop howling. For over a minute Peter Claussen simply stares and stares at Dr. Lund, as if something prevents him from hitting back and crushing this puny opponent: perhaps fear of Dr. Lund's utter fearlessness, perhaps fear of leaving the arena as a murderer. And presently his brothers (or cousins) intercede. Peter Claussen spits on the ground, brandishes his scarlet cap, and rides off, his mission unaccomplished.

From then on the rumor spreads through Curvelo: that the

Danes are fighting about the treasure, the treasure which an Indian chieftain had concealed deep within the Maquiné cave, his spoils of war, including diamonds, gold nuggets, magic parrot feathers which can make water spring from barren rock, young maiden's locks which restore a man to potency if eaten with a coating of golden honey, rings of platinum, strands of beads many yards long, and snakeskins which, when pulverized and inhaled at full moon, ensure eternal youth. Wide-eyed, the children whisper about the treasure and regard Dr. Lund as a mighty sorcerer. The women play up to him, smiling at him with two, sometimes three, loose teeth in their mouths. The venda proprietor treats him and Brandt to free drinks, and their landlord cleans their room extra thoroughly. It is impossible for Dr. Lund to spike the rumor, and in the end he and Brandt amuse themselves heartily with the childishness of these Brazilians who believe everything but are able to do nothing. However, some days later, when Dr. Lund, having completed his treatise, has ridden back to the Maquiné cave to see if he has overlooked any valuable bones, he finds that its entrance has been walled up. Massive boulders have been laboriously piled on top of one another, with pebbles in the joints and red calcareous soil as mortar. Above the entrance on a little rocky ledge stands the proprietor of Fazenda Maquiné, a little hunchbacked Portuguese with arms so long that his hands almost scrape the earth and an infected eye running with pus. Dr. Lund raises his arms in greeting, but the Portuguese responds by raising his rifle to the cheek beneath the healthy eye and aiming directly at him.

When Dr. Lund rides into Curvelo, Brandt joyfully comes to welcome him with a packet of letters from Copenhagen, sent via Rio de Janeiro and Ouro Preto. Dr. Lund snatches the packet irritably, tears it open, and not bothering with his little ivory letter-opener, rips open the first letter with his index finger. He says not a word to Brandt, who persists in asking the reason for his sudden taciturnity. But as he reads the letter from Henrik Ferdinand, his world collapses, and he thinks no more about the Maquiné cave. Just as in Palermo when he had read about the death of his mother, tears roll down his cheeks. Petrea! Only thirty-three years old, a blossoming mother who brought life to everything around her, one of her last projects having been to paint and re-furnish the house on Blegdamsvej. Will this never cease?

Brandt tries to console him, but Dr. Lund cannot explain to his new companion about the dread clockwork which on Nytorv in the heart of Copenhagen ticks on and on. Almost two years earlier, just as Dr. Lund had set off on his expedition with Riedel, news had reached him that Peter Christian Kierkegaard's next-youngest brother, Niels Andreas, only twenty-four years old, had died outside New York in the midst of his desperate attempt to succeed in commerce as a way of breaking free of the family. But Dr. Lund had barely known him and the anguish had not felt then – as it does now – like two thumbs pressing behind his eyes, like pulsating cramps in his stomach, and like a high discordant singing in his ears; a beating more brutal than any he has ever received. Dr. Lund at once sets about packing his belongings. He sends his carefully numbered bones together with the things not yet sent to Rio, most of his instruments, notebooks, stuffed birds and herbariums, to Lagoa Santa, the city which he intends to make his base during the rainy season after a long detour. He writes a long letter to Henrik Ferdinand, seeking to encourage him in his faith that a soul which submits to the will of God is the greatest of all gifts, and that everything which happens is the will of Providence.

It eases him somewhat to write this letter. His energy returns, he hears the call of duty once more. And the next day, September 2nd, he and Brandt ride out of Curvelo, followed by a gang of boys darting in and out among their mules. The boys try to sell them the decomposing carcass of a dog, so rotten that the skeleton juts out, infested with shiny blowflies, a sight so sickening that it could only be seen here in the tropics. The stench of the dead dog wafts up to Dr. Lund's nose, nearly making him vomit. Again his brain is over-whelmed with darkness. First the walled-up entrance, then Markvor Lund, then Mikael Pedersen Kierkegaard once more crossing off a name in his little black book. Now these sickening, insistent, shameless, native boys, near-naked and pubescent, the worst age, with deep hoarse breaking voices and fuzz on their chins. The oldest of them has the effrontery to pretend that he is gobbling up the dead beast as he rubs his belly and rolls his eyes up to the merciless sun which will soon make everything crackle in the barren heat.

Dr. Lund wishes only to leave this wretched town. And Brandt rides three paces behind in silence.

Sun. Sand. The dried mud along the shore of the Rio das Velhas. The panting of the mule. Its smell. Its sweat. Dr. Lund's mind is blank. He rides, followed by Brandt and the two pack mules, mile after mile, dry in the dryness, muddy in the muddiness, with a mute inner pain through the *caatinga*, that stunted forest hampered in its growth by lack of nourishment. The Tormented Forest, as the roaming Indians call it, exposed to the searing sun, lit no longer by God but blazing by itself, a catastrophe of consuming rage which makes the rattlesnakes rattle in the bushes of the caatinga, the birds hush, the fish in the Rio das Velhas gasp for air at the surface of the water, and the muzzles of the mules foam, sticky and salty.

The Sun itself, that is what Dr. Lund is riding through. Soon afterwards he follows its path over salt deserts, among thousands of termite nests several yards high in which termites are waging eternal bloody war upon one another. He rides through parched valleys carved by brooks and tributaries, past the world of the insects, the red earth of the armored ants and the scorpions, and into hamlets with the outward aspect of human habitations. There are no signs of life. Where half-dead dogs lie along the walls of the houses, where mangy cats prowl, where children dig their hungry fingers into the sockets of their eyes, and where gaunt men and women move with the sluggish steps of sleepwalkers. Through the tiny village Papagaio, he and Brandt ride down toward the Rio das Velhas, not far from where it flows into the São Francisco River. They cross over by the village Hipólito, and continue on to the south-east through Piçarrão and Traíras, crossing the river again and entering a new caatinga where prickly shrubs tear at their clothing, hands, and feet when they attempt to press forward. The prospect grows increasingly dreary as the news of their advance in some strange way precedes them.

133

Dr. Lund feels as if every bush in the caatinga knows him. Knows what he is seeking, and whispers the message to all the hinterland caves so that he is frequently met by some squat unshaven fazenda owner who, for a fee, is willing to show him the road to that which he so unremittingly seeks. Those worthless bones which he, covered with grime, scratched to pieces, unheeding his hunger, burned red by the sun, and soaked to the skin by the inner dampness of the Earth, digs out by the light of a torch. Lapa do Mosquito, Lapa Grande, Lapa da Boca Estreita, Lapa do Labirintho, Lapa do Olho d'Agoa, Lapa dos Saraivas: these are some of the nineteen caves which he visits and excavates as he heads for Lagoa Santa. Most of them prove fruitless. Only two of them contain prehistoric bones beneath the calcareous crust. He packs these bones into a couple of boxes which he fastens tightly to the pack animal, entrusting Brandt with a bag of smaller bone fragments. They ride on through the Tormented Forest where now, as an additional plague, flying insects descend upon them in such thick swarms that they cannot ride a hundred yards without being covered by them. The bite of one of these insects instantly causes a violent itchy swelling which, if improperly treated, can lead to gangrene and death. Despite all their precautions, Dr. Lund and Brandt are soon covered with rashes and they must continually exhort one another not to scratch. Even at night the feverish burning allows them but little rest.

Brandt has begun to grumble. He understands neither the purpose of this journey nor where Dr. Lund is leading him. But when he sees that Dr. Lund is suffering just as much, and when he receives in answer a resolute look from behind the scientist's spectacles, he restrains himself and, paint and brush to hand, continues following Dr. Lund from cave to cave. One precious pack mule is bitten to death by a snake. Some days later the other mule is stung by a poisonous insect, paralyzing it for several hours. Once, when Dr. Lund is walking to lighten the load of his mule, he is nearly bitten by a rattlesnake. Hardly has he thanked his lucky stars for being saved by the warning rattle of the snake before a poisonous spider has bitten him on the back of his hand. Never before has he felt such pain. His insides twist and turn as if jagged knives were cutting into his body. He shakes and trembles and twitches and is taken by fever, cramps, and vomiting as he lies on the oxhide which Brandt had managed to throw beneath him just before he fell. His fingers dig desperately into the hard crust of the earth and his legs kick wildly as, in exhaustion, he gradually loses consciousness. He dreams dimly of a fiery stick being pressed into the bite, turning his hand into one great suppurating wound. Thanks to the instant use of the antidote which he always carries, his suffering lasts only six hours instead of the twenty-four hours which, in the end, would have extinguished the last spark of life.

Arraial da Nossa Senhora da Saúde da Lagoa Santa lies slightly more than two and a half thousand feet above sea level, almost exactly on the twentieth southern latitude. This is the region in which the jungle in the east, which here is not called *mata virgem*, virgin forest, because man has long since hewn his way into it and burned it for food, meets the open campos in the west, the ones through which a year earlier Dr. Lund had ridden with Riedel on his way to Ouro Preto.

Crags, even smaller rocks, are rare here. The town is surrounded mainly by red clayey earth covered with yellow-green grass. But Dr. Lund is strongly attracted by Lagoa Santa, which he and Brandt reach on October 17th, not least of all because he has been told of the restorative powers of the lake water. With pleasure he sees once more the tiled houses of the town, many of them with small paths leading down to the lake whose abundant birdlife makes it one of the loveliest he has ever seen in this country of so few lakes. Lagoa Santa will be a good place to live during the rainy season when the caves will be filled with water. Here he can recuperate and arrange his collections, surrounded by the rolling terrain where flat stretches are seldom larger than about fifteen acres, well suited, when it is not raining, for taking walks and finding time to think and forget . . . The red clayey soil is without doubt detritus from the ancient mountain mass and reinforces Dr. Lund's belief that Brazil is the oldest land in the world, a thought which he will explain in detail to Forchhammer now that his field of research is the history of the Earth, which is so closely related to geognosy.

Here God first modeled the surface of the Earth after the Catastrophe. For thousands of years the tropical heat and the moisture have broken down the various types of stones, consisting mainly of gneiss and granite. Clay slate is the proper word for the surface of the earth, with a gleam of copper-red iron which imparts its color to the clay. Dr. Lund recalls all this from his last visit. Now he is back, already refreshed by the pleasant climate of the place even though tornados and fierce squalls sometimes suck up the loose dirt into towering whirlwinds hundreds of feet high in the remote campo regions on the other side of the lake. These presage the rainy season which will soon set in and prevent scientific excursions, dig impassable gaps in the roads in which snakes writhe themselves into exhaustion in their efforts not to drown. The rain submerges houses which, unlike those of Lagoa Santa, do not lie high, and worst of all, sweep away those which are built only of clay and straw.

But Dr. Lund prefers all this now, after the events of the past months in the drought which made his mucosa so dry that he coughed from morning to evening in the caatinga while being bitten by insects and scratched until he bled. Again Dr. Lund can see out over a panorama one-hundred-and-eighty degrees wide which sucks everything into it if he concentrates deeply. Once more he can feel, his appetite returns to him, and with it the pressing urge to work at putting his collections into order. And now Brandt too is beginning to unwind.

They find quarters at a lodging house and are given, along with separate bedrooms, a kitchen with rusty old pots and a fireplace which has not been used for ages, as well as a workroom in an outbuilding. A local hunter is hired to shoot all the species with which he is familiar. Children are set to gathering insects, and on the walls of the workroom and kitchen there soon hang animals, partly or completely skinned, which Dr. Lund starts to classify. Brandt's stack of bone illustrations is growing. Tongue pressed between his lips, he makes meticulous drawings, sometimes painstakingly tinted, of all the bones which Dr. Lund had found on the way between Curvelo and Lagoa Santa. When he is especially satisfied Brandt rubs the bald patch on the back of his head, humming a little tune from the Norway of his childhood and youth as he eagerly discusses ways to improve their diet. He is a cook at heart, with a gift for composing new tropical dishes. However, Dr. Lund has no desire to experiment with his diet, as the eggs which they can now obtain are more than enough for him, together with noodles, porridge, bread, cheese, and strong tea. But he is more and more pleased with Brandt. After having written letters home to Henrik Ferdinand, Christian, and Peter Christian Kierkegaard, as well as exhaustive accounts of his travels to leading scientists in Paris and Berlin, chief among them von Humboldt – whom he praises as the unexcelled pioneer of explorers in South America whose example he humbly seeks to follow – he and Brandt furnish their base as comfortably as possible, having at last found contentment.

The walls of their rooms are made of unfired clay brick covered with straw and wound with paper yarn. The floors are of stamped clay, their beds are still the oxhides, spread out in the middle of the floor so as to avoid the rain coming in through the chinks in the walls when the tornados arrive from the campos. They use their coats as blankets. But even under these primitive conditions they manage to create a homey atmosphere with the help of the flowers and drawings of the lake which Brandt has signed and carefully mounted on cardboard. At sunrise or before dusk, they enjoy a stroll along the shores of the lake, collecting plants and shooting birds, often standing in chest-high rushes. Dr. Lund is particularly fond of the swamp trees. He sees completely new and unfamiliar trees, many of them so dependent upon water that years ago they had begun to wander out into the lake. And among the rushes and the swamp plants live thousands of birds whose songs remind him of the early student mornings at the Gamekeeper's House in Frederiksdal. However, here the birdcalls are staccato and utterly different – *tee-heeeet-tooo-eeet* - *tee-heeeet-tiiit* – calls which would leave a Danish ornithologist agape or even – *sklooood-u-dooot-sklood* – give them a healthy scare. Dr. Lund smiles contentedly. Once more everything is within his grasp. And Brandt is drawing constantly, increasingly in harmony with nature, now that his wounds and cuts from the caatinga have almost healed.

Usually they go down to the lake along a little path leading past the house with the genuine, faintly mud-colored glass panes which Dr. Lund had observed with particular warmth when he had ridden by with Riedel. This house belongs to the priest, a bony Spanish Jesuit with eyes like coals which are not the least averted when they meet him on his way up to church, his worn sandals flapping. He is curiously wary of the two Northerners who have come to investigate everything – even the palm garden which is his passion and which runs from his house all the way down to the lake shore. He himself has planted this garden, except for the towering royal palm which serves as a sort of landmark for Lagoa Santa. Is the priest in fact their enemy? This thought occurs to them one day when he had brushed past them in a cloud of red dust. But the next day they are reassured when, despite his reservations, he allows them access to his palm garden and even gives them much information about the town and the hinterland, doled out in carefully measured doses.

Dr. Lund is especially grateful for his recommendation of a commercial and financial house in Sabará which pays up to three per cent monthly interest. He resolves to deposit some of his money in this institution via the commercial and financial house of Hamann and Co. in Rio de Janeiro through which Henrik Ferdinand forwards his money. The deeper into Brazil he had gone, the higher he found the interest paid on deposits. In São Paulo it was one and a half percent monthly. In Ouro Preto it was two per cent monthly, and here it is three per cent monthly, whereas in Rio de Janeiro it is still six per cent – yearly. Thus Dr. Lund is able to live solely on his interest here in Minas Gerais, and moreover can pay Brandt well. As he cheerfully writes this to Henrik Ferdinand, he resolves to stay on the best of terms with the priest and not, as he would otherwise have enjoyed, to challenge him in discussion about the creation of the Earth.

He still cannot understand why the bones which he had found in the Maquiné cave - along with most of his clothes and all of his instruments - have not arrived by tropa from Curvelo. He assumes that the tropa has taken a detour, perhaps via Oura Preto where the mule train is to pick up goods for families here in Lagoa Santa. But then comes the discouraging news that his goods had long ago been sent all the way to Rio de Janeiro because it was reasoned that no European would ever dream of spending the rainy season anywhere but in the capital. It would be impossible to catch up with the tropa without running into rain on the way back. Dr. Lund will not be able to get his boxes back even by sending express riders. Again his world is shattered. For days on end Brandt cannot coax a word out of him. He lies in a deep depression, staring at the ceiling of palm leaves and old boards, or else he wanders alone through the town, down to the lake, back again, round the church plaza, into the venda to buy eggs, out again, once more down the path past the priest's palm garden and up again. For months he will be forced to wait for his collections and his clothing. The venda carries nothing more than a pair of poorly sewn boots which are not even his size. As he lies in his room with the oil lamp burning, he thinks of the many precious weeks he is losing on his work, in which the Deluge forms the great impassable boundary river between the first and second parts. And suddenly, as if he had called it forth, the flood breaks.

It starts with a light dripping on the roof. Then there is silence again. An hour passes. Suddenly it seems as if the roof is being lifted off, and even though the doors are shut and the windows shuttered, the storm beats in from all directions. Dogs growl in the church plaza, shouts and shrieks are heard, oxcarts rumble, and then, as if all the clouds in the world had gathered above Lagoa Santa, comes the rain. There is lightning and thunder, raindrops like polished rock crystals beat in torrents onto the roofs of the town, hour after hour. Dr. Lund falls asleep, drugged by their noise, and soon after he is awakened by the same unrelenting sound. He falls asleep, awakens – and the rain keeps on falling. For days. For weeks. For a month. At length he has reconciled himself to waiting. Brandt always has some morsel of town gossip with which to cheer him when he twice daily appears in the doorway of Dr. Lund's room bringing hard-boiled eggs, bread and cheese, and sometimes fresh milk. There he stands, wringing wet, smiling and bare-chested, clad in a new pair of canvas trousers of the sort otherwise worn only by the blacks, and does what he can to lift Dr. Lund out of his depression.

Finally one day, when the rain has abated to a drizzle, Dr. Lund arises and emerges from his room with the feeling of having been reborn. For the past weeks he has been hearing within him: *'reculer pour mieux sauter, reculer pour mieux...'* Perhaps it was Providence which had sent the tropa to Rio de Janeiro, thus compelling him to take a much-needed rest instead of ruining his health with constant study and classifying. No, not *perhaps* – Providence *is* protecting him, and in gratitude he puts his arm around Brandt's shoulders and goes out with him to greet the townspeople, with whom Brandt with his frank artistic temperament has become good friends. Often Brandt has made friendly caricatures of them – the proprietors of the venda, a neighboring Portuguese family whose three daughters have an excellent collection of petrified fish from the banks of the Rio das Velhas, a couple of fazenda owners who survive the rainy season by moving to town, a pensioned English non-commissioned officer from Gongo-Soco, as well as people of all ages, both sexes, and indeterminable occupations. Brandt has even become good friends with negroes, both with freed slaves, who wear a gold chain on one ankle, and with those who have just been bought at auction in Ouro Preto or Sabará and who are unable to speak a word of Portuguese.

The freed slaves in particular can tell about many mysterious caves out where the rocky landscape begins. Lapinha and Lapa Vermelha are two of the first caves. In one of them lives a hermit who spews fire from his mouth if anyone approaches him, and in other caves live giant snakes and monsters with eight heads and tentacles as long as the passages themselves...

At last the rainy season is over and the cave expeditions can begin. In the course of the late autumn and the first winter months, Dr. Lund and Brandt visit numerous new caves, many of which are rich in finds. From April 10th to May 15th 1836, they investigate about twenty caves. Lapa Rica, Lapa da Lagoinha, Lapa de Contendas. The first of these had once contained bones, but its soil had such a high content of saltpeter that it had been completely dug out. Lapa das

Palmeiras, some few bones. All of Dr. Lund's strength has returned and, unafraid of snakes and *unzas* inside the caves, he explores each one thoroughly, from the entrance to the end wall. Some caves have only a few passages and modest chambers, others open into halls, but none even approach the majesty of the Maquiné cave.

But Lapa da Cerca Grande in the Indian crag Mocambo, a towering robber baron's castle overgrown by a little virgin forest, rising in the middle of a glorious meadow, almost measures up to the Maquiné cave. As it contains an abundance of fossil bones, Dr. Lund and Brandt are obliged to stay for a time at the nearest stock farm, Fazenda Mocambo, owned by friendly, rational and European-orientated people, two brothers and their wives who spend half of their time in Rio de Janeiro attending concerts of chamber music, the Italian opera, and reading. Without demanding payment, they place a couple of negro workers at Dr. Lund's disposition. The outer wall of the Indian crag, which lies less than half a légua from the fazenda, bears hundreds of colored drawings of animals made by the original primitive population of the country. Dr. Lund knows that he will return to this cave simply because of its beautiful surroundings, and after having nearly emptied it of bones, he and Brandt continue on to new caves. Dr. Lund intends to gather as many bones as possible before the onset of the next rainy season, when at last he will be able to work on his treatises with all his instruments and collections, now being sent back from Rio de Janeiro, within reach.

Lapa de Gamba, about a mile east of Mocambo. The soil here, containing saltpeter, has been partly removed. Traces of fossil bones. Lapa da Aldeia, three miles north-northwest of Mocambo. No yield. Lapa do Taquaral, one légua southwest of Mocambo, a large cliff wall with many caves and two deep entrances. Fossil bones beneath the calcareous crust. Lapa do Morrinho, a little less than half a légua southwest of Mocambo. Narrow winding passages. Bones of small mammals, especially rodents. Lapa da Roça do Mocambo, three miles southwest of the fazenda. Faint traces of fossil bones. Three visits to the imposing cave Lapa da Pedra dos Indios, and one to Lapa dos Mocambeiros on the slope of the cliff which also contains Lapa da Cerca Grande.

From here the route returns to Lagoa Santa, and several more caves are visited. Lapa de Periperi yields notable results, namely numerous bones of the peccary and the paca. Dr. Lund comes to know the landscape like the back of his hand. He can frequently smell his way to smaller caves not indicated on the wretched hand-drawn maps from Lagoa Santa. His instinct nearly always tells him whether a cave will prove fruitful or not. Because of the consistency of the soil at the entrance? Because of the shape of the entrance or the difficulty of getting there? Some mornings, he feels he can almost see the Deluge washing the animal carcases into a cave. He speculates about where in the body instinct lies, for he is invigorated and intent and has not been sick a single day since his depression at the start of the rainy season. In the nerves? Perhaps, but not only there. In the blood vessels? In the cervical vertebrae? Or in the form of a pineal gland somewhere in the still mysterious brain?

From July 7th to July 20th and then from July 20th to August 8th, he and Brandt make two more cave expeditions. Despite its name, Lapa do Milagre yields no bones. Here, for once, Dr. Lund's instinct is mistaken. In compensation, he does find innumerable fossil bones in Lapa Grande de Genette.

Again he visits Lapa da Cerca Grande, on an early morning more fresh and transparent than any he has experienced since he rode with Riedel. Then he returns to Lagoa Santa and the rainy season and his work with two, perhaps three, new treatises with which to surprise the Royal Academy of Science. He has already outlined it clearly in his head. He intends to concentrate on the ancient animals, divided into four orders: *Bruta, Acleidota, Myoidea,* and *Quadrumana.* Each has their families, including the sluggish sedentates, the sloth and the armadillo, the ruminants, the pachyderms, the carnivores, and so on down to the rodents. He is particularly interested in discovering the truth about the nasty ancient apes. Their bones call to mind a legend which he had heard in many parts of the inner highland, in the north and west of the province of São Paulo as well as on the sertão and by the São Francisco River, at the spot where

142

the canoes with the fearsome heads at the prow took Riedel and him across. According to this legend, there still lives in these regions a large animal of the ape family which the Indians call the Caipor – The Forest Dweller. This animal is as big as a human and covered with long curly hair on its body and much of its face. It is brown all over, but on its belly, just above its navel, there is a white spot. It climbs trees with agility but usually remains on the ground, where it walks erect like a human being. When young, it is gentle and peaceable and lives on fruit. Its teeth resemble those of a human. But when it grows older, the Caipor turns blood-thirsty and goes hunting for birds, small mammals – and humans. Huge fangs grow in place of the human teeth, and it cannot be shot because its fur is impenetrable, except for the white spot. The natives shun the haunts of the Caipor and although they can often see its footprints in the earth, they cannot tell in which direction it is headed, for the foot of the beast has a heel both at the front and back.

So much for the legend as it was told in the São Paulo province! At the São Francisco River a new element was added. According to the sertanejos, the Caipor is the lord of the wild boars. If a hunter shoots a boar, he will hear the voice of the Caipor in the distance, and the hunter would be wise to flee from his kill instantly. The mythical beast has even been seen in the midst of a flock of boars, riding on one of the largest of them. And in the canoes crossing the São Francisco River, some of the mulattos described the Caipor, as Dr. Lund and Riedel hid their smiles, as a veritable centaur, fashioned like an ape above, like a pig below . . .

The white spot above his navel – Dr. Lund has the answer: on most of the Brazilian apes the fur grows so sparsely in the middle of the abdomen that its skin is visible when the animal stretches itself. The foot with two heels – Dr. Lund realizes that it is simply a foot which is wider in the front than in the back so that the individual toes cannot be counted. The impenetrability of the fur – Dr. Lund knows that there really does exist an ape, the guigó of the species *Mycetes crinicaudis*, whose fur is so thick that no knife can stab the animal to death except by repeated brutal thrusts. It is impervious to shots from the back and the side, and as if fully aware of its excellent armor, the guigó never attempts to save itself by running away, but simply rolls itself into a ball as if to protect its pale belly. Dr. Lund is nevertheless fascinated by the legend because of the various striking similarities which this mythical creature bears to the pongo of Borneo. Even if no such animal exists in Brazil, might this legend not have been passed down to the living Indians from their forefathers? And does this legend consequently bear witness to the Asiatic origin of the first inhabitants of America?

Dr. Lund will answer these questions along the way. Just now he is writing the first part of his work, so the origin of man must wait. As he carefully arranges all the bones in his bedroom, in the kitchen, and in the workroom in the outbuilding, he is still convinced of the soundness of his Deluge theory. Another rainy season arrives. Now nothing can hinder him in writing his history of the prediluvian world, not even a letter from home relating that Peter Christian Kierkegaard had married, only to become, a few months later, a widower. No more superstition, no more thoughts of the watchwork in the apartment on Nytorv, can concern Dr. Lund now that, after his months of suffering, Providence has once more sent him out on an immeasurably fruitful journey. From Henrik Ferdinand he hears that H. C. Oersted has offered to send two young naturalists to Brazil to aid him in his work with the bones. But Dr. Lund politely turns down the offer and writes to everyone in Copenhagen about his plans for the coming year, grateful that, having Brandt, he already has the best possible assistant.

He must keep a grip on himself so as not to become giddy from this glimpse into the prediluvian world. This glimpse which Providence has afforded him, thousands of miles from home, just as a new rainy season sets in and sweeps everything down to the lake of Lagoa Santa.

7

With a view out over the palm garden and the flower
mountain Serra da Piedade in the distance, with all four
rooms of the house so crammed with bones that he hardly
knows where to begin and where to end in the attempt to
bring order into this multifarious chaos, Dr. Lund, on
November 16th 1837, puts the finishing touches to *A View at
the Fauna of Brazil, Previous to the Last Geological Revolution.
Second Treatise: Mammals.* He is delighted that he no longer
has to spend the rainy season in the rooming house in town
where an endless stream of uninvited guests, most of them
cheeky boys and negro matrons, came at all times of the day
to see the bones, touching and fingering them as if they were
encrusted with jewels and – what was harder to bear –
giggling at him as if he were a madman who might just as
well have collected gravel or old paper.

Here, where the priest had lived so austerely, he has found
peace and quiet and created respect for himself. The house is
neither too big nor too small. The glass windowpanes keep
out the rain and ensure a constant, pleasant temperature,
and the palm garden is a source of joy when he walks in it
mornings and evenings, although he does not approve of the
priest's Latin feudal mania for planting geometric beds and
trimming bushes and shrubs into cubes, as if this were the
park at Versailles. Fortunately, Dr. Lund is not obligated to
preserve the garden as it was when he moved in some
months earlier. The priest, who has become a teacher at a
college in Ouro Preto, laid down no conditions when he let
the house, for a most reasonable rent, to Dr. Lund. He and
Brandt have already bought a primitive piece of furniture
in the baroque style, but Dr. Lund himself built the desk
in the study with the window to the lake. Here at last he
can, in his second treatise on the prediluvian world in Brazil,
conclude:
that before the global Catastrophe the tropical global belt
     was not uninhabited, as otherwise commonly assumed,

that as for the *mammal* class, the prediluvian world was superior to the present with regard to the number of families and species,

that in particluar the families of the armadillos, sloths, ruminants, and pachyderms were more numerous in this period,

that the same holds true of the carnivores and the rodents,

that the lack of *bats* seems to be confirmed,

that the *mammal* class in this part of the world in the period in question displayed the same *curious* features which distinguish it at present,

that the majority of the families of which the *mammal* fauna in that period were composed appears in the present period but

that the existing *species* are all different from the fossil ones, and finally

that MAN DID NOT EXIST IN THOSE TIMES.

From these results, a synthesis of the facts, Dr. Lund advances various general hypotheses. *That* the shapes of the continents in the period in question were the same as at present. *That* the temperature of the entire surface of the Earth was higher than in our day, but *that*, then as now, it decreased from the Equator to the poles. *That* the natural event which caused the annihilation of the numerous, often terrifying, creatures with which he, in his treatise, has already acquainted the Royal Danish Academy of Science, was an event which took place everywhere on Earth. *That* all life on Earth was extinguished, an epoch in the development of the globe was finished, and the innumerable forms in which we today see life manifest itself are the products of a *New Creation*. *That* the epoch which he has studied in his treatise witnessed the culmination of the highest class in the animal kingdom, the *mammals*, but *that* their time is now at an end; after the New Creation, this class is poor and weak in comparison with its condition before the Deluge. The new scene had been destined for the development of a higher creature whose hour of birth had struck, and the raw and brutal mass development retreated to its remotest borders and was in the end swept into the abyss of

Nothingness. Then the high temperature, so favorable to the development of the non-intelligent organic mass of existence, gave way to a milder temperature which allowed for the development of intelligence. After the epoch of the mammals came that of Man, the Lord of Creation. This was the Plan of Providence.

Two thousand half-mandibles of *Mus lasiurus*, four hundred mandibles of *Didelphis murinus*, hundreds of bones of the hands and feet, vertebrae and strong tubular bones of all species of rodents, teeth by the thousands of all species, from small mammals up to *Priodon giganteus*, molars, grinders, jaws with teeth, jaws without, the scapular and lumbar carapace of *Hoplophorus selloi*, sphenoid bones, metacarpal bones, whole and half crania in piles, whole ribs, ungual phalanxes, metatarsal bones, vertebrae in heap upon heap, more crania, still more crania humerus bones, navicular bones, lunar bones, triangular bones, cranial bones, patellaes, whole or crushed to splinters, pisiform bones, calcanea, still more vertebrae, whole spinal columns, the canines of the saber-toothed tiger, and, in hundreds of small wooden boxes: bird skeletons, petrified porcupines, mouse toes, petrified rat claws, fossilized owl casts, and a multitude of soil samples and stone specimens for determining geognostic age.
Bones lie scattered throughout the house. In the large parlor they cover the floor from wall to wall. In Dr. Lund's study they lie beneath the desk, on top of the desk, on top of his books, in boxes, piled in heaps along the walls, and in his bedroom, where they have been pushed far under his bed. This bed is, in fact, the first proper bed in which he has slept since his departure from Rio de Janeiro. Brandt too has bones stored in his bedroom, but he refuses to have them close to his bed. They must remain packed and preferably in sealed boxes only, so that he, with his tendency to have nightmares, can avoid the risk of waking at some ungodly hour of the night to stare at them in the moonlight which makes all things come alive, to see the bones apparently dancing with one another or clattering across the floor like crabs in flight. Every day presents an endless puzzle in which a humerus bone is

suddenly seen to fit together with an antebrachial bone, teeth are fitted into jaws, crania are extended with cervical vertebrae, cervical vertebrae with spinal vertebrae, and femurs set together with tibias. Thus animal after animal from the prediluvian age emerges, here an armadillo, there a paca or a carnivore of the puma family, carefully braced with bamboo sticks, fastened with strings, hung with a label about its neck indicating number and the place where it was found. The fragmented bones are glued together with an evil-smelling waxy substance made especially for Dr. Lund by the proprietor of the venda, of indeterminable ingredients.

Thousands upon thousands of animals from the antediluvian world, excavated from their graves beneath the calcareous crust deep within the caves, now convene here in Dr. Lund's modest house. One animal in particular interests him: out in the garden in a three foot-high pile lie the numberless remains of the giant sloth, bones partly found in the Maquiné cave and especially in the caves closest to Lagoa Santa, the bones of thirty different giant sloths which Dr. Lund, together with Brandt and some local assistants, has worked to gather into one animal the size of a little elephant. It stands in the midst of the palm garden, supported by boards, tied, glued, and riveted together, gazing out over the lake toward the remote campo region where once there grew trees ten, perhaps twenty times greater than those which came after the Deluge, among flowers as big as bushes and insects perhaps the size of small rodents – monster ants, monster beetles.

The giant sloth had dragged itself along there, with its deformed and incredibly muscular supporting tail, its large claws curving inwards; an over-sized cripple from the very start, an idea only half thought through. Ceaselessly, sleepily, it sought after insects in the ground or branches which it tore from the trees by shifting all its weight onto its tail, standing erect after an hour or two, and then slowly letting itself topple forward, into the succulent crowns of the trees. Its claws were a fearsome deterrent. But they were utterly useless against any attacker, especially against its arch-enemy the saber-toothed tiger which from anywhere and nowhere would leap onto it and sink its canines into the rough-skinned neck with its bristly fur. In the death struggle the sloth could not even scream because its larynx too was only the beginning of something which would never be perfected. Its noise, in joy and in pain, was never heard in the primeval forests of the savannah.

Dr. Lund keeps a living specimen of the little three-toed sloth which he knows so well from his first journey to Brazil. He observes it daily while writing the biography of the giant sloth. Lying on its stomach with all four limbs outstretched, it first uses all its strength to brace one hind foot against the ground, thus lifting the same side of its body slightly from the ground. In this way the arm of the same side is freed enough to allow the animal to swing forward somewhat, seeing and not seeing, alert and deaf, all at the same time. And it can only move on uneven surfaces. The animal is helpless if its claws cannot grip something, for example, when it lies on a polished board of jacarandá wood. Closed round its own formidable failure, an unshapely lump of bodily mass, blood which does not circulate rapidly enough, nerve juice which coagulates, it bears witness to its great forefather who also dragged itself through the campo forests of the past. He too was an outcast from the family which included the giant armadillo, which, with its snout pushing in the mud, waddled and poked itself forward through the underbrush, protected by its armor. There was also the ever-scurrying anteater, the sweetmeat into which the saber-toothed tiger could sink its teeth if there were no sloths nearby.

The saber-toothed tiger! Dr. Lund is preparing to write its biography. Large as a lion but proportioned completely differently, with a tail as short as a lynx's and front limbs considerably stronger than its hind ones, it did not, like the great cats of the present, hunt antelopes and fallow deer, but sought its food exclusively among the slow animals. In one leap this beast of prey, to which Dr. Lund has given the generic name *Smilodon*, the scalpel-tooth, and the species name *populator*, the destroyer, would spring onto the back of the sloth. Then with a few violent stabs with its head, borne by powerful neck muscles, it would sink its enormous upper canine teeth like sabers into the fleshy neck of its victim. It was a monster of evil which would have been the first the

149

Creator drowned when he decided to create the world anew. It had vile, receding, almost ape-like nostrils, and tiny divider teeth; it could gape wider than any lion or tiger so as to use its murderous canines which, if broken, would render it as defenseless as the sloth, left to the merciless whims of its own species.

At night, Dr. Lund sometimes wakes with a start, having seen two bones fit together. Leaping from his bed, he lights the oil lamp, and is as a rule rewarded in his feverish zeal. He feels like an invisible spy in the prediluvian world, having been lowered down through a hole in the calcareous crust to study intently a world of horror never before seen by any human being, not even in the caves of Europe. He is poaching in the preserves of Providence. He finds what he is looking for, imagines new connections, lights yet another oil lamp, and proceeds to write a new treatise until strange noises from the lake are heard echoing up through the palm garden, and mysterious feet are heard pattering over the tiles of the roof. There is a tapping at the window. Even the royal palm seems unable to withstand the sudden onslaught of ancient animals which makes him push his chair back as he realizes that he is no longer invisible and that the hole in the calcareous crust has long since been overgrown with vines and the uppermost leaves of the giant ferns. He is running down winding paths, trodden by the giant armadillo, he hides himself behind a tree trunk buzzing with unknown insect life, toppled by the giant elephant. He is sliding down into a half-illuminated cave, pursued by the giant hyena, only to be chased out again by the growling of *canis troglodytes*, the ancient dog, feared even by the saber-toothed tiger, with pus-colored saliva about its mouth, the neck fur bristling, and its tail a whirlwind of insatiable hunger.

And he runs and runs, onward into the forest where unimaginable worms dig beneath the trees, worms the size of vipers, vipers the size of constrictors, and constrictors the size of... He thinks of the Midgard serpent but immediately afterwards he realizes that here, in this world, there is no one to understand him when he gives the animals names, neither mythical nor scientifically correct names. He is the first naked human being, created mistakenly an epoch too early, a trial, an experiment, the laughingstock of the giant apes with the pale-fleshed bellies who point at him and catch hold of each other's tails in malicious delight at seeing him so shamefully concealing his sex with one hand as he runs and runs. Songbirds as large as eagles, enough for a hundred treatises, glaring evilly sideways at him; insects, enough for a lifetime of study; birds of prey in the sky with crocodile teeth jutting from their yard-long jealousy-yellow beaks, waiting only for him to be chased out into a clearing. It is all terror, in a steaming sulphurous heat which drains him of all his strength so that in the end . . . in the end he grips the seat of his chair, clears his throat as if to reprimand himself, reaches for his pen, and again is glad because in his sleep he found two bones which fit together. And he smiles, calmed by the sound of Brandt's deep breathing and incomprehensible mumbling as he sleeps on the other side of the thin whitewashed partition, more like a screen than a wall, allowing as it does the air to pass freely between the rooms from forehead height up to the tiles of the roof on which gekkos swarm.

Here in the moonlight, disturbed only by the flickering light of the oil lamp, after yet another dry season of cave expeditions, this time from Lapa do Baú to the specially profitable Lapa da Serra das Abelhas, Dr. Lund, now no longer a victim of unwelcome fantasies, calculates one night the age of the Earth. From one cave he has supervised the excavation of about seven thousand *barrils* of soil, containing mostly small bones from the antediluvian period. The bones in one barril were counted by his negro laborers. On this basis he arrives at the conclusion that the number of animals represented in this cave alone from the New Creation up to the present mounted up to between seven and eight million! He takes out his rough paper, dips his pen and attempts to calculate how much time must have passed to accumulate the small bones, all of which come from bird cast. As he knows that birds of prey are extremely unsociable animals, he figures that only a pair of birds at a time would have inhabited this little cave, and if he moreover assumes that these two birds would have consumed four animals apiece each day, mice and other small rodents, snakes and songbirds combined, it would mean that at least five thousand years had passed since the formation of the layer of antediluvian bones – probably longer, perhaps, in fact six or eight thousand years as he had always believed and had suggested to Peter Christian Kierkegaard. If he then assumes that God allowed half of this number of years to pass before He decided to send the Flood, then the age of the Earth easily approaches twelve millennia, which is also the conclusion reached by various geognosts in Paris and St. Petersburg.

This is more than twice the four thousand and four years in the Old Testament and the eighteen hundred and thirty-eight years in the New Testament which Peter Christian takes to be true by calculating on the basis of the Bible! Dr. Lund smiles and looks forward to the day in a year or two when he will again resume his conversations with Peter Christian on walks from Blegdamsvej to Nytorv, especially now that letters from home indicate that old Kierkegaard, at the age of eighty-two, will soon be closing his eyes forever without having crossed out the names of his surviving children and kin in the black book. Four thousand and four years! Dr. Lund thinks longingly of the near future when Bishop Mynster and others of his ilk can no longer check the spread of natural science, when all children will learn its fundamental laws in school, and many scholars will be educated in its fields and thus help to combat superstition.

And he returns to bed, as the moon sharply illumines the giant sloth out in the palm garden.

Suddenly the spiny rat is there. To be sure, it is only the left molar of an old individual along with a jaw fragment, but enough to arouse the suspicion that it existed *before* the Flood. At first Dr. Lund says to himself that there must be some mistake. But little by little other teeth are revealed as he digs beneath the broken calcareous crust. There can be no doubt. Soon numerous fossil traces of the animal emerge from the red soil of other caves as well. He is able to make an extremely detailed comparison between the prediluvian and the existing species of the genus *Loncheres elegans,* a graceful animal rustling in the grass, whose color, whose habits, and footprints in the mud by the shores of the lake are already familiar to Dr. Lund. The upper part of its body is a rusty yellow-brown. The lower part is white, and the two parts are sharply delineated. Its abdomen lacks woolly fur and its bristles are stiff, pressed flat and sharp but not prickly. Its scaly tail is thinly covered with hair which increases in length towards the end, where it forms a tuft. The spiny rat prefers to live near pools around the lake, where it builds nests in the grass and clumps of rushes. It swims with the greatest of elegance, using its tail as a rudder. There are no webs between its toes. The fazenda owners are always after it because at night, when it seeks its food, it goes into grain fields, climbs up the stalks of maize, gnaws through the husks of the ears and eats all the grain.

This animal, then, was the only one to survive the worldwide catastrophe and the Deluge. *Why?* And *how?* By a tiny little mistake? For several days Dr. Lund is incapable of working. He leaves the bones to themselves and takes many solitary walks down to the lake and along its shores, leaving Brandt behind in the house and garden to draw the bones for Dr. Lund's planned *Third Treatise* on the animal world of Brazil before the global catastrophe. He sees everything, but with no joy. Here and there are traces of the spiny rat in the mud, gnawed rushes, bits of nests, and, if he stands motionless for a long time, he will see it – first the snout, then its lively fearful eyes. Then its body come into sight. And suddenly it scurries just past the toe of his boot and disappears into the rushes. How could it have survived the Flood? Did it swim up against it? And how many were there? The entire population from some lake, perhaps Lagoa Santa itself? Or only a single family? Was it washed up on the only mountaintop which protruded above the water? *'And God decided to send the Flood over the Earth as a punishment for the wickedness of the animals. But to a single male and single female of the species genus* Lonchere elegans *He said: I shall save you. Gather all the food you have in your nest and run to where the waves cannot reach you . . .'*

Irritably, Dr. Lund interrupts himself in his attempt to find the answer. He will never find it. And he considers abandoning the bones completely and returning to botany, perhaps making a new year-long expedition deeper into Brazil, all the way to Goiás and the lower Amazon country or up to the mouth of the Jequitinhonha River in Bahia. In

Lagoa Santa people are saying that he has changed, that he has become withdrawn and unfriendly. One day he even appears unshaven, contrary to his strictly hygienic way of living. This happens just as he has won the complete respect of the town, having enquired about the price of a good healthy house slave and deposited some of his money on interest with a local moneylender. He has willingly contributed large sums to charitable purposes and is no longer at all reticent – as he was when he lived in the rooming house and felt himself hedged in and stared at – about explaining to those who are seriously interested, such as the proprietor of the venda, an amateur archaeologist who has collected many thunderbolts of the wild Indians in the form of flint axes of all sizes, everything about the rich sinister past about which the bones speak if one can decipher their script. And then came the spiny rat.

But only that. Dr. Lund finds no traces of other animals which may have survived the Flood, and by now he has visited over one hundred sizeable caves. Everywhere the writing says the same thing. Above the calcareous crust: bones from the present. Beneath: bones from the prediluvian era, ever more numerous, ever larger. Finally, without allowing his thoughts to be unraveled past recognition by the spiny rat, he approaches the end of the dry season of 1838 busy at work on his *Third Treatise*. He adds an abundance of new details to his description of the antediluvian world. He classifies scores of new bones, and, just as the rainy season begins unexpectedly early and with rumors of devastating floods inland, he manages to finish his treatise and send it off – with the following conclusions:

that the farther down one goes in the sub-divisions of the system, the greater the differences between the *mammals* of both periods,

that most of the families in the class of *mammals* such as they appear today are only a fraction of those of the vanished world,

that even so the *bats* had relatives in the prediluvian world,

that the general law of a specific difference between the species of the prediluvian and those of the present world must admit an exception, namely the spiny rat *Loncheres elegans*, and

that NOT EVEN AFTER THE MOST RECENT INVEST-
IGATIONS CAN IT BE SAID THAT MAN EXISTED
IN THE ANTEDILUVIAN WORLD.

Dr. Lund informs the Royal Danish Academy of Science that he is still convinced as to the correctness of the conditions which he had described in his earlier treatise in connection with the great event which put an end to the prediluvian world which forever repudiated the natural scientists who base their work on the hypothesis of the immutability of species.

He excavates still more caves either with two or three laborers from Lagoa Santa or by setting a whole team to work with spades and hoes while he, with Brandt, rides along the banks of Rio das Velhas, scouting after even the smallest opening in the cliff walls. He gives some of the caves names, such as Lapa dos Curujês, with its over-whelming quantity of small bones in owl cast. But as the months pass, the new year having long since supplanted the old with the onset of a drought, the like of which has not been seen in the past twenty-seven years, Dr. Lund feels that he is not alone in his quest. More and more caves show traces of recent digging, done almost in panic, and not for saltpeter but for bones. Meanwhile the story is again related to him when he spends the night in small villages or at isolated fazendas. A story usually told by one negro slave to another who has passed it on to a fazenda owner who in turn repeats it to Dr. Lund with an indulgent smile. It is a story of the treasure which he and Pedro Dinamarques continue to fight over as it moves from cave to cave at night when only the Indians can find their way into the innermost chambers.

And as this story becomes more and more fanciful, Peter Claussen still shows no sign of life other than the useless, completely fresh bones which he has left behind, having dug out all the valuable ones. Thus it is related that the Doctor with the spectacles and the clear blue eyes which stick to the spectacles when he removes them, leaving two terrifying holes in his cranium, derives his tremendous strength from the strange flowers which he crushes with his nails and eats from a

155

little bowl which always hangs about his waist. This is the only way to explain why one day in Curvelo many, many years ago, he had only to touch the giant Pedro Dinamarques to make him topple over so that he had to keep to his bed for four days as blood dripped inside his skull. And now, says the rumor, now the Doctor with the blue eyes is hunting him, from cave to cave, out over the campos, down in the buriti valleys, up again and in and out of new caves so that Pedro Dinamarques abandons his hoes and shovels everywhere in his wild search for the treasure and the snakeskin, which, when pulverized and inhaled by the light of the moon, will grant him everlasting life.

What is one to do with such stories? At first Dr. Lund smiles at them and Brandt is highly amused, chuckling in a way which makes his Adam's apple dance up and down and wishing to illustrate them in a fashion which Dr. Lund feels has nothing whatsoever to do with their scientific mission. Gradually the stories weary him. At the same time he is worn out by the irritation he alway feels when, arriving at a cave, he unpacks his implements, lights all the torches, climbs down into the cave, bumps against an unseen stalactite jutting out from the wall, gets soaked to the skin, and sometimes lands in puddles which rise over the top of his boots, only to discover that Peter Claussen has already been there. And when he returns to Lagoa Santa to rest, new problems at once present themselves.

In particular the gold mine Papa-farinha is a constant source of annoyance. He had been so certain that he was doing the right thing when, at the encouragement of its owner, a Hungarian miner and a lieutenant-colonel, he had invested some of his money in the mine as a mortgage. Dr. Lund had carefully inspected the mine, situated near Sabará, with the pensioned English non-commissioned officer from Gongo-Soco, and both of them had arrived at the conclusion that the mine, with its large territory, its well-oiled English machinery, and its gold shimmering in the quartz strata running through all the passages for many fathoms, was both reliable and inexhaustible.

But the venture rapidly proved to be a failure. There was not a drop of water to drive the wheels. It was 'only' a question of waiting for the rainy season – said the Hungarian lieutenant-colonel with the propitious name of Franz Visner von Morgenstern. Dr. Lund waited for one rainy season, then a dry season, then another rainy season, and still the streams did not run full. The waterfalls did not break forth from the mountains, and not even the Indians who were sent around the lands of the mine with divining rods, rat tails, and bird feathers could find the slightest underground trickle. In the end the lieutenant-colonel had to declare bankruptcy, put up the shutters of his elegant house, and let Papa-farinha pass to Dr. Lund, who is unspeakably embarrassed to write this long tale to Henrik Ferdinand who, having married again, is now Director of the National Bank, with the title of Head of the Bureau and a Counsellor, and promptly sends Dr. Lund's money to him via Rio de Janeiro. What must they be thinking of him in Copenhagen? He, the promising PW, acquainted with the most eminent scientists in Europe, until some years ago the youngest member of the Royal Danish Academy of Science, the protégé and special confidant of H.C. Oersted, Reinhardt, and Forchhammer, has suddenly become a speculator owning a gold mine containing enough yellow mica, which, when melted could feed half the population of Copenhagen. If only it could be mined . . .

And if it is not the name Papa-farinha which upsets him, then it is Brandt, who to an increasing degree has plunged into veritable orgies of self-reproach. For hours after awakening with sweat on his brow, Brandt talks about how he has dreamed that Wilhelmine and their three sons are dying of starvation in Kristiania, how the eldest son came up to him with scratched hands palm up, wan, hollow cheeks, and the barely audible reproach on his lips: 'Why did you leave us? Why did you go to Brazil?' Really, Brandt's unhappy life story cannot be of any concern to Dr. Lund. Yet he is touched enough to lend him one thousand species to send to Norway. This too is mortifying to have to relate to Henrik Ferdinand, who will soon be imagining the strangest things about how he spends his money. However, he mollifies his brother by telling him that he has obliged Brandt to repay the loan in regular instalments.

And if it is not Brandt, then it is the slave whom he has now purchased at the market in Sabará and who lives in his own little cottage in the garden, which Dr. Lund has had built specially for him. Dr. Lund permitted him to marry and to have his wife living with him, a little squat Creole woman who in some curious way had come here from Cayenne in French Guiana, permission which few people in Lagoa Santa would have granted. He has furnished him with a decent bed and regular meals and lent him illustrated works on natural science which he can look through and perhaps learn from. He demands of him only that he be always close at hand should he and Brandt have need of his help. Even so, the slave is a daily vexation because, always grinning, he tramps right into the house without knocking, nudges the bones with his toes, filches spoonfuls of Brandt's favorite jam, messes the bookshelves, gets greasy fingerprints on the costly measuring instruments, and leafs through the stacks of Brandt's drawings. He opens his eyes wide, demanding an explanation for every last detail. He uses a corner of the garden as his refuse dump, steps into all the flower beds, vanishes at a trifle, and in addition sings so loudly during the siesta, the oppressive heat of which he adores, that the neighbors are complaining.

And if it is not the slave, then there are the daily corrections which Dr. Lund must make on his first treatises, often in new smaller treatises, because the bones suddenly fit together in a different way, or because he discovers that he had measured skeletons improperly, or has placed the paca's head on the cervical vertebrae of the ancient hyena, or because new classifications insist upon being recognized. For weeks he is absorbed in the painstaking work while again the rain pours down and beats upon the roof. And if it is not the corrections then it is the town – its complete lack of culture, of intelligent society, of learned and inspiring conversation, chamber music concerts, and current literature. Dr. Lund misses Riedel and even the Englishmen in Gongo-Soco, although at the same time he is less and less able to tolerate the pensioned non-commissioned English officer who is telling the whole world about his useless gold mine and has long since absolved himself of any responsibility for Dr. Lund's involvement with von Morgenstern. Whenever they meet at the venda and Dr. Lund asks him to please desist, he responds with a braying *'Hee, hee, hee'*, sways too and fro, already drunk, reaches for his glass, and quotes the malicious dean from Dublin:

So, naturalists observe, a flea
Hath smaller fleas that on him prey;
And these have smaller fleas to bite 'em
And so proceed ad infinitum.

And if it is not Jonathan Swift, then it is the local witch doctor who wields his power over the blacks from his little hovel by the south road into the town. There he lives, surrounded by his spotted swine and his chickens. All about his hut there is a wilderness of poles stuck into the ground and surmounted with bird skulls, ox skulls, and ribs as well as small jars filled with stones and broken bottlenecks, and also with terrifying masks carved from coconuts. At least once a fortnight when the blacks gather at his house for what *they* believe to be a divine service, an indescribable hooting and howling reverberates. They fling themselves on the ground, give blessings incessantly with no tenderness or grace, go into convulsive trances, exorcise spirits, and drain whole bottles of sugar-cane liquor at a gulp as if it were milk or water. Lighting cigars by the dozen, they dance and chant monotonously in African to the accompaniment of a throbbing drum which only ceases when the sun rises and slaves stagger back through town, their eyes even more vacant than when they had come. They do not heed the Catholic procession which often marches forth from the opposite direction, led by the new priest, with every imaginable and unimaginable saint's statue being carried on the shoulders of the strongest men, enveloped in incense, borne on a wave of hymns . . .

And then, as the finishing touch, there is Peter Claussen, *The Dane*, as Dr. Lund thinks of him with clenched teeth. He who rides out into the highland with his hoe and his shovel and his slaves and regularly sends him small offerings – *'From one scientist to another'* – such as a molar, a clavicle, a toe joint, or a metatarsus, brought to his house by a special caboclo messenger and always finely wrapped: 'From Pedro Dinamarques!' 'From Pedro Claudio!' Or simply: 'A molar from Pedro!' The caboclo grins and gallops off.

When all these problems merge, the pains begin, usually as a stabbing ache in his shoulderblades running down through the muscles of his arm and his tendons all the way to his wrists or – worse – like fragments of glass cutting into his gums and tongs pulling out his teeth one by one. Weary, weary, so weary that he almost cannot hold his head erect and yet is unable to sleep, Dr. Lund sometimes sits in bed most of the day and the night, a ragged dog-eared volume of his favorite poet Tieck having slid from his hands into his lap, until the dreadful emetic, Ipecacuanha, which he had scorned in Rio de Janeiro because of its questionable ingredients of which no chemist in Europe would approve, brings relief.

What good is the letter he has received from the consul-general in Rio de Janeiro saying that he has been made a Knight of Danneborg? He writes to Prince Christian to thank him and he writes to the consul to ask him to please leave the medal in the bureau drawer until he comes by to fetch it on his way back to Europe, probably next year. Sometimes letters arrive after a delay of three, four, even up to six years, so that he relives his expedition with Riedel, busily studying botany and pressing specimens into the herbarium with Hornemann and Schouw in mind. To encourage him they write that he has a fine future as a botanist and that they are delighted in Copenhagen with the detailed, rich, and in every way astonishing herbariums he has posted home from Santos. Normally, when the rainy season does not intervene, a letter takes between three months and half a year to reach Copenhagen and it is impossible to guess at the roundabout routes by which the delayed letters were sent before reaching Lagoa Santa. Perhaps they lay in warehouses in Rio de Janeiro. Perhaps they were shipped back and forth over the Atlantic several times before the captain caught sight of the forgotten mail bag. A pang of melancholy goes through Dr. Lund when he suddenly recollects how the years have gone by and how rainy season follows rainy season. Even so, he sends thanks to Providence because he did not stick to botany but found the caves which always fill him with fresh energy. So, after his days of illness, he can once again sit on his mule with Brandt riding behind him.

He has now bought the house for such a small sum that

when he re-sells it before his final departure, he will have saved a good deal of money. In Europe he is being mentioned with admiration in scientific circles, as he learns from letters from de Candolle, Eméry, Owen, von Humboldt, and other leading naturalists. Moreover, they keep him abreast of recent developments in the world of research. In Berlin von Humboldt has published his *Geognostische und physikalische Beobachtungen über die Vulcane der Hochebene von Quito* and his already celebrated *Rede zum Säcularfest der Tronbesteigung Friederich II.* In Paris they have been fighting for eight years now about the scientific legacy of Cuvier and the identity of the true heir. In Copenhagen there are also disputes, especially between the older and the younger botanists. In London Darwin has published his *Journal of Researches into the Geology and Natural History of Various Countries Visited by H.M.S. Beagle*, and there is much excitement about his future works, in which he will concentrate on the purely zoological conclusions which he reached. All this Dr. Lund reads in the piles of letters that arrive in the mail bag brought by the tropa when the rainy season is over. He feels that he is not competely cut off from the civilized world after all. And as an extra piece of good news, he hears from acquaintances of Peter Claussen in Curvelo that *The Dane* has departed on a long trip through Europe, accompanied by a whole team of slaves, boxes crammed pell-mell with bones, gold bars, precious and semi-precious stones, traveling with his little washed-out wife who despite all decided, if that is the word, to stay with him.

Yes, Dr. Lund knows he is at the right spot on the globe, engaged in carrying out a mission which most of his colleagues must envy him.

Some months into the dry season of 1840, new caves have been excavated and new bones numbered and collected in boxes after repeated trips to Lapa da Lagoa do Sumidouro, The Cave by the Lake Where One Vanishes. Dr. Lund discovered this cave while riding along the shore of a large lake, ringed by rushes as tall as a man. The lake was about the size of Lagoa Santa but wilder because no town had grown up around it. In the nearest village, consisting of a mere venda surrounded by some clay huts, it was said that the Indians often sacrificed the hearts cut out of living boars on the shore of the lake. If a white man, or even a mulatto, approaches this sacrifice he will immediately lose his sense of direction, dance four times around himself, with north turning west and east turning south, and wander straight out into the lake to the spot where everything is sucked down to the voracious monsters at the bottom. Only if, at the last moment, the unlucky person is fortunate enough to find a certain reddish-yellow flower by the shore of the lake, pick it, and eat it as he wanders out into the water can he stop himself in time. The botanist in Dr. Lund momentarily awoke at this superstition. He wished he could find the reddish-yellow flower in the hope that, if taken as a strong tea, it would have a healing effect. Suddenly he noticed that the water, which seemed so calm, was being sucked towards a certain limestone rock to the south. The eddy pulled leaves, twigs, and branches down into the depths. Fish flailed their tails desperately to escape.

Now that the dry season is at its height and he is back, his suspicion is confirmed. There is a cave here. All the water in the lake has dried up and he stands by the limestone crag on the bed of the lake while the last water trickles through small cracks in the rock, *sangradores*, which doubtless conduct the water through subterranean canals out into the Rio das Velhas. Roots from several mature fig trees cling to the side of the rock, struggling not to be pulled down into the subterranean canals. Around him, just by the main entrance to the cave, float the branches and twigs which he had seen on the surface of the water when he had first arrived.

The cave itself is one of the richest he has visited, with bones lying everywhere in the coal-black humus, but without the usual calcareous crust which has not yet had time to settle because of the water which Lagoa do Sumidouro empties into it once a year. It does not take long for Dr. Lund to ascertain that most of these bones are fossils from before the Flood. There is enough work here for months, perhaps for a year. This cave, whose forms delight Brandt and sets him at once to drawing, will be his last. Yet another rainy season in which he will work on the material for his most exhaustive treatise so far. And then: Europe, the

the south of France or Palermo, Denmark. Home!

Suddenly the light of the torch strikes some bones, bones unlike the thousands upon thousands which he has already collected and classified. Flocks of bats abandon the cave. An icy gust blows through it. There they lie, in a layer of snail shells from a species still living in the lake, scattered among the fossilized bones of mammals, reptiles, and fish: the remains of a human being. Or rather, of several human beings, for the bones range from the completely fossilized to the light and brittle. Dr. Lund finds the first skull. He finds the second – and soon the third, the fourth, and the fifth. And the skulls stem from two different races. Some are small and well-shaped. Others are large and clumsy in shape with a receding forehead even lower than that of many apes. Entering a second cave, he soon finds even more skulls. And, lying some distance from the fossil remains of deer, peccaries, and pacas, among the teeth and bones of *Chlamydotherium humboldtii, Hoplophorus, Megatherium* and *Smilodon populator*, is a cluster of human bones. All of them are shattered, seemingly from heavy blows. They belong to one individual. They are buried not far beneath the surface, packed into a few cubic feet. They seem to be fossils, for they are very brittle, crumbling, white where broken. The *test* of their antiquity: when he puts them up to his mouth they stick tightly to his tongue! And yet their location seems to indicate a later origin . . .

That night Dr. Lund stays inside the cave, hunched on a little ledge with his knees up to his chest. He breathes heavily, and he knows he must be careful of his health. He brushes away the utterly irrelevant thought of going outdoors and spending the night as usual in a little hut of branches and palm leaves. He lights candle after candle, torch after torch. He cannot fall asleep with the dripping and gurgling from within the cave. Brandt, crouched in a corner, enveloped in his oxhide, is sulking because Dr. Lund should long since have ordered the blacks to build their shelter for the night. The negroes too grow uneasy and ask to be allowed to sleep outdoors, for at night they fear the bones.

Dr. Lund cannot think about anything but this: what was prehistoric man like? How could he survive among the saber-toothed tigers, the giant hyenas, the prehistoric apes, the giant bears, and the millions upon millions of poisonous snakes, giant ants, bird-spiders, and crab-sized scorpions? Was prehistoric man a cannibal, cruelest to his own species, with a black snarl of evil where today there is a heart, a terrifying experiment which the Creator caused to wander in the forests? To evolve into modern Man, so perfect and so liberated? Why this flat forehead which makes him a half-ape, still the worst creature Dr. Lund knows, a filthy, foul, flea-infested, grinning and drooling *caricature*? How large was the brain of prehistoric man? Could he think, feel, remember? Or did he use only his instinct? Did he walk or did he crawl? Could he swing easily in the vines of the trees? Did he use weapons – and which ones? Flint axes such as those used by the first savages after the Second Creation? Clubs? Or did he simply hurl stones and scratch out the eyes of his enemies with his claw-like nails?

The last candle has burned down. But soon morning will come and the first sparrows will flit in and out of the cave. The sun will rise over Lagoa do Sumidouro, all life will awaken except on the dry lake bed where, among the dead fish, snails and small white crabs struggle desperately to survive in the parched mud. Dr. Lund sends his negroes up to the village to buy dried meat, pork, beans, and eggs. He intends to camp at the cave for a long time. He will explore every passage and dig in every recess, more and more convinced that the bones belonged to the first human beings after the Flood, and that they are scattered here among the antediluvian animals only because there is no calcareous crust to separate them. And he keeps on finding more human bones, some of them with such a hard ring that they almost feel like metal casts. He finds the vestiges of at least thirty individuals, ranging in age from newborn infants to decrepit elders. And not a single bone is intact. But perhaps the damage was done after death, by falling limestone rocks or carrion-eaters?

Dr. Lund does not know, but he digs on zealously, while Brandt draws and draws. Again Dr. Lund forgets to eat, and he drinks only a little water or cold, sweetened tea. Most of the human bones lie haphazardly. What does this indicate? Perhaps the water caused this disorder. Most of the skulls are heaped in one pile, while another pile consists only of small bones, finger and toe joints, metacarpal and metatarsal bones. The surfaces of all the uppermost bones are reddish-brown. He also finds a few bones out on the lake bed. A jaw. A nearly intact foot. There is an abundance of old people's bones, lower jaws out of which all the teeth had fallen, jaws so worn that they are nothing but bone sticks. Dr. Lund concludes that the cave had been a burial place and that the tribe or group of ancient people had perhaps not been as cruel as he had first believed. The dead had all been flung into the cave, perhaps up from the rocks, during the rainy season, so that the eddies of water had sucked them down to their eternal subterranean rest. But the question remained: *when*? Before or after the Flood? Once more, Dr. Lund convinces himself that these humans must have been the very first after the Flood, and the first human beings ever in South America. He has found the bones of *Homo americanus* himself, as a special gift from Providence, a reward because he *perseveres*. There is enough for a completely new treatise which will form the introduction to the second part of his Natural History, *The Creator's Plan*.

And now he is again sleeping in the hut, again speaking to Brandt. No longer is his face darkened by a shadow, as Brandt's keen artistic eye has observed when something goes against his will. In fact, he is exhilarated and describes all his observations to Brandt while the frogs croak noisily around them, while the grass rustles where the mischievous spiny rat scurries. Blood-curdling howls are heard in the distance, as if the Caipor really is chasing Indians who have gouged the heart out of its sacred property, the wild boar. With his cigar lit and the pot simmering with black beans and salted pork, Dr. Lund relates that many of the skulls have all the characteristic features of the Indian race. But the teeth are anomalous. Their ends do not form a transverse cutting edge but an oval surface parallel in longitude with the lengthwise axis of the oral cavity. Is Brandt sleeping? Dr. Lund persists: it is well known, and Brandt ought to be aware of it, that a similar abnormal function of the incisors is found, as demonstrated by Blumenback, on the skeletons of Egyptian mummies! All the root growths in Brazil are soft and fleshy!

Thus these people must have been geophagists – is Brandt not even listening? – such as those mentioned by von Humboldt, related to the Egyptian fellahs . . .

Home in Lagoa Santa. After several months during which Dr. Lund and Brandt did not speak to one another as a result of an argument in which Brandt, with the sun seething on his forehead, swelling veins in his temples, and bloodshot eyes, quite unexpectedly refused to draw bones and instead left for more than a week on an excursion around the lake (or to a certain notorious saloon for dancing and amusement in Sabará?), Dr. Lund finished his *Fourth Treatise*. Now all the human bones have been numbered and are lying in a separate room and he has managed to raise complete skeletons with supports and ropes hung from the ceiling. Brandt is again cooperative after a reconciliation effected while the New Year, 1841, was being celebrated with fireworks lit in the church square diagonally across their house. He now illustrates the treatise with extreme diligence and precision. The slave has been scolded so often that he has finally learned to keep to himself in his house with his Creole woman. He has even stopped singing during the siesta. And in Lagoa Santa there is no more gossip about Papa-farinha.

Dr. Lund is able to conclude:

that he has found human bones, mostly fossils, brittle or actually crumbling, but

that he believes, in his new treatise on the fauna of Brazil before the last cataclysm, to have cited enough to show that the bones are insufficient to serve as documentation in the question as to the extent to which Man was contemporary with the extinct animal species whose remains are preserved in the latest soil layers of this country.

Rebellion has long been smoldering. Everywhere in Brazil there is discontent with the conservative centralized government in Rio de Janeiro. Anti-Portuguese feelings have been growing year by year among the people. Spanish Latin America is not fused into one nation, from Tierra del Fuego to Rio Bravo by the Mexican border to the United States, from Peru and diagonally down over Paraguay to Uruguay and

Argentina. Why then should Brazil be one country, among the largest in the world, chaotic, divided into provinces with nothing in common, from Pará in the sweltering Nordeste to the temperate Rio Grande do Sul, from the swampy Mato Grosso to São Paulo with its enterprising immigrants?

One revolution after another breaks out. First *a Rebelião da Cabanagem* in Pará which lasts five years. Then *a Rebelião da Sabinada* in Bahia which lasts one year, and *a Rebelião da Farroupilha* in Rio Grande do Sul now in its seventh year. In city after city, rural district after rural district, the Portuguese merchants and fazenda owners from the colonial period are being plundered, hunted, and sometimes even executed without a trial, often by blacks taking advantage of the struggle between the liberal federalists and the conservative centralists in order to escape from slavery and establish quilombos where the campo merges into impenetrable jungle. Is Brazil headed towards dissolution? Even though the emperor, born in Brazil and therefore popular in the beginning, has acceded to the throne, not yet eighteen years old, under the name of Pedro Segundo, the rebellion has spread from province to province. At last, via São Paulo, it reaches Minas Gerais. From Sabará to Santa Luzia, from Lagoa Santa to Curvelo, all towns are in the hands of the rebels, and the mail is not only delayed but gradually stops being sent and delivered after the emperor has sent his most capable general, the Baron, Count, Marquis, and Duke of Caxias, Luís Alves de Lima e Silva, into the heart of Minas Gerais to crush the rebellion.

This last factor - that the mail has ceased to function - exasperates Dr. Lund. He has just sent off new corrections to his latest treatise and has finished his *Fifth Treatise*, which has caused him the most agonizing inner conflict. After more excavations, he had to admit that not only the spiny rat but five additional canine species which inhabited antediluvian Brazil still inhabit the country. Realizing that he may have to change the general title of the treatises and omit the phrase 'before the last Cataclysm' without having the faintest idea of what to write in its place, he is now in deep doubt as to whether there had been a New Creation, a Re-Creation, or something else entirely which he does not know and which

167

cannot be traced by means of the calcareous crust which has guided him so far. Perhaps there was a process with no cataclysms at all during which certain animal species died out naturally, awkward and clumsy as they were, easy victims for their enemies. The giant sloth, and even the saber-toothed tiger whose murderous teeth cracked so easily, leaving it defenseless, were subjected to a process of tiny steps, from century to century, millenium to millenium. This thought keeps Dr. Lund confined to his bed for days, exhausted as never before and profoundly depressed, feeling that he had wasted years of energy on useless scribblings here among the innummerable bones littering the tables, drawers, boxes, shelves and floors. Brandt is now oscillating nervously between Lagoa Santa and the pleasure-obsessed Sabará because he has no idea how he can help. And then, on top of the nagging doubts, letters arrive, not just one, but two, three, and soon up to ten letters from naturalists in Europe, all of whom write with some surprise about a certain Peter Claussen who has been boasting that it was he who found the bones from antediluvian Brazil in caves which he was the first white man to explore, risking his life at every step.

In London Claussen sells a selection of his bones to the British Museum and allies himself with Owen in challenging essential details in Dr. Lund's biography of the giant sloth. In Paris he sells the remainder of his bones to the Musée de Paris, solemnly promising that next time he will send the human bones which he is tracking after 'various promising finds'. He impresses Blainville so deeply that the latter has Claussen's bones illustrated in his magnificent, newly published *Ostéographie*. In Brussels *the Dane* presents a treatise, *Notes géologiques sur la province de Minas Gerais*, and, armed with the false title of *Membre de l'Institut Brésilien*, he takes all the credit for having discovered the limestone caves along the banks of the Rio das Velhas. The most Peter Claussen will acknowledge is that 'at a certain time' he collaborated with the Danish naturalist Dr. Lund who was passing through Minas Gerais and visited his fazenda.

Collaborated! Passing through! Dr. Lund has written back to all his colleagues in Paris and London and informed them as to who collaborated with whom, but he cannot even send off the letters! For weeks, perhaps months, he can amuse himself by reading them until a new rainy season will further delay their posting. He is ready to pay the tropeiro twice the price or hire an Indian express rider to carry the letters to Rio, but nobody dares to attempt the journey, not even for triple danger money. For now General de Lima e Silva is advancing closer and closer. Brandt has concealed himself in a corner of the palm garden to avoid irritating Dr. Lund, who restlessly paces among the bones, in and out of the house, up and down through the town. While all the able-bodied men are drilling and holding target practice by the lake, the women are instructed to barricade the houses with sandbags. The children are hidden out of harm's way in the church, and the first cannon shots of the imperial army are booming from afar. Horsemen, full of fight, ride back and forth, slaves hide, church bells peal, pigs wake and get in the way of everything and everyone. Across the roads leading out of town, barricades are being built of dining tables, chairs, bureaux, and bedside tables. All is confusion, shouting and screaming. Joyful reports of victory are followed by reports of appalling defeat for the rebels in Santa Luzia and Sabará, which have been razed by fire.

One morning, Dr. Lund, wishing to concentrate on something sensible, sits at the innermost table in the venda and, ignoring everything around him, sends a negro boy to fetch ink, pens, and paper from his house, after which he writes the angriest letter in his life. This letter will await the arrival of Peter Claussen the day he returns from his shameful triumphal progress through Europe. Dr. Lund's spectacles are fogged with indignation as he most respectfully informs *the Dane that* his 'treatise' is a tangle of misrepresentations, *that* he has no right to trespass upon his, Dr. Lund's, long-standing scientific work, *that* he, Dr. Lund, has ascribed him, Peter Claussen, all due credit in connection with the Maquiné cave in an exhaustive note, *that* his, Peter Claussen's, boasting to Blainville is outrageous and disgraceful, *that* he, Dr. Lund, demands redress in the form of a written retraction – *in duplo*! – and *that*, if this is not carried out in legible script, at the earliest possible opportunity, then he, Dr. Lund, will, with the greatest loathing, be forced to avail himself of the

169

influence at his disposal – first and foremost the Royal Danish Academy of Science, the head of which is His Majesty King Christian VIII.

Lagoa Santa is still in the hands of the rebels. From all nearby towns and from most of the hinterland they come, on horseback, on mules, on foot, in ox-drawn carts, to join the townspeople. As a matter of precaution Dr. Lund and Brandt take down the window panes in their house, which is still the only building with real glass panes, and they gather the most valuable bones in the garden, those of the giant sloth first of all, and cover them with oxhides. Still sweating and straining with the question of whether there had been a New Creation, a Re-Creation, or this third possibility which he does not know and which for hours brings the dark shadow over his face, Dr. Lund waits for the rebellion to be quelled so that the mail can be sent off before New Year's Day, 1843. Again he has attacks of dizziness, pains in his teeth, and difficulty eating. Most of the next day he sits on his rickety folding chair in front of the house observing the commotion. The rebels ride back and forth without proper uniforms, young and old together, dirty and unshaven. One early afternoon, in the worst heat of the siesta, a band rides straight up to his house, throws lassoes round the gate, pulling down the picket fence, and demands his house for their headquarters. He tears off his spectacles, stands up furiously, and waves back the rebels with one hand clutching the wide brim of his straw hat, 'I am *Dr. Lund!* I am *Dr. Lund!*'

The sun makes everything swim before his eyes. The dust kicked up by the restless horses chokes his throat. But no one must trespass on his property.

'And I am *Dr. Claussen!*' comes suddenly from the biggest rider on the biggest horse with a silver-mounted saddle and harness. And round and round in a figure-eight, cracking his whip, rides *the Dane*, with his vaqueiro hat cocked, his eyes piercing from his red square face, with a newly-grown full beard and long hair à la Garibaldi and jeweled earrings. Cheered on by his slaves and workers, he grinningly roars to Dr. Lund that his hour will soon come, both as a man and as a scientist. Does the Doctor not know about the latest new theories of evolution in Europe? Does he not keep up with

170

Annales des Sciences naturelles? Does he not own a decent library? Does he not, in short, know that birds are descended from flying fish? Lions from sea lions? And man from mermaids and mermen? And what does he say to the idea that the orchid gives birth to hummingbirds and tiny men? And again the giant grins while his people nearly finish pulling down the fence around Dr. Lund's house.

Then a cannon booms close by. A bullet whizzes into the neighboring garden. The army of General de Lima e Silva has advanced by forced marches from Santa Luzia and is now attacking Lagoa Santa from three sides. Panic-stricken, everyone flees after having fired random shots into the air. The last one to ride out of town is Peter Claussen, and before he breaks into a full gallop toward the lake where he can escape between the shore, and Sierra da Piedade and out onto the campo, he turns one last time toward his countryman, shouting so loudly that he almost drowns out the rumbling of the oxcarts heading out of town:

'*Nous sommes tous des travailleurs de la pensée, Monsieur le Docteur!*'

Those who cannot flee are shot. Right in front of Dr. Lund's house, the pensioned Englishman drops dead, with a single bullet in his chest, a bottle of port in his hand, and a wildly startled expression in the wide open eyes now staring unrelentingly at Dr. Lund. A slave falls just a few yards from him. A caboclo expires on the church steps. Soon afterwards the first soldiers march in under the great imperial banner with a flourish of trumpets. Where is Brandt? Is Dr. Lund the only one left in town, aside from the weeping children in the church? With all the impressions jumbled in his head, his thoughts run wild and all the time he sees the calcareous crust melt like ice in the springtime and hears the echo of Peter Claussen's idiotic taunt, caught by that fool in some anarchist café in Paris. He is so upset that he must do something to keep his guts from boiling over under that white sun. Dr. Lund runs in front of the veranda and takes a handcart for coffee sacks, pushes it back, and with the help of some soldiers cowed by his decisiveness, he casts the corpse of the Englishman upon it.

He pushes the handcart to the cemetery a few hundred

yards behind the church. Half a dozen children fearfully poke their heads out to watch him. He does not have the heart to obey his original impulse of simply letting the Englishman lie in the open to have his liver hacked out by the black urubús circling in growing numbers above Lagoa Santa. Knowing the hopelessness of the task, he finds a rusty old shovel and begins to dig in the stone-hard earth. For half an hour. An hour. A slight coolness comes from the lake. No more shots are heard. Dr. Lund flings aside his shovel. The hole is only a few inches deep. He comes to himself again and goes back to order his slave to bury the Englishman before dark. But the slave, of course, has fled with all the others. Then he catches a glimpse of the Norwegian's bald head behind a window. He hurries over and sees Brandt, trembling with fear, crawling away on all fours from the window. Brandt does not calm down until an hour later when Dr. Lund finally convinces him that Pedro Dinamarques has finally ridden out into the campo where he can be alone with his miserable conscience.

At long last General de Lima e Silva himself arrives. He immediately enters into conversation with Dr. Lund and orders his soldiers to raise and repair his fence. In Dr. Lund's study, over a cup of tea sweetened with jam, impressed at being the first Brazilian to make the acquaintance of *Homo americanus* – now cleaned, numbered, and erect – he solemnly promises to take the Doctor's letters along to Rio de Janeiro when he has crushed the last rebels who have now gathered in Ouro Preto. A simple matter for him. 'Like hunting three-toed sloths,' he smiles, and points to Dr. Lund's specimen, which has spent most of the day creeping from a corner to beneath the desk. Dr. Lund relishes the company of a civilized person with a great love for music and poetry. At last he is calm.

And all the bones are lying in their proper order.

'As the cave expeditions are now at an end . . .' writes Dr. Lund at the beginning of the *Sixth Treatise*. He completes it on November 22, 1844 – without a conclusion. He merely describes his newest finds of bones, directly addressing his treatise to Counsellor of State Oersted. He has excavated over eight hundred caves. Now the question remains, what is to be the fate of the bones, 'these my children', as he writes to Henrik Ferdinand, 'whose future upbringing' he must provide for in the best manner possible. He had originally wished to donate the collection to Christian VIII, but since the king has acceded to the throne he seems to have lost interest in natural history.

Instead, Dr. Lund is now seriously considering selling the collection to Paris, where it will be truly appreciated and where, if he settles in the south of France during the winter, he can continue to work on it and at the same time keep abreast with the newest theories of evolution. Re-Creation? New Creation? He would be mad to think that he would ever find the answer in such a wilderness as Minas Gerais. He must set his thoughts in order. And this can only be done in Europe, if he is not to end up believing in such crazy theories as those of Peter Claussen. The orchid! However, out of gratitude to the Royal Danish Academy of Sciences, which has for many years sent him a fixed sum and also paid Brandt, Dr. Lund finally decides to donate the collection to his fatherland. But on the condition that he will be reimbursed for the nine thousand rigsdaler which he has paid from his own pocket for the excavation of the caves, purchase of the slave and the house which he built for him and his Creole woman, and which also contained the larger bones.

Dr. Lund also has time to write an extra treatise before 1845, *Remarks on Fossilized Human Bones, Found in Caves in Brazil.* Here he is able to conclude *that* the habitation of South America very likely extends back to the geologic epoch, *that* the human race which lived here in the most distant past was the same as when the Europeans arrived here, and, finally, *that* this race may have emigrated from the Old World. Otherwise, his main concern is packing the bones. Boxes are brought from every house in Lagoa Santa, and the first interested buyers have inquired about the price of his house. Brandt is clearly upset by this. He rants and raves that now that Lagoa Santa is again peaceful and quiet, it is the only place to live. For soon all the capitals of the world will be ravaged by the most bloody revolutions. Dr.

Lund avoids discussing the future with him. An excellent solution would be to have Brandt engaged as lithographer for the collection when it is mounted in Copenhagen. But does Brandt wish to return to the North at all?

Dr. Lund cannot get a clear answer from Brandt. Meanwhile, he thinks back over the twelve years which have passed since he rode out of Rio de Janeiro with Riedel, and the fifteen years which have passed since that day when von Humboldt, in the classroom of the Collège de France, in that very city whose cobblestones Dr. Lund is now longing to tread, smacked his palm over Brazil on the wall map. To see intelligent, lively faces around him! Spring in Paris! Rome! The austere museums of Berlin! How will it feel to brush the snow from one's cape on returning to a warm home after visiting the Royal Theater? To sit once more in Madame Børresen's eating house or sip hot chocolate with vanilla whipped cream in Henneberg's Hotel? And Christian and Henrik Ferdinand, who has now moved into a mansion on Gammel Torv with his new wife . . . And Henriette!

Peter Claussen gives no sign of life, but now Dr. Lund does not care. Before the rainy season floods Lagoa Santa, he will be back in civilization, the master of his bones.

One early morning he decides to visit his favorite cave for the last time. He will ride out leisurely over the bluish-green campos. He knows he will miss them always. The morning is radiant. Brandt is mumbling in his sleep. The sun shimmers over the lake. The birds awaken. Whatever may happen, it is all as the Creator has ordained.

Dr. Lund, with his straw hat pulled down over his forehead, is filled with a deep gratitude as he rides off alone on his tired faithful mule, headed towards Lapa da Cerca Grande in the Indian crag Mocambo on the most enchanting meadow in Minas Gerais.

III

And there these people stand, satisfied with their details, and yet they seem to me to resemble the prosperous farmer in the Gospel; they have gathered a great store in their barn, but science can say to them: "Tomorrow I will demand your life," in so far as it is that which determines the significance each individual result will have on the whole. In so far as there be a sort of unconscious life in the knowledge of such a man, to that extent the sciences may be said to demand his life: in so far as it does not exist, his work is like that of the person who with the moldering of his dead body contributes to the maintenance of the Earth . . .

How fortunate you are to have found in Brazil a vast field for your observations, where at every step new curiosities appear, where the screams of the rest of the learned republic do not disturb your peace . . .

Søren Kierkegaard, *Letter to the Naturalist P. W. Lund.*

Of finitude one can learn much, but not to fear except in a most mediocre and pernicious sense. However, he who in truth would learn to fear, he shall go as in a dance, when the fears of finitude begin to strike up and when the apprentices of finitude lose sense and courage.

Søren Kierkegaard, *The Concept of Dread.*

8

He is lying with his head wrapped in bandages so that the light will not disturb him. His whole body is trembling. The slightest sound bothers him. He hears everything. And the sounds come from everywhere. The blowfly is buzzing incessantly in the corner; it is caught in the spider's web. Mice are gnawing beneath the house, rats are following, snakes are writhing in every pool in the garden. Deep subterranean rivers are washing the earth away so the house will soon sink. It has been raining for three months. In the palm garden the coffee bushes have doubtless long since been undermined and are toppling one by one. The sweet potatoes are rotting and merging with the muddy, salty, ugly clay soil. A mosquito comes closer and closer. He reaches out to hit it but in his darkness behind the bandages he has no chance of knowing where it is coming from. There – no, there! Then suddenly it is somewhere else entirely, high up under the ceiling where the gekkos are running. It dies down to a faint tone which feels as if a thread were being pulled through the passages of his ears, as if it were gathering strength to attack him suddenly, followed by more mosquitoes.

He strikes out wildly in the air until weariness forces his arms back onto the blanket, throbbing with pain, a constant itch on his elbows, wrists, and knuckles, as if he had been infiltrated by foreign bodies of which he will never be able to rid himself. Insects abound, so tiny that no human can see them, insects which gnaw their way through even the thickest flesh to reach the bones, their true home, their hunting grounds, their endless rolling wilderness with countless caves whose delicate tissue of lime they consume. There is a festering within him. In the liver? In the gall bladder? An infection? An incurable inner wound? His nerves sting as if drained of all fluid, perhaps even in the arteries where the festering is diluting his blood and will soon reach the heart itself so it will beat at only half strength. No medications help, not even those which the consul-general in Rio de Janeiro managed to send with the last tropa before the rainy season began. He has already taken overdoses of the emetic Ipecacuanha and he cannot endure more bloodletting.

Now he hears the ants, not only in the palm garden but also out from the campos regions and all the way up from Sierra da Piedade. Everywhere they are marching forth, millions upon millions of soldier republics, intent only upon destroying, undermining, and murdering each other, their equally murderous arch-enemies the termites, the beetles, the earthworms, and the butterfly larvae. To murder for the sake of murdering. Not a buriti palm will be spared, not a sugar-cane field will they leave untouched, not a leaf, not a flower will they allow to complete the cycle of life from birth and growth to ageing and natural death. The flower is their enemy. They detest color. The sweetest fragrance irritates them. Trees are helpless against them, and again he hears, as when he had first come to Rio de Janeiro, the sound of leaves falling from the treetops after the ants had cut them off, a muted whispering sound like snow falling, like the still rain over Lake Furesø on a late June evening. But here it is the sound of beauty which must not be allowed to exist, of a longing for life which must be quenched, of colors which must be extinguished in order to turn everthing to rubble. No crystals, no trace of individuality. For that is the opposite of the squares, straight lines, triangles, and rhombuses which the ants form when they march forth and suddenly run into one another to form new squares, lines, triangles and rhombuses. After the day-long battle in the dead rubble, they march onward, in their furious, logically calculated search for more individuality, more colors, more beauty which in anguish will fall to earth and be transformed into nothing.

He hears them. From Lagoa Santa to Curvelo. From Curvelo deep into Goiás. From Goiás to São Paulo and thence to Rio de Janeiro where only the ocean stops them from marching on to the Old World where not a pillar in Saint Peter's Church, not a mountain forest in Germany, not a rush by the Lake Furesø, and not a flower in the old garden at Rosenlund would survive their onslaught. He

180

hears them, as if they were speaking together in a shrill discordant tonal language. A snapping of orders, signals from Nothingness, a crackling of the grinding jaws, a steely scissoring.

And they are in the house itself. Everywhere. He knows their haunts. One republic lives in Brandt's room, within the outer wall. He and Brandt may wall up the hole, but ten days later the plaster will dribble out, fine as sugar, into a thimble-sized heap. And again the first ants will come into sight, scout about, send their scissory signals to the rear, and march forth, followed by ten, twenty, hundreds and then thousands of ants on their way across the floor, under the pile of the bones of the prediluvian cave leopard. Another republic marches diagonally up the wall of the study, from the floor all the way up to the roof tiles, under the roof, down the outer wall, over to the nearest tree, up the trunk to cut off the leaves, back to the house, up to the window, along the window sill, and into the study again, loaded with jagged bits of leaves, day after day, week after week, three times every twelfth hour.

No matter what he sprinkles over them and how many of the citizens of the republic he and Brandt crush to death beneath their boot heels – sometimes so many that the carcasses fill the largest ashtrays of the house – again they come, and again, as if they had placed so many of their resistant eggs beneath the floor that not even an all-consuming fire could wipe them out.

He hears them all. In the walls. Under the roof. Inside the wood of the bed so that its legs will soon crumble. Encircling the inkwell. Beneath his costly writing paper. Inside all the bones, both those which have been packed and are awaiting shipment to Copenhagen just after the rainy season and those which he has not yet numbered, cleaned, and classified.

Evil? *Whose* invention? This is another planet revolving around another sun, such as the Greeks imagined it. The Earth's demonic double globe, as Hieronymus Bosch had painted it with people whose legs are stalks, whose heads are boils, whose eyes flash with terror, in a warped and reeling landscape filled with monsters where only one law applies:

that everyone eat each other. That the first and the biggest will be satiated quickest and can topple over to eat, eat, eat, stuffing a belly which instantly demands more food, more murder, more blood and raw meat. The roar of the belly, the scream of the intestines, the unspeakable filth of the feces. Bones are crushed, flesh torn to pieces, eyes are soulless, all are fleeing, all are hunting. Murder, murder! Perhaps it *is* this planet after all?

He tosses and turns. He will call Brandt to change his bandages, but he knows that he is sleeping now out in the hammock in the rain, which he loves to be soaked in. And the slave would understand nothing because to him this planet is as it has always been and he has no idea of the development of life from the crystal to Man: he himself inhabits that *other* planet where man never stands erect as a liberated I.

Pains, pains. Now in his spine as well, down his loins and within his thighbones. No! He is thinking mad thoughts here behind the darkness of the bandages while on the night table stands a cup of cold tea which he can barely sip. There is a hardboiled egg which has long since crumbled onto his blanket, and bread crumbs which scratch his back exactly as when he was a boy on Nygade. The clock ticks, stops, ticks again. He had bought it for almost nothing at the venda, the heirloom of a Portuguese fazenda owner whom the rebels had managed to plunder before General de Silva e Lima took the town. Ticks, stops, ticks. Why should he care? Till the dry season comes he can simply divide time into weeks and months, with the week as the big hand and the month as the little hand. Brandt will wind the clock when it stops. And still the King has not answered. Why is he in disgrace in Copenhagen? What wrong did he do in bequeathing the bones to his Fatherland?

No! His thinking is delirious. One bad thought intermeshes with another, and only when he manages to sleep a bit, after some gruel and macaroni, does his brain calm down. But only to wake again to a new delirium. The thoughts started the day the caboclo drove him home in the oxcart from the hovel near Lapa da Cerca Grande and he lay for hours on the palm leaves, hunched like a fetus, as if everything within him were crushed after what had happened in the innermost chamber of the cave. There he lay, staring directly up into the clear sky, struggling not to scream from the pain in his bleeding gums and not to think the thought through. The thought sounded like spiteful laughter, *hee hee hee:* it is all an accident, all chaos, the way the Evil One would have it in his struggle against the Creator. The Creator built His house and the Evil One kicked it to pieces. He banished the Creator to another part of the Universe, and among the stones of the ruins, all crushed to rubble and scattered to the winds, he laid down the law: that only the strongest survive – and the shrewdest.

The spiny rat survived because it can slip away from its enemies. The ants survived. But from century to century, one animal species after another has died out, and not only the oversized carnivores with the too large teeth. Murdered, pushed out over abysses or down into hidden holes to the interior of the caves they ended their days – the peaceable armadillo, the perfectly harmless sloth, countless species of the dog, the giant porcupine, certain overly clumsy rodents, lovely but far too delicate antelopes, fallow deer with too great a need of tenderness – they all had to be wiped out to satisfy the Evil One in his delight at the sight of blood. There is no such thing as perfected creation, from species to species, from family to family. The Creator had done only a quarter of the job, and not even that, when the Evil One conquered and made the global bloodbath, the cosmic slaughterhouse which endured from the dawn of time and henceforth for as long as there is life on Earth. The ants – they are only a part of the destruction. Where they stop, the termites begin. Where the termites stop, the flies buzz and spread their flyblow. Where the flies leave off, the spider spins its web, and as soon as it is finished, a silent all-seeing black dot of throbbing hunger, it is caught by a bird who, just as it reaches its nest with the spider, is caught by an even bigger bird so that it ends as a chewed-up bloody mass of feathers and bones in the bellies of the young of the bird of prey. Yes, it was a bloodbath from the very start because the Creator never finished! No! He is thinking mad thoughts!

But they go on. In spirals, like enveloping creepers. He

can beat on his blankets, hoping that Brandt will wake up from his rain-soaked doze. The thoughts refuse to stop, and soon they reach the highest stage of the process, Man. He can picture it, he can hear it in a parody of all music and dance now that they are starting in again at the witch doctor's. Man was never perfected, with the exception of the few individual, unique geniuses who bear witness to what the Creator in His heart of hearts had imagined: a von Humbolt, an H. C. Oersted, the true, liberated Titans of the spirit. But the others. All the others, the millions of *others* – the Creator forgot them when he was chased away by the Evil One. He had to abandon them – outwardly human, inwardly inhuman. The hands are there, the heads, the eyes, the hair, the erect posture, but their hearts and brains were never completed, so they will forever more be susceptible to wild ideas and will kill one another for the sake of every sort of fanaticism, ever ready to invent vile sects, worship stones and feathers, form insane images dictated by superstition. Half animal, half human: they have now been dancing for five hours. They actually believe that the witch doctor can transform them into bears, wolves, or urubús while they swill sugar-cane liquor and fall on their knees before wretched bones and skulls. It may turn into a bloodbath. Human sacrifice, perhaps? Hearts cut out of living infants?

He stares straight into the darkness. A radiance of suns explodes when he presses two fingers hard into his sockets to soothe the burning feverish pain behind his pupils.

Brandt! When will he wake up? Is it still siesta? What time is it? Well, he has decided that time is of utterly no importance anyway. He is awaiting no one, no one is awaiting him. Is it night? Is Brandt not sleeping in the hammock after all? Has he slipped off to Sabará to dance until the break of day with some negro girl or other? But he is over fifty now! He ought to think of his health, eat more fruit and less chocolate, drink milk instead of sugar-cane liquor diluted with coconut milk, and what if he gets . . . *the* disease! He has become fatter, Brandt has, over the past years, and he has lost even more hair. He has also started to borrow too much money and to associate with disreputable speculators in Lagoa Santa. But he has stopped having so many nightmares about Wilhelmine and his three sons. The eldest son is even doing well in business and writes that he will soon be coming to Brazil to buy coffee. Brandt! Where *is* he? He has the urge to shout for him, but it hurts both in his larynx and his ears just to raise his voice, and a word spoken too loudly or laughter which is too shrill spreads in waves deep into his skull which throws the sound back and forth like an echo. Has Brandt packed more bones? Thirty boxes were sent off before the rainy season with the tropeiro Joaquim Dias da Silva, the most reliable of them all. There were over forty mules in the tropa, and the *arrieiro* and the eight *camaradas* to walk alongside inspired confidence. The largest tropa ever to leave Lagoa Santa! Has the consul-general found a ship to carry the bones? And will the King accept them? No! He will not think about the King any more. He feels his mouth. Another tooth is getting loose. He has now lost most of the teeth in his lower jaw and more than half of the teeth in his upper jaw. He will call for Brandt. Brandt must help him.

How can he ever tell Brandt what happened in Lapa da Cerca Grande? Brandt keeps on asking him, and that is why he does not want to tell him after all. His beard itches. He knows that it is chalk-white, just like his uncut hair which now hangs down to his shoulders. Ever since that late afternoon when Brandt, in his artist's smock, had helped him down from the oxcart and into the house and he had seen himself in the spotted mirror by the door, had seen a face with vacant red-rimmed eyes running with age, sunken cheeks, porous parchment skin, and white tousled hair. He has not wished to see himself again. Brandt's horrified expression the first few times he changed the bandages was more than enough. By now Brandt has learned to control himself and has even begun to smile as if nothing had happened. But every day the question is asked, as if casually: what happened? And every day he rebuffs Brandt snappishly.

What happened? What happened? How should he know? How can he describe the flickering candlelight in the cave though there was not the slightest wind, and the rumbling thunder as if someone, somewhere, were beating a gigantic primeval drum or a hollow tree trunk? How can he tell about the three negro boys who suddenly appeared and just as suddenly disappeared? How can he tell about his own colossal shadow on the cave wall which paralyzed him so that he could not take a step and how even so, bellowing with pain, he wrested himself away and reached the exit, and how, when he got outside everything within him gave way so that he felt as if his bones had become so brittle that they would crack at a mere touch? And the mule lying on its side, at the foot of the Indian crag, with the stiffened froth on its muzzle, bitten to death by a snake? And when he dragged himself across the meadow and out over the campo, among the stunted shrubs, and he came to the place where the path divided into three and where the three negro boys again appeared and mutely led him to the home of the caboclo where he spent the night on the clay floor? How? What happened? He himself does not know.

He has been in bed ever since. All the windows are shuttered. Each day brings new pains in the most unexpected places – in his big toe, like an awl piercing the flesh, in his fingertips, under his nails, in his *hair*! He has no idea how to describe his illness to Henrik Ferdinand and Christian in the letters which he dictates to Brandt when the sun has set when Lagoa Santa grows quiet, and the frogs from the lake are heard. He cannot find the words. Because he does not wish to pronounce them from behind the darkness of his bandages? *'I've lost my teeth!'* Or because he is afraid to worry Henrik Ferdinand unnecessarily? *'My hair has turned white and my body is festering. I can bear neither light nor noise. Best wishes to all!'* No, in guarded terms he relates that his health is not quite what he might hope it to be in this pleasant climate, and this at a time when he should relax somewhat after ten years of cave expeditions and after just having sent off the first large boxes of bones. Trouble with his teeth. Fatigue. This he dares to write, for it will not cause them undue concern in Copenhagen.

To Oersted, Forchhammer, and Schouw he expresses his deep sorrow that Reinhardt, the great initiator who in his newly-furnished Royal Museum of Natural History had advised him to travel to the tropics, is dead, an irreplaceable loss to Danish zoology. But his promising son is now following in his footsteps, carrying on the tradition, and who other than the young doctoral candidate Johannes Theodor Reinhardt would be the right man for the position of curator of the bone collection when it will soon be put on exhibition in Copenhagen? As for his *own* future plans? Palermo or the south of France! Again he avoids describing his health, hinting instead at his fear of consumption which still compels him to avoid the cold Danish winter. When new details concerning the bones occur to him, he adds them, mentioning that in Paris and London they would be happy to acquire plaster casts of the pearls of his collection, thus providing a neat sum for its maintenance.

Doctoral candidate Johannes Theodor Reinhardt! Suddenly it strikes him: is it *his* name which irritates the King? All the naturalists in Copenhagen are busy quarreling, particularly the younger ones who have formed schools, launched frontal attacks against one another and especially against their older colleagues. Forchhammer refuses to participate in the polemics. Oersted makes his presence felt in the background. Schouw, who is still wasting valuable talent on an effort to secure a free constitution in Denmark, deplores the new 'brutal' spirit of the times. The parochial mentality. Soon the very flowers will be divided into *democratic* and *reactionary* groups and there will be talk of *popularly-elected* animals as opposed to *privileged* ones. Nothing is surprising when it comes to politics, corrupting even the purest and most objective science. What is Reinhardt junior's stance in all this? Is he still a destructive fantasist? What if the King has sided against the group to which he belongs, which is perhaps the most rabid one, and does not answer because of the supplication in his letter to His Majesty in which he definitively bequeathes the bones to his native country: '. . . *to which position I most humbly dare to recommend Herr Candidate Reinhardt as he who, more than any other of our young naturalists, has concerned himself with these branches of zoology* . . .'

No! Yet another mad thought! A Reinhardt does not get mixed up in politics; the family name is a guarantee of that. But could other lines in that letter have angered the King? Were his opening phrases badly written, were they not respectful enough? *'Most gracious King! Trusting to the great interest which Your Majesty has always deigned to bestow upon the sciences in general and particularly upon the science which has constituted the main focus of my work in this country, I most humbly dare to request the gracious attention of Your Majesty to a matter the purpose of which is to ensure the Fatherland the fruits of these labors . . .'* Had he transposed the phrases 'most humbly' and 'most graciously'? Would it have been more proper to write 'Your Majesty' at the beginning? Is his signature illegible – *botched*, as the King would say? Does the letter not keep the proper margin? Did he make a blot? Did he cross out too much, too carelessly? No! Mad thoughts! He must get that letter out of his mind. Surely the King had replied long ago, but his letter had been delayed . . . or perhaps was lost in Rio where there is, no doubt, yellow fever. Everyone must be dead, even the consul-general, just as the boxes with the bones had arrived! So now the boxes are lying somewhere in the center of town, dropped where the tropa had come in and the tropeiro was struck down by yellow fever. The slaves, who survive everything, will soon break them open, and all the witch doctors in the city will fight over the biggest and best skull. The fruits of his labors will end up on poles or dangle from vines in the trees or be engraved with horrid patterns. They may even be buried in the earth with only the topmost part of the skull jutting out, as is the custom of certain witch doctors in the Rio de Janeiro region.

And thus his work, scattered to the winds, will end up serving the Evil One when the blacks dance about it, invoking their spirits. He cannot even confide in Brandt because to do so would be to confess that everything which he has been teaching him about the development of life since the day they stole away from Fazenda Porteirinhas, has proved untrue. The calcareous crust had no significance. The Maquiné cave was walled up because they deserved no better. All the drawings which Brandt has made are utterly worthless. *Hee hee hee:* every cave they visited was visited in vain, they had been blindfolded, fired by a false faith. *Ho ho ho:* every bone they numbered and carefully placed in a box now bears witness to their foolishness. Never again will this be the planet of the Creator. He lives out in the Universe, out there His thought will succeed on some more fortunate planet. But not here, and certainly not in the interior of Brazil where the Evil One first set foot and smashed the dwelling of the Creator. Wasted - their years. Wasted - every conversation. Wasted - the six treatises, the countless corrections, the treatise on the human bones. Yes, Brandt would break down if he told him the awful truth. It would be the fatal blow - worse than the blow he was dealt back in Wilhelmine's Norway, and worse than the one when he arrived in Curvelo into the clutches of Peter Claussen. Afterwards Brandt too would have to keep to his bed, useless, toothless, white-haired, with long nails and pain everywhere, everywhere . . .

He *must* stop these thoughts! Would it help to have his bandage changed? And the King has *not* forgotten him. He is certain of it . . .

The clock has stopped ticking.

One sound less.

Now Brandt is pottering about by the fireplace. As soon as he has lit the fire for the gruel and the macaroni and put the bread to soak, he will come in to him as he does at precisely the same time every day, just as the sun is setting over the campo. He comes over to the bed, lifts off the blanket and carries it outside to shake off the crumbled egg. Then he tiptoes back, whispers that it is *time* now . . . Brandt puts out his forearm to support him in the painful process of standing up. Brandt puts the slippers on his feet. They were sewn with special care by the wife of the venda owner, and they keep his feet warm up to the ankles. Brandt walks softly over to the fireplace and warms his shirts to the proper temperature, neither one degree too hot nor too cold. Then he warms his trousers to the proper temperature as well. Then he gives him his vest and then his jacket. He helps him stand up. It takes a long time, sometimes fifteen minutes. He is dizzy. Each day he gets even dizzier when he gets out of bed. The slave comes in. He can smell the slave's bittersweet sweat even before he gets close. Together, Brandt and the slave maneuver him outside, round the house, and over to 'the

189

room'. Fortunately there is nothing wrong with his stool. Brandt checks to make sure that the color is as it ought to be, with no blood. He also passes water with no pain, and he thinks that perhaps there is hope left and that before the next rainy season he will have recovered enough to make the trip to Rio de Janeiro – if there is no yellow fever – to stay with Riedel and enjoy the imperial parks. To spend time in his up-to-date library, attend concerts, and then book passage to Europe, having made sure that the last boxes have been shipped off properly, preferably on the corvette 'Galathea' when it touches Brazil on its voyage round the world. If there is no yellow fever, if the witch doctors have not wrecked the collection, if the Evil One does not . . .

On his way back from 'the room' he stops at a certain spot where he can hear the breeze in the top of the royal palm. Sometimes the rain has stopped and he takes deep breaths of the fragrance of the warm steamy earth, the flowers, the lake air, and the dead palm leaves being burned somewhere nearby. Everything within him is aroused, one good memory after another rises to the surface. By turns he is awakening one early morning with Riedel, or arriving in a buriti valley after a long day of riding, and he still has all his teeth.Sometimes his nerves seem to be vibrating with life and the worst pains disappear. But then once more he crumbles to pieces inside, and Brandt and the slave must hold him tight to keep him from falling on the endless way back round the house, through the door, and over to the bed, where it takes yet another quarter of an hour to get him undressed and put to bed. His food and a cup of hot warm tea arrive. And the thoughts begin again.

But Brandt is humming contentedly. A good smell fills the air.

Thus pass the hours, each day. Month after month.

The dry season has arrived. It will soon be his birthday, and Brandt persuades him to try walking around inside the house, preferably without the bandage over his eyes. At first he refuses. He knows that the light will dazzle him, even though the shutters are still up. But he agrees to let Brandt cut his hair, with the utmost care, lock by lock. He fears that the scissors will touch him on the neck, just where the jaw begins, and send a chill through him. It takes Brandt most of the day to cut his hair so that not a single hair slips under his nightshirt to irritate his skin. When Brandt has finished, he is also permitted to clip his nails, which are now so long that they have started to grow the wrong way, curving back into his fingertips. Here Brandt must exercise even greater care. The clipping of each nail is a complicated operation. Wherever the scissors cannot be used, Brandt must file with strong thread because everything within Dr. Lund trembles at the slightest touch. At last Brandt declares himself satisfied and says encouragingly that now . . . now he *really* looks like himself again! Wouldn't he like to remove the bandage?

In two days, perhaps. In a week. When the heat is at its worst. But first, paper must be pasted over all the shutters to prevent the sun from coming in through even the tiniest slit. And his spectacles must be set out in the sun several hours in advance so they too can be warmed to the proper temperature. After ten days, he finally agrees to have the bandage removed. It must be done so carefully and slowly that Brandt must anticipate several hours of work. After almost five months in darkness, he sees again. It does not hurt as much as he had feared. He can make out most of the furniture, the shelves with his scientific works, the remaining bones. His desk has not been disturbed. No one has removed the paper, the inkwell, the pens, and his letter-copy book. He sees his feet move upon the carpet. He holds his hands up to his eyes and recognizes them even though the bones of his fingers are nearly fleshless and the knuckles shine white under the skin. His spectacles are carried in on a plate, and when he slowly puts them on there is no pain: on the contrary, the warmth of the sun spreads in pleasurable waves into his temples and down his cheeks. He wishes to be shaved. His beard hangs down to his chest. It prickles worse than ever. Brandt and the slave must help him with this too. He still refuses to see himself in the mirror. He gets up carefully from the bed. He is able to walk, two steps, five, ten, and soon all the way around the bedroom. Brandt smiles at him in the half-light. It is so beautiful in the palm garden just now, he whispers. In a few minutes the sun will be setting...

The next day he sits once more in his favorite chair in the study. He wants to get used to the light gradually, so a single shutter is opened very slightly, and he can see a ray of sunshine dancing over a pile of paca bones. For a week he sits like this when he is not asleep in bed. He can now eat cheese and bread which has not been soaked in water. He is looking forward to the arrival of the tropeiro with the mail bag. Yet another shutter is eased open a trifle. There are just a few days till his birthday. Then at last the mail bag arrives. Brandt sorts through all the letters and reads them aloud, one by one. Among them is an answer from the King.

He has this letter read to him many times, last on the June day when he turns forty-five. Brandt has lit all the oil lamps to create a festive atmosphere. He has taken extra pains with the porridge and spiced the macaroni. The house is pleasantly warm. The slave is busy sawing firewood by his cottage. His Creole woman has been sent into town to fetch fresh milk.

Over and over Brandt reads, patiently, word by word, with approving nods and pauses where appropriate, as he crouches on the floor:

'Herr Doktor Wilhelm Lund!... The directors of the Royal Museum of Natural History have been commanded to accept the shipments from you, both those which have already arrived and those which are still expected. These will remain unopened until doctoral candidate Reinhardt returns from his voyage on the corvette Galathea, on which he departed in June of last year, and which in the Spring of 1847 will call at Rio do Janeiro on its return voyage.

In the meantime, rooms and cabinets for the mounting of the collection are being fitted up, and doctoral candidate Reinhardt will be appointed as Curator, with a fixed wage, of this collection, which the Museum owes to your devotion to the sciences and your love of Fatherland.

Your treatises with their accompanying illustrations, published by the Royal Academy of Science, have already aroused the particular attention of learned naturalists, as has been the case with the shipments which I have earlier received from you for my private collection.

It would give me much pleasure if your health would allow you to visit your Fatherland and give me the opportunity of repeating in person this expression of my gratitude and of my appreciation, the proof of which I send you in the form of my medal, 'Ingenio et Arti' which you as a scientist have made yourself so worthy of possessing.

I remain with high esteem and favor, Herr Doktor Lund, your faithful and respectful,

Christian VIII

Suddenly, from out in the garden, a call is heard:

'Troglodyte! Troglodyte!'

Brandt jumps up and runs outside. He is soon back to say that four boys with jumping jacks shaped like skeletons had been trampling the sweet potato beds. Unable to catch up with them, he sent the slave to chase them. They will get their well-deserved punishment.

Dr. Lund must take to his bed again. But he does not put the bandages back on.

He loses another two teeth.

193

9

Death has bandages round its skull and Death has moved to
Lagoa Santa. He came from the cold lands, bringing with him
strange instruments in small boxes lined with purple velvet, a
hoe which can shatter the rocks all the way down to where the
monsters live, a shovel which can throw the earth a hundred
leguas away, and gilt spectacles with colored glass which he
puts on when he removes the bandages and rides away from
his house by the lake. Death sees everything and yet no one can
see him because he always turns his head away. When he takes
off his spectacles, his eyes gush out and lie like two small watery
spots on the earth. They cannot dry up and that is why one can
always see where Death is riding if one looks closely. Death is
neither young nor old, and when he removes his spectacles and
looks out over the lake and up toward Serra da Piedade with
his two black holes, it hurts everywhere in his bones because he
sees without being able to see, hears without being able to
hear. Death is tired of being death, but as long as the sun shines
in the daytime, the moon shines at night, and dry seasons
alternate with rainy seasons, he shall never find rest.

Death is not a skeleton. Thin flesh clings to his skull and
bones, but if he forgets to put on the winter clothes from his
cold homeland, the Sun will burn his skin to ashes and
without being able to see and without being able to hear, he
will wander out over the campos to the place where the São
Francisco River is so wide that it takes ten days to sail across.
There he will fall down in the sand and molder away. Then a
new time will come and two suns will shine in the sky.

Death is the man with the skeletons. He searches and
searches as if he were looking for someone. Even the animals
fear him when he looks at them without seeing them. Even
the Caipor flees when he approaches on his mule.

And Death lives in Lagoa Santa.

Death eats bones. From far out on the horizon he comes
riding on his mule, followed by his humming and red-

cheeked color-magician, who gives him images of all the bones he consumes when he reaches a cave and gets off his mule and steps down into the darkness of the Earth where he sees everything and hears everything. He brings the bones which he has not eaten back home with him. He makes furniture of them, and in a gigantic cauldron he boils the biggest ones, so there is an eternal steam in his house. Death is a man with no colors, with no dreams, with no day or night, and no flesh clings to his skeleton. He winds damp rags round his body beneath his coat and he puts on the spectacles with the painted eyes only because he is afraid of being recognized. Death is afraid. Death carries a terrible secret. Should the Sun strike him on the forehead just when it rises between two palm trees near the river, it would burn a hole just above the left spectacle lens, and he would stiffen on the spot. A new time would come and no one need descend into the caves of the mountains and die there in fear of Death.

Death is *um velho esqueleto.*

And Death is afraid to show it.

Death will soon die. Saint George chases him from country to country, over all the mountains, over the seas and the rivers, across the sertão, into the caatinga, in and out of the virgin forest, and from village to village. Once, Death was the strongest and needed only to touch Saint George with his skeleton hand to topple him. But Saint George found the secret treasure in a cave far to the north, where the Rio Cipó runs into the Rio das Velhas. While the full moon was shining in the sky he ate the powdered snakeskin which gave him everlasting life. With his hoe and his shovel he now rides after Death, flourishing his red cape and his silver-handled whip, and one day he will catch Death. When the rainy season is at an end, the rushes round the lake have died, and Death has eaten the last bone in his house with the big garden where the flowers are as pale as the white man's flesh, then Saint George will ride up in front of his door, kick it in, and with jangling spurs on the most beautiful embroidered boots in all of Minas Gerais, he will go over to the bed where Death lies and strike the skull from his skeleton.

A new time will come, and Saint George will cure the sick and make the old young.

Death watches over his bones like a beautiful woman over her jewels. No one is allowed near them. Death is so old that no one can count his years, but he is never tired. He is bow-legged, with large bare feet and an eye in the middle of his forehead. He is covered with flesh, except on his right hand. Growling like a bear, he sits deep in the heart of his caves and scratches his neck with his skeleton hand. He comes to everyone. But he does not like it, and therefore he always hurries back to his caves. One never knows which cave he is living in. But he likes some caves better than others. The ones he likes best are those where the Indians have painted red armadillos on the walls. One must never disturb him, and he who takes his bones will be punished in a way which is worse than being buried alive or bitten to death in a snakepit. Slowly Death will crush the insides of the thief, dilute his blood, and send half of his soul away on an endless ride over the plateau. The little that is left of the soul is not enough to keep the body erect. The thief will no longer be able to see colors, and everything around him will turn to ashes. But live he must, longing for the rest of his soul.

Death is a cheerful gentleman and he knows many ways to punish, although he does not like it.

And he can make mountains roar.

He no longer knows what to dictate in the letters to Copenhagen. If he told them all the tall tales Brandt comes home with, most of them overheard in the venda, they would think him mad to suddenly pay heed to such things. To Henrik Ferdinand he writes that he is recovering from his tooth disease and that he has had to lend Brandt money again – to be repaid with interest. Most of his capital can remain in Copenhagen. He knows that this will set his brother's mind at rest. Sometimes he senses that the family believes Brandt – 'that Brandt' – is the one influencing him to stay, and therefore he emphasizes that Brandt is a great help to him and that *he* too hopes to be able to leave soon, to assume the position of lithographer of the collection when, with the blessing of the King, it is mounted. Brandt nods, smiles a little, scratches the back of his neck, yet seems hesitant to write. A new suspicion rankles inside Dr. Lund until he must also chase this one away by saying to himself over and over: you are sick! You are sick! Sick as never before! Sick in Brazil where proper physicians are unknown. In the province of Minas Gerais where the houses only look like real houses, where the roads are overgrown with weeds and every day brings surprising new evil noises. Sick here in Lagoa Santa where not even the Church is able to educate the people because it too is pervaded by superstition, sick here in this house, in these four cluttered walled-up rooms which were only to have been a temporary station but which have long since grown accustomed to him and now demand that he remain here forever. Sick, sick – it is only because he is sick that this thought now arises, together with the others, especially when Brandt is taking dictation and suddenly hesitates, gets a strange expression in his swimming eyes, smiles distantly, and emits his strange little grunts. Does Brandt *want* it to be like this, runs the thought – and continues: has Brandt done something to tie him down to this place? Has he been lying when he declared himself ready, after all, to travel back to the North? How has he done it? Has he conspired with the walls? Entered into a pact with the furniture? Bewitched the floorboards? Invoked the tiles in the moonlight?

Dr. Lund cannot recognize Brandt. All at once he sees him in a way he has never seen him before. Before, he was *Brandt*. Lost Brandt, unhappy Brandt, the garrulous and imprecise artist, flurried, grateful for his regular wages, faithful in his work as an assistant. Now his way of walking has changed, as if he were constantly concealing something or other. He also hums as if he were up to some trick. Who are these 'tradespeople' he is hanging about with at the venda? And his glance! There is a greenish tone to it! It has become penetrating! It knows something he, Dr. Lund doesn't know! His smile is no longer shy, marked by pain. It is mocking. His adam's apple is swelling with pleasure about something he has no business being pleased about. He is into

197

something, *up* to something! For ten years he has supported this Norwegian on his monthly interest, this Bohemian whose dream it is to drink burgundy with poets. He has saved him from the brink of disaster with Peter Claussen, and now Brandt is paying him back by imprisoning him in this miserable house which not even the former priest wished to keep.

The worst is when Brandt is in Sabará, especially when he is away a day longer than promised, leaving Dr. Lund to the mercy of the slave and his Creole woman. And when at such a time the slave suddenly makes himself scarce, Dr. Lund is convinced that Brandt has evil intentions. Summoning all of his energy, he sits up, swings his legs over the edge of the bed and slowly gets up. The shutters in the bedroom are still shut. But the slave has been there, so quietly that not even a mouse could hear him. The bones are in disorder. And, making his way to the fireplace, he discovers that all the jars of Brandt's jam are gone. Thus the cheater is also cheated! Leaning on his cane, Dr. Lund makes a decision which weighs heavily upon his conscience, but there is no other alternative, he must know the truth. He enters Brandt's room. Changes his mind in the doorway. Retreats. Then makes his decision again and enters Brandt's room, opens the shutter as he covers his eyes with one hand, lights the oil lamp, goes over to the desk and opens his letter copy-book. He must find out whom Brandt has plotted with, plotted, no doubt, to make the house the headquarters of some ignoble business venture when and if...when and if...

Cautiously he turns the pages, feeling that he is committing the worst sin of his life. There are letters to Wilhelmine and his sons in Norway, full of excuses but also assuring them that he, Peter Andreas, never betrays them in his thoughts and that his benefactor, the Danish naturalist Dr. phil. P. W. Lund, a man whose goodness he cannot describe in a letter, poor in words as he is, has again lent him money to enable the eldest son to start his career as a merchant. In one very angry letter, Brandt reprimands his wife for threatening to write to the Danish king and the Royal Danish Academy of Science for means of sustenance after having 'voluntarily relinquished her husband in the interest of natural science'.

Dr. Lund leafs further, afraid that the oil lamp will suddenly shatter and burn the letter-copy book, the desk, and with it the whole house as a punishment for his crime. But he *must* read what Brandt has written in the small memorandums scattered among the copies of his letters, mostly notes for his excursions to Sabará. If he finds a clue, Providence will forgive him because it understands that he must try every way to escape from the clutches of the Norwegian. But no note indicates anything of the kind. In one, Brandt reminds himself to enquire about various sorts of medication for the Doctor, in another to find out whether there is water in the Doctor's gold mine after all. And he is continually reminding himself to repay the interest on his loan punctually.

Slowly Dr. Lund feels a shame which nearly makes his heart stop beating. When he ends by reading two letters to Forchhammer which he had no idea Brandt had written, he knows that he deserves more misery than that which he has already suffered. In his childish stiff Gothic script, full of Norwegian spellings, and as if every word had cost him great pains, Brandt gives a detailed account of the misfortune which has plagued the little house in Lagoa Santa and how Herr Doktor - who, proud as he is, refuses to make a murmur of complaint to those at home - is so ill that he cannot bear the slightest contact with objects of glass or metal. The tiniest insect which takes the notion to buzz about his room can awaken him from his uneasy sleep and 'then sleep is hours and not rarely a whole night away'.

Brandt describes how cautious he must be not to awaken him: '. . . the sound made by the mere turning of the pages of a book in the quiet of the night awakens him from sleep, which is why I must keep as quiet as if I were in my grave,' or '. . . I put down my brush and pen to creep like a chambermaid to conceal as much as possible the negligence and carelessness of our wild negro, as the Doctor, after having been compelled to give him a well-deserved slap, either personally or by me, is very grieved thereby and an increasing indisposition lasts several days after such scenes have taken place in our cheerless hermitage.' And the inhabitants of Lagoa Santa regard them 'the way exotic animals in the menageries in Europe are regarded; our movements, as when in conversing I pace up and down our narrow room, or when they hear me reading aloud for the Doctor . . . are utterly incomprehensible to these children of nature.'

In closing, Brandt proposes the idea of ordering from Norway a carriole in which the Doctor can drive out, with Brandt himself on the back seat 'till the Doctor acquires sufficient confidence to be able to drive alone.' It must have a comfortable seat. There should be a fork on the wheel axle to prevent the carriage from rolling backwards on steep inclines. It must have good springs and be oiled in such a way that it can withstand the Brazilian heat. The rear seat must be removable and the reins must be easy to control. Thus, hopefully, the Doctor could venture out on new cave expeditions. In expressing this wish, Brandt concludes: 'If in the course of time it should appear that the Doctor does not profit from the intended usefulness of this *voiture*, I will take its expense upon myself.'

Dr. Lund shuts the letter-copy book. He blows out the oil lamp. He considers doubling, tripling, Brandt's monthly wages. May all the powers forgive him! And may Brandt never have the least suspicion that he has looked at his papers! On his way back, he very nearly falls to his knees to pray for forgiveness. Then he suddenly wonders what Forchhammer's reply is to Brandt's letter. Surely he has alerted Oersted who in turn has alerted the King. His brothers consult together as Henriette stands listening in the doorway and at night dreams awful dreams about him. At the Royal Academy of Science he is the sole topic of conversation. One adds, another multiplies. Soon all sorts of stories about his condition will be rampant in Copenhagen. They will guess at consumption. They will guess at something far worse. In the 'liberal' circles they will surely invent wild stories about how he has become deranged by living in the tropics, or worse, that he has been infected by . . . *the* disease. Yes, he knows Copenhagen. He has always despised gossip. He must show them that it is not true, that he is still himself.

And he goes into the study with a determination which momentarily makes him forget all his pains. Feverishly he

200

begins to re-arrange his books, and he actually gets his appetite back by holding them in his hands. Owen: *On the Mytodon Robustus*. Linnaeus: *Systema natura*. Wagler: *System der Reptilen*. Burck: *Magellan oder die erste Reise um die Welt*. Cuvier: *Cours de l'histoire des sciences naturelles et de la philosophie de l'histoire naturelle, professé au Collège de France*. And all of Oersted's, Forchhammer's, von Humboldt's, Réamur's, Ampère's and Milne-Edward's most important works and treatises. And Kant. And Auguste Comte, who in Rio de Janeiro is being talked about as the shining new star in the firmament of European philosophy, whose book Riedel sent him last year as a birthday present with a long and cordial dedication, expressing the hope that they soon meet again.

It is in the company of these men that he belongs, with his own great treatises which perhaps simply need to be polished, corrected, and divested of the worst misunderstandings in order to emerge as The Work. In this alliance of Spirit and Knowledge, with Linnaeus as the one who started it all and handed on the torch, he will once again find inspiration and incentive. He reads again. He savors the ingenious and brilliant ability of the letters to form that irreplaceable quality which is called Meaning. He recalls the smell of the great libraries of Paris, the muffled coughing from a reading table, the sound of subdued voices from the front rooms, and the shower of brightness which always went through him when he stepped out into the slush after having read Cuvier's most recent treatises.

He rejoices over all his old underlinings and the scraps of paper with notes inserted between the pages. He recalls conversations with Carsten Hauch, Oersted's lectures, and the auditorium in Kiel where he defended his doctoral dissertation. *Alles lernen*. This will be his motto once more. And as he goes over to the fireplace to fetch the pot of cold macaroni from the day before and then opens the cigar box, taking out a single bone-dry cigar which he places on the desk as a reward for later, he again sees the coherence of Reason. The light literally dawns on him. He is again on the right track, and he has the urge to write. Outside, with the start of the dry season, the plants are parched, the cicadas are singing as never before, and the geckos beneath the tiles are vibrating silently. A sabiá is calling in the garden and its cry goes through his brain without bothering him. Already one foot is feeling better.

Dr. Lund finds all of his printed treatises. He nods to them in recognition as he gingerly opens a shutter a crack. He knows that he could not have been completely mistaken. Even a von Humboldt must have had his moments of terrible doubt. He places fresh writing paper on the desk after having scraped the macaroni out of the pot and drunk a glass of cold boiled water on the night table. He will write his *Seventh and Concluding Treatise*, the one which will synthesize it all, during the most pleasant time of the dry season. He will have it ready when young Reinhardt arrives in Rio de Janeiro on the Galathea and hopefully keeps his promise to come directly to Lagoa Santa to pay a short visit. Calcareous crust or not: there *are* two worlds, the one with which the Creator experimented and the one which he finally chose. But perhaps the Deluge was not global. Perhaps it ravaged the continents one by one so that certain animal species, perhaps more than he realizes, could flee.

Now he knows! And as he makes outlines in his head and plans his schedule thus: – morning: *reading, notes*; afternoon: *writing, at least two pages*; evening: *corrections and fair copies* – the anger within him grows, making his armpits sweat and his beard itch in a very irritating way. What was it Brandt had written? Like exotic animals in a menagerie? As people in Europe regard . . . apes, monsters, dwarves, bearded ladies and . . . yes, that negro from Saint Thomas whom so long ago the circus director had displayed on Gammel Torv and whose two foreheads had delighted the boys of Borgerdyden School, led by Carl. And Brandt has kept all this to himself. Not once has he complained about the way the people of Lagoa Santa have treated him.

Dr. Lund decides to double his assistant's wages as he wonders whether he will be able to shave himself. He still does not wish to see himself in the mirror.

Are they looking at him through the windows? He senses it. His anger grows to rage, and he takes the pot and flings it against one of the shutters. Luckily there is no one.

There is still a long way to go before he gets well...

The next day, as Brandt has still not appeared, Dr. Lund resolves to break out of the darkness. He tints his glasses with ink and opens the shutters another crack. Then, with some difficulty, he puts on his boots. For the first time in nearly two years he will visit the garden. His straw hat is on his head again, and the ink on his spectacles makes a pleasant light-blue tone which filters out the brightest rays of the sun. The garden looks very nearly as it had done before. Fewer coffee bushes than he had feared have been washed away by the rain. Water is trickling everywhere. One day it is hot and the next day the humidity returns, as if the dry season this year cannot make up its mind. Soon spring will arrive with a multitude of green shoots and the tyrannids and all the other birds will chase one another in the mating dance. The clouds are drifting in one stratum of air for northwest winds, another for southeast and east winds. The campos are burning, and here and there the entire landscape is swathed in dark smoke which completely hides Serra da Piedade. Dr. Lund senses that by August the heat will be sultry. Lightning will dance on the horizon. And this year there will be many fireflies, especially lampterids and elays, those sparks of fire which are periodically snuffed out when they speed through the air or out of their hiding places in the bushes.

From all the water-filled holes he hears the rapacuia, the frog which lives closest to the houses. It is midsummer, and the last winter rain, the *chuva de São João*, often gentle and nordic, will bring cooler nights. So he must dress warmly. Dr. Lund feels all the seasons at one time. From his bed he has calculated the average temperature, the amount of rain, the solar incidence. He has listened to the building of nests, the rustling of the spiny rat, and the movements of the snakes. Now he is back in nature, nature which is never the victim of confused thoughts. Once more he will live by its regularity.

A procession passes. It must have started down by the shores of the lake. He sees the statues of the saints, led by the black Virgin Mary, swaying past the wall which Brandt had had built to keep out the impertinent negro boys. He hears

203

footsteps, mumbling, the rumbling of the oxcart carrying flowers to decorate the church. He hears the priest at the head of the procession sending up his Latin prayers to Heaven. Dogs growl and incense rises to the treetops. Dr. Lund has the urge to see Lagoa Santa again and to prove that he is no exotic animal, and he walks slowly up through the garden, and round the house, emerging just as the procession is turning past the fence in front of the house. A few children catch sight of him and hurry over to their mothers, who hug them tightly and nudge them into the midst of the procession. '*O homem das cavernas*' he hears the mothers murmer as they cover their faces with their shawls in fright.

Quietly he follows them. He passes the lodging house where he had stayed when he first came to town. Nothing has changed in the past two years. The same pigs are drowsing by the door, their snouts pressed into the red muck. Hens and chickens run on and off the path leading to the filthy guest room. On a chair under one of the windows sits the old landlady, her long black whiskers hanging down over her puckered lips, the sparse white hair on her head bristling out of the pink scalp, and the same grimy dress she had worn ten years ago when he had taken rooms at her house. All her life she has been sitting there, ancient from the very start. She will be sitting there for another hundred years. She is the only one who pays no attention to him, whereas everyone in the procession has by now turned round to look at him. Even the men appear anxious, as a low wondering whispering is heard:

'*O homem! O homem!*'

He enters the venda. Caboclos and sertanejos step aside as he approaches the counter. The venda owner behaves as if nothing had happened and hands him a dish of boiled eggs, a bottle of boiled water, and a bit of dry bread. The Doctor is welcome back! Hopefully the Doctor will soon be completely well! The whole town has been so worried about the Doctor! There are no limits to the hospitality of the venda proprietor and he even serves a little dried meat and some small sausages – courtesy of the house. Waving away the flies from a gash on his forehead, he eagerly tells about several Indian *coriscos* – thunderbolts – which he had found while the Doctor was bedridden – so many of them that he has started to sell some to an interested buyer from Ouro Preto. And he has a story which may interest the Doctor. Yes, it is true. Just where the Jequitinhonha River runs into Bahia, there lies a strange city, with houses of hewn stone and gilt roofs, a city which is thousands of years old and where all the inhabitants are old, white-haired, and thin-skinned. Even the children are old, over ninety when born. But everyone is happy because they can grow as old as they please and there is no sickness in the town. Every day for three hours and forty-five minutes they worship the sun which, in gratitude, shines on them without being too warm and without being too cold. It is forbidden to eat meat, but tea made from the twelve-fingered herbal bush keeps away all evil thoughts. Everyone lives in houses containing furniture more beautiful than that of the governor in Ouro Preto. In the center of town is a high pillar on which the statue of a human points northward. If one chances upon the town, one must undergo fearsome trials to be worthy of entering it. One must wrestle with the cave bear and swallow a live snake, but then the gate will be opened and the new arrival will be accepted on an equal footing with the others and live hale and hearty for as long as he pleases.

Why is the venda owner telling him this story? And is he the one who has told Brandt all the other cock-and-bull stories? Dr. Lund senses that they are still afraid of him at the venda, and soon tiring of their childish fantasies, he seats himself in a corner. Perhaps it was unwise to rise from his sickbed so quickly. He is a bit dizzy. Everyone is casting sidelong glances at him, except for the young couple sitting next to him, kissing one another. They are no more than sixteen or seventeen. He is a Portuguese, she is a mulatto. She is perched on his lap, scratching his neck, toying with a lock of his hair. Every so often she laughs aloud, and her laughter has a familiar ring to Dr. Lund. Round about him everyone is dancing, there are Venetian mirrors from floor to ceiling, and in them he can see a myriad of costly candelabras and elegant Italian guests coming and going. Most of them are wearing half-masks, as is the black-haired girl next to him who now touches his neck softly, twists a lock of his hair, and leans back her head, laughing to him with her dark almond-shaped eyes behind the mask. She asks him to walk her home and he says yes. He is vibrant with happiness. He kisses her, very lightly. Then he catches sight of a little mirror on the wall among all the others. No one is dancing in it. There are no candelabras, no elegant guests coming and going, only a crust of greasy fingerprints and flyspecks. Underneath the crust the mulatto girl is still kissing the boy as he slides his hand all the way up under her dress and then greedily licks the sweat from her thigh. Next to them sits an old eccentric with blue-tinted spectacles, white hair sticking out from under his straw hat, a thin layer of skin clinging to the sharp lines of his skull, and a toothless sunken mouth behind the white wispy beard.

Terror strikes Dr. Lund, terror which turns to panic, making his blood pound hot and wild as he suddenly feels a swelling between his thighs. The heathen within him is aroused. He is no longer a human being. Can they *see* him? Sweat runs down his body. He presses his hands into his lap, hard. The light blue shrouding all forms is at once the color of hell, and when the sun vanishes behind the clouds, everything is transformed into whispering contours and telltale shadows. He pushes the table forward and stands up when he is once more in control of his body. He walks straight to the door.

The sun is shining again when he gets outside. He knows that he must cross the long deep ruts dug into the road by the rain last November. He walks and walks, one step to the right, one step to the left. Catching sight of a group of negro boys down by the fence of his house, he walks faster and tries to straddle the ruts. He is still dizzy. Do the boys have skeleton jumping jacks which they will jerk about with shouts and screams as he gets closer? And are they putting rat skulls up on the fence? And is that Brandt just now coming into view on the road into town, riding his mule as the slave runs alongside?

His forehead strikes the ground. The straw hat flies off. He tries to get up to catch it, but everything is spinning and all he can see are water-colored eyes glistening like little lakes all the way down to his house. And the house stands just above the entrance of a great cave. It is choked by gigantic ferns. The giant sloth is crawling up on the red-brown tiles to escape the saber-toothed tiger which is leaping toward them over the campos. He hears a roar of delight and slowly he steers toward it, through the caatinga, across the plateau. He must find out who is roaring . He can still glimpse the house in the distance. The sun is about to rise and then there are two suns scorching the earth.

When it is evening he arrives. The suns have set on opposite horizons. The frogs awaken, and the giant sloth keeps sliding off the roof. He arrives, and there he sees himself in the middle of the entrance to the cave. There he sits with bandages round his skull, his straw hat in bits and pieces, roaring with delight as he tears at himself between his thighs the way only the foul apes do.

Several yards away, Brandt gets off his mule and watches with revulsion.

10

Henrik Ferdinand is waiting for him by the entrance of the National Bank. H.C. Oersted has called the members of the Royal Academy of Science to a special meeting, at which tea and sherry are served, where they will gather to pay homage to him. In his letters, the King has promised to receive him personally, to present him with the great cross of Danneborg. It would be inadmissible for him to arrive at these events even half an hour late. There is talk of a torchlight procession in his honor through the streets of Copenhagen. Henrik Ferdinand must have spent hours, days, in buying flowers, arranging them in vases with the help of his female assistants, and ordering baking chocolate, and having vanilla cream whipped at Henneberg's Hotel. In the Royal Museum of Natural History the most imposing halls have been cleared and the floors freshly varnished. Silver-plated exhibition cases have been ordered from Berlin and St. Petersburg. All the zoology students, with Christian's son Henrik at their head, are waiting only for the last boxes of bones to arrive from Lagoa Santa so that they can be unpacked and if possible assembled into whole skeletons which will bring scientists from Paris to Calcutta flocking to Copenhagen.

Dr. Lund has always known it: by a stroke of magic, as when Constantine the Great made Christianity the state religion, Copenhagen will become the Athens of the North, the Nordic Byzantium, the home of all true science and philosophy; a city permeated by the touch of the Creator. Only in the very coldest months will he, Dr. Lund, stay in Monaco so as not to risk consumption, as he had promised his mother at their last meeting, in the garden sloping down to Peblinge Lake. She had smiled at him so tenderly in the candlelight, certain that he would be the one to restore the family to the pinnacle of honor. Now she is with him once more. He must never betray her. In Monaco he will furnish a special room to her memory, with her combs and brushes, her summer gowns, her jewelry, her shoes, her letters to him bound with lavender-scented ribbon, and the golden lock of his hair which she had proudly cut when he was two years old and kept for him in a heart-shaped envelope.

And Brandt dares to question all this! Really, he ought not to speak to his assistant at all. He ought to keep to himself his excitement about the reception they are preparing for him in Copenhagen. But now that he feels healthy and energetic in anticipation of the final departure from Lagoa Santa, and now that the last bones are ready to be sent off with the tropa, he cannot help but every now and then let an exhilarated word pass his lips about everything he will return to, a world which Brandt of course knows nothing about, a world in which family unity and intelligent conversation are prized, in which concerts are held weekly, and in which nature offers daily delight to anyone who wishes to read its enchanting script. But whenever he says anything of the kind, Brandt stares at him, reprimandingly, sometimes even dumbfounded, as if grudging him the triumphal return to Copenhagen.

Over and over he has told Brandt: he will *not* leave him high and dry. *Brandt* may sell the house if only he will promise to send on the remaining boxes of bones. *He* may keep the money from the sale as extra wages, a reward, which will enable him to buy his passage to Copenhagen, where nothing will prevent him from assuming the position of lithographer. Does Brandt not share his wish to see the Old World again? Does he not know that he too will be received with admiration in Paris, in Rome, in Berlin, and in Copenhagen because he has helped unearth the bones of prediluvian Brazil, hidden beneath the magical calcareous crust which the two of them were the first in the world to break through? Never again need Wilhelmine fear the morrow when it is reported far away in the little town of Kristiania that her runaway bankrupt husband has now returned from Brazilian America as a pioneer, venerated by all. Is *that* wrongly said? Oh, yes! Apparently! First Brandt refuses to hear more about the reception which Oersted is preparing. Then he brushes aside talk of Henrik Ferdinand's reception. And it took him two days to buy a new mule for him when he could have done it in just a few hours.

Is the old Norwegian feeling of inferiority being turned to sabotage?

Brandt will just have to fend for himself. Dr. Lund himself certainly has the cleanest conscience in the world as he rides rapidly down to the lake. From here he will ride along the shore halfway around and then head up the closest path leading directly to Rio de Janeiro. There Riedel is awaiting him impatiently with all his imperial parks illuminated and the Emperor himself will head the reception committee consisting of all the European consul-generals. He has his bag in his lap, which is the safest place. He had to literally tear it away from Brandt, who had suddenly snatched it from him and tried to hide it after he had, with great difficulty, packed it with his shirts, his underwear, his treatises, Linnaeus and Owen, and bags of eggs, salt, and sugar. Brandt even had the impudence to call for help from the slave so that he had been forced to threaten to give the latter the soundest beating ever if he did not get out at once. As a result, the black baboon had opened his eyes so wide that the pupils had turned into two rolling dots in a sea of white, leaped into the air, and nearly flown over to the door to run away again – this time, perhaps, for good.

But it doesn't matter in the least to him. Brandt may keep the house, lock, stock, and barrel, with the fireplace and the pots, the ants, the bandages, and the unwashed bedding, the poisoned medications and the wretched coffee, the palm garden and the fence. Even when Brandt ran after him far down the path to the lake, and the moment had come when he no longer needed to pay him any regard, he had politely turned for one last time to his assistant, whom the tropical sun and an excess of sugar-cane liquor had clearly flustered to an alarming degree, and shouted with all the restored power of his lungs:

'From now on, everything of *mine* is *yours*, Herr Brandt! Except for the bones! *Send* them to me!'

But he has the feeling that not even that last offer helped. Soon Brandt will be riding after him, perhaps after summoning help from town, where he has been conspiring from the very start. So Dr. Lund urges on his new mule, whose smell is hard to get used to and who trots more nervously than the mule which had so faithfully carried him from cave to cave. He sees a cluster of trees in front of a rocky ledge. Here he crouches behind the mule, his arms resting on the bag. Sure enough, Brandt soon comes riding by at full gallop, his painter's smock having been tucked hastily into his trousers, the tufts of hair round the bald head all tousled, and his wild bloodshot eyes scouting frantically in all directions.

Dr. Lund laughs to himself, satisfied that his little tactical ruse has succeeded beyond all expectation.

It was Immanuel Kant from Königsberg, the philosopher of moral duty, the denouncer of aberrations and daydreams, who had saved him at the last minute. Early one morning, when still lying in bed after a fall which Brandt kept insisting he had incurred after leaving the house alone like a sleepwalker, with a mounting anger over all the cock-and-bull stories with which Brandt kept bothering him, he remembered the four fundamental questions which Kant had posed as a touchstone for his age. Questions which long ago Headmaster Nielsen had drilled into the oldest classes at Borgerdydens School, sometimes by writing them on the blackboard:
1. What can I KNOW?
2. What shall I DO?
3. What dare I HOPE for?
4. What is MAN?
What can he KNOW? Dr. Lund concentrates on excluding all inessentials, all irritating, unimportant questions, every confused chain of thought. He can KNOW that someone – something – is out to get him. How does he KNOW it? The bed! The bandages! The house! The ants! The slave! The people of Lagoa Santa! The pain! The letters which have still not arrived with invitations to all the receptions! The words which elude him while he is dictating his own letters to enquire when the festivities in Copenhagen are to take place! Brandt who at the most unexpected times refuses to take dictation! All this he adds together, as Immanuel Kant

advised, with no false analogies. What can he DO? Calmly, calmly think, fully knowing that the bad is always balanced by the good. Elsewhere in the world, where the streets are clean and children laugh merrily, people wish him the best. They are longing for his return – and for him to arrange his unique finds. What shall he DO to reach there? *Continue as he has started* after pretending to be ill so that during Brandt's noontime nap outside in the hammock he could in all secrecy pack his bag with the most essential items.

It is still the dry season. Nature is helping him – again. What can he dare HOPE for? *That his escape will succeed.* And it will if he never lets Kant out of his thoughts and for every step he takes *think more carefully than ever before*, not allowing himself to be *distracted*, either by the wayside flowers, or by the birds, *or even by the sight of a new cave*. The time for that is over. He knows his mother would agree. Now is the time for years of interpretation, maturity, and perspective, when he, *at the meridian of life*, the age which von Humboldt lauds as the golden summer following the gay spring, will write, day after day, the work about the nature of MAN. This same work which Brandt and all the townspeople of Lagoa Santa are trying to prevent him from writing because it would reveal their own backwardness, show that they are nothing but torn-up pages in the Creator's Plan, useless even as experiments.

Brandt has now shrunk to a cloud of red dust, and Dr. Lund rides on, halfway round the lake and up the path leading directly to Rio de Janeiro. The sun is scorching, and the mule is already thirsty. This he can KNOW: that he must push on, defying all odds. This he can HOPE: that the mule will survive the hardships and that a little brook will soon appear where it can quench its thirst. This he can DO until the brook appears: talk to the mule, encourage it with fond words, pat it gently. The Biblical beast, Balthazar. Companion of prophets and the saints, praised in psalms and hymns, the very opposite of the heathen and belligerent Arabian stallion, the mule possesses perhaps a bit of human soul which enables it to understand the inspiring and guiding words of reason. Now he has accustomed himself to its gait and its smell. Now the animal knows him to be its protector. It understands him and in gratitude will carry him, delivered, to the illuminated imperial parks of Rio de Janeiro.

It is growing hotter. Sweat is pouring down his temples and the bridge of his nose so that his spectacles keep slipping off. There are pains in his thigh and in his spine. But they are only after-effects. And his bag is still safe. He may be a little dizzy and the path may be swaying, but it is only *because he had made the most important decision of his life*, to save himself from annihilation at the last moment. Nature understands him and does everything to help him. The plants nod approvingly, the crystals glitter in the sunshine far ahead on the path. The birds, the bem-te-vi, the sabiá, and the first tyrannids, whistle him onward, fully aware that at this decisive moment of his life he has no time to study them. They are his fellow conspirators, grateful to him for having classified them so thoroughly, just as the plants thank him for all the times he pressed them into the herbarium.

'Take care of the bag!' whisper the stunted trees to him. 'Tell of us in Europe!' hiss the snakes, which have all agreed not to bite his mule, as one afternoon by Lapa da Cerca Grande, one of them did in a fit of wickedness, bewitched by the man in the mountain with the eye in the middle of his forehead and no flesh on the bones of his right hand. 'Forgive us for the torment we caused you! Every cut! Every attack of fever! Forgive us, forgive us!' whisper all the animals and plants. Dr. Lund greets them all, even the vultures, and forgives them, happy to have gone several miles out of Lagoa Santa, having already halfway succeeded in his flight. Someday, he thinks, someday many years hence, this country, this wildlife, will also be civilized. Many naturalists will follow in his footsteps, inspired by his example, to study and classify, and when that day comes, in the autumn of his life, he will receive them in his library, either in Monaco or in Rosenlund, happy for the greetings they will bring him from the sabiá, the bem-te-vi, and from the stunted bushes and the shy crystals. Slowly he slides down over the neck of the mule. Startled, it bolts off, leaving him lying on the dusty path.

The sun is inside his head. It splinters everything. He

213

reaches out to extinguish the thousand tiny flames, red, yellow, white, light-blue, orange. His hair is on fire. He cannot find his straw hat. A thick layer of dust coats his tongue, and he can hardly breathe. The ants march directly in front of him in a column stretching as far as he can see. They crawl over the back of his hand, beneath his shirt. Soon they reach his sweaty armpits. They bite him and spray their poison into the wounds. He screams, but not even the sabiá hears him. Then he is falling again, but now without impact. He is falling through the thick porous calcareous crust, which , here and there, is almost pulpy. All around him animals are falling, legs stiff in the air, faces distorted by fear – all must die to satiate the Evil One in his desire to see blood. Tigers and cave leopards, showers of geckos, prediluvian and antediluvian antelopes jumbled together, dogs and rats – everywhere the calcareous crust is splitting open beneath them and they will fall till they are crushed in the innermost recesses of the caves. But in mid-fall he stops – although the animals continue to fall. Something bears him aloft. He floats up to the light again, up to the sun now searing the surface of the Earth. The bushes, shrubs, and even the tiniest tufts of grass flame into torches. A cool breeze blows from the north to try to quench the fire and rain drizzles down. But the fire is still burning, now again in his head, in his abdomen, and in his skin which will soon be a caustic charred layer of nothingness round his bones.

Little by little, he is laid down in a bush or onto a pile of dry palm leaves. He glimpses a face. He thinks he recognizes the small eyes, the broad nose, the lips. The rain is falling harder on him, and when he tries to open his sticky eyelids, he makes out a cloud above him, blood red. Lightning strikes from it. He is lying on sugar-cane. He can smell it now. He is being jolted and his neck keeps banging against a piece of hard wood, the handle of a spade or a hoe. The face has vanished. He is falling again. Beside him is the saber-toothed tiger, spitting as it is sucked into the abyss. Even the ants must perish. Wherever he looks, their ruined anthills are whirling through the calcareous crust like leaky sacks of dust.

Upon waking, he sees the children first. They have swollen bellies and the eldest has the *papo*. The gigantic tumor growing out of the larynx will soon be the size of a melon. In the corner sits a negro woman, her legs wrapped in layers of cloth. She must be leprous, and she too has the papo, although the tumor on her throat is only the size of an orange. All at once he realizes where he is – in the village Rio Manso, fearfully called Arraial dos Papos after the dread disease which causes a swelling of the tissues of the throat, the disease of the limestone regions which is almost always followed by *o mal de São Lázaro*. He lies motionless. Now and then the woman comes over to him to fan him with a palm leaf and wet his lips with a moist cloth. He shuts his eyes so as not to see her. He knows that this is a trial he must endure, the ultimate test before all the receptions, a terrifying stop on the road back to Rio de Janeiro and Europe. If he can only collect his thoughts and exclude all analogies, his mule will soon come for him and cautiously nudge open the door with its muzzle so he can get up and ride away.

And now Carl is calling and imploring him not to give up and not to confuse nightmares with reality. Carl, who was always with him on the way to school and who protected him, keeping the gypsy woman from the mysterious land of the Common, from snatching his heart hand and reading his future with her evil smile. Now Carl is trying to approach him, his arms stretched out and his mouth contorted with pain. No longer does he urge him on. For now it is Carl who needs help, caught as he is somewhere between heaven and earth as a punishment because *he*, Wilhelm, that day in the Gamekeeper's House, had peeled a little green twig to make it look like a larva and quivering with triumph, had banished a student, who was a bit too cocky, to the loneliness of self-reproach with the words, 'Well, it seems that student Beck cannot *classify!*'

He tosses on the oxhide. Now the hour of reckoning has come. Now his punishment will be meted out because he had chosen to follow in the footsteps of Markvor Lund instead of seeking the light, and he will forever hear Carl calling and see him coming toward him. He wakes. He

215

gazes straight at an ox skull hanging on the wall, surrounded by chains from which dangle, by strands of parrot feathers, stones, the teeth of many animals, and strange symbols of tattered cardboard. His body is aching all over. The children are still there. The woman brings him a bowl of water, a wizened orange, and a morsel of bread crust. He can barely swallow two sips. The bread turns to ashes in his mouth, and the orange catches in shreds between his remaining teeth. He continues staring at the skull. He recognizes it. But where he saw it before he does not know. And when he stands up, groggy with hunger, he sees more skulls, long candles sticking up from empty bottles, piles of feathers, and a box of tiny mouse skulls.

Again he pictures the face which had floated above him when he lay among the sugar-canes. Who was it? He goes toward the door. Behind him, the woman is wailing that he is to lie still, but he knows he must flee, whatever the price. In the withered garden patch in front of the hut more skulls gleam dully, laid in patterns, stuck on poles, hung from bushes. All the people he slips past have the papo, and many are leprous. He can hear the faint jingling of the small copper bells tied round their necks. Some of them have no legs. Now he feels a tumor swelling out of his own larynx, first as big as a nut, then an orange, and finally as big as his own head. He must hide it quickly, and in confusion he searches after his mule so he can find a shirt in his bag. No one must see him like this. If they hear in Europe that he has been stricken by the papo, they will have nothing to do with him. His bones will be removed from the silver-plated exhibition cases and sold by the King to inferior museums all over the globe for fear that the bones too carry the infection.

He avoids everyone and everyone avoids him. Staggering among the slave huts, in a glitter of sun and dust, he glimpses brick houses and a church in the distance. He heads toward them, but hardly has he escaped the hell of the slaves here in the Village of the Damned before The Giant, wrapped in a crimson cape, emerges from a house and strides straight over to him. He must run away from him. He must shout for help. Somebody must be able to hear. They cannot desert him here, with a swelling tumor, with the

216

white sun scorching away the last of his vision, blurring all
contours, casting black shadows. He stoops to grope after his
spectacles, lying somewhere near him. Children are shrieking
at him. He is accustomed to that, but not to his own
fumbling like a blind man, sensing ghosts at every other step.
The nightmare continues, but The Giant is no specter. He is
Punishment. He is Revenge. And he towers before him,
grasping a bottle, his mouth reeking of guts and liquor,
surrounded by his wretched brothers, cousins, and slaves.
His huge body momentarily blocks out the sun. Even before
the Giant has opened his mouth, Dr. Lund knows the words
which will come out of it, the question which will strike
violently, as if his skull were being knocked off his spine:

'Well, Doctor! Can we no longer *classify*?'

People are thronging round The Giant. An ancient crone
falls on her knees before him, kissing his cape. Children offer
him fruit. Someone hands Dr. Lund his spectacles and now
he sees that *the Dane* is wearing an imperial officer's uniform
beneath his cape. And then he sees the houses, the venda,
the church plaza, and, right beside him, Brandt, his
painter's smock still tucked awry into his pants and his tufts
of hair still disheveled. Brandt gently takes his arm to lead
him away. The Giant snatches his cape away from the old
crone, knocking her over, and orders his followers to mount.

'The sea lion, Doctor! I tell you, the sea lion!' he grins,
flinging the bottle away.

Then he gallops down the road leading from Lagoa Santa
straight to the Rio das Velhas.

He is riding over the highland, and he can find no rest. He
sits on his mule, unable to quench his thirst, unable to satisfy
his hunger. He is doomed to ride like this for all eternity,
dressed in an old faded blue jacket and ragged canvas
trousers through which his charred flesh can be seen. From
cave to cave he rides, but whenever he reaches a cave
entrance the mule veers away. His straw hat is pulled down
over his eyes, yet he is dazzled by the sun. He rides eastward
though the road seems to run westward, northward though
it seems to run southward. The untiring mule takes him
wherever he wants to go, but 'wherever' may be anywhere,

and he dares not think about the mule's eyes because he fears that they are not its own. No froth ever gathers on its muzzle, no snake can bite it to death. Its ears face backward and its forehead flashes white. Every morning it nudges him awake at a certain time, and no matter how weary he is he must rise, roll up his oxhide, put out the fire, and ride onward from nowhere to nowhere, along paths strewn with letters fluttering like dead leaves, invitations bursting into flame at his glance, concert tickets which scorch his fingers, and the torn pages of books printed with the truth which he seeks, crumbling to dust at his approach.

For years on end he has been riding like this. He will keep on riding although the other half of his soul can no longer hold up his head or even lift a finger now that he is again lying in his bed shrouded in a darkness not of bandages but of eyelids which he cannot open. Pains choke whatever has not been burnt away within him. Sometimes, forcing his eyes open, he sees a world drained of color. Black geckos scurry along the black tiles. Now they seem like the dread lizards of Greek myth, venomous, poison-spewing, their darting tongues able to turn clear well-water into black sticky fluid. The geckos multiply and race down the walls under his bed and up the shutters, emiting their hungry little shrieks. Their molted tails rain onto his bed. Wriggling like eels cut into three pieces, like a thousand earthworms, like snakes possessing only heads and tails, the black reptile trails cover him with a slithering slimy layer. Brandt has no time to wipe it away, absorbed as he is in painting or cooking macaroni or carrying on long whispered conversations with the priest.

That lisping, tonsured priest, he has suddenly started daily visits. With Brandt hovering behind him, the priest peers into his room, black like everything else, his black prayer book clenched between his black fingers. When the priest is mumbling some incomprehensible Latin prayer over him, he himself is speechless because his voice is out riding with the other half of his soul, out where all is whiteness just as here all is blackness. But what should he say to the mule? No affectionate word can rouse it, yet it carries him where he knows not. Color has vanished. The ants are white. And now not only the mule's head but also its body is white as chalk, white as stinging, itching lime. Flowers wither. Trees are white and lifeless. And the mule plods on, to the Jequitinhonha River, whose waters are churned white as milk, foaming white, raging white. The mule swims him across and they soon come to the white stone city with roofs which once were golden. But he is not forced to eat a snake nor to wrestle with the cave bear to be allowed inside. The gates of the city swing open for him. The mule carries him to the entrance of a great hall where, at the end of a resounding stone floor, the people, seated round a long table, are drinking tea, waiting for him. Above them hangs a tapestry showing a group of strong young naked naturalists, shouldering their instruments, on their way into a jungle.

They are all there – Oersted, Cuvier, von Humboldt, Milne-Edwards, Rudolphi from the Museum of Natural History in Berlin with the sealed jar containing the entrails of the black urubú, Linnaeus with *Flora suecia* open in his lap, and Schouw with all his precious herbariums. Students from Kiel, holding torches, line the walls behind the silver-plated exhibition cases displaying the bones in scrupulous order, freshly numbered and labeled. The skeleton of the giant sloth towers in the middle of the hall. It reaches up to the ceiling. It is daybreak somewhere in the arctic, although he can hear the rush of the Jequitinhonha River. And suddenly color floods in. Oersted's face is red, Linnaeus's Roman cape glows dandelion yellow. Cuvier, clad in a blue silk dressing gown, smiles. They are waiting for him to come closer and accept their thanks. He takes three cautious steps toward the giant sloth, passes between its legs, and continues up to the table at the end. The students cheer him, raising their torches high. Oersted is still smiling at him. Then each man unbuttons his embroidered shirt. He whirls round, dashes desperately back under the giant sloth to the waiting mule standing with its hindquarters toward him. The students fling their torches at him and rip open their shirts too. They all have the papo.

Brandt drops his brushes and rushes to his bedside.

Several weeks later, Dr. Lund is able to sit up in bed, eat

regularly and sip lukewarm tea sweetened with honey or jam. The priest no longer comes to plague him with his mournful prayers, scared away, perhaps, by Dr. Lund's remark that having once rejected the Protestant faith he was not about to convert to the Papal variety. Even more boxes full of bones have been sent off, and soon only duplicates will be left in the study. Dr. Lund cheers up at the thought that Reinhardt is now in Lagoa Santa, after a long and perilous voyage around the world. As he lies in bed, he tells Brandt how to re-furnish and decorate the house to make it presentable for the guest of honor. Pots are to be scrubbed three times. The three-toed sloth is to be chained in the cottage where the slave had lived. The weeds by the door are to be pulled up, and perhaps the fence ought to be given a fresh coat of paint. Brandt's easel may stand in his room, but the paint jars are to be set out neatly on the shelves and the bones nicely arranged so as to show Reinhardt that scientific work is still being done in the house. Dust is to be wiped away, books ordered in rows, and shutters opened. No chamberpots. No spittoons. But a bottle of port is to stand on a table; Brandt should send a negro to Sabará to buy it from the Englishmen.

Again Dr. Lund is bathed and given a haircut. Brandt takes out his best shirt from the traveling bag, which a black boy had delivered this afternoon – God only knows where he had found it. Every step is carried out according to a carefully-laid plan. No detail must be overlooked, and Dr. Lund is pleased to see his assistant co-operative again. Perhaps he will not have to buy a new slave after all. Soon the invitation can be sent to Reinhardt, who is no doubt suffering in that filthy rooming house. Dr. Lund impresses upon his assistant a proper respect for the distinguished guest they are to receive. Without Reinhardt, there would have been no zoology in Denmark, nor in Norway for that matter, because it was in Guldbrandsdalen that Reinhardt as a young man became aware of nature and abandoned theology. Without Reinhardt the Royal Museum of Natural History would not exist. Indeed, Cuvier refers to him as his Nordic Peer. Why, the Professor Emeritus must be over seventy now, but because of his love of nature, he is still going strong.

Brandt simply does not understand. He looks doubtful. He asks odd, even impudent questions, although he had seemed so obliging. But the Norwegian's sabotage can no longer bother him.

He KNEW it: that titular Councillor of State, Professor and honorary Doctor of Philosophy Johannes Christopher Hagemann Reinhardt, his benefactor and advocate, he who in the name of science had advised him to travel to the tropics to avoid the risk of consumption, would one day come to him here in Lagoa Santa, now that he is unable to make the journey to Copenhagen.

11

The young man comes to the older man. Once he had come to him in the new Royal Museum of Natural History on Stormgade. There Peter*wil*helm, or PW as he was now called, listened to the older man's lectures about the new day heralded by the Creator when science, having liberated itself from theological speculation, would truly show how spirit permeates matter and how even the tiniest flower, the tiniest insect, are links in the Creator's Plan. Wilhelm knew that Reinhardt was not only his friend but also his ideal. After the lectures, as he walked out to Vibens Hus, he planned his two competition papers with Reinhardt in mind.

Now again the youth comes to the older man, and the latter is an old man of forty-six. It is July 1847, and doctoral candidate Johannes Theodor Reinhardt, newly-appointed curator of the bone collection and responsible for mounting this collection upon returning from his voyage round the world, realizes that something has happened to Dr. Lund, something which cannot be explained simply. For days he and Brandt discuss how to shake Dr. Lund out of his confusion and persuade him to return to Denmark. Reinhardt is living in the same lodging house room in which Dr. Lund had slept and worked twelve years earlier. While waiting for Dr. Lund to receive him, he makes excursions to the Rio das Velhas to catch, study, and mount specimens of the countless river fish. He fears that he will not meet his father's favorite student after all.

Dr. Lund is off on a long journey. It takes him from the Sicilian coast to the translucent mornings of Ile de France, from Rue Corneille and revolutionary uprisings on foot up through the German states to Denmark and thence, after embraces with Petrea and Henrik Ferdinand, to Hamburg, where a brig sets sail to carry him to Brazil. Episode after episode come to mind and gradually fall into sequence. He recalls the harbor of Rio de Janeiro, the crustacea's glowing script in the water, the black boys rowing out to the ship to sell mangos and oranges. He studies weeds outside Rio de Janeiro and then rides through the virgin forest, up into highland. He crosses rivers, hears natives describing the Caipor, suffers fevers, recovers, and at sundown carries on deep discussions with the German botanist Ludwig Riedel. He leaves the monsters of the São Francisco River – those embellishing the canoes and those hidden on the river bottom – and experiences the melancholy Baroque atmosphere of Ouro Preto, after which he returns to Curvelo. And he remembers the butterfly *Psyché* suddenly fluttering up from a dusty doorstep just as he had read that Petrea had died. Motionless, it hung in a sunbeam, as if borne up by the wind. Then it flew just above him and vanished into the sky.

After Curvelo he toils through the Tormented Forest, to Lagoa Santa with its red-roofed houses. And he is young and able to perceive a range of one-hundred and eighty degrees. Slowly he comes to himself by dreaming memories which arouse happiness, by re-living the loss of time and place and the disappearance of color and smell. He travels further. He is on the road to himself, and after sleeplessly, repeatedly, reliving the days and nights of Brandt insisting that it was not old Reinhardt but his son who had come to Lagoa Santa, his thoughts grow clearer. He even smiles at himself for having forgotten that two years earlier he had written home to express his deep sorrow at the death of the elder Reinhardt.

No longer does his other half roam the campos. He can now hold his head erect, move his fingers, take nourishment, and ask Brandt with curiosity about this young Reinhardt. Is he content in Lagoa Santa, despite the shabby lodging house? Is he diligently studying the shores of the Rio das Velhas? And has he brought greetings and letters with him from the Galathea?

He insists on hearing everything about the voyage round the world. When at last Reinhardt visits him, sits smiling on the edge of his bed, his sunburnt fleshy cheeks fringed by well-trimmed whiskers resembling brushes, and whispers how happy he is to meet *him*, the most celebrated man in Danish science along with Oersted, Dr. Lund eagerly asks about London, Paris, and Berlin. He then demands that young Reinhardt tell all, skipping not even a week, about the corvette Galathea's voyage during the same three years which Dr. Lund hopes, if not to forget, then at least to view in the proper perspective. Every word penetrates and stimulates his sick body to life. He delights in the equipping of the corvette, asks about the newest scientific instruments, the firing range of the cannons, and the size of the scientific team and its composition. Is Kamphoevener a promising botanist? Is Rink a geologist whom Forchhammer vouches for? Is Kjellerup a reliable entomologist? And Professor Behn, the King's personal choice as zoologist, now traversing the interior of South America after debarking north of Chile – is he a scientist or an arrogant adventurer? Will he be passing through Lagoa Santa? Fortunately Reinhardt praises most of this new generation of naturalists, for they carry on the best traditions and have no intention of suppressing their inquisitiveness just to please Bishop Mynster and his followers. And they all support a free constitution.

At this latter remark, Dr. Lund frowns. Politics and science must never be mixed, he reproaches Reinhardt, even as he jubilantly sails past Elsinore, hearing the band on the deck blowing melancholy valedictions to Kronborg Castle. Danish wind! Danish sea! He hears the courses of the Galathea fall. He sees the studding sails billow out from the spars, and hears the great top sail cast back. Plymouth! Britain! He will never see England, so Reinhardt must describe his stay there in great detail.Dr. Lund still admires the *godems,* who are now planning the first railway from Recife to São Franciso and will soon be followed by others, so that in a few decades mule travel and tropa transport will be a thing of the past. English words are cropping up even in Minas Gerais – *budget, deficit, bill, funding loan.* The few cultivated families in Lagoa Santa are reading such books as *Viagens de Gulliver* and *Robinson Crusoé.* And English port wine! Suddenly Dr. Lund has a craving for a glass, so Brandt cheerfully dashes off for the crooked dusty bottle which he had managed to buy. Now Dr. Lund sits bolt upright. His eyes flash.

'Welcome and *skol*, Reinhardt! *Tell more!*'

On August 24th, 1845, they passed the Tropic of Capricorn. The first Cape pigeons were sighted. As the Galathea slowly neared the southern tip of Africa, the albatross appeared, and the black swallow called Mother Carey's chicken. These birds glide restlessly about the sky, coming out of nowhere. Where is their home? Where do they build their nests? In Mother Carey's chickens dwell the tormented souls of the damned, those who can find no peace in the ocean waves, and no self-respecting sailor would ever dare to shoot one of those black swallows. For then he too would perish.

'And you? Did *you* shoot them?' demands Dr. Lund.

He is weary. He sees blood. But he insists on hearing more. No, neither Reinhardt nor the other naturalists have ever managed to shoot a black swallow. But in calm weather, when the birds rock in the wake of the ship, they can be caught with fishing lines which they bite into most greedily. On deck they heartily amuse the crew with their pitiful waddling about on their webbed feet, unable to fly without having the sea to launch themselves from. Only the second-in-command disliked them because they often vomit train oil, as if these lost souls grow landsick in a foreign element.

'Did you *kill* them?' asks Dr. Lund.

'Only those we needed for museum specimens,' answers Reinhardt.

'How many?'

'About ten or twelve.'

'That's not good . . .' whispers Dr. Lund.

He dozes off. One of these days he will give Brandt orders to throw away the old piston rifle. There must be no lethal weapons in the house, nor a drop of blood, not even in an egg yolk. Dr. Lund will never again allow meat in his house. Reinhardt must make the best of it. Maybe a fish, one of Reinhardt's own favorites – but no more meat. Dr. Lund has nightmares again. He sees himself skinning the fur off live animals, and his arms are spattered with blood. He stuffs birds while their hearts are still beating and fills the three-toed sloth with sawdust while it slowly moves a hind leg. The next day he asks Reinhardt if he believes the sailors' tale about Mother Carey's chickens.

'If you believe everything you hear, you might as well forget science,' answers Reinhardt, vexed because he cannot have an egg for breakfast.

Land is sighted, and aboard the Galathea there is jubilation after seventy-seven days at sea. Anchor is dropped off the verdant coast of Coromandel, near Tranquebar. Here lies the Dansborg fort. The Danish swallow-tailed flag flies as it has done for over two hundred years. Now the colony is being given away.

'What a shame that Denmark does not . . .' begins Dr. Lund.

He is also pained to hear of the failure to colonize the Nicobar Islands. Denmark ought to have its own Singapore, and the jungles of the Nicobars interest him. Early one morning the Danish naturalists gather on a beach there. Together they penetrate a jungle which even the natives fear to enter because of its countless poisonous snakes, perhaps the most dangerous in the world. But neither Reinhardt, Behn, Kamphoevener, Kjellerup, nor Rink are afraid. They collect plants, soil specimens and stones, shoot birds, break off twigs, make notes, and write numbers. Abruptly the terrain shifts to an impassable tract covered by stinking brackish water lapping round high mounds swarming with the detested white ants. Mangrove trees shoot their branches into and their roots out of the earth. The air is sultry. Not a breeze stirs the jungle and pestilential vapors fill his lungs. He is deserted by the other naturalists, led away by Reinhardt. With his ebbing strength he pushes on southward – only to discover that the situation worsens. He falls. He breathes his last. Natives approach and drip some coconut milk into his mouth. Women and children wail loudly, and an hour after his death, they wrap eight pieces of cloth around him, each of a different color, and bind them with a cord to his elbows, hips and feet. Messengers race out to bid the inhabitants of nearby villages to come to his funeral, and they come, carrying spears. A three-foot-deep grave is dug amidst the anthills. The natives take off their ornaments while the procession carries his bones, a handful of glass beads, his pots, and his blank papers over to the grave. Bark of the *upeh* tree is wrapped around his corpse. A live chicken is tied to his chest. The first cackle of the chicken starts the natives lamenting. His corpse, with the dangling chicken, is lowered and a pig is slaughtered. Its blood is sprinkled on the edge of the grave.

'No more *blood*! No more *blood*!' he pants.

Brandt gently supports his neck as Reinhardt anxiously asks if they ought not send for a physician – if there is one. But Brandt is calm. He has seen how much Dr. Lund has improved since Reinhardt's arrival, and, sure enough, Dr. Lund soon opens his eyes. For a moment he has no idea who is sitting on the edge of his bed, wearing a starched white shirt with buttonholes entwined with a gold watch chain. Then he recognizes young Reinhardt. He can even discern features resembling his father's. Now he wants to hear more, especially about the Chinese folk theater so unlike the European. He has reached Pulo-Pinang. He is like the wandering stranger arriving at an Oriental court who through his courage saves the kingdom from great danger and is rewarded with the hand of the King's daughter and her dowry of vast fertile lands, flowering mountains and valleys, and waterfalls which can make gold mines work.

Pulo-Pinang. He murmurs the name and Reinhardt smiles with relief and wipes the perspiration off his neck with a handkerchief elaborately embroidered with his name in orange and royal blue. Nutmeg, cloves, and sugar are cultivated everywhere. In the towns, carpenters, cabinet-makers, smiths, tailors, and bakers are busy in their open-air workshops. The fresh breeze rustles the long paper strips painted with Chinese characters – golden mottos summing up ancient wisdom – which people trade on the New Year. Fruit vendors sell peeled sugar-canes, not gnawed through by ants, red wild bananas, oranges of all sizes, pineapples. watermelons, and mangos. There is a celebration with song and music, a wedding feast, and the bridal couple has long since retired behind soft draperies. There is a pagoda, and across from it an open-air theater. The smoke of incense sticks spices the air, and the actors are nearly indistinguishable from the spectators, some of whom are drinking their tea up

on stage. A princess lies in chains in the midst of this crowd.
A knight is trying to save her, and his arias can make even
the heaviest prison doors spring open. Pulo-Pinang. Singapore.
The Gaspar Straits. The Philippines. The Chinese mainland.
Amoy. Tscusan. Shanghai. The Pacific Ocean. The Sandwich
Islands. The Van Dieman Straits. Bay of Jeddo. Oahu.
Tahiti. And then ... Valparaiso with its forty thousand
inhabitants, lying like a vast amphitheater on a mountainside
and, as Dr. Lund is distressed to hear, stripped bare of
vegetation. Not a garden. Not a tree. Instead swarms of
carriages, landaus, and ox-drawn carts heaped with chalco-
pyrite and copper bars.

Dr. Lund glances at Brandt, who is chuckling and
nodding his head in recognition at Reinhardt's description.
Did he meet this person and that person? Is the editor of the
newspaper for which Brandt had worked still in prison? Are
there still murderous duels down by the harbor? But now
Dr. Lund is impatient to hear how the Galathea rounded
Cape Horn to sail via Montevideo and Buenos Aires to Rio
de Janeiro, the last stop but one before the return to
Copenhagen. Again he feels a powerful surge of joyful
recognition when from the sea he sees the fertile slopes of
Brazil, with the high peaks of Gávea, Dois Irmãos, and
Corcovado. He glides serenely past the islets of Pai and Mãe –
Father and Mother. He passes the forts of Santa Cruz and
Lago, and there ... there gleams the white beach of
Botafogo with the elegant country homes in the distance and
negroes, laden with sacks of coffee, trotting rapidly among
the palm trees. The city now has nearly two hundred
thousand inhabitants and is more glittering, more imperial,
more European than ever.

Riedel sends him cordial greetings, as does the Emperor
who admires him greatly for his lonely labors in the caves in
the heart of his immense realm. Claussen! No, not the Dane,
but a brother of his who had run away from Curvelo and in
fact proved most helpful to Reinhardt in buying and
packing mules and giving good advice about the journey to
Lagoa Santa. Reinhardt scoffs at the tropa, deciding instead
to travel on his own with five mules, costing six hundred
milreis in all. Dr. Lund thinks this an exorbitant sum to pay

for the foolish idea of shortening a Brazilian journey by a few weeks. Not to mention the superfluity of bringing along a special 'animal preserver' – a sailor from the Galathea who doubtless has no idea of how to stuff birds or preserve fish and snakes in jars filled with solution. He can understand why the captain of the corvette, Steen Bille, was reluctant to send one of his men along to Lagoa Santa, and that he probably did so only because Reinhardt had secured permission from the King himself for his odd plan.

Times are changing and a new generation with new ideas arises. But the nature of Brazil is unchanged, at least to judge by Reinhardt's vague description. Serra da Estrela and Serra dos Orgãos still stand sharply against the sky. They are visible on the horizon, with their rounded peaks, their luxuriant forests as virginal as when the Creator brought them into being, with lush masses of bushes, vines, orchids, aroids, bromeliacaes, and pineapple-like plants vying for space, and innumerable brooks trickling through gorges in the shade of giant ferns. Dr. Lund is happy to see again the melastomaceae and the lasiandras with their big rosy-red or purple five-leaved crowns. And the celebrated fig tree near Petropolis which he never reached but which Auguste de Saint-Hilaire had wonderingly described earlier, in the second decade of the century – perhaps the only tree to survive the Deluge! – and still standing! Young Reinhardt saw it with his own eyes! And although complaining about the hardships of travel, he is trying to persuade Dr. Lund to also make a journey, but in the opposite direction, together with Reinhardt, who would do anything in his power to bring him back to Denmark.

'In a month?' Perhaps! Who knows! 'In any case, *before* the rainy season!' insists Reinhardt. Why not? Maybe! Dr. Lund will not make up his mind about a departure date just yet, and he feels that Brandt understands him. So Reinhardt must go on, telling now of the last stage of the journey. Long before he reached Lagoa Santa, he had heard about *o illustre sábio dinamarquês* with the straw hat, spectacles, and countless boxes filled with bones. Dr. Lund is gratified to recognize himself. He is now resting comfortably in his favorite chair in the study, and through the half-open shutters he can see the palm garden.

'So we finally made it to Lagoa Santa,' he says, lighting a crackling-dry cigar. 'Reinhardt! You've whetted my appetite!' Lost in thought, he gazes at the remaining bones.

The red-roofed town lies flooded in late afternoon sunshine and reminds him of southern France. The lake brings memories of Furesø, and now Reinhardt is teaching him about fish – a subject he had neglected earlier – and revealing an admirable store of scientific knowledge. Reinhardt has rapidly discovered over twenty different species, and he estimates there to be at least twice as many more. In town, people nod warmly to them. Dr. Lund is relieved that the little black boys have stopped taunting him now that he has a visitor from Denmark. So it didn't take much after all. Strolling through Lagoa Santa for an hour every afternoon is enough to stop the gossip about him.

The church stands with its three tiny windows peeking out high up beneath the moss-grown red roof, and the cicadas are singing more gaily than ever in the golden tufts of grass surrounding its sun-baked walls. A young couple leaving the church hand in hand smiles at him shyly, impressed by Reinhardt's whiskers, his elegant attire, and his rings, flashing expensively. The priest, a dusty-black figure emerging from the back door of the church, greets them amiably, although his ragged straw hat gives the impression that he sometimes forgets that life is more than just Latin. He even has regards from the old priest, now rector of Colegio Duval in São João d'El Rei, where he instils in his oldest students respect for the Doctor in Lagoa Santa, whom he calls a living model of knowledge and diligence for all Brazilians.

The rich, pungent air hints at the approach of the rainy season, and every bird salutes Dr. Lund as Reinhardt talks on about his fish. New houses have been built down by the lake. Lagoa Santa now has over two thousand inhabitants: slaves, freed slaves, and whites. Merchants are moving into town, and one of the most reliable is a cultivated young Frenchman, Monsieur Foulon. He has offered to help Dr. Lund invest his money and to order modern scientific instruments from the Swiss colony of Nova Friburgo, where he has many good contacts.

All this raises Dr. Lund's spirits. Slowly, slowly, he is emerging from a dark tunnel, impossible to describe even to himself. But why should he? The very mention of Nova Friburgo clears his vision. The greeting from the old priest sharpens his hearing. And the talks with Reinhardt exhilarate him by bringing him up to date with the latest scientific developments in Copenhagen. The newly-founded Society of Natural History has become most popular. To be sure, it had been mentioned in letters, but now he can imagine the meetings, often held on Sundays (to tease Bishop Mynster) in the Stock Exchange auction hall. A gathering of not only naturalists but also the most distinguished ladies of Copenhagen and philologists such as Madvig, philosophers such as Sibbern, and lawyers such as Kolderup-Rosenvinge – all men he had met in passing at Bakkehuset. Natural science is at last considered a vital part of an all-round education. The Botanical Gardens are flourishing, but the cramped Royal Museum of Natural History must be enlarged to make room for his bone collection. Fortunately the King warmly supports the idea.

The bickering among the younger scientists is, feels Dr. Lund, a result of that epidemic of democratic opposition which is sowing the seeds of discontent in Paris, Berlin, and once again in Brazil, in Pernambuco.

'Reinhardt! A free constitution would lead to disaster. We would end up like Mother Carey's chickens, but no ship would save us.'

'Dr. Lund . . .'

'I'm just giving you my opinion!'

He has no strength to debate. Words exhaust him – at least, when he has to pronounce them. So he asks Reinhardt to return home, where Brandt will have dinner ready – macaroni, porridge, and boiled water. And coconut milk for the guest!

He can see, he can smell, he can hear. And there are colors.

'What a shame we have to leave this place,' says Reinhardt, placing his hand on his chest, gazing dreamily out over the lake. Yet not a minute goes by before he is distracted by the sight of a beautiful negro woman walking

231

through town, balancing an Indian vase on her head and smiling at him, revealing a mouthful of nearly-intact teeth.

The sailor is busy stuffing specimens at the venda the next day. The negro woman whom Reinhardt had more than once alluded to during dinner, sits by him, helping him with cotton, sawdust, thread, and needles of all sizes, little copper-pointed ones, strong crescent-shaped ones, barbed ones. Boxes filled with bones stand stacked in front of the venda, waiting to be sent off by tropa. Dr. Lund wishes to keep only the bones with sentimental value: a cuneiform bone from the Maquiné cave, a lower jaw from Sumidouro, a tibia from Lapa da Cerca Grande, a canine tooth from the saber-toothed tiger, and four crania. Brandt's merry new way of whistling amuses Dr. Lund because he knows that the Norwegian has long been dreaming of flinging out the last bones so he can paint the house and buy new furniture in Sabará. Watching the sailor working in the venda, Dr. Lund wonders what Brandt is planning to do. Does he want to go along to Europe? Or does his whistling mean that he intends to stay? It's up to him. If he stays, Dr. Lund will make sure that Henrik Ferdinand sends him a permanent annual pension.

The eager venda owner dashes to and fro with pot after pot of *chá de pedestre*, with biscuits, cheese, and thick jam made from his own garden flowers. Townspeople stream into the venda to watch the Europeans, above all the lively sailor who keeps them laughing at the way he clicks his tongue and pounds his chest in mock pride when he has finished stuffing a bird. Dr. Lund, sitting next to him, must admit that he is good at his work. Row upon row of specimens, birds of all shapes, sizes, and colors, flanked by jars containing fish delivered to the venda by panting black boys sent down to the lake by Reinhardt. Dr. Lund will never again stuff another bird. He means to keep his vow of forbidding blood in the house, and sometimes a pang goes through him when a bird shot that morning by Reinhardt suddenly twitches its tail or blinks an eye.

But the sailor is a most likeable fellow. His neck is fiery red, his nose peeling, and his thick dark eyebrows bristle above his cheerful blue eyes. He often bursts into lusty songs such as the one about the sailor and the three Arabian princesses, the one about the mother who finds her lost son after thirty years, or the one about the solitary Spanish soldier from the Napoleonic war on the Danish island of Funen. At the end of his song he winks at Dr. Lund while hugging the black woman so tightly that Reinhardt's well-trimmed whiskers quiver.

'So, Doctor, you didn't know that one either?'

Thus September passes. New boxes containing Reinhardt's collection are heaped onto boxes filled with bones. Reinhardt sits for hours on end studying the fish brought him by the black boys as in turn the sertanejos and the caboclos study him, as intently as if gold dust glittered beneath the scales which Reinhardt is counting one by one. His monocle set firmly in his right eye and the sleeves of his immaculate shirt rolled neatly up to his elbows, Reinhardt examines each fish with a pair of tweezers before handing it over his shoulder to the sailor, who seals it in a jar. And now at last he has discovered where Cuvier was mistaken! The question has been bothering him for some time, and he asks Dr. Lund, who has been dozing over his teacup, to please move a bit closer.

Now that his eyes cannot make out details, Dr. Lund feels useless. But to oblige Reinhardt he obediently pretends to peer at the fish as Reinhardt agitatedly explains how the *Lepipterus francisci* from the São Francisco River is identical to the *Pachyurus squamipennis* described by Agassiz – contrary to what Cuvier had believed and taught! Don't they both have the same enormous spiny ray in the anal fin? Doesn't the edge of the fore operculum in both of them bristle with tiny thorns down to the bottom corner? A close study of old specimens in Paris and Munich would hardly do the Baron credit!

'Well, now we know *that*, Doctor!' grins the sailor.

Reinhardt gasps for air and, unable to control himself any longer, bursts out, 'Mind your manners, Poulsen. Mind your manners, please!'

Next day, the sailor has vanished. They wait one hour, two hours – still he does not appear. At the lodging house no one has seen him since early morning. And at the house where the black woman lives – she is, as her gold anklet shows, a freed slave, and she works for a fazenda owner and his aged mother – he has not been seen. Nor, what is worse, has she. Some of the townspeople claim to have glimpsed them on mules on the far side of the lake. More reliable sources, including a newly-arrived caboclo, report having seen them galloping on a horse in the direction of Diamantina, he roaring out songs in his outlandish language, she clinging to his back. Reinhardt demands that a rider immediately be sent out to catch them. If the runaway man does not return, it is a clear case of desertion which must be reported to Steen Bille, the captain of the Galathea.

'Police! There must be *police* about!' splutters Reinhardt as he rubs his whiskers on his sweaty cheeks, glaring from one to the other, but the only response is a resigned shrug. The venda owner pours him a glass of lemonade which he irritably pushes over to Brandt. Dr. Lund cannot help him either. He withdraws from the commotion, hears with but one ear, sees with but one eye, sensing only a shadow which suddenly falls over him. He raises his eyes and is once again astride his mule, riding away from Lagoa Santa, roasting in the sun for hours, crushed inside. Then that same shadow falls over him, and as he is lifted up and gently laid down onto the sugar-canes, he glimpses a face with a broad nose, lips cracked by years of sun, and expressionless eyes. That same face is looming above him again. The shadow moves away and the witch doctor goes over to the counter to buy some bottles of sugar-cane liquor. In two hours the slaves will dance down by his hut where skulls dangle from bushes and form strange patterns in the withered garden patch.

Reinhardt refuses to mention the sailor. Instead, as Dr. Lund lies in bed and Brandt washes the dishes, he describes a fish which he is most fond of. Its lower jaw, longer than its upper jaw, protrudes when the mouth is shut. It is silvery white, toned gray along its back, from which faint dark stripes extend diagonally down to the lateral line and ... Dr. Lund, aren't you listening? ... there are precisely one-hundred-and-thirty scales along the body to the caudal fin.

If the Doctor does not mind, he, Reinhardt, would like to name this fish after his father's beloved student: *Pachyurus lundii!*

Wouldn't the Doctor be happier if he decided upon a date of departure for home? The rain will be coming soon . . .

Dr. Lund is not listening. From the remote highland he hears the Caipor howling, and he falls into a long deep sleep.

12

And the years pass.

The bones lie untouched in their boxes in three attic rooms in Christianborg Castle, and now that Christian VIII is dead it seems the collection will never be exhibited. The new king has enough problems without having to worry about the advancement of natural science. For reasons unknown the collection is even banished from its three storerooms to desolate cellars in Copenhagen as dark and dank as the caves the bones came from. One thing is linked to another, and in the largest Minas Gerais newspaper, *Jornal do Comércio*, Dr. Lund, now titular professor of the fifth degree, peers through his costly new spectacles to read reports of the three years' war between Denmark and the rebellious duchies. He learns from Henrik Ferdinand's and Christian's letters about the electoral reforms which, he agrees, are 'pernicious'.

No doubt democracy will also be introduced in Brazil, although the revolt in Pernambuco has been quelled. But Dom Pedro Segundo had to submit to the liberals in allowing the prime minister to appoint ministers. France has flung itself into another unhappy revolutionary episode, and the new Germans, striving to unify their country, are as foolish, in Dr. Lund's opinion, as the fantasists dreaming of 'Denmark to the Elbe'. The devil with politics. What he does like is Holstein, although he never really explored the countryside, focused around his mother's Lohbech. What he does like is Zealand, when he recalls Denmark, its lakes, woods, and shores. Why divide and re-unite with meddlesome rulers between one's fingers? Why change the Creator's Plan? Do trees *vote*? Do birds respect *borders*? When is a mouse's nest New German and when is it United Monarchy Danish? And why destroy nature as well in the name of equality? Is a lion not a lion, a lamb not a lamb? Struggle, struggle! Can Man only be happy when he is in harmony with . . . what? His deepest instincts? His will to power? The spirit of the world? But which world? That of the Creator or that of politics?

'The world-spirit, my dear Dr. Lund, operates beyond the fickle caprices of Reaction.' declares the New German, Burmeister.

Burmeister had announced his visit a year in advance, having learned from Riedel that Dr. Lund does not receive uninvited guests. This young naturalist, whose conversation Dr. Lund likes at first, has come to Lagoa Santa because he plans to devote an entire chapter of his *Reise nach Brasilien* to the celebrated Danish naturalist. Burmeister can rattle off more statistics than anyone Dr. Lund has ever met, and as he talks he taps his polished nails against his gold-rimmed teeth. The pudgy Burmeister with the deep-set eyes and twitching legs which give him the appearance of running even when sitting, gushes on about comparative statistics, point statistics, general statistics, and an advanced sort of statistics which entails making statistics about statistics. *Statistics*, claims the New German, is the foremost science of the new age, offering undreamed-of opportunities to its devotees. Statistics enable us to measure, calculate, add, and even – *predict*. Numerical quantities dating back to the Romans can be deciphered to tell us of the population of Berlin, for example, in the year 1937. Pure reason. Science.

Dr. Lund is amused to hear this, although he cannot share Burmeister's belief in the crucial significance of numbers – but at least it is better than discussing politics. The number of coffee sacks in Rio de Janeiro, of casks of genever exported from Holland to Brazil between 1840 and 1850, of whites, freed slaves, slaves, men, women, and children in even the most obscure quarters of Rio de Janeiro, and of fish in the Amazon based upon measurement of the depth of the water multiplied by the number of waves per hour. Statistics can reveal all this. Statistics have the answer. Burmeister's legs start jerking, he jumps up and paces to and fro past Dr. Lund, who is seated in a new garden chair built for him by Brandt. Now Burmeister has launched into politics.

And statistics have shown that races and nations are fated to wage war against each other. A united Germany, including Holstein, has a unique universal mission, and statistics, united with *sociology*, united with *craniology* (a science unfortunately dominated by Frenchmen, due to the famous *instruments craniométriques* of Monsieur Maurice Maurice) can help accomplish the necessary elimination of inferior races. The negroes of Brazil are doomed to destruction. The New German speaks with a peculiar agitation – a physical disgust which makes him oblivious of his surroundings, his eyes fixed inwards, as his cheek muscles twitch – about the blacks whose origins he can pinpoint at first glance. Angola, Guinea, or the Congo. That nose, from Angola. That hair, if such a kinky mat is hair, from Guinea. And the ones from the Congo – the most repulsive of all. Their smell. Their underdeveloped brains, half-gorilla, half-reptile, with only certain nerve centers resembling those of humans. Perhaps Dr. Lund would like to hear what he has written about the negroes of Rio de Janeiro. Or read the pages himself. Or have copies made for reference and inclusion in his scientific files.

Dr. Lund agrees to the latter suggestion. For he suddenly feels drained after several months of having been up and about most of the day, having found strength to weed the garden, to decide where new vines should grow, new tea bushes be planted, and new beds be laid out in terraces down to the lake and edged by large stones to protect them from the rain and planted with roses sent from Nova Friburgo. The air is buzzing with vexing words and his head is whirling as he wonders whether Burmeister is a true expression of the New Germany, now including Holstein, or whether he is simply an over-eager dilettante in science who leans too heavily on imagination and politics.

Yet he cannot control his anger when Burmeister arrogantly repudiates God and every form of faith. God is dead and has always been dead, no matter what He is called, Kuni-Tsu-Kami, Zeus, or Jehovah, He belongs to the *reaction*. He is opium for the masses, invented by kings and emperors, and if it were up to Burmeister, all churches in Germany, Catholic and evangelical, would be converted into Temples of Reason, just as Robespierre converted the French churches. *Temples of Reason*! Dr. Lund protests indignantly, he refuses to hear such talk in his own garden, however much he may have divorced himself from the Church. Burmeister swallows his words and apologizes deeply, his legs twitching.

Soon after the visit of the New German, which ended when he broke his leg en route to Congonhas where he was bedridden for several weeks, reportedly in a constant state of rage, an English humanitarian organization in Rio de Janeiro asks Dr. Lund to report on the condition of the slaves. Now he does not object to dealing with politics, for this has nothing to do with the Emperor abdicating mass rule in the cities, estates being burned down, despotic executions, and other such events in Europe which, as he increasingly agrees with Brandt, does not exactly seem to be the most desirable place to live.

Dr. Lund is asked to answer seventeen detailed questions and is pleased to take pen in hand again. He writes to the director of the organization: *that* the slaves work from sunrise to sundown, often longer; *that* their food consists solely of vegetables and fruit: rice, beans, maize, manioc roots, sweet potatoes, cabbage, bananas, and oranges served three times daily and seasoned with salt only; *that* the slave owner furnishes them only with work clothes, shirts, and canvas trousers, whereas they must sew their own Sunday clothes; *that* their religious upbringing and education consists only of learning prayers by rote and imitating meaningless ceremonies; *that* they are punished chiefly by whipping, although certain lenient laws do exist to protect them from the worst cruelty; *that* they have fewer children than freed slaves and whites; *that* they treat their children with great tenderness; *that* they have far more diseases than whites; *that* their diseases are mainly *sarna*, smallpox, scarlet fever, measles, and dysentery; *that* female slaves are relieved when their children die so they will not have to grow up in slavery, and that this is perfectly understandable in view of the hopeless conditions of the slaves; *that* most Brazilians would like slavery abolished but fear the national economy would collapse without it; *that* the slave trade will continue until an alternative to this evil is found; *that* most of the freed slaves are not good workers; *that* they are very poor but do not worry about the morrow; *that* freed slaves can afford no better clothing than the slaves; and finally, *that* the slaves at the English-owned goldmine of Morro Velho are treated more kindly than those at the Brazilian-owned goldmines.

For some reason, the leader of the humanitarian organization had asked Dr. Lund, in a personal postscript, about the emetic Ipecacuanha. Dr. Lund is able to inform him that it consists of the plant *Cephalis ipecacuanha*, which grows in the jungles, with the addition or substitution of campo plants such as *Polygala poyaya*, *Jonidium ipecacuanha*, and *Ricardonia alba*, *rosa* and *scabra*.

Dr. Lund gardens for several hours every morning while Brandt hammers away on a little house built on piles out on the lake. Each plant must be cared for individually, each bush pruned in its own way, and if Dr. Lund accidentally cuts off a live branch or even a green leaf, the plant's pain spreads up through his arms and paralyzes him till the bush begins to breathe again and stretch out to the sun. He rakes the paths scrupulously, careful to let the most crystalline pebbles lie as they please. Then step by step, he hobbles up to the house. Behind a screen green with rambling roses, he undresses slowly for his daily twenty-minute 'air bath'. His skin is cleansed by oxygen, sunshine, and the light breeze enriched by the restorative water of the lake.

He places his spectacles on a stone facing the sun to keep them as warm as when he took them off. Just one degree colder gives him shivers which may confine him to his bed for days. Entering the house, pausing long between each step, he must take new precautions. Twenty-three minutes after the sun has reached its apex and the siesta heat has settled over Lagoa Santa, the house is at last as warm as when he worked in the garden, and he can enter the rooms. Brandt comes up from the lake house and they eat lunch together. Dr. Lund has discovered that it is unhealthy to swallow liquid and listen to words at the same time, so he has forbidden Brandt to speak while he drinks from a glass or takes a cup of tea or of that coffee he loves so much, with generous doses of milk and sugar.

Brandt, now sixty years old, unexpectedly receives a visit from his eldest son, who had been in New York on business for the Bergen commercial firm which he now owns and which is so successful that Dr. Lund will actually be repaid the thousands of species he had once lent to Brandt to get his son started. Tall, flaxen-haired, with a merry contagious laughter, well-dressed without being foppish, athletic, and strong enough to swing his father around four times in the excitement of seeing him again, chattering about everyone and everything, delighted more by the kaleidoscopic street life of Brazil than by its alternately parched or green hell of a landscape, the young Brandt breathes fresh life into the little house in Lagoa Santa. The townspeople are charmed by him and bring him gifts of semi-precious and gold-glittering stones, whittled dolls, soapstone armadillos, and tiny embroidered pouches containing magic powders to safeguard him from evil spirits. After a few weeks, his father, despite his gray tufts of hair and his poor teeth, seems five years younger and even walks jauntily.

The lake house, which the son helps finish in a few weeks, is a wooden structure, a veritable Norwegian Viking house whose roof is embellished with a fire-spewing Viking dragon artfully carved of jacarandá wood, gazing out over the lake toward Serra da Piedade. In this imposing house Brandt has at last fulfilled his dream of having his easel standing amidst a wilderness of paints and brushes through which only the artist can find his way. There is not a bone in sight. Brandt takes great pride in inviting Dr. Lund to lunch, and to heighten the anticipation, he invites him a week in advance to his feast, at which he serves fried fish, mashed sweet potatoes, fragrant herbs, and a bottle of burgundy from the cases his son had brought. Dr. Lund sticks to his porridge, macaroni, bread, eggs and cheese, which are carried down through the palm garden and punted out to the lake house by the new slave bought by Brandt and carefully instructed in how to prepare the Doctor's food.

But the rich smells of Brandt's food enliven Dr. Lund, reminding him of the south of France, and it is only because he does not wish to interrupt Brandt's torrential conversation with his son that, to Brandt's relief, he refuses to drink anything at all, and instead leafs through the books and illustrated journals brought by Brandt's son from Europe and New York, among which he reads about Honoré de Balzac, who in *Guideâne a l'usage des animaux qui veulent parvenir aux honneurs* and elsewhere pokes fun at naturalists. He especially satirizes Baron Cuvier, whom he calls Baron Cer ... Cercuea ... Cer*ceau*, judging by the words which Dr. Lund can barely decipher, despite his strong new spectacles ... *A ... parquer les animaux ... dans ... les ... des ... di ... divisions absolus ...* Yes, Balzac's meaning is clear enough, and Dr. Lund closes the journal again. And smiles anyway. He remains in the lake house an hour longer then he had intended, put in even better spirits because Monsieur Foulon, waving a brand new barometer, appears in the late afternoon sunshine over in the palm garden. He and Brandt now have increasingly cordial relations with the townspeople, who are full of praise for Brandt's lake house, designed so he can roll right from his hammock down into his canoe and glide out onto the lake to draw and paint the watercolors which he has now begun to sell to the fazenda owners. Monsieur Foulon, having been poled out to them by the slave, even promises to hold an exhibition of 'the master's' best paintings and to advertise it in the '*Jornal do Comércio*'.

The son left as quickly as he had come. That whirlwind of nordic summer and enthusiasm has returned to Rio de Janeiro on his way back to the Hardanger Fjord. Once more Dr. Lund confines himself indoors when Brandt is out on the lake, fortunately within hearing distance, should the slave have to call him. Dr. Lund's failing eyesight forces him to hold books and newspapers right up to his eyes. After yet another rainy season he must give up reading, obliging Brandt, who long after his son's departure had been dreaming up all sorts of new projects of starting (a palm oil factory and portable herbariums for Minas Gerais schoolchildren) to read aloud to him for one hour before Dr. Lund's noon nap and again one hour after supper.

The most interesting news, to Dr. Lund, is the struggle against the Pampas Tiger – that monster criminal, that destroyer, that personified terror of humanity, namely the dictator Rosas who has been undermining for years the Brazilian economy by damming the southern rivers, usurping power in Uraguay, Paraguay, and Argentina, and re-creating the Spanish vice-royalty in a grotesque, perverted form, with an army of unshaven, brutish scoundrels. Brazil, ruled for the first time in many years by an effective government which in no time at all has transformed the sluggish deficit of the country into a bustling surplus, has sent forty thousand of General de Lima e Silva's men against the monster. This, the most impressive South American army since the wars of independence, has chased the bandit away, destroyed. Pedro Dinamarques, who had swindled scandalously and fought the other Curvelo fazenda owners, went with his remaining brothers (or cousins) and his slave regiment to serve the Pampas Tiger and can never return to Brazil. Rumor has it that he has fled to England, a broken man, afflicted by *the* disease in its most horrible form . . .

In Copenhagen, the bones are still not on exhibition. But the city ramparts are being demolished and working-class quarters are mushrooming to keep pace with the growth of industry. Perhaps they stretch out to Vibens Hus and Rosenlund? The Schleswig-Holstein problem has still not been solved and a new war is brewing.

In England these days every genteel family owns shell collections, stuffed animals, and scientific reference works. Popular pastimes include gathering shellfish along the coasts and botanical specimens in the dunes. Aquariums are turning up in private homes, and bird cages of all shapes and sizes are selling for high prices. Nearly every child owns a globe.

In Brazil, the slave trade has finally been abolished. People are whispering about fabulous new gold finds, and not many leguas from Lagoa Santa the main vein may have been found. But no water flows at Papa-farinha.

The years pass, and Dr. Lund has *not* become fat.

His house is cluttered with fish of all sizes, lying on brown paper, palm leaves, cardboard scraps, and straw mats. There are fish in sealed jars, ready to be sent by tropa to Rio de Janeiro. Snail shells and reptiles litter the shelves once lined with bones.

Reinhardt is back in Lagoa Santa, still not having succeeded in following in his father's footsteps by becoming director of the Royal Museum of Natural History. This torments him. He feels persecuted in Copenhagen, like a scapegoat for some unknown cause. But he is able to relax in Lagoa Santa. He often refers to Brazil as *terra minha* – although he is forever criticizing its customs. If truth be told, he loves India best – a culture thousands of years old. If only he had been born English, he would carry out his work there. Dr. Lund listens to his complaints. He cannot understand Reinhardt's goal in life. The inner forces pulling Reinhardt down are stronger than his search for the light, and something in his character makes him utterly unsuited for life in the tropics. When the sun sets over the lake, and he comes home laden with fish from the Rio das Velhas, he seems content and says he dreams only of a 'quiet diligent life in the service of science.' But he soon grows restless, and in town he is regarded with suspicion because he flirts with married women in a 'modern' way, as if everything were allowed. And now Christian writes to Dr. Lund that he heard from Henrik Ferdinand who heard from some naturalist who in turn . . . has heard that he, Dr. Lund, has become *fat*. Reinhardt must be the one spreading these falsehoods. Dr. Lund resolves to have a word with Reinhardt when he returns from Rio das Velhas.

A shot rings out, and Reinhardt leaps through the doorway, his whiskers dripping with sweat. He is entangled in fishing line and his arms glisten with fish scales. Terrified, he crouches behind the door of the study. Another shot is fired. The bullet whizzes over the roof. Dr. Lund immediately orders the windows be taken down, for new panes would take months to arrive, despite improved transportation, and he shudders at the thought of a draughty house. Who has started the uprising? Where has it started? Are the liberals up in arms or are the slaves in revolt? Reinhardt is trembling too violently to utter a word, but Dr. Lund is determined to find out. Silence falls and finally, at suppertime, as Brandt is fixing the food because the slave burns the porridge and overcooks the macaroni, Reinhardt admits that . . .

'. . .they were shooting at you alone?,' asks Dr. Lund. In his agitation he swallows his water down in three gulps, forgetting that Reinhardt's answer may upset his digestion.

'Well, yes,' admits Reinhardt, looking away.

'This is a *Catholic* country, Reinhardt!'

'I know, I know!'

'A *South* American country!'

'I know!'

'Reinhardt!'

'Yes?'

'We don't do things like that here!'

'Good Heavens, it was just a glance...'

'I said we don't do things like that here...'

Cholera has broken out only sixty or seventy leguas from Lagoa Santa. It had spread from Rio de Janeiro to Minas Gerais, where it has carried off a third of the population. Hardest hit is the town of Paraíba, where each day eleven or twelve people die, including the tropeiros bringing goods and mail to the heart of the province. Yellow fever has reportedly struck the capital. So Reinhardt has had to prolong his stay for the third month, and Dr. Lund thinks that this may have unbalanced him. Yet hardly a week goes by without his mentioning all the intrigues making life in Copenhagen unbearable for him.

'How wonderful it would be to stay,' he says presently. 'But we'd better start thinking about the trip home. They say the cholera is almost over...'

'*We?*'

'You know how your brothers are longing for you to come back. Their children as well, the grown ones, the young ones are always talking about meeting you at long last. But it certainly would be wonderful to stay.'

'*Your* place is in Copenhagen!' answers Dr. Lund. 'With the bones! And one more thing, Reinhardt...'

'Yes?'

'I have *not* grown fat! Now, would you kindly put the windows back up...?'

Sure enough, the cholera was stopped a few leguas out of Paraíba, and Reinhardt can prepare to leave. In the last weeks he works like a beaver, mentioning neither Copenhagen nor that unfortunate incident. Fish after fish is put into its preserving jar after he has described it and counted its scales. He keeps away from the town, particularly from the venda, where tongues would start wagging if he as much as showed his face. Dr. Lund, taking his weekly stroll through town, is relieved to hear that the Danish fish collector with the impressive mutton-chop whiskers has been forgiven, although by whom is unclear: the heat sometimes causes uncivilized outbursts. Dr. Lund keeps this information to himself, for fear that Reinhardt would simply do something foolish again. Reinhardt, however, plunges into his work. With true objective enthusiasm he describes his favorite new fish, a tiny catfish only a few inches long, a most unusual creature which seems to live in the gill opening of the large catfish. Reinhardt finally hits upon the right name for this tiny fish, the crowning glory of his work in Lagoa Santa – *Stegophilus insidiosus.*

'A curious fellow,' he says in a low voice. 'Represents a *completely* new genus.'

'What's his name? inquires Dr. Lund sharply.

'Who?' Reinhardt, bewildered, glances at Dr. Lund, sitting in the corner of the study with his straw hat perched on his head.

'Trouble always has an address, Reinhardt.'

'Kroeyer . . . the zoologist . . .'

'There's always some spiny rat botching up the works.'

Dr. Lund rises and goes into his bedroom for his afternoon nap.

And several years pass, and now there is real shooting.

The first bullets crash through the windows even before Dr. Lund has time to order the slave to take them down. Yet Lagoa Santa has become one of the most respected towns in Minas Gerais, a fact which Brandt proudly ascribes to the presence of the Doctor. The new arrivals include a French circus rider and his family who with their white horses have toured both Copenhagen and Kristiania and have for the past two weeks been performing in a circus tent. In the midst of a performance the notorious fugitive bandit from Ouro Preto, Joaquim Domingos, nicknamed Veneno, bursts in, blocks the exit, and demands sanctuary in the town for several days. From all over the hinterland, slaves, escaped and freed, come flocking to join him. In no time Veneno has command of most of the interior of the province. His men plunder the gold mines and crush the resisting English to a gory mass in the gigantic water-powered hammering pistons of the goldworks. In Sabará, trading companies are again burnt to the ground, and in Lagoa Santa, Monsieur Foulon is forced to hand over his entire stock of goods, including an aquarium ordered by Dr. Lund, to avoid being skinned alive on the church plaza. Black urubús glide through the sky. The scoundrels even pay a visit to Dr. Lund, and without bothering to knock on the door, they kick it in.

'Your name and purpose here?'

The black man does not answer.

'Your *name*, I said.'

The black man grins.

Dr. Lund blocks his way. For some reason the black man does not push him aside. The neighbors have fled, but Dr. Lund does not intend to leave town, and certainly not to flee, even if he is knocked down. He recalls his father at Sunday dinner in Rosenlund telling about the English cannonball which crashed into his office on Nygade: 'A Lund is *never* afraid!' The black surveys the room. Veneno appears in the doorway. Ignoring Dr. Lund, he motions the black back to him, and soon his men are heard storming one of the finest houses. Screams pierce the air. Furniture comes flying out the windows. By now, most families have sought refuge in the church, where the priest is kneeling by the door, raising a cross up toward heaven.

After some days, the authorities in Ouro Preto send a detachment to Lagoa Santa to restore law and order, but just in front of Dr. Lund's house they are attacked by a group of runaway galley slaves from Bahia who have been ravaging the countryside for years and have now joined up with Veneno. It is the most gruesome sight Dr. Lund has ever seen. Every last soldier is slaughtered. The galley slaves, wearing nothing but grubby canvas trousers and gold rings dangling from their ears, murder the soldiers one and all. They play ball with their heads. The growing heap of corpses sends a horrible stench through the smashed windows into the house.

Dr. Lund cannot take his afternoon nap, cannot eat, and dares not drink, what with all the shouting and shrieking. A bullet slams into the back of the three-toed sloth and Dr. Lund sorrowfully asks Brandt to wipe up the blood stains and put the animal out of its misery as gently as possible out in the garden. The slave has run away, knocking Monsieur Foulon's barometer down from the shelf in his haste so it will never work again. From his headquarters in the grandest house in town, Veneno issues a flood of new orders. He is decked out in a dead soldier's uniform which he has put on backwards and pinned with painted cardboard medals, handles of broken coffee cups, and gold and silver coins. Teeth of butchered government soldiers dangle from strings round his neck. As he rides up and down the town, on a white horse confiscated from the circus rider, he brandishes the imperial banner, bellowing bawdy songs so loud that they echo as far as Serra da Piedade.

The authorities will not stand for it any longer. A new, well-armed, well-organized detachment of soldiers moves in, led by the Ouro Preto chief of police himself. Some days later, Lagoa Santa is as tranquil as ever. The corpses have been buried in the slave cemetery, and Dr. Lund can now stand to eat and drink, although he is so shaken by the cruelty of Man that for days he is unable to utter a word. He very nearly has to stay in bed from morning to evening. And the light bothers him so badly that he fears he will have to use bandages again for the first time in many years.

But at last he manages to block out the sight of the rolling heads and the din in his ears dies down. In letters home he describes the rebellion in measured phrases so as to allay the fears of Henrik Ferdinand and Christian, and to Reinhardt he relates local anecdotes now that town life has returned to normal.

He enjoys writing to Reinhardt, whose letters tell how much he longs for Lagoa Santa as he plods through the melancholy slush of Copenhagen on his way to the museum whose director he realizes he will never become. Perhaps he really did lose his heart here. Perhaps that glance was just a forgivable mistake. Dr. Lund describes to Reinhardt everything he hears and sees on his weekly stroll through the town. There is a band, the first of its kind in Minas Gerais, blaring out with its trumpet, clarinet, trombone, and kettledrum, devised, dressed, drilled, and directed every Sunday afternoon on the church plaza by the flamboyant circus rider, who has settled in town and dreams of making Lagoa Santa the musical center of the province. There is the mystery-monger Ilídio, by turns liberal and conservative, who has left for Sergipe in hopes of furthering his political career. There is Filobertinho, who is suffering from hallucinations of vampires. Pedro, wanted by the authorities, is back in town on bail. Manoel has left for France. The jury in Santa Luzia has acquitted the rascals Bonzo and Neves, but Luís Alves has been sentenced to twenty years in the galley. Manoel Bonito has bought his fazenda. Monsieur Foulon has built a rancho next to his house. José is raising Paraguay tea . . . and a glass piano has come to town together with an extremely affable Senhor Américo Fonseca and his charming little daughter. So everything is going well . . .

Hordes of goldpanners have arrived after stupendous finds of gold, and a diamond of over one hundred carats has been found by an old negro woman in Rio das Velhas. There is still no physician in town, and Dr. Lund writes to Henrik Ferdinand, not without pride, that the sick often come to him for advice – as the blind come to the one-eyed man. As a rule he prescribes ginger tea with honey, a miraculous drink which he recommends to everyone at home, a drink which does not vex the nerves. A new war threatens and the cost of living has soared. In that respect Reinhardt left Brazil in time. In Rio de Janeiro, Riedel is seriously ill, and yellow fever may break out at any time. The stream of German colonists to Petropolis is not enough to improve the national economy. Hopefully, these New Germans are not like Burmeister, who, having long since returned to Europe, has published his *Reise nach Brasilien* with a few paltry pages about his visit in Lagoa Santa. 'Thus,' writes Dr. Lund, 'all that glistens is not gold.' But the study of the other chief part of the world order, morality, is a source of happiness.

A letter from Henrik Ferdinand, delayed by over two years, tells that the youngest Kierkegaard is dead. Those angry articles he had published in 'Faedrelandet' were certainly not to his credit. Too much theology. To Henrik Ferdinand Dr. Lund had earlier lamented that the unmistakable talent revealed by the articles had been led so far astray. 'Perhaps', he had written, 'official duties and the concerns of a married man could have freed him of that unhappy absorption in his own self which, it is to be feared, will ever increase and at last come to bear ruinous consequences for spirit and body.'

Dr. Lund is most unhappy that his prediction has now come true. With a certain tenderness he recalls the young awkward *quodlibetarius* in the red-cabbage-colored coat, with his all-seeing eyes, his wheat-golden hair brushed forward, and his snoutish mouth, galloping toward the university, fleeing from Nytorv and his father's heavy pacing round the dining room table up in the murky flat. It seems like an eternity ago. Dr. Lund would have liked to answer the letter, but now it is too late. And Peter Christian Kierkegaard never writes, for reasons known only to himself. More than oceans separate them.

But, gazing out of the window, Dr. Lund catches sight of the butterfly *Psyché*, and, like that time in Curvelo, it is for a moment borne upward without moving its wings before it flutters up into the sky and the late afternoon sunshine.

Down at the witch doctor's hut at the end of the town the dance is once more beginning.

Tempora mutantur et nos mutamur in illis.

New panes have long since been set in the windows. Dr. Lund can now tolerate being spoken to while he is drinking, and his eyesight has improved slightly. In Copenhagen, the bones have still not been put on exhibition, and on the desk in the study of the little house in Lagoa Santa, Charles Darwin's *On the Origin of the Species by the Means of Natural Selection, or the Preservation of Favored Races in the Struggle for Life* lies open. Brandt has read most of its chapters aloud to him during the rainy season, but he frequently has the urge to read the book himself, although he knows it will strain his eyes. He is more irritated and indignant than sad at the thought of how badly mistaken a highly gifted naturalist can be. But he must admit his admiration for the immense wealth of detail and the keen observations, especially the comment that all domesticated animals have hanging ears because their muscles are so little used.

The irritation which maddens Dr. Lund so much because

250

he cannot rid himself of it, is caused, above all, by a single remark in a chapter on the succession of identical types about the 'wonderful collection of fossil bones made by MM. Lund and Claussen in the caves of Brazil'. Messieurs! Although Darwin has the courtesy to mention him first, he has omitted his title of 'Doctor' thus leading the reader to believe that either both or neither are doctors. Where has Darwin seen the gentlemen's 'wonderful collections' (his!)? When they are still hidden away in the cellars in Copenhagen? At best he may have seen some illustrations in the works of Blainville and in journals, perhaps some duplicate specimens here and there, or even Claussen's unsystematic and unclassified collection, bought by the British Museum. Or had Darwin seen Brandt's illustrations in Dr. Lund's treatises? If so, why does he not mention the treatises? His work pretends to know everything and has become the leading topic of conversation in Europe, having been sold out on the day it was published: admired and attacked, and guilty of dire consequences if taken literally.

A sentence! A parenthesis! A footnote! So that is what he has dwindled to, and to add insult to injury, in the company of Peter Claussen. So that was why Claussen had gone to England, to ingratiate himself with the flat-nosed Charles Darwin in a final attempt to impress the scientific world! It is a poor consolation for Dr. Lund that, according to rumors in Curvelo, *the Dane* has died in a London poorhouse, raving mad. Their names will now be forever linked in a work which may give rise to all sorts of mischief, which perceives struggle and destruction where the Creator's order and harmony ought to prevail, which can unleash a new morality excusing all evil, postulating that the weak exist in order to be crushed by the strong. Doesn't Darwin believe in anything at all? Is he merely a wildly fanciful compiler of facts and specimens? Does he derive aesthetic pleasure from the vision of one vast everlasting bloodbath?

Nonsense, nonsense, and more nonsense. To say that the species have developed 'naturally' (whatever that means) from 'some few original forms' or perhaps from 'one single form'! Hocus pocus - and the fish turns into an amphibian. Abracadabra - and the amphibian crawls onto land and turns into a mammal. Presto – and the mammal turns into a man . . . Is this what Darwin is driving at? That man was not created as the ultimate step in the succession of development but descends (that very word!) from . . . the ape perhaps? It is almost like hearing old Fabricius from Kiel! *Keine Hexerei, nur Behändigkeit!*

What are they saying in France?

All these thoughts weary Dr. Lund, and in the end he tells Brandt to remove Darwin. 'D' – he is put on the shelf just before de Candolle, who is undeniably more worthwhile reading, and just after Cuvier, who is certainly a match for his abundance of detail. Brandt has begun to visit the witch doctor a good deal, and has a somewhat dreamy air, now that he is nearing seventy. He still seems to be getting younger, and Dr. Lund, soon sixty, feels like the elder of the two. What goes on in Brandt's head? And why is Dr. Lund himself growing more and more melancholy? Not because of Darwin. He will be put in his place in time. But Riedel is dead. And von Humboldt, the essence of all that was good in the old German countries. And Henrik Ferdinand's second wife is dead. And Søren Kierkegaard who died much, much too young, haunted by the memory of his father. Dead, they are all dead. And he himself? There are days when he feels the approach of his own death. He closes his little medical practice, leaving the people of Lagoa Santa to nurse their own ills, he lies in bed, and his only wish is to talk with Brandt.

'What do they actually *believe* in, Brandt?'

'Who? I?' answers Brandt in his melodious Norwegian.

'The blacks. I mean the slaves . . .'

Brandt doesn't really know what to say, and Dr. Lund doesn't really know what sort of answer he wants. And the months pass. The sabiá sings in the palm garden. The rain pours down from morning to night, and the air smells sweet. Dr. Lund, in bed with a board on his lap, is writing to the Royal Academy of Science about the tea plant *Neea theifera*, which the Brazilians call *caparrosa-do-campo*. This plant grows profusely in the Lagoa Santa region, and he has always been fond of it. As an infusion of its leaves lacks fragrance, he suggests adding leaves of the vine *Mikania*, and he encloses specimens of both in a little packet. He would be grateful if the Royal Academy of Science could analyze the theine content of the tea. Benzine can be used to extract it.

He writes to Henrik Ferdinand that he will send him his sizeable wood collection together with the Indian bows and arrows he has had for many years. If the family is not interested in keeping these curiosities, they can be donated to the Museum of Ethnology. The bows, made of brejuba palm wood, are tightened by pressing one's feet against them. The long arrows are for shooting big game, large birds, and fish deep in the water, whereas the stumpy ones are for shooting small birds and fish up on the surface of the water. These arrows can hit birds perched high in treetops where a shotgun cannot reach.

In conclusion, Dr. Lund asks his two brothers to send him the following note, signed by them both: 'We, the undersigned, the sole heirs of our brother Peter Wilhelm Lund, hereby pledge that in the event of the death of our said brother, we will pay to P.A. Brandt a life annuity of five hundred rigsdalers in silver, an obligation which we willingly assume in recognition of the faithful service P. A. Brandt has rendered our brother, and which in the event of our deaths will be transferred to our heirs until the death of the aforementioned Herr Brandt.'

He does not mention this note to Brandt, who is now pottering about the fireplace. At suppertime, Dr. Lund is pleased to hear that Brandt's son is doing well. He goes back to bed, and Brandt, sitting in the study, reads poems aloud for him by the light of the oil lamp.

He is especially fond of Bouterweck:

The heart is our true country.
All our strivings are a dream
Wherein the world beyond us disappears.
Within its borders lies reality.

13

Dr. Lund makes sure that Brandt's jars of paint, and his easel are not removed from the lake house. Everything must be as it has always been. But the elegant canoe, painted in a rainbow of colors and furnished with a parasol, cushioned seats, and a little Viking sail in the prow, this canoe he has given to the witch doctor's boys. He often sees them, out on the lake, fishing. They sing and shout, walk on their hands or dive into the water, and when they raise the sail they skim swiftly from one end of the lake to the other. So life goes on very much in Brandt's spirit with his deep faith in the young generation and his lack of fear of dying, despite his timidity, despite the way he had trembled with fear at one thing and another, especially during the two years when he had wandered without his inner compass, starving and feverish, through the swamps and wilds of Brazil, plagued by the icy shadow of a guilty conscience about what he had left behind.

A peaceful smile was on his lips, as if he were completely prepared for the long journey, as if he had just been lifted up and swung round in the air four times by his jubilant son. Brandt lay there, some months after the start of the dry season of 1862, beneath the royal palm in the sunset, in harmony with the nature which in his last months he had depicted in ever more glowing paintings. Dr. Lund knelt awkwardly by his side, tenderly closed Brandt's eyes, and for a long time held his heart hand against his own breast. He had moistened Brandt's lips with a few drops of the orange wine which Brandt had proudly begun to make, a sample bottle of which he held in his hand, no doubt a gift to their neighbor.

The funeral lasted almost all day. The neighbor's slave and his own slave had carried Brandt up to the house and laid him out on his bed and dressed him in his Sunday clothes. The next day he was placed in a coffin lined with royal blue velvet and containing a red pillow edged in white: the Norwegian colors. For two days Dr. Lund had sat by the coffin from morning till evening. Early the third day the coffin was carried out and put on an oxcart. Dr. Lund, leaning on Senhor Fonseca, followed the cart as it slowly set into motion. Senhor Fonseca's little daughter held his hand, and now and then she looked up at him with her dark almond eyes and whispered that she was certain that Brandt, that kind man who had drawn such nice pictures of her, was up in God's heaven. More people joined the procession. When the oxcart reached the hillside with its view out over the endless campos, the place in the red, red soil where Dr. Lund also wishes to be buried, Brandt was given a Christian burial, in accord with the faith of his childhood which he never lost, conducted by Padre Adriano, the third priest in town since Dr. Lund moved here. The coffin was lowered into the earth and covered by a shower of bouquets, picked and tied by all Brandt's friends. Slaves shoveled earth over the coffin. A cross was hammered into the ground, and the chorus of song which arose could be heard over the roofs of the town and out over the lake. Dr. Lund, with Senhor Fonseca's daughter, was the last to leave the grave, and afterward he was invited home by her father. That evening, nearly till midnight, he played Schubert on the glass piano worried at first that he may have forgotten how to play and read music. He had not touched a piano since Italy.

As his fingers slowly got acustomed to the keys, he saw Brandt's smile.

He knows that they will meet again.

In Copenhagen the bones have at long last been put on exhibition, after a rather embarassing controversy in the newspaper 'Faedrelandet'. Dr. Lund is chargrined to see his name the focus of angry attacks and counter-attacks. An anonymous person who has signed his articles 'k' wrote column after column about what a scandal it was that the bone collection had still not been unpacked despite the fact that for the past ten years Reinhardt had been receiving wages as the curator of the collection. Why has he done nothing? Does he not know that Dr. Lund is an internationally-acclaimed name? Does he not know that in Paris and London these collections would be eagerly received and exhibited in the finest showcases? Reinhardt had responded in the same indignant tone that he would not stand for such personal attacks, that there was a reason for everything, and that while 'k' was writing his article the decision to exhibit the collection already *had* been made.

Dr. Lund has no wish to be drawn into the fray, as he makes clear to Reinhardt. At the same time he complains about a newspaper serial depicting his life and scientific acomplishments. Well intended, to be sure. But would Reinhardt please inform the author of the serial that his early fame was not due to having discovered and described 'birds without stomachs'. Such childish misunderstandings would make his name a laughingstock, especially if people think that he and the author are in league together. This in turn might lead people to believe that he is the mysterious 'k', the initial having been arbitrarily chosen from the alphabet. But Dr. Lund must confess that if all the fuss could help 'his children' find their place in the sun, be admired by a constant stream of visitors, be fondled by naturalists who understand their background and their uniqueness, then much progress would have been made.

And he tells more about life in Lagoa Santa, in letters with town maps, drawn by Brandt before he died, with crosses, arrows, and notes showing who lived where and the locations of new houses. Ilídio is back in town after having made a fool of himself in Sergipe. He has hatched up a new political party which he thinks will make Lagoa Santa famous throughout Brazil – the Imperial Democratic Party. He has succeeded so far in enroling three freed slaves as members. Monsieur Foulon has been very unlucky in his transactions with German colonists in Petropolis and now lives solely from raising turnips. The circus rider has bought a circus tent twice as large as the old one and is still conducting the band with gusto. Rita has married Carlos. A new postmaster has taken Bernardo's place. A diamond mine has been found not far from Padre Adriano's fazenda. Manoel Bonito has died. And now Brandt . . .

The lake is becoming choked by vegetation. The remarkably severe dry season, without a sprinkling of rain, not even the *chuva de São João*, has gradually dried up much of the lake. The lake house can be reached on foot now. Fortunately Brandt was spared that sight, and also the news that Wilhelmine in Norway is in dire straits again. Brandt died a happy man in his last years, but Reinhardt must not alarm either the Royal Academy of Science or the family. Dr. Lund is being taken care of by the townspeople, especially by a certain Senhor dos Santos, a mulatto whose little boy possesses quite extraordinary talent and sings like a *Wiener Sängerknabe*. Senhor dos Santos supplies him regularly with food and other necessities; if not he, then Senhor Fonseca; and if not he, then an old acquaintance from Sabará, the Swiss Behrens who is now considering moving into the little house in Lagoa Santa.

But, adds Dr. Lund wearily, if Reinhardt and the Academy of Science know of a talented young student, preferably a botanist who would like to spend a few years in Brazil, then his door – which is a new one made of glass, protected by a screen! – will be open for him. Finally he tells of a new preparation for getting rid of ants which he had read about in *Jornal do Comércio* and which has excellent chances of winning the competition arranged by the Emperor himself in hopes of eliminating Brazil's worst pest. This insecticide consists simply of acetic cupric oxide, verdigris. The ants die after contact with this preparation. The powder is sprinkled in a ring around an anthill and in a semi-circle in front of ant holes in a house. The ants emerge, unsuspecting, fierce, ready to plunge into their daily destruction. Undaunted, they pass through the verdigris and set about their work. But after two days, the scene changes cruelly. Instead of carrying in leaves, sugar crystals, bits of macaroni, and congealed porridge from the cooking pots, they begin to carry out corpses and grains of poison. The sick drag themselves about among their dead and dying fellow soldiers. After another three or four days the first two acts shift to the third and final act, and a deathly silence reigns. Corpses lie everywhere. Curtain.

New scientific expeditions equipped with modern measuring instruments have come to Brazil. The many scientists passing through Lagoa Santa include a well-known entomologist from Berne, a craniometrist from Munich, the brothers Camargo from Lisbon, three English crocodile hunters en route to the Amazon, and an anthropologist from Pamplona who believes the Brazilian Indians to be direct descendents of the Basque sailors who may have come to the New World as early as the seventh century. But most of them must wait in vain down at the venda, for Dr. Lund cannot bear the mental strain of receiving them.

He trusts they can understand this at home.

The botany student Johannes Eugenius Bülow Warming, son of a rural priest from South Jutland, robust and stocky, a graduate of Ribe Cathedral School who since childhood had dreamed of becoming a botanist, has landed in Rio de Janeiro, loaded with instruments, books, herbariums, and – a camera. At Praia dos Mineiros, one of the northernmost quays in the imperial city, he boards the little steamboat Inhumerim. After sailing for several hours, the boat reaches the flat northern coast of the bay and continues straight up the Inhumerim River. Some days later, Warming and the other passengers disembark from the steamboat, which blows three farewell whistles. Now he is truly in Brazil. In the forty years which have passed since Dr. Lund rode from Rio de Janeiro to Fazenda Rosário, the way of traveling is unchanged. Dom Pedro Segundo's realm contains no more than a few railway lines and one single macadam road, twenty-five leguas long.

Unlike Reinhardt, Warming cannot afford to hire his own mules and guides, so he travels with the tropa. He reaches Porto d'Estrela in May 1863. Several tropas are staying at this large rancho. Noisy shouts and yells are heard among the boxes, bales, barrels, and pack saddles strewn everywhere. Fires over which hang pots of beans or coffee kettles blaze here and there. Some blacks are tightening oxhide straps round goods just arrived from Rio de Janeiro. Others are crouching, smithing horseshoe nails on portable anvils. Many are rolling cigarettes; in fact, Warming has never seen a people who smoked so much. From morning to evening he photographs everything, often scaring the negroes badly when the magnesium flare of the camera explodes.

Then the mule train heads for Lagoa Santa. Warming notices each flower, even the tiniest ones which grow in the bark of the trees. He knows that he has come to the right place at the right time of his life, at the age of twenty-two.

258

He is bringing many greetings to Dr. Lund, for whom he hopes he will not have to spend much time reading aloud and about whom he has heard so many queer things. That he does not tolerate being spoken to when drinking. That he sometimes raves and afterwards sits slumped in his favorite chair, not uttering a word, gazing vacantly at the little handful of bones which bear witness to the work of his prime. That if he so much as steps on a drop of water spilled by the slave he will be laid up for days with an attack of arthritis, and that he has the odd notion that one can speak to the flowers if one understands their secret language, an idea which slipped out in a conversation with Reinhardt before Dr. Lund quickly changed the subject.

Warming is eager to give Dr. Lund an album of family photographs, the best pictures of which show Henrik Ferdinand's children by his two marriages. Warming also brings greetings from the elderly bishop of Aalborg, Peter Christian Kierkegaard. Thus, excited about meeting the hermit in Lagoa Santa, clad in his Indian poncho, with his accordian strapped to his back, deep in talk with the tropeiro Manoel de Sanso and proud of being able to understand and entertain him with tales of his Atlantic crossing because he had quickly picked up Portuguese in Rio de Janeiro, he rides his mule up through the Atlantic jungle. He presses on toward Petropolis and thence gradually out into more open terrain dotted by the trees which nourish the three-toed sloth, and the white-leaved cecropias shining through the rest of the tropical profusion. He passes through a vast garden, a desert, a deep valley, and at last the blue-green *campos cerrados* open up for him. Nowhere can he see a trace of man. Silence and emptiness prevail, till suddenly, from behind a ridge, another tropa appears, plodding to the capital with sugar and cotton cloth, whereas his own tropa carries porcelain, stoneware, kitchenware, cloth, and foreign medicine.

Then the red-brown roofs of Lagoa Santa come into view.

Dr. Lund trembles with emotion when he sees the photographs. He takes them out of the album. He sits with them one by one, day after day. He forgets to take his 'airbath', he forgets to take his special precautions in leaving and re-entering the house for visits to 'the room'. His family is with him. Surely photography is one of the greatest inventions of mankind. A face, a soul, is captured on a piece of cardboard simply by pushing a button and releasing a puff of magnesium into the air. Perhaps one day it will even be possible to capture voices? Feature by feature, he recognizes Henrik Ferdinand and Christian, both round-cheeked, gray-haired, and sober-eyed, with waistcoats draped with watchchains, well-tailored jackets – and wrinkles. He finds little Henriette in the mature regal woman looking straight at him, serious, perhaps solitary, and yet in harmony with her innermost nature. Her hair is parted in the middle and drawn tightly into two buns by her ears, and she stands between her cheerful vigorous brothers from Henrik Ferdinand's marriage with Petrea. The squire Wilhelm, the cavalry captain Christian, and the youngest, the Bachelor of Divinity Peter, whose eyes are the clearest and whose smile is the most boyish. And Ferdinand, Ole Henrik, and Troels, the young historian: Henrik Ferdinand's three grown-up sons from his second marriage. And Christian's children, on their way into life, confident of their future and obviously delighted because the little magnesium bomb exploding in front of them is imprinting their features forever on cardboard.

It is overwhelming, all these vivid faces looking out at him, almost *speaking* to him. He is astounded to hear that they are no longer children, especially Henriette who can be heard above them all, asking him to tell of the sloth. And he can still hear her voice in the spacious parlor of the house on Blegdamsvej. Tell me, Uncle Wilhelm! Tell me! Yes, it *is* she! It *is* Henrik Ferdinand! It *is* Christian! It *is* all of them! Even those whom he had only heard of through letters and had pictured quite differently as he rode through the Brazilian interior or returned home from a cave expedition with Brandt. Those who often combine the features of his parents with those of the Kierkegaards. To one, he had given his mother's forehead. To another, he gave Peter Christian's heavy-lidded eyes. But nature can make such astonishing leaps. A nose may appear from three generations back, a pair of eyes may have the same expression as four generations earlier. It is overwhelming.

Dr. Lund paces round and round the study to allow the impressions to sink in, and he refrains from weeping only because of Warming's intent gaze. He pushes all the books on the shelves back to the wall and stands the photographs in front of them, with Henrik Ferdinand and his children from right to left and Christian and his family from left to right. Warming leaps up to help him, but Dr. Lund, aroused, snaps that he can stand up by himself. Then, in a milder tone, he asks the young botanist to play 'La Parisienne' on his accordion. When Warming has set off on his first botanical tour around the lake, Dr. Lund writes to Henrik Ferdinand that he feels a whole new chapter in his life began that late afternoon when the tropeiro Manoel de Sanso knocked on his glass door to announce the arrival of a most talented, most attentive young man, with his magic package containing the album of photographs which at once evoked his dearest memories from home. One tap on the sonorous figure in his heart and the powder arranged itself into the loveliest pattern. Then it occurs to him that he ought to have some proper food in the house. So he sends a slave to fetch a sack of beans, a sack of rice, spices of all sorts, bags of meal, oranges, bananas, and – as long as he can be spared the sight of the yolks being broken – twenty fresh eggs. Along with coffee, José's Paraguay tea, milk, sugar, and a bottle of sugar-cane liquor for Warming.

The next day he introduces Warming to the townspeople. From the venda they go to visit Padre Adriano, who dramatically relates, as he threateningly gestures toward the horizon, how his fazenda had been ravaged by shooting and knife-throwing bandits lured by rumors of a diamond mine. From the priest they stroll to the modest house of the mulatto dos Santos, where the gifted boy, now being tutored by Dr. Lund in writing music and singing from a songbook, receives them with delight. Continuing up the main street, they encounter Ilidio, who instantly tries to enrol Warming in his Imperial Liberal-Democratic People's Party, as he has now named it, and who talks about the great interest his activities have met with everywhere in Brazil except for

Lagoa Santa. Warming smiles, but fends him off, and Dr. Lund is impressed both at his command of Portuguese and at the resoluteness behind his courteous façade. They greet Senhor Fonseca and his daughter. And they greet the new postmaster, and the circus rider, who has ordered a bear cub from St. Petersburg. And they go back through the blacks' quarter at the end of town. There sits the witch doctor in front of his little hut, pulling straws through his old straw hat, ageless as always. Their eyes meet and for a moment Dr. Lund is at a loss as to how to present Warming to him. They each nod, and the Danes start back to the house.

Dr. Lund has not felt so invigorated, so energetic, for years, and this feeling lasts for months. He often sits on a little folding chair by the glass door, studying the photographs which Warming has taken of him and developed. Some are blurred like white gruel, others have coal-black shadows or lines crossing his face. But some of the photographs have turned out well. One shows him in profile by a corner of the house gazing out over the palm garden and the lake up to Serra da Piedade, the flower mountain which Warming has already visited and considers to be the most magnificent revelation of his life. Another shows him full face not wearing his straw hat with the floppy brim, a photograph in which as if by magic he again looks as he did in his prime. Before . . .

As he fondles his accordion, Warming dreams about a completely new way of studying botany, for he does not like herbariums which press all the sap out of plants. The house is filled with plants and fresh flowers in all sorts of vases, cups, buckets, and basins. It is a fragrant orgy of color which the house has never before known. In Warming's opinion, and he excuses himself for not being able to express it more clearly, the new botany ought not content itself with merely classifying and describing a plant in isolation from its surroundings. The divine fitness of a plant, developed in its struggle to survive, is comprehensible only through knowledge of the soil, neighboring plants, bees, and other insects with which it has contact, climate, shade and sun and the night dew. It must be seen in its *niche*, a term which Warming is a bit hesitant to use in a strictly scientific context. *The great chain of being* which the Thomists had so long ago mentioned: if a single link in the chain is lost or forgotten, then the vision of the sum total of fitness is destroyed or blurred.

Dr. Lund is happy that Warming has the courage and conviction – particularly in this age – to use the word divine. But he is critical of the term fitness, developed from the 'struggle to survive'. It smacks a bit too much of the brutal doctrine of arbitrary descent introduced by the *godem*. Yet it may not be Darwin who has influenced Warming, though one day out in the garden, before Dr. Lund could interrupt him, he had declared his interest in Darwin's work. It may be . . . 'Lamarck?' asks Dr. Lund abruptly, with an uncanny instinct.

Warming nods.

'Lamarck!' he answers, blushing slightly, as if the very name were shameful.

'A strange fate,' says Dr. Lund, indicating that on this topic Warming is allowed to speak. Dr. Lund has never studied Lamarck's *Zoological Philosophy*, attacked in the most disparaging way by Cuvier, who nevertheless composed a most stirring eulogy about his rival when he died. Can acquired characteristics be passed down? Has the giraffe developed its long neck because for thousands of years it longed to eat from the treetops? The thought is far more beautiful than the Englishman's idea of the world as an evolutionary bloodbath, and Lamarck's unhappy fate resembles that of many other great unappreciated naturalists and artists. But before Warming has a chance to open up and tell about his secret hero, Dr. Lund has told the strange story of the poor carpenter's son from Ouro Preto who during the Baroque period in Congonhas carved the twelve Hebrew prophets on the façade of the basilica Bom Jesus de Matosinhas. First acclaimed, later an outcast when stricken with leprosy so that he was forced to carve his statues at night by torchlight, isolated from the world, with his hammer and his chisel tied tightly to his aching hands, Antonio Francisco Lisboa, popularly called Aleijadinho, created his masterpieces despite his cruel fate.

'Character, my young friend! Character means everything!

To those who say "descent" or "evolution" or "fitness", I say . . . *character!* Just look at Aleijadinho's Hebrew prophets!'

And Dr. Lund tells about the Jews, whom he has admired ever since reading Lessing and Baggesen. Forever persecuted, condemned, forced to wander, subject to the 'law of mutability', 'the struggle for survival', and yet in all respects the same people down through history. Has the Jew become German by living in Germany? When he came to Denmark, did he acquire blue eyes, apple cheeks, and wheaten hair? And even if ten generations should pass, would he turn into a giraffe if he were suddenly forced to live on the savannahs of Africa? No. More than any other living creature, the Jews, God's chosen people and God's chastised people, His favored and the victims of His wrath, are proof of the immutability of species and proof of God-created character:

'Observe the Jew's face, Warming! Does he look like a descendent of the – *perch?*' concludes Dr. Lund. Ordering the slaves to close the shutters for the night, he puts out his cigar, a new, very mild brand which Warming had brought from Rio de Janeiro, and leaves the tropical night to his hard-working guest. But Dr. Lund has a hard time falling asleep. He hears the incessant cries of the geckos. So many thoughts are germinating within him, growing and unfolding after a year of reading nothing, thinking about nothing, sick with the loss of Brandt. Now too the photographs on the shelves are speaking to him. They call forth one memory after another until at last, in the early morning hours, as the sabiá begins to chirp and Warming, in Brandt's old bed, rolls over, Dr. Lund falls asleep to the laughter from a crowd of dancing masked guests reflected in Venetian mirrors as she – the girl, Sarah – sits beside him, telling him what the word *Schekhina* means in the language of her people.

Everything we come from.

Everything we shall return to.

The rainy season is soon over.

Dr. Lund is eager to send the little son of the mulatto dos Santos back to Denmark with Warming. Dr. Lund has decided to spend some of his money on educating this child of nature whose talents are unfolding more each day. It would be a sin not to do anything for such a gifted boy. Dr. Lund writes to Henrik Ferdinand, asking him to suggest a place for Nereo to live and the best school for him (Borgerdydens, most likely?) and whether there would be a risk of his being teased by the Danish boys for his dark skin? Nereo can sing the Danish national anthem 'King Christian' and the soldiers' song '*Den Gang Jeg Drog Afsted*' almost perfectly. He can speak a little Danish and French after weekly one-hour lessons in each language at Dr. Lund's house. He is knowledgeable about plants and flowers, having accompanied Warming on expeditions over the campos and even up to the peak of Serra da Piedade, where he sang Gregorian chants which floated out over the landscape. The boy has bought a guitar with money from Dr. Lund, and sometimes he and Warming play duets. Dr. Lund only wishes that he himself could accompany Nereo on the glass piano.

However, he is helping to name Warming's plants, and he is pleased to discover that he still knows his Latin. Yellow-blossomed, twining, climbing campo plants with all sorts of biological peculiarities. Primary and secondary forms of vegetation. Bushes, shrubs, and roots. Thistles, orchids, pea flowers. He recognizes most of the plants and becomes acquainted with a few new ones, many of them planted in a generous corner of the palm garden which he has given to Warming.

Not the tiniest flower can be forgotten, nor the ugliest thistle. Not even the thorny twigs from the Tormented Forest must be omitted from the work which Warming hopes to write some day, the complete description of the flora of Lagoa Santa in which each plant, each flower, is placed in its unique niche. Is the nature of the tropics as unsociable as European scholars often claim, after having studied only herbariums in museums? Can what they say be true? Warming thinks not. Every single living plant is dependent upon the others. Not a bush can be isolated, not even the strange eriocaulácea with its long-scaped inflorescence up to three feet high, crimson red.

'*Praepalanthus claussenianus!*' suggests Dr. Lund.

Warming smiles. He seems to know whom Dr. Lund

has in mind, and the name is approved.

For the third time Dr. Lund sees the butterfly *Psyché* hang immobile in a sunbeam, this time in front of the photograph of Henrik Ferdinand's youngest son Peter. The butterfly flutters out of the window and into the sky. Several months later Dr. Lund receives a letter telling how Peter, mortally wounded in the retreat from Als, has now been buried in Ulkebøl cemetery, beneath the epitaph which his comrades had written on his tombstone: 'Faithful unto death'. Peter had enlisted as a volunteer, and to the very last he had preserved his merry spirit. He had been about to embark upon his career, teaching at the university the language he loved best – Hebrew.

'*And so peace/Peace be with your dust and stars in your memory*' are the closing words of the commemorative poem for Peter Lund which accompanies the letter from his father to his uncle in Brazil. Dr. Lund places the poem in front of the photograph, and for several months he speaks but little to Warming. He had known that an accursed war would come as a result of the national liberal fantasists' abortive policies, but that it should carry off young Peter is more than he can bear. Again he is overcome by weariness. Again he collapses, unable to understand why he is still alive, here among Warming's flowers and herbariums, alive in an age becoming more and more cruel, just as the New German, Burmeister, had predicted with relish, an age to which he does not belong. Peter's clear eyes! His boyish smile! Why Peter?

There are questions which must remain unanswered. When in the evening, in a new rainy season, Warming plays his accordion while Nereo becomes better at playing his guitar, a joy slowly wells up again in Dr. Lund, joy because of all those who are still alive, especially Henriette – and Troels, who has now begun to write to him and has revealed that he had been the mysterious 'k', joy because of Warming's skill and joy because of the life which for the past two years has filled his house. Dr. Lund can sit for hours in his folding chair in the front garden, greeting passersby, offering good advice about herbal tea for the sick; or by the corner of the house, lost in the view over the campos from which smoke rises incessantly, like an exclamation mark, like a question mark.

It is as if he can smell all the flowers on the peak of Serra da Piedade – as if he can hear them whispering softly to one another. And time passes. Soon Warming must set off for home, although he keeps postponing his departure, first with one excuse, then another. Dr. Lund would like nothing better than to have him stay, but Warming has a great future as a scientist, and only in Europe can he develop his new botany, the general idea of which Dr. Lund now understands. Niche! Oecological! Not bad, those terms! But if Warming prolongs his stay with yet another dry season and yet another rainy season, the tropics will claim him forever. So Dr. Lund encourages Warming to leave as soon as the rainy season of 1866 is over – and to take Nereo with him.

But suddenly Nereo does not want to go. He cries for days as the departure approaches. His father has packed all his belongings, putting his guitar in a case which can protect it from even the roughest handling. For weeks Nereo had chattered about the country far to the north where he was now going to see snow and millions of migratory birds, boys and girls with sky-blue eyes, and lots of green islands to which he would sail in a Viking ship when the big icebergs had melted. Now he cringes behind his father, stays for hours in the canoe out on the lake, and once even howled in anguish when his father took him on his lap and told him of the beauty of the country from which the Doctor came.

Warming must return to Rio de Janeiro alone with the tropeiro Manoel de Sanso. Warming is more convinced than ever of the rightness of his theory that all things must be seen in their proper context and that no link can be isolated from the chain. As a parting gift, Dr. Lund gave him a pouch of his own favorite tea, his old herbariums, his closely-written, faded travel diary, and a copy of the Brazilian poem which he loves most, *Cancão do Exílio*, written in exile by Gonçalves Dias. Its closing lines especially touch his heart:

Permit me not to die
without returning there
to taste the beauties
I have not found here,

to glimpse the palms
once more from afar
where the sabiá *sings,*

And the years go by.

A son-in-law of the Emperor, Duke August of Saxony Coburg-Gotha and his brother Philip visit Lagoa Santa with a photographer. They take pictures of Dr. Lund's house, of the lake house, of the palm garden, and of the town. Dr. Lund himself refuses to pose with the last of the bones in his lap for the distinguished guests, and he must unfortunately declare himself unable to help them find the entrance to the Maquiné cave, even if he were to be carried there in the most luxurious sedan-chair. The group had come at the request of Dom Pedro Segundo himself, and via his son-in-law the Emperor informs Dr. Lund that he will have all his treatises translated and printed on fine paper if Dr. Lund would please send him copies. Duke August also hints that the Emperor is considering presenting the Doctor with the highest Brazilian order, but nothing could interest Dr. Lund less than any formal mark of honor. His Danish chivalric cross is still lying in the drawer of the consul-general in Rio de Janeiro, and the cross of the Commander of the Order of Danneborg will also end up there if he is awarded it – as Henrik Ferdinand has 'heard a little bird tell'.

Duke August and Prince Philip depart with copies of the treatises, and soon reach Curvelo, where they cannot find the entrance to the Maquiné cave, not even either with the help of Peter Claussen's surviving slaves or of his swarm of illegitimate children, mulatto girls and boys with frizzy wheaten hair. This news relieves Dr. Lund. He smiles with satisfaction as Senhor Fonseca tells how the duke had ordered his ducal tent erected somewhere near the cave, summoned all the local inhabitants and in vain promised a generous reward to the first person to find the entrance by the big telltale eriodendron. But either trees have grown up around it, or rain has washed it away, or it has been hidden by vines. The duke did not find what he so zealously sought and soon he is back in Rio de Janeiro and again, from Curvelo to Lagoa Santa, rumors fly about the precious treasure which when pulverized and sniffed by moonlight could grant Dom Pedro everlasting life.

In Lagoa Santa great changes have occurred. Newcomers have moved in, others have moved away. There is talk about a school opening in town and much speculation as to whether a good teacher can be found so far out in the country. Monsieur Foulon is dead. Rita has left Carlos. The postmaster's wife has given birth to twins, and tongues are wagging because one child is as black as the other is white. New methods of cultivation are yielding a double coffee harvest for fazenda owners, but the earth has begun to erode dangerously. Sugar-cane liquor is being distilled more purely, and Dr. Lund has sold his gold mine to an English immigrant who intends to use steam machines to get the pistons working.

Many of the houses in town now boast real glass panes, but not even the miraculous new powder has been able to exterminate the ants. If they die in one anthill, they come to life in an adjacent one. The most genteel families have acquired cameras, aviaries in the garden and aquariums in the parlor. In the venda the new proprietor advertises that he can develop and copy photographs perfectly. Ilídio now accuses everyone he meets of conspiring against him, and even the renowned explorer Richard Burton who had come to town to meet Dr. Lund was shaken roughly by the arm and forced on the spot to give his opinion for or against the Imperial National-Liberal Unity Party, as it is now called. Richard Burton had to leave without having met Dr. Lund because the Swiss, Behrens, who now lives in the little house with the palm garden, informed him that Dr. Lund had long been ill and that he cannot tolerate excitement. What Behrens does not realize is that Dr. Lund is silently waging a nerveracking battle not to get upset – about Behrens.

At first, their relations were cordial. Behrens was overjoyed to get away from Sabará. For here in Lagoa Santa he could finally write his novel about a colonist from Central Europe who goes to pieces in the suffocating vine-choked tropical forest, forgets Mozart, forgets Goethe, at last takes his own life, and is then devoured by the pig mites which can make a rat bite off its own tail when they have lodged themselves on it. A publisher in Berne specializing in exotic stories has promised to publish Behrens' book, and at first, for most of the day, except when fixing food for Dr. Lund, Behrens had worked in Brandt's old room. But after three months he had begun to turn into the person who haunted his mind and his pen. Empty bottles stood on his night table, ink-spattered paper was strewn everywhere, he cursed Brazil in long incoherent tirades, and he grew more and more unshaven, unwashed, and drunk.

Afterwards, he tidied everything up and became his old self again, but after three months during which Dr. Lund managed to forget the unpleasant episode, it happened again – only worse. Like a simmering cauldron of self-reproach for having wasted his life in Brazil, having been enticed here by lies about easily-won money, Behrens either splutters in tearful self-pity or hurls such vicious curses against the world that the slave hides himself in his cottage. Dr. Lund, in bed or in the garden raking or planting or taking his 'airbath' – once more a necessary part of his daily rhythm, is bombarded by the abusive words of the Swiss. They make his body ache, they lodge themselves as migraines or stomach cramps or pains in his esophagus. Behrens has now ripped to shreds everything he has written. He kicks the furniture, throws himself, drooling onto the floor, or dashes down to the venda and back with new bottles under his arm. He raves on about having found 'the method', the best, the fastest, better than being consumed from within by pig mites or strangled by vines. A bottle of water, right? A handful of acetic cupric oxide, *nicht wahr?* And then a plunge into the lake. No more Behrens. The earth freed of one more parasite, one more failure. Brazil. *Scheisse!*

Long after Dr. Lund had dismissed Behrens as his companion, he lies in bed without getting up. He cannot eat, cannot drink. He feels that the house has begun to sink into a morass of garbage, seething from centuries of putrefication. The house is permeated with the stench of alcohol and vomit. Behrens' spirit still seems to haunt the rooms even after his body has moved up to the lodging house, and it brings back all the memories which Dr. Lund thought he had managed to forget – memories about the time after *it* had happened, that which he will never find words to describe. Again he rides out over the campos though he is still lying here, empty, empty, gazing up at the geckos. One moment the world is white, the next, black. There are no colors anywhere, yet his shadow is everywhere, even where it is utterly dark. The shadow spreads over the walls when he sits up in bed, as if it would nail him to the spot. He turns, and now the shadow lies across the floor, from the bed all the way over to the door of the study with the photographs which he shall never see again, never speak with again.

He stands up, but scarcely have his feet touched the floor before he is paralyzed, just as that time in Lapa da Cerca Grande. The slave entering with the food sets the pots down on the floor in fright and disappears. He cannot even reach the food. The shadow has caught him. He falls. For four days he lies unconscious on the floor until, suddenly opening his eyes, he glimpses her almond eyes in the dusk. He tries to reach out for her:

'Koblenz! Koblenz!' he murmurs.

'But Dr. Lund! Dr. *Lund!*' he hears presently, the voice of Senhor Fonseca, who with his daughter has come to see how he is. She is now seventeen, and she smiles at him. They visit him every day during the rainy season, no matter how much it pours, and sometimes her hair clings to her cheeks.

No more does it stink of liquor and rottenness in the house, and with Senhor Fonseca's daughter holding his hand he is able to shuffle into the study to look at the photographs.

One day as he thinks of her, her fragrance, her eyes, her rain-wet hair, grateful that he does not have to ride restlessly out over the highland for a second time, he musters his courage and asks the little *banda* to come to his garden early the next morning, before the sun rises. Suddenly he dares do what he had not dared when Warming was here and certainly not when Reinhardt was his guest. For the latter had almost giggled outright when Dr. Lund had mentioned this idea. For years he has been thinking of this, especially while planting. He knows that he cannot be mistaken. The banda comes, three caboclos with a marimba, a viola, and a wooden flute. He seats himself on his folding chair by Monsieur Foulon's roses from Nova Friburgo. It happens just as he had hoped. When the banda begins to play the roses open up. They understand him. And the three caboclos do not laugh at him.

The sun has risen.

14

Twice a week he teaches natural history and geography to the children of Lagoa Santa. Sometimes he also tells them about art and poetry, from the time the first person made paintings in caves to Aleijadinho's statues in Ouro Preto and Congonhas, from the blind Homer in ancient Greece who sent Odysseus out on his perilous voyage, to Gonçalves Dias who can make the sabiá sing like no other bird.

He is accompanied to the school, which he supports with a regular sum, by Nereo Cecilio dos Santos, whom he has adopted as his legal son. Nereo is a young man in his early twenties. By now he writes French, reads Danish, and masters his own language so fluently that he is able to help the townspeople write letters. In school, two small rooms in what was once the miserable lodging house, Nereo sometimes teaches Portuguese and arithmetic. But the children prefer the old Doctor who many many years ago came riding to town, bought a house, fought with the Evil Man from Curvelo over the secret treasure which moves from cave to cave, and let it lie when he finally found it because the thunder of the mountain told him that powdered snakeskin inhaled by moonlight demanded a fearsome price in exchange for providing eternal life. Afterwards, when the Evil Man had departed and was frozen to ice in the cold lands, the Doctor sat down in his garden and found out how to speak with the flowers. Each flower must be spoken to in a certain way. To the rose, the words must be hummed. To the purple creeper on the wall, one must whistle after every fourth word. To the thistles, one must growl very softly. All the flowers unfold when the Doctor wishes them to. But he does not teach this in school. This is his secret.

There he sits in a corner of the classroom, wearing his straw hat and the gold-rimmed spectacles which enable him to dimly make out faces, although many years earlier he had become nearly blind in the deepest of all the caves. He tells the children about the interior of the Earth, where a fire burns because once the Earth was a flying star and the present did not exist. A multitude of strange animals have lived on the Earth. Before them it was empty and deserted. Uninhabited because it was uninhabitable. *'Tell us! Tell us!'* And he tells them about the time when there were earthquakes and melting masses of earth and stone and lava cracked the Earth in a thousand places, lifted and shifted and transformed it. Crash! Land became sea and sea became land when the young Earth, like a molten mass, enveloped in steam as from millions of pots of boiling beans, moved through the immensity of space. And this fluid mass became a ball, which was most rounded at the Equator and in Brazil, whereas it got squashed at both poles, where the seals and penguins live. And then he tells about the life which arose when the ball was hardened and now only revolved about itself and God saw how lovely it was and said, 'Let there be light! Let there be life! Let there be joy!' And all the animals came forth; the racoon and the sloth which at first was so enormous that it could crawl over the roofs of Lagoa Santa. The tiger which once had fangs as long as sabers. And the hummingbirds which the old troll deep in the virgin forest says can make orchids give birth to small men, small good spirits that watch over every single sleeping child.

'Tell more! Tell more!' And he tells about the cold countries, where there is snow most of the year so that you can see all the animals' footprints, the bear's and the deer's, the wolf's and the tiniest bird's step, step, step. There you can track them across the fields, down into valleys, into forests and up to their nests and caves where some of them lie down to sleep till summer comes. You can even pat the bear on its belly while it sleeps, as long as you have some honey to rub on its nose. And he tells about Denmark and the town where he had been a little boy and what it is like to be a boy or girl in a city where the snow falls over the roofs like blue-white wads melting against the panes and turning into drops of water playing tag with one another. Ringing bells are heard from wheel-less wagons pulled through streets by horses whose breath comes like cold steam out of their snorting nostrils. And he points to Denmark on the globe

which has now been brought by tropa from Rio de Janeiro and which he has donated to the school. The globe stands just beside his chair, and none of the children can understand that Brazil is two hundred times larger than tiny Denmark.

And the old man stands up and hobbles slowly back to his house and sits on the folding chair, waiting for Nereo to come back from visiting his sick father or from the lake, where he is bracing the little house with new posts.

The lake house must remain as when Brandt lived.

'Did you say *damn?*'

'Yes, the Devil take me if I didn't!' answers Dr. Lund.

'I didn't think you swore!'

'Yes, the Devil take me!' Dr. Lund bounces gleefully in his chair on the little porch which he has added on to the study. Here he can be both indoors and outdoors at the same time. Once more he has told the story of how he lay down to sleep in the venda and *the Dane* stepped inside, filling the room with his presence as he poured out a glass for Riedel and said that luckily no one in this wilderness understood his mother tongue, whereupon he, Dr. Lund, quietly propped himself up on one elbow, placed his straw hat on his head, cleared his throat, caught the stranger's eye, and commented dryly, 'Don't be so damn sure of that!'

Willum de Roepstorff, a young Danish dentist who had come to town hoping to open a practice but now dreaming of becoming a palm-oil manufacturer after having discovered how indifferent Brazilians in the interior of Minas Gerais are about oral hygiene, seems to remember that the last time the Doctor had told the story, that little 'damn' was not mentioned. But the Devil take Dr. Lund if it wasn't. He is not one to embroider on his experiences. He knows better than anyone else what has happened in his life, and every glass in the venda, every bottle, every sack of coffee, and every single bunch of sugar-cane he remembers as if it were only yesterday, *damn it all.* But aside from Roepstorff's desire to instruct him, especially in matters of religion, this dentist – who has agreed to be his part-time secretary and is about to move into the house across the way with his Brazilian wife in hopes of soon getting underway with the manufacture of palm oil – is a sympathetic person whom Dr. Lund thanks Providence for having met in his advanced age. However, their first exchange of remarks was:

'Did you say *dentist*, Herr Roepstorff?'

'Yes.'

'Then you've come thirty years too late!'

Dr. Lund has re-arranged his daily schedule but he does the same things as before. He no longer minds if one raises one's voice when speaking with him. But he still cannot bear the slightest touch, and therefore he refuses to shake hands, giving the excuse that he has eczema up to his elbows. He wakes up every morning between five-thirty and six and drinks a cup of milk flavored with a dash of coffee. At nine o'clock on the dot he eats breakfast: a large bowl of cream and very strong coffee – so strong and so much that it is talked about in town. They say the Doctor is drinking himself to a heart sickness and that for hours afterward his face is coppery red.

For an hour and a half, he reads with a magnifying glass or else is read aloud to by Nereo, to whom he has begun to teach Latin. There are mostly letters and scientific treatises sent to him by Reinhardt, who apparently has managed to find consolation by describing new fish and – after all these years! – the campo fires in Minas Gerais in a way which Dr. Lund does not agree with but which he respects nevertheless. He hears from Warming only once a year. From what he understands, Warming has now gone to Uppsala to carry on his career after having fallen out with his colleagues in Copenhagen, who seem to have become even more petty, although the town is now acquiring the status of a major city and there is talk of a new sort of 'naturalist' literature.

At ten-thirty he eats his lunch, just a few bites of salad or beans. After lunch he can neither read nor write. Not until evening does he wake up and drink a glass of lemonade or a cup of tea and devote himself to literature unrelated to science. Word by word he reads the least known poems of Schiller and Goethe until his eyes are strained. Or else he listens to the letters of Peter Christian Kierkegaard read aloud. He has suddenly resumed contact and has the notion of converting Dr. Lund to the fashionable liberal Christian doctrine in Denmark called 'Grundtvigianism'. Meanwhile he describes with grief his son Poul Egede Pascal's violent attack of melancholy which makes him revile the family, the Church, life – everything. That theology! That family! Will the curse never cease?

Dr. Lund responds in a letter which takes over fourteen days to write. He still refuses to divide God into three parts, still insists that the first article of faith is more than enough for him, that Christ was unique for the very fact that he was a *person*, and that he has always nurtured a 'childish' but invincible faith in Providence, in the Christian sense, which has always stood by him. He will leave it at that. There lies his Rubicon, and on the other side of the river he sees Christianity shattered into countless fractions. Instead of the clear light of learning, the murkiness of mysticism. Instead of the spirit of love, that of hatred and intolerance. And as he writes – now with a generous scrawl over a few shaky lines per page whereas as a youth he could write so minutely that each page could contain a whole treatise – he again recalls Copenhagen and the everlasting discussions with Peter Christian whose eyes always gazed far into the distance, where there was, perhaps, a door leading to eternal peace. Never could he see a flower by the wayside, not even an imaginary flower, without recalling the magnificent hymn *Pangue, Lingua* – 'Speak, Tongue!' – which he, Dr. Lund, always carries with him, and which he now sends, in a copy written out by Nereo, to his old friend, the disputant devil.

Rubicon! No, Dr. Lund will not cross it. And yet he is tempted for the first time in his life to participate in such a struggle when the Church, abetted by the government in Rio de Janeiro, launches a fierce campaign against the Freemasons. Now, why shouldn't *they* be allowed to exist? What harm do they do? What wrong is there in letting intelligent people form their own society, regardless of national boundaries, to support one another on life's arduous path? Is helpfulness now prohibited? Burmeister also had a grudge against these freethinkers, although for entirely different reasons. When Dr. Lund reads that the Church has sharpened its attack against the Freemasons, in the name of orthodoxy, he decides once and for all that he will not allow Padre Wellington, the fourth priest in his time, to give him a Christian funeral. He wishes to belong to nature and nature alone, as he writes in his will. Here he also bequeaths his house and possessions to Nereo, and arranges that from his capital, which is not inconsiderable, Nereo shall be paid a lifetime annuity which will later be paid to his children, should he establish a family. In a letter to be opened by Nereo after Dr. Lund's death, he describes how he wishes his funeral to be.

'Are you sure of what you are doing?' asks Roepstorff.

'Don't try to correct me!' answers Dr. Lund, somewhat irritated at Roepstorff for having let himself be rushed into conversion to Catholicism so that he could get married. When Dr. Lund sits in front of his house, he thinks of everything other than words. He forgets what he had written home and who had written to him. Again he feels as if he were split in two, but now without the pain he felt that time when for eternities he had ridden the highland on the mule which took him from nowhere to nowhere, and he saw without seeing and heard without hearing. He stands up although he is still sitting, cautiously pushes open the gate, and goes into town, seeing all and hearing all. The plants round the church wall, the stones, the bushes, the shrubs, the snakes in the holes in the path down to the lake. He is everywhere at once, and he has no desire to give things names. Everything speaks. The flowers unfold when he looks at them, and the ants cannot kill them. People pass by, most of them blacks, caboclos, and sertanejos, with ragged straw hats pulled down over their foreheads, in shabby canvas trousers, leading mules loaded with sugarcanes. He is on his way out over the campos cerrados. He sees the palms in the valleys and he sleeps beneath them, and even the Caipor does not harm him when he has discovered its tracks which face both ways. The sun rises, the rain pours down, and from somewhere a whistling is heard. There are children playing round their mothers' skirts. Even though they have no teeth, they smile at him and ask him to show them the animals' footprints leading to the nests and caves where they sleep away the rainy season and do no harm if one tickles them on the nose with a flower. Then he hears music and he is back in town. He enters town at the foot of the hill and slowly goes by the witch doctor's little hut with all the ox skulls which the blacks dance around, going into trances one after the other and driving the evil spirits from their bodies. The witch doctor still says nothing, but their eyes meet. They nod to one another. The witch doctor does not mind him standing there, watching, and he stays till the sun rises and the blacks return to their huts. With blissful empty eyes, they whisper now and then a last incantation in a language which he does not understand, words from the heart of Africa where the last primeval monsters live in hidden fern forests. Then he continues up the road, and the sun slowly dries the red kneaded clay into hard steps in front of his feet. He comes up to his house, and now all the flowers in the garden have opened up. The roses. The twining plants. The thistles. And rainy season follows dry season and a new dry season comes after the rainy season. Sometimes the night frost covers all the plants with a delicate layer of crystal-clear sugar which quickly turns into a necklace of dew. Can the stones also speak? They glow, each with its own color, from Lagoa Santa to the primeval forest outside Rio de Janeiro. The crustacea draw their glowing tracks in the sea. He sees them, one by one. And he gets up to the house, sits down, and no longer waits for anyone or anything while now the sun hangs vertically above the red-brown roofs of the town. Geckos hurry past his feet and church bells chime Ave Maria. It is growing late. A breeze comes up from the lake, and he can hear the rushes rustling and the rats scurrying among them. It must be the witch doctor's boys whose shouts are heard from out on the lake where they are diving into the water from Brandt's canoe. He hears the wind whip the sail.

'*A vida real não existe . . .*'

'Whatever are you *saying*, Dr. Lund?' Roepstorff has come across the road.

'*Soli Deo gloria!*'

'Good heavens, Dr. Lund!'

That evening he has the urge to tell Roepstorff about how he had once walked along Vesterbro and had seen God's glowing word in the sky. Just as he is about to reveal what it said, he realizes that Roepstorff would not believe him, would laugh at him just as passerbys would have laughed if he had not hastily risen to his feet again after kneeling in the mud, exclaiming, 'Glory to God alone.'

Henrik Ferdinand and Christian have both died, in the same year in fact. But Dr. Lund knows it was the will of God, and each died peacefully in his sleep after a long and faithful life. And the children are well. Dr. Lund likes to receive letters from Troels especially. Troels is now making a name for himself as a historian, a different sort of vocation, rather more 'straight' as the *godems* say, than studying spiritual categories and that subject which had infected Peter Christian in Germany . . . *Hermeneutics*. Troels describes his projects in detail, he too is fascinated by the thought that a link cannot be isolated from the chain, and that the smallest detail is as important as the greatest event in the history of a nation. Behrens is also dead. Dr. Lund has not the heart to deny him his last wish, to be buried beside Brandt. In his last years he had regularly visited the little house in Lagoa Santa, where he had once caused so much havoc. According to his own account his dreadful novel was progressing and he had more or less managed to tame those inner demons which had driven him to the bottle. Dr. Lund did not attend his funeral. For he now stays indoors all the time, moving at the very most from his bed to the porch, where a profusion of plants, given him by Senhor Fonseca's daughter before she left for the girls' college in Ouro Preto, filters the sunshine into a lively green play of light. But Nereo, who is thinking about getting married, brought a bouquet of the loveliest garden flowers whose composition of colors Dr. Lund had approved from the window of his study.

The schoolchildren sometimes come to visit him, after having asked permission several days in advance. Again he talks about nature, mostly about the Danish migratory birds which continually flutter before his eyes when he is sleeping. With cries and gestures he describes the golden plovers, the turnstones, the godwits, the sandpipers, and the gray plovers. The children laugh merrily to hear about all these queer birds with their funny names. If they could fly to Brazil, they all would – also the ruffs and reeves, the snipe, the swallow, the warbler, the wagtail – *see*-veet! – *see*-veet! – and the redstart, the lark, and the meadow pipit. About November the migrations slowly ebb out to the last starling. Yes, he can remember them all. When the children have gone, after leaving a piece of chocolate or a bag of sweets on his night table, he watches the birds in the sky from the meadows edging Lake Furesoe or from the Gamekeeper's House as Carl chops wood in the shed or fills the lamp with oil for the night. And soon the darkness falls like silk, unless it is June with its white nights and cuckoo calls until the morning light. Then the pain stabs in his chest. He begins to cough the way Carl had coughed when he'd come home from Sweden. And his mother, bending over him, is redolent with vanilla and freshly-washed linen. He smiles at her, and he is happy. She whispers that he is sure to get better, but that he must travel to the warm countries. Again he coughs. And he sits up in bed with a start. He is all alone.

He gets out of bed, searches for his piston rifle, his saddle, his bags, vasculum, insect forceps, barometer, saucepans, boots, and the oxhide to cover the boxes and to sleep on at night. He goes to the glass door, throws it open, and looks about for his mule. He calculates the track of the sun. He goes out through the front yard. He must go onward, but first he has to find Riedel. Riedel must be sitting at the venda writing letters to the Emperor. For months they have been riding but there is still a long way to go, and the mule must be rested now after the trek through the Tormented Forest. So many birds he has not yet classified! And the exhaustive biography of the three-toed sloth! He will work on it as he lies by the campfire. The sun has shifted exactly as he had foreseen. But where is his rifle? He looks around. His skin is burning. Everything swims in front of his eyes. And the saddle? And the bags, the vasculum, the forceps, the barometer, and saucepans, the oxhide – and the boots? Hasn't he put his boots on? Where are the black workers? Never before has he felt such energy. All his senses are aroused at the thought of everything he will accomplish on the rest of his journey. He calls for Riedel.

Nereo, now married and the father of newborn twins, dashes up through the palm garden and reaches Dr. Lund just in time to keep his head from hitting the ground as he falls. It is May 25th 1880, the dry season has just begun, and it looks like it will again be more severe than usual. Nereo fetches Roepstorff, who is busy painting his house while his wife is in Sabará buying French perfume. Together they carry Dr. Lund inside, and carefully they lay him on his bed. They can see that he has coughed blood. For several hours he lies there, unconscious. Then, quite suddenly, he opens his eyes, and looks straight at Roepstorff.

'Have I been baptized?'

'Yes, you have, Dr. Lund.'

'What am I really?'

'You're a Protestant.'

'Oh, I am? But that won't do here.'

Dr. Lund says this softly. He dozes off. Then he wakes again.

'What am I?'

'You're a freethinker, Dr. Lund.'

'But what are you, Roepstorff?'

'I'm a freethinker, as I've always been.'

Dr. Lund smiles. For a moment he is fully conscious. He looks as if he would like to leap out of bed.

'Oh, it warms my heart to know that you aren't a hypocrite! They're the worst, those hypocrites. Yes, I'm a freethinker. But Providence, Roepstorff, Providence, that I do believe in. It has been with me every moment of my life. God has been with me always and he is with me now. So I can die peacefully! Roepstorff?'

'Yes?'

'Hold me!'

But Roepstorff remains seated. He remembers that Dr. Lund cannot bear the slightest touch. Nereo, standing nearby, listens. Setting down the medicine, he goes quietly over to the bed and places his arms firmly around Dr. Lund's neck. Slowly Dr. Lund pulls him close and whispers something in his ear. He is crawling up a high mountain, and the wind is tearing the oxhides off the boxes on the pack mules. Then, reaching the summit, he sees a summer meadow blooming with golden flowers. She is standing with her back to him, gathering basketfuls of blossoms. In the midst of the meadow stands the chapel. Now he knows where he is. Sarah Lisa is picking flowers for Linneaus. No longer does he freeze.

'What did he whisper to you?' asks Roepstorff in awe.

'*Amor, amor, amor.*'

Down to the last detail, Nereo Cecilio dos Santos fulfills Dr. Lund's instructions for his own funeral. In the letter written in his large shaky handwriting, he specifies that he will have no religious interference, but that for three days and three nights, food and drink is to be served freely to everyone in Lagoa Santa. And he means *everyone*. He asks to have the little caboclo banda which made the roses open play, as his coffin is being lowered into the earth. No funeral ceremonies in the house, no professional mourners, no black mourning attire. Nereo gets busy arranging everything as best he can. Dr. Lund now lies in his coffin, dressed in his riding clothes, and by his side is a little box containing the most cherished letters from his family, while on his breast is his doctoral dissertation, dedicated to his mother. The banda arrives and when the oxcart with the coffin is pulled through town it plays at the head of the procession. The circus rider musters his band into place, following the coffin, playing whenever the banda takes a rest. Thus the two bands take turns playing melodies sprung from the parched soil of Minas Gerais, and the deep melancholy tones of the Tormented Forest are followed by '*La Parisienne*' and '*Dengang jeg drog afsted*', which Nereo whistles for them.

The townspeople come to join the procession. The oldest can still remember the day when the Doctor came riding into town. The schoolchildren are in their Sunday best. The oxcart creaks past the venda where the proprietor instantly closes the shutters and leaps into the procession, promising to shoot off all the fireworks he has been making over the past weeks in memory of the Doctor. Padre Wellington cannot refrain from ringing the church bells as the cart turns past the church. And at last the procession reaches the hill where Dr. Lund will be laid to rest, with Brandt next to his heart. From the foot of the town the slaves, led by the witch doctor, come up. Many townspeople make little speeches as the coffin is lowered. The longest eulogies are by Nereo and Senhor Fonseca, whose daughter, home on holiday from the college in Ouro Preto, has brought the loveliest bouquet in the Danish colors, red and white, which she has gathered and tied. Ilídio desists for the time being in his attempt to enrol members into his Imperial Conservative Congress Party. Rita and Carlos are re-united in honor of the occasion.

The caboclo band plays as bouquets of flowers, more than ever seen before in Lagoa Santa, cover the coffin, filling the grave to overflowing. There they will lie during the celebration till earth is shoveled over the grave. The witch doctor drops seven parrot feathers into the sea of flowers. A tree is planted and a humble wooden cross, unadorned, is erected. Then everyone goes back to town, swaying in time to the rhythm of the circus rider's band.

For three days and three nights they dance and drink, and there are no mishaps. Lagoa Santa resounds throughout Minas Gerais. On the last day, the venda proprietor runs out of fireworks and has no more paper to make new ones. But Nereo and his wife, who is as dark and plump as he, come to his aid, and after nightfall fireworks again explode over the lake. Blainville's *Ostéographie* bursts into a spluttering shimmering sun. Two thick volumes of von Humboldt's *Kosmos* float down in a purple shower. Darwin evolves into a twin sun, swiftly followed by Buckland's *Reliquiae Diluviae*, while Baron Georges Léopold Crétian Fréderic Dagobert Cuvier's *Discours* is a dud which drowns among the rushes. Schouw's *Plantegeografi med Atlas* soars so high into the sky that it disappears with the howl of a stuck pig. Milne-Edwards, de Candolle, Rudolphi, Owen, Biot and Ampère, Réamur, Linneaus, Fabricius, Forchhammer, Charles-Lucien Bonaparte, and H. C. Oersted all are transformed into a shower of stardust which bids farewell to the Doctor out of the dark tropical sky.

Wilhelm is sleeping.